T0305022

# THE
# FIRST
# MURDER
# ON
# MARS

*Also by Sam Wilson*

Zodiac
The First Murder on Mars

# THE FIRST MURDER ON MARS

## SAM WILSON

ORION

First published in Great Britain in 2024 by Orion Fiction,
an imprint of The Orion Publishing Group Ltd.,
Carmelite House, 50 Victoria Embankment
London EC4Y 0DZ

An Hachette UK Company

1 3 5 7 9 10 8 6 4 2

A CIP catalogue record for this book is
available from the British Library.

ISBN (Hardback) 978 1 4091 9917 5
ISBN (Export Trade Paperback) 978 1 4091 9918 2
ISBN (eBook) 978 1 4091 9920 5

Typeset at The Spartan Press Ltd,
Lymington, Hants

Printed and bound in Great Britain by Clays Ltd.
Elcograf S.p.A.

MIX
Paper | Supporting
responsible forestry
FSC
www.fsc.org   FSC® C104740

www.orionbooks.co.uk

For Kerry

**OUTLIER TERRITORY**

Janus •

+

+

+

Loyola •
Olympus •
Jayan •
Wellington •

+

+

• Destiny

Binan Suo •
Ben-Gurion •

Shiloh •

Randtown •

• Rothschild

New Gusev •
Hunter •

• Azania

Galt •

• Marcus

The Orange Fortress •

Rael •

+

• The Wintergarden

• The Hanging City

Company Outposts +

+

• Tharsis

**THE FREE SETTLEMENTS**

Mangala •

• Titov

Hong Bao •
Whale Rock ∆

Plymouth •

• Pavonis

Clarke •

• The Ruby Palace

• Indis

• Solidaritas

• Harmony

• Hope

Michigan •

• Leonov

Kepler •

• Huoxing Cheng

• Sunrise View

Athena •

Syria •

Sinai •

• Burudan

• New Prague

• Rayleigh

• Novvy Mir

• Nazarovo

• The United Fortress

Aries •

Euler •

• Mariner

**COMPANY TERRITORY**

• Calico

• Wollstonecraft

• Ferne Stadt

• Fortune Point

• Lu Bao

Challenger •

0
400
800Km

# Part 0.5

———

# The First Birth

**Rosemary Olivia Fuller and Archimedes Escher Fuller (Birth)**

(Marspedia entry created at 15.15 on D 67 Y 2103)

Rosemary Olivia Fuller and Archimedes Escher Fuller were born in Aries Base at 4.15 a.m. and 4.17 a.m. respectively on day (sol) 96 of 2034 to Kelly Anne Fuller, the wife of Alexander Fuller, the founder and CEO of Fuller Aerospace. At birth, Rosemary was 2.2 kilograms (Earth weight) and 32 centimetres from head to toe, and Archimedes was 2.3 kilograms (Earth weight) and 34 centimetres.[1] They were delivered by the base surgeon, Doctor V. S. Narayanan.[2]

CONTROVERSY [edit]

Leading up to the birth, Alex Fuller repeatedly said that it was his intention to deliver Rosemary and Archimedes himself, in his private quarters in Aries Base.[3] On day (sol) 81 of 2034, fifteen days before the birth, he released a video stating how important it was that the birth was natural, saying 'I need everyone to see that Mars is a healthy and safe place to start a family.'[4] However, during the birth the twins were found to be in a breech position, and, against Alex Fuller's wishes, Dr Narayanan took Kelly Fuller to the base's medical bay to deliver the children by Caesarean section.

In the weeks following the birth, Dr Narayanan's actions became the subject of intense online debate. The controversy began[5] on the Alex Fuller fandom subreddit r/EmperorFuller, where several users strongly contested the necessity of the medical intervention, since Alex Fuller had trained himself to perform the home birth, and could have performed an <u>external cephalic version (ECV)</u> to bring the twins into a <u>headfirst position</u>.[6] The debate was quickly picked up by mainstream news organisations.[7] Opinions were sharply divided along political lines, with <u>pro-science</u> news sources generally praising Doctor Narayanan's swift action, and <u>alternative health</u>, <u>pro-family</u> and <u>pro-business</u> groups condemning it.[8] An editorial in <u>The International Quarterly Journal of Medical Science</u> called the Caesarean section 'sensible, considering the difficulty of performing an ECV on twins, the uncertainties around how low gravity effects gestation, and Alex Fuller's total lack of practical experience in assisting childbirth.'[9]

National Patriot News called it 'a transparent attempt by a member of the medical establishment to steal credit for one of the greatest achievements of the human species.'[10]

Forty-three days after delivering Rosemary and Archimedes Fuller, Dr Narayanan voluntarily ended his contract with Fuller Aerospace. He claimed that he had received multiple anonymous death threats, and that he no longer felt safe or welcome working for the Company. [11] Rather than returning to Earth as he had originally intended, he relocated to the newly built Mariner Base, where he ran a private practice until his death during the Collapse in 2058.[12]

In an interview conducted in 2055 for the documentary film <u>Mars Natives</u>, Narayanan maintained that he had made the right decision.

'People were obsessed with Rose and Archie, even back then. Fuller wanted their birth to be a symbol, but they were real human children, facing a real biological risk. Put aside the politics for a moment, and look at the facts. They were in breech, I performed the surgery, and Rose and Archie Fuller both survived. The first two human beings were born on Mars. That's all that matters.'[13]

# *Part 1.0*

——

# Dylan

# Chapter One

Dylan steps around the sleeping bodies in the storage bay. Some of the evacuees have blankets, but most are wrapped up in sheets of cheap orange plastic that are usually used to keep the dust off the floor around the airlocks. They're resting their heads on backpacks and rolled-up bundles of clothing to keep them from being stolen in the night. Dylan walks carefully, trying not to stand on any stray fingers.

From the far side of the dark chamber she hears a panting, gasping moan. She doesn't want to interrupt anyone having sex, but it's her job to keep these people in line, so she grudgingly swings her flashlight to the noise. As the light whips across the bodies, she catches a glimpse of a halo of white hair and a face streaked with blood. She steps closer, picking her way between the sleeping evacuees. An old man is propped up in the hatch leading to the east wing of the base. His cheeks are red, and a rag is shoved into his mouth.

Dylan kneels down at his side, and her sputters as she tugs the gag out.

'I've got to find them,' he says. 'They took…'

'Shhh. It's okay.'

'They took my money.'

Dylan sweeps her flashlight over him. He looks to be in his early seventies, with thin white hair and sunken cheeks. His nose is bleeding, and his breathing is short and sharp. He's dressed for the wrong planet, in a white button-down shirt, jacket, dress pants,

7

socks and heeled shoes. Dylan gets a glimpse of milky blue eyes as he winces in the light.

His hands are behind his back. She leans over him and sees them bound with a thick black cable tie, the same type that she has hooked onto her belt. His fingers are puffy, and turning blue.

'Who did this to you?'

'Guards. They jumped me outside the docking bay. They had grey and blue uniforms—'

'Like this?'

She turns her flashlight onto herself, revealing her base uniform and knife-proof vest.

'Shit,' says the man.

One of the sleepers behind Dylan coughs, and a plastic sheet rustles.

'Relax,' says Dylan, more quietly. The evacuees around them could become unmanageable if they're disturbed. 'I'm here to help you, but I need you calm. Are you calm?'

The old man rests his back against the side of the hatchway.

'Calm,' he says.

'Describe the guards.'

'An Asian-looking guy with acne, and a vicious little white shit with bad teeth.'

'Chen and Raul,' says Dylan. 'Okay. If I cut you free, are you going to cause trouble?' she says.

'Not for you.'

She leans behind him again, and saws through the cable tie with her serrated knife.

'They followed me from the docking bay,' he says. 'Beat me up and took my money. Twenty ingots of titanium.'

The black plastic snaps under Dylan's blade, and the old man massages life back into his hands. He grits his teeth.

'Fuck. I think they broke a rib.'

'Come on then.'

She puts an arm around him, and keeps him steady as he slowly stands. He barely weighs anything in the low gravity, but he still groans as he stumbles onto his feet. Someone mumbles in the darkness.

'This way,' says Dylan. 'Let's let them sleep.'

She slides the storage bay door open on its rails. The corridor lights outside are dimmed for the evening, except for a single LED bulb that's bright and flickering. Dylan pulls the door closed behind them and steers the old man down the corridor towards the medical bay. The carpeting below their feet is worn through, with exposed patches of the black rubberised floor. The edges of the corridor are strewn with empty biopolymer coffee cups and food wrappers from the Company canteen.

'Will you help me get my money back?' says the man.

'No, sir, I won't.'

He gives her a sidelong glare.

'Why not?'

'Raul and Chen didn't do anything illegal. They can confiscate your property if they have reason to think—'

'I know how asset forfeiture works,' he says. 'I wasn't committing a crime.'

'Was it after 11 p.m.?'

'Yes.'

'Then you were breaking curfew and carrying untraceable currency.'

'Bullshit. It was a mugging, pure and simple.'

'There's nothing I can do, sir,' Dylan says evenly. Five months on the evening shift has given her a lot of practice with handling frustrated civilians.

'You could arrest them.'

'Were you born on Earth?'

'What does that mean?' the man snaps.

'I don't think you've learned how to live in a closed system.'

They walk into the central hub of the base. The administrators have their private rooms here, and the carpeting is clean, blue, and new. Three workers in ancient grey and khaki uniforms are picking up litter, and scrubbing graffiti off a mural of a Martian landscape painted back in the tourist days.

'Hey,' she mutters to the workers. They ignore her. She knows them all through her dad, and a few years back they had been friendly enough, but they haven't spoken to her since she signed up to be a guard.

The old man limps alongside her sullenly. He's giving her the silent treatment too.

'I know how it must look to you,' she says. 'But the base is dealing with an air leak, and we've had to close the foundry wing. We've got two hundred evacuees without beds or jobs, making Mars-shine in the bathrooms and vandalising the air ducts while they wait for the repairs. They're getting violent. Raul and Chen aren't great, but bad guards are better than no guards.'

The old man snorts.

'Seriously,' says Dylan. 'Let it go. Complaining will make you a target, and the security manager will take their side. Just take the loss and be glad you're still on your feet. Hey, look where we are.'

The corridor ahead is brighter. The regular late-night crop of drunks and addicts are lined up outside the medical bay, moaning and muttering, looking to have wounds stitched and broken teeth pulled. One of Dylan's shift-mates, a guard called Riyad, is leaning against the wall panels and keeping an eye on them while casually tossing a knife to himself overhand.

As Dylan approaches, he glances at the old man on her shoulder.

'What have you got there, Freebie? Another stray? You're a soft touch.'

'Just doing my job.'

Dylan pushes past him, and leads the old man to the back of the line.

'The medics have a little production line going in the evenings,' she says, taking his arm off her shoulder and lowering it carefully at his side. 'You won't have to wait too long. Half an hour at most. When you're done, talk to Riyad there and he'll escort you to the traveller's quarters. Don't go wandering around by yourself again. Will you be okay if I leave you?'

'I'll manage, I'm a big boy,' the old man says flatly. He's still holding his hand across his ribs with his right arm, but he offers her his free left hand, and she shakes it awkwardly.

'Thanks for the lift,' he says. 'The name's Clifford.'

'Dylan Ward.'

She tries to break the handshake, but he keeps his grip and holds her still as his eyes dart around her face.

'Have we met?' he asks.

'I don't think so,' she says, pulling her hand free.

'Well, thanks for your help, Dylan Ward. And for your honesty.'

'Are you still going to try to report Raul and Chen?'

He smiles tightly. 'No. It wouldn't solve anything, would it?'

'Right,' say Dylan, relieved. She doesn't want to see him come to harm. 'Then goodnight, sir. Stay safe.'

# Chapter Two

Dylan wakes up the next afternoon, just after 3 p.m. The late night patrol shift is stealing her days, but at least she gets paid extra for working during the slip – the thirty-seven minutes tacked on at the end of the day to make Earth standard time work on Mars. The overtime isn't much, but the recharge capsules for her dad's insulin pump aren't cheap and she needs every extra dollar she can make.

She rolls up the privacy screen of her bunk and drops down onto the rubberised floor. It sucks at the soles of her bare feet as she pads over to the dorm's desk. She picks up the guards' shared pad, which is tethered to the wall by a short length of cable, and swipes the screen to scroll through her morning alerts.

WELCOME BACK ONLINE, DYLAN WARD!
Your next shift starts in 57 minutes.

3 new messages from Security Manager Merrick (Read Now)
1 new message from Frank Ward (Read Now)

HEADLINES FOR DAY (SOL) 205, 2103:

MARS
Five dead in Outlier attack near Orange Fortress
Riots quelled in Sinai Base

EARTH
War casualties approach 60 million
Miami sea wall repaired

Russia vows return to space 'within 30 years'

Exercise Goals:
HIIT 0 / 30 Mins
Steps 0 / 10 000
Dietary goals: 0 / 8600 kJ

You have earned 23,480 exercise reward coins!
  Trade them in here.

YOUR DAILY AFFIRMATION
By doing your duty, you make Mars a better place for all!

She taps the exercise tracker icon to begin her daily routine. She starts with star-jumps, and after a minute is greeted by a chime and a message on the pad.

CONGRATULATIONS! You earn 20 Exercise Reward Coins!

Next are squats.

CONGRATULATIONS! You earn 20 Exercise Reward Coins!

Push-ups.

CONGRATULATIONS! You earn 20 Exercise Reward Coins!

Lunges.

CONGRATULATIONS! You earn 20 Exercise Reward Coins!

As she's doing step-ups on the metal dorm chair, a privacy screen rattles behind her. She looks around to see Ortega from the morning shift lying back in his bunk and watching her. He's naked, but thankfully the lower half of his body is draped in a yellowing

sheet. Behind him, Dylan sees a tangle of blonde hair and a pair
of embarrassed eyes peeking out at her.

'Hey,' says Ortega. 'How long is that going to take?'

'I'm just doing interval training. Seven more minutes?'

He looks her up and down.

'Fine.'

He slides the screen closed, and Dylan goes back to her step-
ups. A minute later, she hears quiet sounds of sex from the bunk
behind her: grunts, gasps, moans and wet lips, all in time to the
rhythm of her exercise.

With her cheeks burning, she logs out of the pad and grabs
her uniform from the shelf under her bunk. She storms out of
the dorm and towards the communal washrooms, to shower and
change.

*CONGRATULATIONS!* she thinks. *You earn 20 Spineless
Reward Coins!* But she's spent two years letting the other guards be
assholes to her, and she can't waste all that effort by snapping now.

She washes herself clean in a gunmetal grey bathroom stall, puts
on her uniform, and straightens out her collar in the mirror. Her
wild black hair takes a few minutes of combing before she can
contain it in a bun at the back of her head.

Some workers from the foundry are playing cards in the base
cafeteria. She hears them laughing from down the corridor, but
when she enters the room they go silent and watch her guardedly.
She picks up a foil container from a stack on the counter, and
takes it into a dark corner. When she peels off the lid, she discovers
that today's meal is a grey-green mass of algal curd that tastes
faintly like boiled cabbage. The card players resume their game,
punctuated with coughs and whispers and glances in her direction.

She finishes as quickly as she can, and drops the container in the
trash chute by the door on the way out. Her next stop is the guard
office, to catch up on her incident-and-arrest reports before the
next shift. The other guards make fun of the time she puts into her
paperwork, but the truth is, she gets a zen-like calm from it. Every
day she encounters people going through the most traumatic and
chaotic moments of their lives – domestic violence, assault, mental

breakdown, overdose, loss of family. Even as an outsider it's hard to deal with, but when Dylan fills in the forms then life's greatest horrors become small enough to fit in a check-box.

The guard office is filled with frantic activity. At the front desk, Security Manager Merrick is scrabbling through a plastic crate, picking out documents and feeding them into a whining shredder. The afternoon shift guards are shouting at each other by the weapons locker. As Dylan enters, they all fall silent and stare at her.

'Ward,' says Merrick. He doesn't have to raise his voice. 'What the hell happened last night?'

'Nothing, sir,' says Dylan.

'Really?'

He slides an envelope to her across the desk. It's made from good-quality paper, not the cheap translucent vat-grown cellulose that the guard forms are printed on. It's already torn open.

'They were two of our best, Ward,' Merrick says. 'They had families.'

Dylan pulls the letter out of the envelope. The handwriting is neat and orderly, and it's addressed directly to her.

# *Chapter Three*

Dear Dylan Ward,

Thank you for your help last night. I'm sorry that I didn't introduce myself properly, but you were being wonderfully candid and I didn't want to spoil it.

My name is James Clifford, and I'm the head of Internal Affairs at Fuller Aerospace. The cases I investigate are usually rather complicated, so dealing with your friends Raul and Chen was satisfyingly straightforward. Thanks to the state of emergency, I have full authority to keep the peace in any way that I see fit, so I have ordered your security manager to throw them out of the airlock. I know the rot goes deeper than those two, but my time is tight and they're the ones who made the mistake of trying to rob me.

After our meeting last night, I felt compelled to look through your personnel file, and you have a history that I'm extremely curious about.

Please meet me in the greenhouse at 5 p.m. I told the security manager to give you clearance and clear your schedule. Also, bring the ingots that Raul and Chen stole from me. There should be twenty of them, all titanium. If there are fewer than that in the evidence locker then please alert the security manager again. I'm sure he'll be able to pull them back from whatever cracks they may have slipped into.

Again, thank you for your assistance, and see you soon,
James Richard Clifford,
Internal Affairs,
Fuller Aerospace

# Chapter Four

Strips of thick transparent plastic hang down over the entrance to the base greenhouse. As Dylan pushes her way through them, she's hit in the face by warm, humid air. This is her first time in the greenhouse, and the sight makes her catch her breath. All around her are vast stacks of transparent trays of gel substrate, held up in racks that tower overhead, rising up to the roof of the dome. Between them, every ten metres or so, are tall white columns with leafy green vegetables growing out of their sides: lettuce, kale, arugula. Through the leaves and the beehive structure of the dome's frame she can see the sun, and the rusty Martian sky.

She takes a deep breath of faintly chemical air. There's no sound but the thrum of the water pumps and the beeping of distant electrical systems. White-suited gardeners are dispersed through the dome, pruning leaves and transplanting seedlings in reverent silence. Dylan raises a hand in greeting to a group of gardeners, and one of them acknowledges her with a nod. The greenhouse is off limits to most base inhabitants, but she's in uniform.

She adjusts the bag over her shoulder and walks through the foliage. The metal walkway clanks under her boots. She runs her hand lightly across the seedlings in a tray next to her, and feels their delicate stems bending under her fingertips. Her dad once told her that people need to be around plants, on a deep and primal level. He says injured people heal quicker when they're around vegetation. Instinctively, their bodies know that if the nearby plants are green then food will be abundant, and they can put all their energy into healing without holding anything in reserve.

Such wisdom from a man who lives on caffeine and deep-fried crap.

There's a label on the side of the plant rack, just below eye level. Dylan leans down to read it.

```
BASE - RICE PLUS (v5.3) BATCH 4465
HYDROPONIC - SQUASH PLUS (v.0.7.1), CUCUMBERS (NAT), MOD.
   PEPPERS (v3.11)
AEROPONIC - GOLDEN TOMATOES (v1.22)
```

'Ward!'

She snaps her head up and sees Clifford beckoning to her through the foliage from the far side of the dome. He's leaning against a plant rack, with one hand held over his broken rib, and he's dressed for the heat in light khaki-coloured slacks and a button-down short-sleeve. She winds her way to him through the racks, and he smiles as she approaches.

'What do you think?' he says, waving a hand at the surreal scene. 'One of the advantages of my job. I hold my meetings wherever I like.'

Dylan doesn't answer. She slings the bag off her shoulder and opens it to show him the twenty bars of titanium, polished and cylindrical, each one the size and thickness of her thumb.

'Your ingots, sir.'

'Thanks, but you'd better hold on to them. I shouldn't carry anything right now. Come. Let's take a walk.'

He strolls over to a rack of plants, and looks into the lower-level trays, one by one.

'So,' he says. 'According to your file, you were born in the Free Settlements.'

'Yes, sir.'

He looks back at her. 'You want to talk about it?'

'No, sir.'

'Why not?' he asks.

'I've got no loyalty to the Settlements,' she says. 'They're just a thousand tiny bases at each other's throats. I've lived here since I was nine years old. I'm a Fuller employee. This is my home.'

Clifford raises an eyebrow.

'Does anyone give you a hard time for being from the Settlements?'

'Sometimes. Minor things. The other guards call me Freebie and stick pictures of Red Rose on my bunk. It's good natured, mostly. They know which side I'm on.'

'Good to know. I'm not here to question your loyalty, though. I just wanted to know how much you remember about the Free Settlements. Who is Azania at war with?'

Dylan's brow furrows as she dredges it from her memory.

'The Orange Fortress.'

'How do you greet someone in Novvy Mir?'

'*Privet.*'

'Who was the Saturday Accord between?'

'All the Chinese-speaking settlements.'

'Good. Who split off from the Enterprise League?'

'Rand Town and Galt.'

Clifford beams. 'Excellent! You're doing better than most of the trainees back in Mariner Base. Could you locate a hidden underground base if you had to?'

'Probably,' she says, cautiously. She doesn't like where this is going, but she knows better than to lie to Internal Affairs.

'How?'

'Rover tracks,' says Dylan. 'They sweep them away, but they can't replace the stones they kick up. You can track the indentations that the stones left in the ground. And if there are no tracks, you just have to think like a base-builder. Look for terrain that's easy to dig in, close to high ground where they can mount a defence, not too near to any major rover routes or shifting dunes. If it's a good spot, then chances are there's a base there.'

'Fantastic,' says Clifford, and rests a hand on one of the plant trays. 'I think you can help me. I'm searching for something.'

'What is it?'

'Strawberries,' he says with a grin. 'I haven't tasted one for years.'

He looks back down at the trays of growing plants.

'Nothing here,' he says. 'Check those racks behind you.'

Dylan looks in the trays on the other side of the walkway. She isn't exactly sure what a strawberry plant would look like.

'One of our census takers in the Free Settlements has gone missing,' Clifford says over his shoulder. 'He was last seen in Pavonis Base. I'm going out there to find him, and I need a bodyguard who can convincingly pass as a Free Settlements trader.'

'I'm not keen to go north again,' says Dylan.

'I can tell,' says Clifford, and goes back to looking in the racks. 'But I need a bodyguard, especially now that I'm injured. I'll tell you what. This base is going to need a new security manager. If you come north with me and we find the census taker, there's a promotion in it for you.'

'Can I get that in writing?'

'No.' He smiles again. 'I appreciate your paranoia, but if you can't trust me, I can't trust you. Aha.'

He pulls one of the transparent trays, and it slides out of the rack like a filing cabinet drawer, revealing dozens of bright red berries nestled in the green leaves. He plucks one, and tosses it to Dylan.

'Take it,' he says. 'How often do you get a chance to taste a strawberry?'

Dylan rolls it between her fingers. It's plump, and covered in a diagonal grid pattern of tiny seeds.

'Is it safe?'

'Of course.'

She bites, and the juice fills her mouth. It's more sour than she expected, and it doesn't taste anything like the strawberry flavouring she's used to.

Clifford plucks a handful of the berries, and puts them in his pocket.

'How long do you think we'll be?' says Dylan.

'A couple of weeks,' he says. 'Don't worry, we won't be taking any unnecessary risks. I value my life quite highly.'

Dylan rubs her forehead.

'Come,' says Clifford. 'Let me show you something. It might make you feel a bit better.'

He leads her over to the acrylic-glass composite wall of the dome. Red-brown dust is piled outside it, up to chest height. Beyond it, Dylan can see all the overground structures of Syria Base: a satellite dish with half its panels gone, a radio mast, a rover bay, and processing plants for all the chemicals too dangerous to hold underground. Scattered between the buildings are stripped skeletons of old rovers and piles of trash from the base below. No one bothers cleaning it up. There's no ecosystem to destroy.

'There she is,' says Clifford proudly.

He's pointing towards the blocky docking bay. Pressurised tubes come out of it like spokes, hooking up to some of Mars's ugliest rovers. There's a giant wheeled beetle with a mining drill face, a cargo hauler that looks like a ribcage filled with scrap metal, and a top-heavy crane on caterpillar tracks.

In front of them all is a much smaller rover, only two decks high, with angled outer walls and six ridged wheels at its base. It looks ancient, in a good way.

'She was built in the twenty-fifties,' says Clifford. 'Back when safety was still a thing. She's got a titanium alloy frame, reserve oxygen, and back-up power. There's even a layer of radiation shielding. She's regularly serviced, and built to last.'

Dylan looks it over. The outer surface is covered in red dust, but it's still cleaner and sleeker than all the monstrous vehicles behind it. The profile of its body is a flattened hexagon. There's a hatch at the back, and a wide-windowed cockpit jutting out the front. On either side of it, antler-like structures hold up cameras for a self-driving system.

'That's my baby,' says Clifford. 'The Calliope.'

To Dylan, it looks more like a Rudolf.

# Chapter Five

Sealgair sees the Company rover from a kilometre away. It's a small white beetle hooked onto the central hub between the three small greenhouse domes of his private homestead.

He sighs, deep and low. His hunting trip is barely over, and subordinates are already invading his private space. They couldn't even give him a day to recover. He can see his next week filling up with meetings and negotiations and performance reviews, and all the other little traditions of corporate power. It's tiresome, but necessary. The Company needs a constant steady hand.

He looks through the side glass of his buggy's cockpit at the three security rovers riding beside him. All of them are the same dusty red as his buggy, and the afternoon light glints off the barrels of the cannon-mounts bolted to their sides. A body is tied to the front roll-bar of each rover: three smugglers that his patrol caught trying to take a functional gene sequencer out of Company Territory. Hunting them down had been a thrill, the kind that Sealgair rarely gets from running the company.

He flicks on the radio connection.

'Okay,' he says. 'That's close enough. You're dismissed.'

In the side window of the closest rover, Heron, the head of his security entourage, raises two fingers to the side of his head to salute in acknowledgement.

'Yes sir.'

Sealgair approves of Heron. He's a large man with a ginger beard, and he's too muscular to fit comfortably in the cockpit of a rover. He's quiet, obedient, and willing to do what's necessary to protect the Company.

The rovers of the entourage peel away, heading east towards

Challenger Base, and Sealgair continues ahead down the track towards his homestead. Five hundred metres from it he passes the metal warning sign.

## TRESPASSERS FORBIDDEN
## PRIVATE RESIDENCE

A quiet chime in his headset and a blue light on his dashboard tell him that his home's security system has recognised the buggy, and the explosive charges buried under the path ahead are disarmed. He lowers his speed as he approaches the domes of the above-ground greenhouses. Through the polished glass, he sees the mechanical arms silently tending to the crop of dwarf wheat.

He has been looking forward to getting back all week. Isolated homesteads like this are scattered around the dusty Solis Planum, but none of them are as large, luxurious, or private as his. He was hoping to be able to take off his out-suit, have a hot shower, sleep in a real bed, and eat a meal that doesn't come through a straw. He was hoping to be left alone.

He pulls his buggy to a stop next to the Company rover. It's a white dome with the windscreen at the front, not much bigger than his own buggy. A Fuller Aerospace Solis Mk3, seven years old, in reasonably good repair. Capacity for a single occupant, probably waiting to bug him as soon as he gets downstairs.

He detaches the umbilical tubes from his out-suit one by one, raises the hood of the buggy, and drops down onto the rocky ground. After giving the vehicle a final check for damage, he picks up his rifle from next to the driver's seat and carries it into the homestead's airlock.

The door of the metal chamber closes behind him. Air hisses in from grilles above and below, blowing off the toxic dust coating his suit, and after a few minutes the inner door slides open. He flips the catches on the neck of his out-suit, pulls off his helmet, and breathes in the air of his home. He runs his fingers over his face, then scratches his cheeks, his nose, his ears, his chin, and his forehead. He closes his eyes and massages the lids. He unties the bun at the back of his head, lets his hair free, and runs his fingers through it. He removes the rest of his suit methodically, piece by piece, and stows it on the rack next to the airlock until all that's left on him is the suit's yellowing underlayer, stinking of dried sweat.

He slings the rifle back onto his shoulder, and walks down the spiral staircase into the sunlit atrium. It's exactly as he left it. The floor is polished hardwood, made from vat-grown cellulose richly scented with camphor. Sunlight streams in from above, rippling slightly. The homestead's transparent water tank is above, providing a buffer against ionising radiation from the sky and infusing the room with subtle, mesmeric ripples.

A visitor is on the other side of the atrium, sitting in the chair next to Sealgair's collection of printed books. He's young, in his mid-twenties, wearing a blue-and-grey guard uniform that denotes a low rank. Black hair, weak chin, and a mild rash of acne.

'Stand,' says Sealgair as he walks down the stairs.

'Wha–?' the young man stutters, looking up from the book in his lap. He's dumbfounded, like he's never been spoken to like this before. The new recruits are being coddled.

'That's my chair,' says Sealgair. 'And that book is my property. Get up and put it back.'

'Sir.'

The man gets up and hastily puts the book back on the shelf, with the rest of Sealgair's collection on the military history of the twenty-first century.

'Sorry, sir. I know you said we should only come in person if it was urgent—'

'Stop,' Sealgair says, holding up his hand. He goes to the weapon display on the wall and places his rifle on its mount, just below the row of out-suit gloves he collected as trophies from the Free Settlements.

'Wait here,' he says, 'and don't touch anything.'

He goes through to his bed chamber, and seals the hatch closed behind him. The room is warm. The carpeting is soft, the lighting is subdued, and a robot arm in the corner is slowly tending a bonsai tree. Sealgair hasn't slept for thirty hours, but he needs to deal with his subordinate first. He turns on the shower in his bathroom and strips out of the suit's yellowing inner lining, a one-piece undergarment threaded with bio sensors and tubes of fluid for temperature regulation. This is the part of undressing that he enjoys the least. His suit was designed to be worn for days at a time and it's reasonably fit for purpose, but there aren't many good ways for an out-suit to handle elimination. He peels off the adhesive tube attached around his groin, and the other one attached to his rear, and steps into the shower to wash away everything that had accumulated there over the last week. When he's clean, he checks his body for sores. His skin is calloused, but intact.

He turns off the water, dries himself off with a towel, and examines himself in the mirror. His blonde hair is definitely grey-ing, no question, but he still has a fair amount of muscle mass. He uses his electric razor to trim his beard back down to a goatee, and clips his fingernails. When he's neat, clean and dry, he puts on a robe, and walks back through to the atrium.

The guard is sitting on the steps at the bottom of the spiral staircase. He jumps to his feet and stands expectantly as Sealgair enters. Sealgair ignores him, and goes over to a small table with a tea set. He puts on a kettle, and scoops tea leaves into a pot made from factory-grown jade.

'This is a remarkable residence, sir,' the guard says. He's trying to ingratiate himself.

Sealgair doesn't respond. He pours the boiling water into the jade pot and lets it brew, then pours himself a cup of black tea. He doesn't offer any to his guest. He sits down in his reading chair, puts the tea on a side table, and stretches his legs out.

'Tell me why you're here.'

The guard stands with his hands behind his back. He's a little too close for Sealgair's comfort. It's a problem with his whole generation: they've grown up in crowded bases, and they aren't accustomed to keeping their distance.

'Sorry sir. My name's Baikonur. I'm one of your agents...'

'I guessed,' says Sealgair.

'I didn't want to disturb you, but I couldn't tell you about it over the Company network...'

Sealgair taps the armrest of his chair thoughtfully. 'You've been shadowing one of my executives? Someone with decrypt access to the network?'

The guard nodded. 'Yes sir. James Clifford, Internal Affairs.'

'What's he done?'

'The security manager of Syria Base reported that he ordered two of their guards to be executed yesterday.'

Sealgair picks up his tea. 'He's Internal Affairs. He can execute anyone he needs to.'

'Yes sir,' says Baikonur. 'The question is what Clifford is doing there.'

Sealgair lowers the cup, slowly.

'Go on.'

'He travelled to Syria in a private rover, without a Security Services escort. He didn't tell anyone he was leaving, or where he was going. He isn't answering any calls or messages. All the computers in his office have been wiped clean. I know you didn't want to be disturbed, but...'

'Yes,' says Sealgair. He leans his elbow on the armrest and stares at the far wall. 'I can't have my department heads disappearing without warning.'

'Shall I tell the Syria guard manager to hold him?' says Baikonur.

Sealgair shakes his head. 'No. I don't want to cause any unnecessary talk. Let's find out what Clifford's playing at first. Room?'

'Yes sir?' says an ambient synthesised voice, and Baikonur glances up, alarmed. The technology is from an earlier time, and the young man clearly hasn't experienced it before.

'Call Heron.'

'Yes sir. Calling Oscar Heron.'

There are seven quiet beeps, and Clifford's orange-bearded right-hand man answers, his voice coming from the upper corners of the room.

'Sir.'

'Delay your leave, Heron, we have one more job. Meet me outside the homestead's perimeter.'

'Yessir. What should we do with the bodies?'

'Cut them loose and drop them.'

'Yes sir.'

The call disconnects. Sealgair puts his cup back down on the side table, and stands. 'All right.'

He goes to his weapons display and picks up his rifle, and three fresh clips of ammunition.

'Sir?' Baikonur says. His brow is furrowed. 'Permission to ask a question?'

'Go ahead.'

'Why do you risk your life out there, driving around in that little buggy?'

'Because it's fast.'

'But why do you have to go out yourself, sir?'

Sealgair powers up the rifle and checks the calibration on the auto-aim. The gyroscope inside it spins up with a low hum.

'I like to stay sharp. I patrolled the Company border for fifteen years, back when I was still in security. Getting out there keeps me sharp. It reminds me why we do what we do. We need to defend ourselves from the chaos of the Free Settlements and the carnage of the Outliers.'

He tries to recall as much as he can about James Clifford. Old, white hair, a competent administrator. Not someone likely to do anything impulsive. Smarter than he lets on.

'What we have here is valuable,' says Sealgair, slinging the rifle over his shoulder. 'Civilisation needs protection.'

# Chapter Six

Raul and Chen weren't popular, but they were local, and if there's one thing Mars teaches it's loyalty to your base. For the next three days, everyone Dylan squeezes past in the corridors or sits next to in the canteen acts like she isn't there. Conversations die as she approaches. The other guards don't even bother making fun of her any more. There are over a thousand citizens on Syria Base, and none of them will look her in the eye.

But she's keeping herself busy. Clifford is restocking Rudolf for the journey into the Settlements, and with his broken rib, Dylan has to do the bulk of the heavy lifting and stowing.

She tries not to think about what she's lost. Fourteen Earth-years' worth of following the rules, and taking crap from the local bullies. Fourteen years, wasted. She prepares for the journey diligently, familiarising herself with every centimetre of Rudolf's interior. If this mission isn't a success, there'll be nothing on Syria Base for her to come back to.

Except for Frank, of course. There'll always be Frank.

The lower deck of the rover holds the life-support, two small cabins, and a chemical toilet. The walls are white plastic, the flooring is clean and unscuffed, and the air blowing from the vents is scented with artificial mint. Even the sheet in her cabin is neatly folded. Near the rear hatch she finds Clifford's out-suit, secured in place by white plastic webbing. There's a place next to it for a second suit. On Clifford's instructions, Dylan gives her measurements to the base suit-merchant to get one custom-fitted to her smaller frame. Behind an access panel she finds the hydrogen-boron stacks, reserve batteries, $CO_2$ scrubbers, heat exchangers and water purifiers. She disconnects them one by one and carries them up to Clifford, who is sitting at the galley table on the upper deck. He tests them with a pocket diagnostics kit and puts aside anything that needs to be replaced. When they're done, Dylan scrubs and refills the water tanks, repressurises the oxygen tanks, and carries crates of frozen food up to the refrigerated storage lockers in the galley.

'Lunch time,' says Clifford as Dylan unpacks the crates. 'Are you joining me?'

'Sure.'

Dylan stows the supplies while Clifford goes to the tiny stove-top at the back of the galley. Soon there's the crackle of frying food, and a smell that makes Dylan's mouth water.

She stacks the empty crates by the ladder and sits down at the table. The sunlight shining in from the cockpit lights the galley with a warm glow. After a few minutes, Clifford brings over a tray of food and slides it onto the table. He sits down opposite her, and points to the food containers.

'Fried tofu,' he says. 'Modified sweet potato. Garlic kale, from the Mariner hydroponic farms. Bon appétit.'

Dylan sticks a fork into one of the containers. The tofu is crunchy on the outside and silky in the middle, with a coating of soy sauce.

'We don't get this in the canteen.'

'I should hope not. We don't want the Company going bank-rupt. Oh, I almost forgot.'

He gets up again, and after a minute comes back with two white plastic cups, and a bottle of amber liquid.

'Whisky,' he says.

'Not for me.'

His eyebrows rise. 'A teetotaller? In the Company?'

'I'm on duty.'

'More for me, then.'

He pours himself a quarter of a cup and takes a swig.

'So,' he says. 'Want to know about our missing census taker?'

'Of course.'

He reaches into his shirt pocket and takes out a pad. All pads were manufactured on Earth, so it must be close to fifty years old, but it's shiny, black and well maintained. He unfolds it, and after some tapping, a face appears on the screen.

'Chris Unwin,' says Clifford. 'Thirty-one. One point six metres, black hair, brown eyes and glasses. Slightly overweight. He's been a census taker for about three years. He travels through the Free Settlements, getting information about population, imports, exports, political views, that kind of thing.'

Dylan looks at Unwin's face, wearing an uncomfortable smile for the camera.

'I can't imagine that many Free Settlement bases like Fuller Aerospace employees snooping in their business.'

'True,' Clifford says.

'So why do they let him in?'

'Some don't. But he's harmless enough, and most of the bases don't want to risk antagonising us.'

'So, where did he disappear to?' says Dylan.

'That's the question. Like I said, his last transmission came from Pavonis Base, just over a week ago. He said he'd found something interesting involving one of my pet projects, and then he disappeared.'

'What did he find?'

'He didn't say.'

Clifford swirls the cup, and takes another gulp.

'So what's this pet project?'

He fixes her with his blue eyes.

'A cold case. Historical interest only. Nothing to do with him.'

Dylan understands. She stops asking questions, and finishes her meal in silence. Clifford stares down into his cup.

'Have you ever been to Pavonis?' he asks eventually.

'When I was young.'

'It's a rough place. The only good thing I can say about it is that it's big, and it's in the south, so it's safe from the Outliers.'

'We never got close to the Outliers when I was riding with my father,' Dylan says. 'I heard stories, though.'

'Yeah?' he says. 'Whatever you heard, the truth is worse.'

'You've seen them?'

Clifford slugs the rest of his whisky, and breathes in through his teeth.

'No,' he says, 'but I've seen what they can do.'

He pulls out a locket from his pocket and hands it to Dylan. It's a dull grey metal rectangle, about three centimetres wide, at the end of an aluminium chain. It looks cheap, with weld-marks at the edges, like it was manufactured in the tool shop of some small Free Settlement base. There's a tiny clasp on the side. Dylan clicks it open and sees the picture inside: Rose Fuller, airbrushed and flawless, staring into the distance. Dylan didn't know who she was expecting to see, but it wasn't Mars's most famous terrorist.

'Red Rose?' she says.

Clifford nods.

'I got it seven years ago. The Company had just set up the first of the outposts along the border of Outlier Territory. Many of the Free Settlements in the north weren't happy we were there, so I had to go up and convince them that it was for their own good. A couple of weeks into my stay, we got a radio call. It was from a small faction of English-speaking residents on one of the old European Union bases, just three families, who wanted to leave and join Fuller Aerospace. I checked their skills and they had a few biochemists and engineers we could make use of, so I told them that if they could make it to Archimedes Outpost on their own, I'd make room for them on the rover train back down to Company Territory.

'The day before I had to leave, the group of settlers sent a message that they were on their way in a convoy, and that they would be at the outpost by sundown, but the sun went down and they weren't there. They weren't there the next morning, either. We tried to call them over the radio but we didn't get a response, and by the afternoon I was getting impatient, so I took out a guard patrol to see if there was any sign of them.

'We found them. What was left of them. Their buggies and out-suits and weapons were gone. The only thing they had left on them was these lockets.'

Clifford reaches across the galley table, and Dylan hands it back. He holds the chain, and lets the locket dangle between them, spinning slowly.

'There was a rumour going around at the time that the Outliers respected Red Rose as much as the Free Settlements did. I guess the settlers thought that if the Outliers saw they were carrying her picture, they wouldn't harm them. The thing is, there's no mistaking an Outlier attack. Sometimes people find a rover in the middle of nowhere, stripped bare, and they think maybe the Outliers did it. No. When the Outliers attack, they want you to know it was them.

'The bodies were tied to metal poles right at the top of the ridge so we could see them from a distance. Scarecrows, the guards call them. Their hands and feet were chopped off and laid out around the base of the poles. Their eyes and lips were gone. It looked like they were grinning. Their abdomens were sliced open, and their intestines hung from pole to pole, strung up like decorations.'

Clifford drops the locket into his open hand, and makes a fist around it.

'I keep this on me as a reminder. Don't put faith in symbols. Not on this planet.'

Dylan doesn't know what to say. The meal she just ate isn't sitting so well. She pushes her plate away.

'Don't worry,' he says. 'The Outliers aren't our problem. Not today. Just be happy we're staying in the south.'

# Chapter Seven

That evening, it takes Dylan forty minutes to find her dad. He isn't in the gym doing his doctor-mandated exercise like he's supposed to be. He isn't in his dorm, or the canteen, or the medical bay. Less than an hour before the curfew starts she finds him in the south wing common room, leaning back in a soft chair with his book in his lap and his guinea pig on his shoulder. His grey hair is tied back in a pony tail, and his beard is getting bushy.

'Before you say anything, it wasn't my fault,' he says.

The common room is quiet this evening. The poker players who usually dominate the place have gone off to the bar, leaving the tables free for the other base residents. There's an elderly couple playing dominos in a side booth, and one lone kid playing a fighting game on the last console on the base that hasn't succumbed to radiation damage. The rest of the room is empty.

Dylan sits down on the couch opposite her dad and stretches out her legs. When she was a child, she used to wonder if he was really her father. Apart from their obvious difference in skin tone, she finds his carefree attitude to life exhausting.

'What wasn't your fault?'

'Getting kicked off the scrubbing crew.'

'You lost *another* job?'

'It wasn't really a job, was it? It was a way to keep me out of the corridors. Anyway, they don't want me any more, so it's over.'

Burma the guinea pig tightrope-walks down her dad's arm. Mice and guinea pigs are the only available pets on Mars, and genetic disorders are common in their small breeding populations. Burma is mostly hairless except for a fuzzy patch around his snout.

He gets all the way down to Frank's hand, and his beady eyes stare unblinkingly at Dylan as Frank feeds him a stick of carrot.

'Are you looking after yourself?' she asks.

'Of course,' he says. 'Fit as a fiddle.'

Frank Ward has broken his own body with a lifetime of bad decisions. Years of deep-fried junk food and cheap dorm-brewed booze have ravaged his internal organs. Dylan has to pay for all his medication, and for his bunk in the workers' quarters. Oh, and all his fines. Frank resents being helpless, and he expresses his resentment by causing trouble.

'Don't worry about me,' he says. 'How are things with you? What's this about a field-trip with a corporate fat cat?'

'We finished prep this afternoon. I'm heading out tomorrow.'

'Hmm.'

Frank nods, absently running his fingers along the bridge of Burma's nose.

'What's wrong?' says Dylan. 'I thought you wanted me to go back to the Free Settlements. You've been bugging me about it for years.'

'Yeah, seeing the real Mars will do you good. I'm just not so keen about your travelling companion.'

'We had a chat this morning. He's fine. A bit macabre, but mostly kind of charming.'

'Psychopaths usually are. He hasn't dug too deeply into your past, has he? Don't let him look into your family.'

The guinea pig drops out of his hands and scurries across the table. Frank watches him for a while. He's spacing out.

'Hey,' says Dylan, clicking her fingers. 'Is your insulin pump working?'

Frank blinks. 'What? Yeah, yeah,' he says.

'What's up, then? Are you drinking?'

'Why? Can you smell it?' says Frank.

'Dad.'

He looks embarrassed. He's treating diabetes like another set of rules to break.

'Just a sip of rum,' he says. 'Guthrie distilled it in his room. I didn't want to be rude.'

'Really, Dad.'

'I just missed doing what I want,' says Frank. 'It was a one-off. Oh, hey. I brought you something you might need.'

He feels around next to his chair, and pulls up a roll of crispy grey paper.

'What's this?' she says as he pushes it into her hands. It's stained in a dozen places, and the edges are torn.

'The map I used when I was a trader. It has the locations of a few out-of-the-way bases, if you ever need somewhere to run to.'

'I'll be fine.'

'Take it,' he insists. 'But don't show it to your psycho boss. I quite like those little bases, and I don't want a Fuller Aerospace exec hassling them.'

Dylan unrolls the map and sees all the handwritten notes. The memories rush back: kneeling over it as a child on the floor of their old rover, tracing her finger along the machine-printed elevation contours and reading names that sparked her imagination: The United Fortress. New Prague. Sunrise View. Solidaritas. In the north, above Olympus Mons, is the word *Outliers*. And in the south, where they now live, is the warning *Here Be Corporates*.

'I wish I was going back out there with you,' says Frank.

'You wish you could go back into the past,' says Dylan, rolling up the map. 'It's not the same thing.'

She stands up and kisses him on the top of the head.

'Thanks for the map,' she says. 'I'll call you from the road. Tell Guthrie to keep his rum to himself. And just … stay alive until I get home, okay?'

'Don't worry, I'll be fine.' He picks up Burma and leans back in his chair. 'Have fun.'

As Dylan heads out, she looks back at him from the door. He's staring down at Burma and letting the guinea pig run forward, swapping his hands under him like a treadmill, again and again and again.

# Chapter Eight

At seven minutes past ten the next morning, just as the first shift of workers are heading out of Syria Base towards the magnesium mines, Rudolf undocks from the rover port and drives through the scrap heaps, heading north. Dylan keeps catching glimpses of trash blown out across the landscape: plastic packaging, old napkins, and scraps of paper. If humanity doesn't survive for the long term on Mars, at least it left its mark.

Clifford shows Dylan around the cockpit.

'The good news is, we don't have to do much. The Calliope's self-driving system is fully operational, which is a bit of a miracle considering I've had to replace most of the rest of the controls from radiation damage. You set the destination on this screen here, and click here to activate it. If there's a problem, she'll sound an alarm and switch over to manual control. I used to be able to steer her from both cockpit seats, but the manual controls on the left side aren't working any more, so if you're driving you need to sit on the right. All clear? Good.'

After the briefing Clifford goes down the ladder to his cabin and Dylan stays up in the cockpit, acclimatising to above-ground life. The raw sunlight hurts her eyes, and she can't fully focus them on the horizon. She can't work out if it's because she's exhausted after months on the midnight shift, or whether a decade underground has ruined her eyesight permanently.

A lot of memories about life in a rover are coming back to her. The queasy feeling of suspension bouncing over rocky ground, for one. Technically they're on a road, but all that means is that they're on a path of kicked-up dust, where a few of the larger stone slabs have been moved aside by the earlier travellers. The ground is still an uneven mix of shale and head-sized stones, and Dylan's stomach drops every few seconds as Rudolf bounds over another obstacle.

At around midday Dylan goes back to the galley to make lunch. She microwaves two packets of high-protein ramen, and the galley fills with the savoury smell of cooking. A few minutes later Clifford comes up from his cabin below. Dylan tips the noodles into two ceramic bowls that she found in the stowage, and carries them to the table.

'Bored of the landscape yet?' he says as they eat.

'A little.'

'I've been picking up the news from Earth,' he says. 'You know there's a conspiracy theory that life on Mars is a hoax? They think that Alex Fuller is still alive, and he's filming all this in the desert outside Hollywood. Wouldn't that be something? Some director calls "cut", and we all find ourselves in Joshua Tree.'

Dylan doesn't know where that is, but she nods politely.

Clifford chews for a while, then says, 'What do you remember about Pavonis?'

'Big crowds,' says Dylan. 'Stinking machinery. Actuators that fell apart the day after my dad bought them.'

'That's about right. It's an industrial hub, so they won't have too much of a problem with letting strangers onto their base. Still, we'll need to use false identities.'

'Are we expecting trouble?'

'No, but it'll be easier to dig around if they don't know we're working for Fuller Aerospace.'

He takes some documents out of his jacket pocket, and pushes them to her across the table.

'Here we go. Cargo inspection certificates, base IDs, and clearance forms from Rand Town. Easy to forge now that Rand Town has stopped using digital authentication.'

Dylan flips through the papers. They all look convincingly realistic, with the right anti-counterfeiting measures – raised ink, embedded security thread and microprinting. She finds a Rand Town ID with her face on it, and the name *Merrin Shay*.

'You think you can pose as a Rand Town trader?' Clifford asks.

Dylan has never been to Rand Town before. All she knows is that it was founded by a group of libertarians shortly after the Collapse. There's a joke that every Rand Town citizen owns their own life-support system, because using a big one for the whole base would be communism.

'I can try,' she says. 'What are we going to do? Poke around Pavonis and see what we find?'

'I have a connection there we can talk to. He doesn't want anyone to know he's working with us, and I don't want to blow his cover. That's the other reason we're going incognito.' He smiles at her with the confidence of a salesman. 'Don't worry. We'll go in, get the information we need, and get out. If we run into any trouble then we'll pay a little bribe. Easy.'

# Chapter Nine

The next morning, a kilometre south of Pavonis Base, the self-driving system chimes with an obstacle warning and Rudolf crawls to a stop. Dylan climbs up to the cockpit and looks out the window. A line of medium-sized boulders is stretching across the landscape ahead, evenly spaced, with gaps half of Rudolf's width. It looks like a fence set up specifically to block rovers.

She takes the driver's seat and grabs the control stick. It's been years since she's taken manual control of a rover, but after a couple of jolts she gets the power level to the wheels right and eases Rudolf forward.

'This is new,' says Clifford, arriving at her shoulder. He's wearing orange overalls, the unofficial uniform of Free Settlements traders.

Fifty metres to the right, there's a gap just big enough to squeeze through. Dylan drives over to it, and stops. The word WAIT is crudely carved on a boulder at the side.

'Do we obey?' says Dylan.

'Of course. We're good little traders.'

Dylan powers down the motors. Through the gap, the above-ground structures of Pavonis are jagged teeth on the horizon. Huge clouds of vapour are billowing up from vents over its manu-facturing bays. After ten minutes, a rover crawls down the track towards them. It's a similar size to Rudolf, but it's a more recent model and it isn't nearly as well maintained. The outer cladding is gone, and so have the antlers of the self-driving system. The real difference, though, is the star symbol on the front, and the cannon welded to the roof.

'What's that?'

'A landing harpoon,' says Clifford. 'The Free Settlements have a ton of them from a Fuller asteroid-mining scheme that never got off the ground. Looks like Pavonis found a use for this one.'

The vehicle edges forward until it's bumper to bumper with Rudolf. Dylan can see two people in the other cockpit: a dark-skinned middle-aged woman sitting at the controls, and a beefy looking man with a moustache standing behind her. They both have humourless expressions which Dylan instantly recognises as the public face of law enforcement.

The woman at the controls holds up a piece of card for Dylan and Clifford to see. *27MHz.*

'Is that a radio frequency? Can't they use wi-fi?' says Dylan.

'Their computer's probably burned out. But they've got radio, the hottest technology of the nineteenth century.'

Clifford points to a metal box welded above the control desk. It has some switches on the side, and a pair of 3D-printed dials on the front marked *vol* and *freq*. Dylan flips a switch on the box, and turns the frequency dial. The radio crackles.

'Good morning,' says Clifford. 'This is rover Zero Zero Niner Calliope. How can we help you folks?' He says it with a happy lilt, like this obstruction is the best thing to happen to him all day.

'Rover Calliope, this is Pavonis law enforcement,' says the man opposite them. Dylan sees his lips moving, half a second ahead of his voice. 'State your business in our territory.'

Clifford keeps it going. 'Pavonis, we're looking to buy some of your fine ceramic tubing to sell up north in Olympus and Janus. It should be a quick trade, goods for ingots. We won't outstay our welcome.'

'And how're you going to pay for your air during the stay?'

'What currencies are you taking?'

'Pavonis dollars, but only if they're minted in the last five years.'

'Then what am I meant to do with all these forgeries?' says Clifford. Dylan can't believe how thick he's laying it on, but the corner of the man's mouth twitches upwards.

Clifford sighs theatrically. 'Okey-dokey. Then we've got Rand Town Dollars, or the ingots we're trading with. Titanium.'

The woman in the driver's seat looks back at the man with the moustache, and shakes her head. She takes the mic from him.

'Rover Calliope, this is Sheriff Laurie Ravine of Pavonis,' she says. 'We'll give you twelve hours inside the base to exchange your ingots for Pavonis dollars and then report to my office. The docking fee and a week's worth of air for two people is three hundred dollars in total. If you don't pay within twelve hours, we'll confiscate your rover and sell it to recoup our costs. When you're on the base, you'll abide by our laws and you won't cause us trouble. If you're not sleeping in your rover then the lodging will cost extra. Do you agree to all the usual Ts and Cs?'

'We surely do,' says Clifford.

'Wonderful,' says the sheriff, deadpan. 'Let the wheels of commerce freely turn.'

The man picks up a clipboard and runs his finger down the top page. He says something that Dylan can't hear, and the sheriff frowns.

'Just a moment. My deputy says that your rover isn't on our whitelist. Y'all are first timers at Pavonis?'

'No ma'am,' says Clifford. 'We used to come with the convoys. Only the rover's new.'

The woman sighs.

'You're set on making this difficult for yourselves, aren't you? What are your names?'

'I'm Dan Reckling,' says Clifford. 'And this here is my bodyguard, Merrin Shay.'

The deputy slowly writes the names on his clipboard.

'You've got your previous entry documents?'

'Yes, ma'am,' Clifford says.

'I go by *sheriff*,' says the woman. 'Okay. Bring your rover in through the boulder fence and pull over on the left. We'll need to give you a proper once-over. Prepare for boarding.'

The radio clicks off again.

Clifford stares ahead. 'Huh. I don't remember them being this paranoid before. What's got into them?'

The other rover reverses out of the gap. Dylan drives through it and pulls over on the side of the track, as instructed. The sheriff's rover turns until it's facing in the opposite direction, then reverses until the two rear hatches are aligned. There's a clunk of metal and a whir of motors as the automatic docking process begins. Clifford and Dylan climb down the ladder, and along the narrow corridor of the lower deck. They stand together by the rear hatch.

'Anything on board that we need to be worried about?' says Dylan as they wait for the inspection.

'Not a thing,' says Clifford, but he doesn't take his eyes off the hatch, and the playfulness in his voice has gone.

After a few more minutes, the whirring ends and an LED over the door turns green. Clifford unbolts the hatch and it swings inward, revealing Sheriff Ravine and her deputy, who is resting his hand casually on the butt of a holstered bolt gun. It's the most common projectile weapon on Mars, a modified riveting tool that can tear a hole in an out-suit or a human, while not being quite powerful enough to puncture the wall of a rover or a base.

'Welcome aboard,' says Clifford with a smile.

'Well thank you,' says the sheriff. 'Now would you mind standing the hell aside so we can do our job.'

Clifford backs up, and the two of them squeeze past him and Dylan into the corridor.

'What's all this new security for?' he asks.

They ignore him. The sheriff goes into Dylan's cramped cabin on Rudolf's port side. She empties Dylan's travel pack out on the berth, and rifles through her clothes and toiletries. The deputy goes into Clifford's cabin, opposite Dylan's, and searches through his shirts and pressed trousers. When he's done, he flips over Clifford's mattress and looks underneath. The sheriff pulls off the access panel in the corridor to inspect Rudolf's power stacks and air and water tanks, then shepherds Dylan and Clifford back up the ladder.

'Show us your documents.'

Clifford lays the travel papers out on the galley table, and opens a case holding his precious titanium ingots. The deputy makes handwritten notes on his clipboard while Sheriff Ravine walks around the upper deck, tapping on the walls with the butt of her flashlight. She stops at a metal panel behind the driver's seat, and prods it with the toe of her boot.

'Looks like you've had some modifications done. This shouldn't be in a first-gen rover.'

'I wouldn't know anything about that,' says Clifford. 'It was like that when I bought it.'

'Yeah?' says Ravine, folding her arms. 'Well looks like whoever sold it to you left you a little treat. I bet you can't wait to get a screwdriver and find out what's inside the secret compartment that you never knew you had.'

The deputy rests his hand on his bolt gun. Clifford's eyes dart to Dylan. She goes and gets a screwdriver out of the toolbox in the galley stowage.

'Do the honours, please,' says Ravine. 'I'm not setting off any booby traps.'

Dylan kneels down by the panel and unscrews it. She lifts it to reveal a hollow space below floor level, with a metal case inside.

'Open it.'

Dylan pulls the case up onto the metal floor of the rover, and lifts the lid. The deputy leans over to look, and gives a low whistle. Inside are three Earth-style handguns. Extremely dangerous and incredibly illegal, everywhere on Mars.

'Now that's a thing,' says the sheriff, almost impressed.

'I didn't know about them,' says Dylan. 'I swear.'

'Then I guess you're criminally unlucky,' says Ravine. 'Put your hands behind your head. Deputy Marchant, get the cable ties.'

Dylan does as she's told. The deputy binds her wrists, then grabs Clifford's hands and pulls them forcefully behind his back.

'Fuck!' says Clifford. 'I've got a broken rib!'

'Shut up,' says the deputy, binding his wrists with a thick black cable tie. He pulls it tight, and Clifford winces.

'This isn't necessary,' says Clifford. 'Just confiscate the weapons and let us go. We're barely in your territory. No harm done.'

'Ms Shay, Mr Reckling,' says sheriff Ravine. 'What you've got here is some serious grade-A contraband. They're weapons of mass destruction. These things could puncture a life-support system. I can't think of a single base in the Settlements, friend or foe, that would forgive us if we let you go free with something like this.'

'What's the penalty?' asks Clifford. 'Some kind of fine? Because if that's the case then we could work out a deal, here and now, just between us.'

He tilts his head towards the table, where the case of precious ingots is standing open.

The sheriff shares a look with the deputy.

'Let's be straight,' says Ravine. 'You want us to overlook your transgressions, and take the metal?'

Clifford looks her in the eye. 'If that's the way things are done in these parts.'

Ravine strolls over to the case, and puts a hand on the lid. She slams it shut.

'It ain't. Come on, Marchant. Let's get these two shit-bird smugglers into the bubbles.'

# Part 1.5

---

# The Prince And Princess
# Of Mars

# Chapter Ten

**Q: 'Why do the Free Settlements still think that Red Rose is a hero?'**

Posted by User 45861 on allq.mars, the questions-and-answers site.

Top Answer (45 Votes) from User 02167:

A: Red Rose was the founder of the Free Settlements. She was also, more famously, a terrorist and a murderer. So why do the Free Settlements still worship her? The answer lies in psychology.

Rose and her brother Archie were famous from birth. They were the children of Alex Fuller, who was himself a living legend, and they were the first human beings born on another planet (Chiang Lee was born on the moon three years earlier, in 2031). Throughout their childhoods they were subjected to intense media scrutiny, and their lives were treated with an almost mythic significance. When Archie broke his arm aged six, the news speculated that his bones had been made brittle by the low gravity, and that everyone on Mars going forward would be weak. When Rose showed higher-than-average reading comprehension, a dozen editorials said that future Martians would be more literate than their Earth contemporaries.

The first Mars-born generation were raised to see Rose as a living incarnation of their own future. So when she turned out to be just another human – a deeply flawed one – her followers wouldn't accept it. They had a cult of personality around Red Rose, and any suggestion that she was less than perfect was written off as disinformation and

47

propaganda. An attack on her was considered an attack on the Free Settlements, and on all the humans born on Mars.

In summary: the Free Settlements' continued respect for Red Rose is tribal thinking, pure and simple, and it will only end when they are finally reintegrated back into Company Territory.

This answer has been confirmed factually accurate by the Fuller Aerospace Media Centre.

# Chapter Eleven

Grace Chiwasa sat on a rainbow-coloured bench at the side of the playground and let the joyful shrieks of the children wash over her. This was her favourite place in Mariner Base. As the tourists arrived from Earth, life on Mars was feeling less like being trapped in a bomb shelter, and more like being trapped in a mall. The tight corridors and folding tables were being replaced by white-walled caverns filled with shops selling food and trinkets. But the playground was different. It wasn't there for survival, and it wasn't there to make money. It was a collection of swings and climbing-frames in the corner of the base where young humans could practice being human. It was an unpretentious, primary-coloured step towards a genuine future.

Grace watched the children as they bounded in the low gravity, whooping with joy as they leapt between the bars of the climbing frame, gliding through the air in ways that were impossible on Earth. If anything was worth leaving the planet for, it was this. She had been born in Zimbabwe and had travelled the world, moving to South Africa with her parents, getting a scholarship to the University of Toronto, studying human–machine interactions at a tech firm in Shenzhen, but nothing on Earth had been as fascinating as these children. They were the first generation to grow up on Mars, and Grace had the professional privilege of watching humanity adapt to a new planet. It wasn't just that they were developing new physical skills; Grace could sense a new culture bubbling under the surface. The children were learning social skills far quicker than they would on Earth. They were growing up in enclosed bases where everyone knew everyone else. Selfishness wasn't as easy as it would have been on Earth, because there was nowhere they could go to escape from the consequences of their own bad behaviour. They were developing attitudes and social norms that would one day shape the future of Mars.

This morning, Takeshi and Haru were being hounded by a three-year-old girl, a daughter of some recently arrived billionaire tourists from Germany. Grace disapproved of exposing children to the physical and mental harm of space travel, but the little girl wasn't showing any major signs of trauma. She had started out the morning playing blocks with Grace's daughter Netsai and her friend Bailey, but got bored with children her own age and soon started chasing after the older boys, yammering at them and trying to order them around. At first they ignored her while they played on the trampoline and the climbing wall, but the girl was persistent. After a while the brothers acknowledge her, and now Haru was holding her steady as she pulled herself up the climbing wall, shrieking with delight. Haru looked in Grace's direction and saw her watching. He grinned, and she smiled back approvingly.

Behind the climbing wall, the doors of the playground chamber slid open and a pair of security guards strode in, followed by Kelly Fuller and her two famous children. The other parents sitting on the benches around the edge of the playground saw them, and went silent.

Kelly was holding a biopolymer coffee cup from the base canteen. Her son Archie Fuller's arm was in a blue plastic cast. He grinned widely when he saw the playground, and roared ahead of his mother. Rose Fuller stayed at Kelly's side, with a stuffed toy elephant under her arm.

Kelly looked around the playground and locked eyes with Grace, who acknowledged her with a nod. Kelly leaned down to talk to Rose, then gave her a gentle nudge towards the play area. Rose walked over to one of the swings and sat, twisting it from side to side and hugging her elephant. She had reddish-brown hair with a low fringe, and was wearing a white and blue sailor-suit that made her look like a toy doll.

As Kelly approached, Grace pulled herself up on her walking stick. The long flight from Earth had destroyed her back, but it was easier to stand than it would have been on Earth.

'Is the playground safe?' Kelly asked. 'I don't see any padding under that climbing wall.'

'Children need to learn to manage risk without fear. Anyway, there's only so much harm they can do to themselves in this gravity.'

'Archie had better not get hurt again, that's all I'm saying.'

Grace knew Kelly, just like everyone knew Kelly, from the Fuller Aerospace commercials and magazine articles and late-night talk show appearances. She wasn't wearing her usual fake smile today. She dropped down onto the rainbow bench without shaking Grace's hand, and took a swig of her coffee. On the other side of the play area, Takeshi and Haru's mother had her pad out and was pointing its camera at Archie and Rose. One of the security guards went to talk to her quietly, and took the pad away from her.

'We shouldn't be meeting in public,' said Kelly.

Grace nodded. 'I understand. But everyone sees everything on this base. If you brought Rose to my rooms then they would instantly know the story. Here, we're just having a nice chat while our children play. Will the father be joining us?'

Kelly frowned and tapped a long fingernail on the plastic bench. 'Alex was meant to be here already. He said he'd try.' She took a pad with a zebra-print case out of her white handbag, and tapped on the screen.

'Give me a second,' she said. She turned away from Grace and cradled her pad to her ear. She spoke into it quietly, shielding it with her hand.

'Hey. It's me. Where are you?'

Grace tried not to listen. In the play area, Archie Fuller reached the top of the climbing wall and dive-bombed off it. Takeshi and Haru laughed at him, and climbed up so they could do it, too. They abandoned the little girl they had been playing with, and she shrieked in annoyance.

Rose Fuller didn't seem to notice any of them. She got off the swing and wandered over to the toy shelf, where she found an astronaut doll. She held it in one hand and shook it, making it talk to her toy elephant, then waggled the elephant in response. Grace wished she could hear what she was making them say.

'You agreed that we needed to—' Kelly said, and was cut off. She glanced at Grace, and got to her feet.

'Well, she's the best I could find on Mars,' she hissed into the pad. 'And Rose needs this.'

There was another pause.

'It isn't normal, Alex.'

Grace could hear a raised voice on the other end of the line.

'That isn't fair. I'm the one who's here for her. I—'

Kelly was cut off again. She looked down at the screen, and bit her lip as she pressed the disconnect button.

'He's in a meeting,' she said, sitting back down next to Grace. 'He said I should handle this for both of us.'

She clenched her jaw as she tapped on her pad for a few seconds, and handed it to Grace.

'What's this?'

'An NDA.'

'That won't be necessary,' said Grace gently. 'Doctor-patient confidentiality.'

'You don't understand,' said Kelly. 'You can't say anything to anyone about this. You can't even write about Rose or Archie in a notebook. The news sites will find it.'

Grace skimmed through the pages of legalese, and signed with a digital thumb-print.

'All right,' she said, handing back the pad. 'What difficulties is Rose having?'

Kelly took a deep breath.

'Rose is socially ... weird,' she said. 'She's a good girl, she does what we tell her to do, but ... She doesn't like speaking to anyone. She used to have a little friend called Dominic who was the son of Alex's CFO, but the family had to go back to Earth, and now ... she just hides from other children. She used to burst into tears every time we took her anywhere, especially when Alex needed her to look happy, because can you imagine what would happen if people thought that living on Mars was making her depressed? So he laid down the law, but now she's just … nothing. Look at her.'

While Archie and the other kids were whooping and chasing after each other, Rose was alone, lying on the floor and looking into a doll's house. It had a pitched roof and a chimney, which was totally different from any home on Mars. Rose seemed fascinated.

'If I tell her to go and play with anyone else then she just clams up, and she won't tell me why. It's this planet, isn't it?'

'It might be,' Grace said tactfully.

'I want to take the kids back Earth, but Alex says that Archie and Rose are the prince and princess of Mars. He's joking, but serious, you know? If they leave, it's like we're admitting that this place isn't enough, that there's no future here …' She stared into the middle distance. 'Anyway. How do you want to do this? Are you going to talk to her?'

'I'd prefer to talk to you first,' said Grace. 'I'd like to know Rose's full history. As much detail as you can tell me.'

'I thought you did research,' said Kelly irritably.

'This isn't about the facts, it's about how you see things, and the stories you tell Rose about her own life. If I know those stories, then I know how she sees herself.'

'That's a bit touchy-feely,' said Kelly.

'As a psychologist, I assure you that touchy-feely things matter.'

Kelly took out her pad to check the time, and put it back into her handbag. 'Where do you want to start?'

'From the beginning,' said Grace. 'Were Rose and Archie planned?'

Kelly laughed hollowly. 'They were the most planned children in history. You know what Alex is like. He was going to have the first child born on the moon, so I uprooted my life on Earth to join him on Selene Base. Then Chiang Lee was born on that Chinese base, so Alex got us on a flight here, and the twins were conceived on the way.'

'And what were things like after they were born?'

'A nightmare. It was ridiculous. The Aries dome was loud and cramped and there was no one around who would help me. I was trapped. I couldn't go anywhere or do anything except stare at a pair of squalling kids all day. And Alex was no help, he had a company to run. It was hell.'

'What were Rose and Archie like as babies?' asked Grace.

'What do you think? They cried and drank milk and shat all the time, and I didn't sleep for a year. I couldn't even shower, you know that? Alex wouldn't waste cargo space on disposable nappies, so I had to use most of our water rations to clean the reusables. What's the point of being the richest family in the solar system when you can't even shower?'

'What about milestones?' said Grace. 'When did they start talking?'

'I can't remember.'

'And walking?'

'I said I can't remember, okay? I see where you're going with this. I'm not a bad mother. It was years ago and it wasn't a great time for me, so I'm sorry if I didn't memorise every detail. If you want to know any of those things, look at all the promotional videos.'

'I'm not judging you,' said Grace. 'But if I'm going to help your daughter then I need to know what her world is like.'

Archie had found the slides, and was climbing up one of them as Haru was sliding down. They collided, and Haru yelled in complaint. Archie laughed as he tumbled back down to the bottom.

Kelly ignored them. She folded her arms.

'Would you like us to wrap this up for now?' Grace asked.

'Yes.'

'All right. Then I'd like to talk to Rose in person.'

She pulled herself up on her cane again, and walked with Kelly to Rose, who was still playing with the doll's house.

'Rose, baby,' said Kelly. 'This is Grace. She's a friend.'

'Hello Rose,' said Grace, kneeling down to Rose's level. Rose looked at her warily.

'It's okay,' Kelly said. 'Grace would just like to talk.'

'Dad said I must never talk to anyone,' said Rose seriously.

'Grace is different. You can say anything you like to her.'

Rose inspected Grace's face. 'Is it for a video?'

'Grace is a doctor,' said Kelly.

Rose's brow furrowed.

'Don't worry, you're not sick,' said Grace. 'I'm just a talking doctor. Is it all right if we talk?'

'Okay,' said Rose, looking down at the colourful foam padding of the playground floor.

'Can we have some alone time?' Grace asked Kelly.

Kelly looked relieved. 'Of course.'

'Mom, look!' Archie called from the top of the slide. 'Look at this!'

He dived off the side of it, and landed on all fours on the padding, giving her a wide grin.

'Don't do that again, okay?' said Kelly, glancing at the watching parents.

Grace turned her attention back to Rose, who had pushed her toy elephant into one of the rooms of the doll's house, next to a plastic toy child with an oversized head.

'That's a nice elephant,' said Grace.

'Her name's Plumpy. She comes from Juggle Jungle.'

'What's Juggle Jungle?'

Rose frowned slightly, like she didn't quite know how to explain it.

'It's toys from Earth. They sent me Plumpy in a box, and wanted to see me open the box and play with her.'

Grace's heart sank. So Rose was an influencer, on top of all her other troubles.

'Who is Plumpy's new friend?'

Rose wobbled the big-headed toy through the doll's house.

'This is Maia. She's six years old.'

'And is this Maia's house?'

'No, it's her Mars Base.'

'I see.' Grace examined the scene carefully. Two astronaut dolls were lying face down on the play mat outside the doll's house.

'Who's that?' she asked.

55

'Maia's parents. They don't like Plumpy. Maia sent them outside.'

'And are they going to stay out there?'

Rose nodded. 'I'm taking all the furniture out, so there's space inside and Plumpy can stay forever.'

'So Maia wants her parents to stay outside the Mars Base, in the cold?'

'Yes,' said Rose firmly.

Grace nodded. 'It can be hard sometimes with parents, can't it?'

Rose didn't answer. She kept playing with the toys inside the doll's house. Grace lowered her head to see her face. There were tears coming down Rose's cheeks.

'Hey,' said Grace. 'It's okay.'

Rose took the elephant out of the house and swung it furiously at the astronauts, knocking them off the play mat. They clattered across the white tiles outside the playground, and slid to a stop. Rose looked up at Grace, and the fury on her face turned to fear.

'It's all right,' she Grace calmly. 'You're allowed to be angry.'

Rose took a shuddering breath and wiped her eyes and nose on her forearm.

'Hey,' said Grace. 'I've got something for you. Would you like to see it?'

Rose nodded warily. Grace took a stick out of her jacket pocket, and held it out on her open palms. She wanted to give the moment some ceremony.

'This is my magic wand,' she said, 'I'm going to let you borrow it.'

Rose picked up the stick and turned it over in her hands. It was a piece of driftwood, bleached almost white, thirty centimetres long and the thickness of Grace's finger. It had just enough of a twist in it to look magic. Grace had found it on a family trip to the south coast of Mozambique many years before, and had taken a great fondness to it. It had cost her thousands of dollars to ship it with her to Mars, but its professional value was far higher than that.

'You can use the magic wand on anything,' Grace said. 'Just

56

point it, and you can make things go away, or come back, or change completely.'

'Really?' said Rose. 'For real?'

Grace hesitated. 'For pretend,' she said gently. Some children took to this naturally, but if Rose had trust issues then she would need to have her expectations managed.

Still, Rose looked disappointed.

'We can't make things real until we imagine them first,' said Grace. 'But this really is a powerful magic wand. With this wand, you can imagine things so strongly that it's easy to make them real. Look, it's made from real wood, from a tree on Earth. There's nothing more magic than that.'

Rose turned the wand over in her hand, examining it seriously, then she held by its thicker end and bounced it up and down, waving it like a conductor's baton. Her eyes followed its tip.

'You can wish for whatever you want. It can be a secret, if you'd like, but it works better if you tell me. It can be good or it can be bad, and I won't tell anyone, not even your brother or your mom or your dad. Okay?'

Rose's cheeks flushed, and she gave a small, solemn nod.

'So, what's the first thing that you want to change, Rose?' said Grace. 'If you could fix anything, what would it be?'

# Part 2.0

---

# The Bubbles

# Chapter Twelve

'Sorry for the mess, sir,' says the Syria Base security manager, wiping his brow. 'We weren't expecting you.'

The office is a mess. The security manager's desk is stacked with clutter: coffee cups, documents, deodorant spray, and a foil container holding a half-eaten bean protein wrap. The walls are white plastic, yellowing with age. The manager is overweight, balding, with sweat patches under his arms. He's hurriedly tidying up in front of Sealgair, grabbing litter from the desk and tossing it down into a bin at his feet.

Sealgair turns away from him and looks out of the window with his hands behind his back. The office is on the surface level, in what must have once been the docking bay's observation deck. He looks down on his buggy, parked next to the Marscrete slabs of the Syria Base graveyard. It's surrounded by the three rovers of his entourage, waiting patiently for him to conclude his business.

Four out-suited figures come out of the base carrying a shape wrapped in black plastic. They pause when they see the buggy. It's sleek and smooth, nothing more than a seat, a canopy, a power supply, an electric motor, four thick wheels, and an auxiliary life-support system that can be plugged directly into Sealgair's out-suit. It's red-brown, making it harder to see coming, and it's fast, much faster than any other vehicle on Mars. It's one of a kind, and the graveyard workers clearly recognise it. They back away, giving it a wide berth as they carry the body towards a shallow grave.

'You're getting caught off-guard a lot lately, aren't you?' says Sealgair.

Security Manager Merrick says nothing. He keeps tidying his desk.

'What was Clifford doing here?'

'Restocking his rover, sir.'

'Where did he go?'

'He didn't say.'

'It's your job to know where everyone comes from and goes to. Stop that!'

Merrick winces, and puts down the foil container. Sealgair takes a breath to calm himself.

'He restocked his rover and he left yesterday morning,' says Merrick. 'He was heading north. That's all I know.'

'What did he take?'

'A couple of weeks' worth of food, water and air, sir. And one rookie guard. Dylan Ward.'

Sealgair nods. 'That's something. Does this guard have friends or family on the base? Someone they're likely to communicate with?'

Merrick wipes his brow again.

'Yes sir. Her father. Do you want me to bring him in?'

'No. I don't want to spook him just yet. But watch his incoming calls. As soon as she contacts him, I want to know what she has to say.'

# Chapter Thirteen

Long ago, during his training for Mars, Clifford was put through a tactical awareness course. His instructor, an overweight ex-cop with a crew cut and no neck, drilled Clifford to observe the whole environment without tunnel vision, tally the threats, resources and opportunities, predict what would happen next, and revise his assessment as the situation evolved. The instructor was the kind of man who confused repeating something with understanding it, and whenever Clifford asked for clarification, the instructor would bark 'Observe! Tally! Predict! Revise!'

Even so, Clifford sailed through the course. His situational awareness was already excellent, thanks to his natural paranoia. At the time he thought the instructions were worthless, but after forty-five years of survival on Mars, they've wormed their way into his brain as a personal mantra. He repeats them often, to calm the fear gnawing at his core.

*Observe. Tally. Predict. Revise.*

*Observe.*

The sheriff leads Clifford and Ward away from Pavonis Base, along an inflated tube that extends out from its thick red outer wall. On either side of the them, the dusty, pebble-strewn ground stretches away to the horizon. About twenty metres ahead are a cluster of five transparent polymer mini-domes. Each of them is about ten metres in diameter, and they're joined like petals to a central hub. Through the milky walls of the tube, Clifford can see that every one of the domes is filled with human bodies; standing, sitting and lying down. The transparency of the domes makes the people inside look vulnerable and exposed.

Clifford has seen domes like these before. They're used across the Free Settlements as temporary living-spaces, and as a highly effective method of imprisonment. The bubbles are surrounded on all sides by the near-vacuum of Mars, so escape would be lethal. The smallest tear in the plastic would mean death.

'What the hell is this, now?' the sheriff mutters as they get closer to the bubbles.

Two armed guards are waiting for them in the central hub. They're in blue uniforms and polished black boots – a far cry from the sheriff and deputy's brown shirts and aluminium name badges. One of them is leaning against a hatch, and the other picks his own fingernails with the tip of his knife.

'Hey!' the sheriff says as she approaches them. 'What are all these folks are doing in my bubbles?'

The guard with the knife shrugs. 'Gotta keep them somewhere.'

'You don't get to keep people here,' says the sheriff. 'You ain't cops. You're private security.'

'We're just keeping the peace while you're out of the base. The mayor says, "You're welcome."'

*Tally.*

Threat one: the sheriff and her deputy. They're an obstacle for sure, but they also seem to be strictly and unimaginatively law-abiding, so they probably don't harm people in their custody. Law is slow. They don't pose an immediate danger.

Threat two: the private security guards. They aren't intimidated by the sheriff, and they've got a swagger that comes with author-ised cruelty.

Threat three: the inmates in the bubbles. They're packed in tightly, mostly wearing dirty orange workers' uniforms. Clifford can see angry bruised faces, and fresh knife wounds on arms and chests.

Resources: Dylan Ward. She's still at his side, in her grey shirt and work trousers, with her bushy hair tied back, and she's watch-ing the situation unfold as attentively as him. She's slightly shorter than average height, but she's young and fit and she has guard training. If it comes to a fight, he rates her chances higher than his own. The only question is how much she still trusts him, and how long that will last.

*Predict.*

'Stay close when we get in there,' he mutters to Ward. 'There's going to be trouble.'

The sheriff pushes Clifford and Ward towards a hatch, and the deputy turns a handle. As it opens, the hub fills with the yells of fifty inmates.

'We've got people bleeding out in here!'

'Where's my family?'

'Call the medics!'

'Get back!' shouts one of the guards, pointing a curved knife blade at the hatch.

The deputy looks in at the prisoners.

'You sliced the hell out of them,' he says to the guards.

One of the guards gives a lazy half-shrug.

'Like we said. Gotta keep the peace.'

The deputy cuts the cable ties from Clifford and Ward's wrists, and shoves the two of them into the bubble. Clifford collides with the hard shoulder of an inmate, and stifles a scream as his broken rib clicks in his side. Grey spots appear in front of his eyes. He barely hears the hatch slam closed behind them. All around, prisoners are shouting and threatening each other and howling in pain. The metallic whiff of blood hangs in the air, mixing with the stench of panic sweat. Some of the inmates eye Clifford and Ward, but the attention doesn't last long. They're quickly pulled deeper by the current of moving bodies, and in the heart of the chaos, no one gives them a second glance.

Clifford feels something bump against his legs. A wounded boy, about thirteen years old, is kneeling on the ground, gasping in pain, while a bearded man holds a rag to his bleeding face. Ward crouches down next to them.

'Hey!' she shouts to the man over the noise. 'Need help?'

The older inmate looks at Ward curiously, then up at Clifford. His beard is an untrimmed explosion of hair, and he has tattoos of the crests of a dozen Free Settlement bases down each arm.

'Sleeves!' he says.

'What?'

'We need bandages! If you want to help, tear off your sleeves!'

As Ward straightens up, Clifford grabs her arm. He follows her as she pushes her way through the crowd towards the edge of the bubble.

'What are you doing?' he shouts near her ear.

'Helping,' she shouts back.

'These people aren't your friends.'

'But we're stuck with them, right?'

The thin polymer wall of the bubble doesn't retain heat. Clifford shivers as they approach it, but Ward doesn't seem to notice the cold. She pulls free from Clifford's grip and faces the empty Martian landscape. With her back to him, she strips off her grey T-shirt, turns it inside out, and bites at the shoulder stitching until a thread comes loose. Clifford sees her bare back, and looks away.

*Revise.*

Clifford had been working under the assumption that Dylan Ward was loyal to him, or at least to Fuller Aerospace, but her first instinct was to help the inmates. If she wants to connect with the people around her more than she wants to protect him, it could be a problem.

He feels a tap on the shoulder, and turns to see Dylan with her shirt back on and her arms bare.

'I'm going back to give these to that man,' she says, holding up the detached sleeves. 'Are you going to stay here?'

Clifford looks around. Over the heads of the inmates, at the top of the round metal frame that surrounds the hatch, he sees a small black dot.

'No,' he says.

Ward squeezes back into the heaving mass of bodies. Clifford follows, staying close behind and letting her clear the way. His broken rib is aching, and he walks slowly, protecting his torso with his arms.

Ahead of him, Ward finds the bearded man, who's now tending to a middle-aged woman with a gash above her eye.

'Thanks,' he says as he takes the sleeves and presses them on the woman's wound. She sucks air through her teeth in pain, but the blood stops flowing down her face.

'Are you a medic?' Ward asks.

'Nope. I'm the foreman for the bioplastic vats. Just doing what I can.'

'What happened to you all?'

'The usual. Pay cuts. Protests. Stabbing.'

Clifford squeezes away from them through the bodies, wincing in pain each time an inmate bumps into him. Here in the heart of crowd, everyone is dripping with sweat. He keeps pushing until he's directly in front of the hatch, and stares up at the coin-sized circle of shiny black plastic set in the circular frame. After a few minutes, Ward pushes through the bodies behind him. He keeps his eyes on the dot.

'What are you looking at?'

'That camera,' he says, pointing to the dot. 'I hope someone's watching us.'

'I'm going to help out some more,' says Ward. 'There's a load of badly injured people. You need me for anything?'

'No. I'll be fine here.'

She squeezes back into the crowd. Clifford stays as still as possible in the jostling inmates, staring at the dot, barely blinking, until his legs begin to ache. The crowd keeps shoving him but he stands his ground, fuelled by his fury at himself. What was he thinking, coming here? The noise is unrelenting. Three inmates carry a body past him and lower it gently to the ground at the side of the hatch. It has a brown plastic jacket laid over its face, and is wearing a worker's uniform, torn and bloody. The three inmates sit around it, heads hanging down. The other prisoners around them back away to give the mourners some respectful distance, but Clifford doesn't move. He feels their resentful eyes, but he stays where he is, just outside their circle, and keeps looking up at the camera.

The afternoon wears on into evening. After decades on Mars Clifford is still caught off-guard by the sunsets, the way the sky turns from orange to blue as the sun drops down to the horizon.

With a final glow the sky turns to black, and the inmates are left in darkness. The only light comes from the lumpy moon Phobos hanging in the sky above, and from out of the windows of Pavonis Base.

The noise in the bubble dies down to a low murmur, interspersed with sobs. Clifford feels the inmates bumping into the back of his legs as they curl up to sleep on the ground sheet.

From the darkness behind, he hears Ward's voice.

'Are you still staring at the camera?'

'I assume it has night vision. Where are you going to sleep?'

'I don't know,' says Dylan.

'Stay here. I'll make sure no one steps on you.'

She curls up on a bare patch of ground in front of him. He feels her body shifting against his shoes.

'What's the matter?'

'I can feel the rocks under the ground sheet,' she says.

But she settles down, and within half an hour, she's still.

Clifford keeps staring up into the darkness. He imagines what he must look like in night vision: green and black, with glowing eyes, surrounded by prone bodies.

Without the sunlight or the movement in the dome, the air gets cold. Moisture drips down onto his shoulder from above. All the breath and sweat of the inmates is condensing on the plastic. He steps out of the dripping water, keeping his face pointing to where he imagines the camera to be, and waits.

Before dawn, the eastern horizon starts to lighten. The first of the inmates wake, and the murmuring begins. The ones that can stand get back to their feet, and the noise in the dome builds up again, rising with the sun.

He takes a short break to use a stinking bucket-toilet at the far end of the dome. As he presses his way back through the crowd, a roar comes from the inmates. Through the transparent polymer wall he sees more blue uniforms walking down the tube towards the central hub.

The crowd surges to the hatch, pulling Clifford forward. He

looks around for Ward and catches a glimpse of her wading towards him through the inmates.

'Stay with me,' he shouts, reaching out a hand.

The hatch clicks, and an LED above it turns red. After a few seconds it swings inward, pushing back the mass of bodies. Four blue-uniformed guards block the hatch with their weapons raised. One of them is holding what looks to Clifford like an electric cattle prod, with a battery pack wired to the handle and the tell-tale grooves of cheap 3D printing.

The crowd pushes into Clifford's back. A man in front of him loses his footing and stumbles into the guards. There's a flash and a crackle, and he falls to the ground, shaking. The air fills with the smell of burning hair and fabric.

'Get the hell back!' the guard yells.

The inmates grab the man by the legs and pull him to safety. Clifford sees a growing dark patch on the shaking man's trousers.

'Where are Reckling and Shay?' another guard yells.

'That's us,' Clifford calls, and beckons to Ward.

The crowd shouts in desperation. He feels hands grabbing him, trying to hold him back. The guards reach into the bubble and pull Clifford and Ward towards them. Clifford stumbles out into the hub, and falls to the ground.

'Close it!' shouts one of the guards. The hatch slams shut, silencing the roar of the inmates.

From the ground, Clifford looks up through the transparent walls of the hub and the bubble. The bearded man that Ward helped is looking down on him with his arms folded. His face is stone.

The guards holster their cattle prods. One of them offers Clifford his hand, and helps him to his feet.

'This way.'

They lead Clifford and Ward down the tunnel, towards the dusty red outer wall of Pavonis Base.

'Where are they taking us?' Ward mutters.

One of the guards hears her, and looks back with a grin.

'You're in luck,' he says. 'You're special guests of the mayor.'

# Chapter Fourteen

One of the guards spins a handle, and the hatch into the base swings open. Clifford and Ward follow the guards through an airlock, and down a shallow ramp into the processing room.

*Observe. Tally. Predict. Revise.*

The room is a mess. The white enamel coating on the walls is chipped in a dozen places, and cables are hanging down from a broken conduit. A ceiling light is flickering. There are rows of storage lockers against the far wall, and a quarter of their doors are torn off. A yellowing counter divides the room, littered with handwritten forms.

The only potential threat that Clifford can see is Deputy Marchant, standing behind the counter. As the mayor's guards enter the room the deputy lowers his head and takes a step back, and Clifford gets a flash of a memory from his childhood: an encounter with a feral dog in the streets of Miami. His parents had brought him there while they helped his aunt during the final evacuation, and he found a Dalmatian hiding behind the dumpsters outside his aunt's crumbling apartment block. The strays were everywhere, abandoned by their owners as they fled the city. The Dalmatian was skinny and trembling, and it cowered away with its tail between its legs when Clifford reached out to pet it. He thought it was being submissive, but when he got too close, it snapped.

The deputy gives off the same feeling, but the guards aren't reading his body language. They stroll into the processing room casually, chests out and elbows swinging. Ward isn't paying enough attention to the danger. She's looking around at the tattered posters on the walls, instructions for what to do in the case of an air leak or power outage.

'These two are under the mayor's jurisdiction,' the lead guard says to the deputy. 'Get their personal items.'

The deputy's jaw tightens.

'You want to release them? On what grounds?'

'On the grounds that the mayor can do what he likes to keep the peace. If you did your job better, he wouldn't need to use his special authority.'

One of the guards leans on the edge of the counter. The deputy bristles.

'Me and the sheriff follow the law.'

'Your law lets rioters take the whole base hostage,' says the lead guard smugly. Clifford knows his type. When there isn't a pecking order, this guy will make one.

The deputy puffs through his moustache. 'The mayor can't just free whoever he wants. This isn't his jurisdiction.'

'That's your opinion?' says the lead guard. 'Who's going to stop him?'

There's a moment of stillness. Clifford sees the deputy's hand twitch over the knife on his belt.

Ward is aware of the danger now. She plants her boots apart, the way Security Services guards do to keep their footing during low-gravity fights.

The lead guard bursts out laughing.

'Really? You want to take us on? Then draw your knife, lawman! Enforce the law!'

The deputy's eyes dart from guard to guard. There's four of them, and they're half his age. Slowly, he lowers his hand.

'There you go,' says the lead guard. 'You see? There's nothing unlawful going on here. We're all friends. Now give us their belongings.'

The deputy's face is grey. He backs away from the counter, and returns with Clifford and Ward's bags. Ward takes them and slings them both over her shoulders, one on each side. The lead guard taps his palms together in mock applause.

'Good boy,' he says with a grin.

# Chapter Fifteen

The Pavonis concourse is a flood of humanity. It's a new workday, and grey-suited workers from the night shift are spilling out of the wide loading doors of the manufacturing bays and bioprocessing vats, pouring through the base towards the living quarters. The stall-keepers at the edge of the concourse call out, offering them breakfasts of crispy seaweed and fried protein cakes, and beggars limp at the edges of the crowd, showing their missing teeth and limbs, and holding out their palms for any spare chips of copper or steel.

'This way,' the lead guard calls, pushing his way onto the concourse. The guards clear a path for Clifford and Ward through the human torrent. The few workers who don't back away fast enough get shoved aside with nightsticks.

The morning crowd isn't all local. Among the crush of bodies, Clifford spots citizens from across the Free Settlements. Mormon missionaries from Destiny Base are talking earnestly to a trinket hawker. A woman in a tight-fitting burgundy uniform, surrounded by a security detail, is instantly recognisable as an emissary from the militaristic Huoxing Cheng. Migrant labourers are swigging coffee from cardboard tubs, and singing the anthem of Nazarovo Base. The Free Settlements generally hold each other in contempt, but the cheap goods from Pavonis bring them all together.

Clifford hears a crunch underfoot. Shards of broken glass and plastic are scattered across the concourse floor. Overhead is a sculpture of one of the Thunderhead passenger liners, twenty metres long, and the front half of it is burned black. Melted plastic has dripped down to the floor and hardened into warped disks. The walls are plastered with shredded posters. On a scrap that remains he sees a smiling face, and the word *Kohler*.

Clifford walks faster, until he's level with the lead guard.

'So you're the mayor's private security?' he asks. 'He pays your salary from his own pocket?'

'He's a great man.'

'Looks like you've had your hands full lately.'

'No more than usual,' says the guard.

They walk past a boarded-up bar. A yellow out-suit helmet is riveted over the entrance, and a hand-painted sign next to it reads *The Blowout*. The proprietors are moving aside a flipped-over table and some sheets of corrugated metal that were covering its entrance. Leaning on the wall outside the bar is a trio of gaudily dressed sex workers. The lead guard points at them.

'Hey,' he says. 'We warned you lot. Stay off the concourse.'

The three of them give him a sour glare as they slouch away. Clifford looks over his shoulder in time to see one of them flipping an elegant finger at the backs of the guards.

The concourse opens up into the central hub of the base, and sunlight streams down from above. A glass composite dome arches overhead, letting in the morning light through a layer of dirt and a grid of electromagnetic shielding. The food stalls are packed densely below it, selling breads, vegetables and protein cultures to the pedestrians coming up from the base's main stairwell. Clifford smells a dozen different foods stewing, baking and frying: tofu curries, rice flour cakes, umami algae, seitan burgers and deep-fried mushrooms. The scents are intense and conflicting, and Clifford breaths them in deeply. They're a welcome change after the sterile air of Company Territory.

On the far side of the stairwell, a mural is embedded in the plastic wall panelling, assembled from triangular shards of glass about the size of Clifford's thumbnail. It's a picture of Rose Fuller when she was a teenager. She's wearing an out-suit, with a helmet under her arm, and she's pointing up towards the stars with an expression of hope and awe. All around the image are handprints of red paint, ranging in size from child to adult. It looks like an explosion, or a vast blooming flower.

Under the mural are the words:

## RED ROSE
## 2034 – 2058
## NEVER FORGIVE, NEVER FORGET

The stark, two-tone image has reduced her eye to almond shapes, but the sight of them still makes Clifford freeze in his tracks.

'What's wrong?' says Ward, coming up behind him.

'Nothing,' he says. 'It's just a surprise.'

She follows his gaze.

'Yeah. It's weird that they treat her like some kind of martyr.'

'I remember the original photograph that mural's based on,' Clifford says. He keeps walking. 'It was a marketing shot to promote the Company. Ironic, isn't it?'

The escalator is broken, so they walk down unmoving steps to a darker lower level. The guards lead them out from the hub into a narrow tunnel, where the floor is marked with lines of dried glue that once held down a carpet. The ceiling is low, and most of the lights are broken. After fifty metres they come to a round hatch, unmarked and painted the same shade of grey as the wall. The front guard unlocks it with a key card and pulls it open.

'Sir, ma'am,' says the lead guard. 'This way, if you please.'

Clifford and Ward step through it, into one of the most extravagant rooms on the planet.

# Chapter Sixteen

For a world founded by billionaires, Clifford is often surprised by how non-materialistic Mars can be. The truth is, there just aren't many good ways to display wealth. Tourism has been dead for the last forty-five years. Luxury goods are rare, partly because they require supply chains that don't exist any more, and partly because anything that takes up physical space on a Mars is basically clutter. Most rich people demonstrate their power in direct ways, like bullying or coercion. A few get respect by donating free air and food and water to their bases. The more imaginative ones learn to master a talent like painting or music, because it proves that they're in the rare position of not needing to worry about survival.

But the mayor of Pavonis has found another way to prove his wealth. The room Clifford and Ward walk into is two storeys high, and over fifty metres long. The walls are bare, and there are no paintings or artistic flourishes of any kind. In the centre of the room is a long table set with a plain white cloth. The mayor is flaunting the most valuable thing on Mars: available space. He's claimed a huge chunk of the base, enough for a hundred dorm rooms, and is keeping it empty just to prove that he can. It's obscene.

Next to Clifford, Ward takes a deep breath.

'What's the matter?' he says.

'I feel exposed.'

'Me too,' he says.

He looks back at the guards, who have lined up on either side of the hatch.

'What should we do? Stand around? Make ourselves uncomfortable?'

'The mayor won't be long,' says the lead guard.

Clifford rocks back and forth on his heels. After a few minutes, a door clanks open on the far end of the room and Kohler strides in. He's a little more round-faced than Clifford remembers him from his last visit, but he's still cosplaying a CEO from old Silicon Valley, in a black polo-neck and blue jeans.

'My guests of honour!' Kohler calls out, spreading his arms. 'Welcome! What do you think of my dining room?'

'Cosy,' Clifford calls back.

The mayor strolls towards them, dragging his feet slightly. As he gets closer he smiles, and points to the ceiling. 'I'm recreating the feeling of being on Earth. The sensation of space. That feeling that you could close your eyes and just walk.'

Clifford glances at Ward.

'Kohler's a Terraphile,' he says.

'You have no idea,' says the mayor with a grin. He rolls up his sleeve, showing a thick metal band around his wrist. 'Lead weights on my arms and my legs, to simulate Earth gravity. Keeps me healthy. Reduces ageing.'

He shakes Clifford's hand.

'Good to see you again, Mr Clifford.'

'And yourself, Mr Kohler. I'm going by Reckling on this trip.'

'Of course,' says the mayor, and shakes his head. 'Sorry for the cold welcome. The sheriff is one of the old guard from before the election. She hasn't come around to our new way of doing things. She won't be a problem for much longer, though. I hope your night in the bubbles wasn't too unpleasant.'

Clifford puts on a smile.

'I'm just glad someone finally noticed the surveillance cameras.'

'Please, let me make it up to you. I'm having a private dinner party tonight. Join me, I insist.'

Clifford feels Ward tensing up next to him, but he nods anyway. 'We'll be delighted. This is my bodyguard, Dylan Ward.'

The mayor shakes her hand, smiling, and keeps holding it for a little too long.

'Charmed. If we have time today, I'd love to show you my Earth memorabilia. I've got lockets, phones, collectible figurines, playing cards. Anything people brought with them on the ships. Three pens, too. One still writes. But enough about me. Can I offer you anything? Breakfast? Coffee? A drink? I hired a distiller from Huoxing Cheng. She infuses her gin with botanicals from their local greenhouse. You should taste her work, she's an alchemist.'

'That's very generous,' Clifford says, 'But if it's all right, we'd like some time alone to recover. Maybe some breakfast in our rooms. Is that all right with you, Ward?'

Dylan Ward nods firmly.

'Absolutely.'

# Chapter Seventeen

The room that the mayor gives to Clifford is the size of a small hotel suite on Earth, which makes it huge for Mars. There are no windows, just a desk and a bed. The walls are covered in fake wood panelling, and over the bed is an oil painting of hunters on horseback, riding through a lush green landscape.

A white-jacketed servant brings Clifford a breakfast tray of soya tenders and cultured egg protein, and a glass of lemon water. When Clifford's finished he locks his door, takes off his travelling clothes, and sleeps.

He wakes in the evening to a tapping on his door.

'Yes?' he calls.

'It's Ward, sir. The mayor's calling us to the party.'

'Hold on,' he says, swinging his bare legs off the bed.

He swiftly showers in the tiny en-suite bathroom, then unpacks his bag and puts on his suit. The suit is necessary. It lets people know that he's from Earth. After all these years of separation, there's psychological power to being from a different planet. People aren't sure what he's capable of, and treat him with a little more caution.

His jacket and tie weren't refolded properly after the deputy rifled through them, but the creases aren't noticeable in the bathroom mirror. He takes a deep breath, and goes to open the door. Ward is leaning against the corridor wall outside in the same clothes she wore in the bubbles: work boots, trousers with tool pockets, and a travel jacket over her grey shirt to cover up her torn-off sleeves. He looks her up and down, and she folds her arms defiantly. 'I didn't know we'd be attending a soirée when I packed. You want me to sit this one out?'

'No,' he says. 'It's perfect. It tells the mayor never to invite me to another party.'

She scratches absently at a patch of dried glue on her cuff.

'I don't trust him,' she says.

'Of course you don't, you're not a fool. But we have to keep it a secret that he's working for the Company.'

'So we're still from Rand Town?'

'Exactly.'

When they return to the cavernous dining room, they find that the first of Kohler's guests have already arrived. They're milling around in small groups, clutching their drinks and looking uncomfortable in the open space. The lights are dimmed, and some anodyne ambient electronica from Earth is playing, full of swirling synths and the sound of crashing waves. Blue-suited guards stand to attention in the corners of the room, as still and silent as statues. Mayor Kohler is talking with a woman in a green gown, and he beams at Clifford as he approaches.

'Ah! Here he is! Mr Reckling, meet Margot. She's just won the contract to dig out an expansion for the western habitat.'

Clifford shakes hands with the woman. The mayor brings over the next guest, and the next, showing them off to Clifford like a child trying to impress an adult with his favourite toys. The guests are all overdressed, charmless and vapid, but Clifford memorises their names and listens politely as they talk about themselves. It's all part of the job.

'This jacket?' says a young man with complicated hair. 'It's from the twentieth century. Genuine stone-washed denim. It was antique before it got here.'

The conversation in the room cycles through the same old topics: the Outliers, the economy, rumours of when the space flights will start again. The wars on Earth are always a few months away from being over. Some country or entrepreneur is always talking about sinking money back into human space flight. The ships are always five years away from coming to rescue the people stranded on Mars. Nothing ever changes.

Clifford sees the guests circling Ward suspiciously.

A man in a waistcoat offers her a hand. 'Bethany said that you work in security in Rand Town. What's your position? Settlement Commissioner? Chief Marshall?'

'Patroller. Night shift.'

The man is caught off-guard by the directness, and laughs with surprise.

'Isn't that fun! You must be full of stories,' he says.

She smiles grimly. 'You have no idea.'

Ward starts describing her evening patrols in ghoulish detail, leaving out anything that would locate her stories in Company Territory. She soon gathers a small crowd of listeners, and Clifford is delighted to see the shock on their faces.

'The worst are the ones who get sliced open in knife fights. Gut-spillers, we call them. They crawl through the corridors, holding in their own intestines, bleeding and begging for help. Most of them are petty criminals or drunks, so no one wants to touch them. Sometimes they crawl all the way to the guard quarters, thinking we'll be able to do something. They end up slumped over outside our doorway. The guards just step over them.'

'Can't you help?' one of the listeners asks in an appalled whisper.

'We're not medics,' Ward says. 'We can't put anyone's insides back in. We used to call for the base doctors, but gut-spillers never live long enough for them to arrive.'

Clifford is sure that Ward is exaggerating, but the squeamishness of the guests is wonderful to watch. He has misjudged her, again. She isn't nearly as dull or obedient as she's pretending to be. Back in the bubbles he had assumed that she had a compulsion to fit in at all costs, which made sense for her profile. After coming from the Free Settlements to Company Territory, she's probably learned not to stick out from the crowd. But Dylan Ward isn't quiet or compliant. She sees through these people, and she isn't intimidated by them.

The mayor taps an empty glass with a fork, and calls the guests over to take their places at the table. When they see their plates, they clap their hands and compliment him on his ingenuity. The appetisers are chicken drumsticks, deep-fried and served with a side order of barbecue sauce. The vat-grown meat is moulded onto ceramic bones to make it seem like it came from a living bird. Clifford knows what actual chicken meat looks like, and he isn't impressed.

The mayor clinks his whisky glass again. The table quietens, and the few people still talking get nudged into silence by their neighbours.

'Thank you. Before we go any further, please, charge your glasses.'

The guests pour themselves more drinks, and the mayor stretches out a hand towards Clifford. 'Allow me to introduce a special guest, my old friend and business associate, Mr Reckling, from Rand Town. I've worked with him for over a decade and I can quite honestly say that without his help, I wouldn't be in the position I am today.

'Yesterday, as Mr Reckling returned to this fine base, our very own sheriff Laurie Ravine took the opportunity to throw him in the bubbles for trivial reasons. This is unacceptable. The sheriff isn't keeping the peace, she's following old laws that just don't apply in the modern world. I have tried to work with her, but she has undermined me every step of the way. I had to use my own guards to bring order and stability back to the base.'

The party guests murmur their approval. The mayor raises a hand to settle them down.

'The sheriff is forcing my hand,' he says. 'We don't need two separate arms of law enforcement fighting each other, when only one of them does the real job. Tonight, I'd like to make a proposal. I believe it's in the best interests of the base to disband the sheriff's department. My guards will be relieving her of her duties, and if she refuses to cooperate then they'll be placing her under arrest. But you all are the backbone of the base. I rule with your consent. So if any of you have any objections to this plan then let me know, right here, right now, in front of everyone.'

The guests are suddenly sober. Clifford sees them looking around at the armed guards in the corners, as if they're seeing them for the first time.

'We need law enforcement that isn't bound up by rules and red tape,' says the mayor. 'You're my closest friends. We've all come a long way together, and we have a great journey ahead. We rely on each other. If one of us falls, we all do. So I'm glad that you're supporting me in this troubling time. Thank you.'

He raises his glass.

'To peace in Pavonis!' he says.

The dinner guests echo his words. They drink together, and the conversation slowly babbles back to life. Soon, they're all chatting and laughing as if nothing has happened. Margot, the woman in the green gown, leans over and talks to the mayor quietly.

'Well, Iain,' she says with a smile. 'You really out-do yourself with your little surprises.'

# Chapter Eighteen

At the end of the evening the lights dim and the volume of the ambient music goes down. The few remaining guests take the hint. They finish their drinks and their meaningless chatter, and stagger out of the dining room, towards their own residences. The mayor signals to the guards and they file out too, leaving Clifford and Ward alone with the mayor.

Clifford sips water from his glass, and watches Kohler. The mayor's been drinking whisky, and his head is nodding slightly. He doesn't seem to notice that he's being stared at.

'So,' says Clifford. 'Arresting the sheriff. That's ... bold.'

Kohler waves a hand dismissively.

'If the law doesn't protect the powerful, then the powerful have to protect themselves.' He leans back in his chair and puts his hands behind his head. 'But don't worry about my business. What brings you to Pavonis?'

'You had a visitor from the Company,' says Clifford. 'A census taker.'

'Ah, yes! Unwin. Skittish little man. Glasses.'

Clifford nods. 'That's him. He dropped out of contact after coming through your base. I'm trying to locate him.'

Kohler tilts his head at Clifford, and their eyes lock. He isn't as drunk as he's pretending to be.

'You lost an employee? That's a little careless, isn't it?'

Ward is looking from Kohler to Clifford uncertainly. Kohler grins at her.

'Have you asked your boss why he's so interested in one missing person?'

Ward glances at Clifford. 'Not yet.'

Kohler doesn't look at Clifford. He keeps smiling at Dylan.

'Really? It's the first question I'd ask. Why did the head of Internal Affairs need to come out here, in person? Whatever he's really looking for, it must be valuable.'

'All right, Kohler,' Clifford warns.

Kohler raises an eyebrow.

'What's the matter? We're all friends here. I'll tell you where Unwin went when you help me out with a few small things.'

'The Company hasn't been generous enough?' Clifford says, waving a hand around the cavernous room.

'But this is more of a personal thing for you, isn't it?' says Kohler, leaning back in his chair. 'This is about Project Granite.'

Ward looks at Clifford again, questioningly. He keeps his face still, making sure that Kohler doesn't see he hit a nerve.

'I'd like five Company rovers,' says Kohler. 'You're sending hundreds of them north to deal with the Outliers, so you must be able to spare a few for an ally. Fully armed with base-bursters.'

'Why base-bursters?'

Kohler shrugs. 'Just a show of power. Some of the bases nearby have been poached by Huoxing Cheng for trade and protection. Helena, Founder's Gully, and Combine are traditionally ours. We want them back. It's in the Company's interest, when you think about it.'

Clifford stares at Kohler unblinkingly.

'Two rovers.'

'Three.'

'Agreed.'

They shake.

'So where's Unwin?'

Kohler relaxes, and smiles again.

'Last I heard, he was heading for the Twins,' says Kohler. 'Better him than me. I have a letter that he wrote to you. It's in my office, I'll send for it if—'

The lights cut out. A moment later, so does the hiss of the air system. They're caught in darkness and silence.

Clifford feels on the table in front of him, and his fingers find the steel handle of a carving knife. He grabs it and stands, listening to the room, ready to lunge at anyone who gets too close.

'What the fuck?' says the mayor. There's a clatter as his chair falls over in the dark.

There's a faint roar of voices coming from the corridor outside, and a repeated metallic thud, like a dull steel drum.

Red emergency lights snap on. Everything in the room turns stark black and red, like a propaganda poster. The mayor is on his feet, and his eyes widen at the sight of Clifford's knife.

'Did you do this?'

'Not me.'

The inner hatch swings open and the lead guard runs in followed by three of his men. The moment they see Clifford, they draw knives of their own.

'Put those away,' Kohler says. 'Hillard, what in fuck's name is this?'

The lead guard's eyes are wide. His swagger from the concourse has evaporated.

'Sir, we didn't want to disturb you during the party, but the sheriff released the rioters from the bubbles.'

'When?'

'A few hours ago. She's calling for your arrest.'

'So? We outnumber her. It's her law against mine, she can't do shit.'

'We tried to round her up, sir,' the lead guard says, 'We sent forty guards. They're all detained or dead.'

'How?'

Hillard's face is drained.

'Sir. She deputised the entire workforce.'

'Bullshit. She can't do that.'

'She did, sir. She unlocked the weapons cache. She's arming the rioters.'

Hillard touches a finger to his earpiece, and his eyes wander as he listens.

'They've taken over the central base controls,' he says. 'They sealed the emergency doors.'

A metallic bang comes from the outer door of the mayor's quarters.

'They're breaking in,' he says, and puts a hand on the mayor's arm. 'Sir. We need to get you out of here.'

'All right,' says the mayor. 'We'll regroup in the guard quarters. It's better defended.'

'No, sir,' says Hillard. 'We need to get you into a rover.'

'What?' says the mayor, shaking himself free. 'No! I'm not going to be intimidated by rioters! This is my fucking base! We're not running. Get out there and fight!'

Clifford sees a muscle twitch in Hillard's cheek. He's barely keeping himself under control.

'Sir. They're armed. They outnumber us.'

'Oh, come on!' shouts the mayor. 'Do I have to do your job for you? Use your bolt guns! Shoot out the windows! Suffocate them!'

There's another boom from the outer door, and the roar of the crowd gets louder.

Hillard grabs the mayor by the arm again, firmly, and pulls him towards the inner hatch. The other two guards come in close to shield the mayor with their bodies. This time, Kohler doesn't resist.

Clifford passes the knife to Ward. 'You'd better take this.'

They follow the mayor out of the dining room and into the metal-walled corridor. One of the guards seals the hatch behind them, and Hillard holds a hand to his earpiece again.

'The rover bay's clear. We can go.'

'Wait. We need ingots from the store room,' says the mayor.

He scrambles down the corridor ahead of his guards. Clifford is about to follow when he sees an open hatch opposite the dining room, and catches a glimpse of a wide desk covered in papers.

'Hold on,' he says to Ward, and runs into the mayor's office. She sticks her head in behind him.

'What are you doing?'

The office has a desk, a side table, two bookshelves and a whiteboard. The right wall is covered with a glass fronted cabinet filled with curiosities: old laptops, cellular telephones and children's toys. In the red light, they look like artefacts excavated from Hell.

Clifford gets to the desk and searches through the stack of documents, tossing aside invoices, quarterly reports and draft treaties.

'Sir?' Ward says urgently.

He doesn't answer, but keeps searching. The filing is incredibly sloppy. Half-written speeches. Personnel files...

The metallic battering starts again, much closer this time. Dylan Ward puts a hand on his shoulder.

'Mr Clifford. It's my job to keep you safe.'

He lifts up a stack of intelligence reports, and finds an envelope with *James Clifford* on the front. It's been torn open. He takes out the letter, and slips it into his pocket.

'Let's get the fuck out of here,' he says.

# Chapter Nineteen

Ward takes her hand off his shoulder, and he follows her out of the office. Up ahead, the passage splits left and right. There's no sign of the mayor of his guards.

'Which way?' says Ward.

'Shhh.'

Clifford holds his breath, until he hears a faint metallic screech from the left. They follow the sound down a narrow corridor. Doors on either side lead into store rooms with shelves stacked with ration packs. The noise is coming from an open hatch ahead. The mayor and his security team are on the other side, bathed in the red emergency lights. One of the guards is using an electric screwdriver to remove a floor-to-ceiling wall panel, and the others are standing over a pallet holding three bundles of titanium, wrapped in layers of transparent plastic. It looks like at least a thousand ingots: an untraceable fortune. The mayor looks up at Clifford and Ward as they approach, but his eyes slide off them. They no longer matter.

The last of the thick metal screws falls to the ground and the guard pulls the panel away, revealing a walk-space lined with supply tubes and cables.

'This way, sir,' says Hillard, ushering the mayor into the walk-space with a flashlight. The three other guards strain as they lift the pallet, and haul it after the mayor. The fortune clinks in the darkness. Clifford and Ward follow after them, uninvited.

The air in the walk-space is hot, and it stinks of ammonia. The red light from the room behind them fades to black. Clifford follows the clinking and the guards' straining breath. He runs a hand along one of the pipes to keep himself going straight. Ahead, he sees flickers from Hillard's flashlight, shining between the moving bodies.

The dark path winds through the guts of the base. At every turn, Clifford expects an ambush. The guards stop ahead of him, and he hears the butt of Hillard's flashlight tapping on a wall panel. Someone taps back, and a bright streak of light shines into the walk-space. The mayor and the guards disappear into the light, and Clifford and Ward follow after them, into a loud, brightly lit chamber.

Clifford recognises the Pavonis docking bay. A row of hatches on the far wall lead out to the rovers. The mayor's guards are clustered around one of the hatches, loading power packs and oxygen tanks into it with a human chain. They're moving fast, and their expressions are grim.

At the far end of the bay is a wide security door, set with a glass-composite window. Through it, Clifford sees a mass of moving bodies. Voices roar faintly, and hands hammer on the glass. The mayor flinches.

'Don't worry, sir,' says Hillard. 'They're not getting in. I ordered my guards to tear out the control cables.'

Ward looks down the row of docking hatches.

'Which one's Rudolf?' she says quietly.

'Who?'

'I mean the Calliope.'

Clifford looks at her askance. 'The second hatch on the left. Seriously, "Rudolf"?'

A barely audible voice shouts on the other side of the security door. Clifford can't make out the words, but through the slit windows he sees movement. The sheriff's deputy is forcing his way through the crowd, carrying a foil package towards the door. The protesters all back away. They're clearing the room.

Hillard's face goes grey. 'We've got to go now, sir,' he says.

The mayor turns to run, and collides with a guard carrying supplies. Frozen ration packs scatter on the ground. On the other side of the door, Clifford sees the deputy hurrying away after the rest of the protesters, leaving the room empty. The foil package is propped up next to the door.

Clifford turns to Ward.

'Run!' he yells.

Before they can reach the Calliope's hatch, Clifford is hit by a noise so loud that it can only be experienced as pain. He sees the security door flying towards them. It clips the side of the pallet of ingots, tearing the plastic and spraying metal bars across the docking bay. Then, suddenly, he's on the ground, watching debris falling all around him. His shoulder, rib and ears are in agony.

Ward is standing over him. She reaches down, and her lips move silently. He takes her outstretched hand, and she pulls him upright. At the far end of the docking bay there's a hole in the wall where the security door used to be. Titanium ingots are scattered everywhere, among the fragments of supply crates and the water spilling out from a cracked plastic barrel. Some of the guards are getting back to their feet, but most are lying still. The air is hazy, and smells like burning plastic.

Clifford can hear distant sounds again. Ward is talking to him.

'—need to go,' she says. 'Are you with me?'

He feels his shoulder for damage. It's bleeding from the impact of the debris, but he'll survive.

'Go,' he says, knowing that he's speaking too loud. Ward goes through the hatch, and Clifford follows. It's a relief to be back in the Calliope's familiar lower deck, next to the out-suits stowed behind their white plastic webbing.

'I'll start Rudolf,' says Ward, climbing the ladder to the upper deck. 'You close up.'

Clifford grabs the handle of the outer hatch, and pulls. The hatch barely moves. Outside, the protesters are swarming into the docking bay. The mayor's guards stand ready with their cattle prods crackling, but the protesters have the numbers on their side. The first wave of bodies falls to the ground, twitching and screaming, but more pour in behind them from the hole in the docking bay wall.

Clifford yanks on the handle again. His broken rib screams at him, but the heavy metal hatch begins to close. There's movement on the docking bay floor. Clifford sees the mayor crawling towards him, bleeding from his arms and chest, and the red drops splash and swirl in the pooling water from the barrel. He looks up at Clifford, and his face is twisted with pain and anger.

'Fucking help me!'

The hatch keeps closing. The mayor's mouth is open in scream-ing fury as protesters spill into the bay behind him. The outer hatch slams, and the rover is sealed off from the base.

Clifford pushes the inner hatch closed, and locks it in place.

'Drive!' he calls up to Ward.

The Calliope shakes around him. He hears the wheels throwing up gravel, but a lurch of forward motion doesn't come.

He runs up the passage, and climbs the ladder up to the cockpit. Ward is sitting at the controls with her jaw clenched.

'Why aren't we moving?'

'The docking clamps are locked. They're holding us—'

She's cut off by a bang from the rear of the rover. The Calliope swings violently to the right, and Clifford grabs onto the seat's headrest to stay upright.

'That was one of them,' she says.

With a second bang the Calliope swings the other way, and starts fishtailing left and right while the wheels throw up dust and rocks. The remaining clamps around the Calliope's rear hatch are creaking, but they don't break.

'Go slower,' says Clifford. 'Get traction.'

Dylan lowers the throttle, and the treads stop skidding. The wheels hook into the regolith with a metallic crunch, and the Calliope's nose bucks upwards. With a final snap they drop down again, and they bounce on the suspension.

'Go!' says Clifford, reaching over Ward to push on the throttle. The Calliope lurches forward into the darkness.

'I've got it,' says Ward, nudging his hand aside. She flips on the headlights and steers until they're riding parallel to the wall of the base. Just as Clifford begins to relax, Dylan pulls hard left on the control stick, and they skid sideways on the loose rocks. He grabs the seat's headrest to stay upright.

'What the hell?' he says.

Up ahead is a group of about ten people, standing in the darkness outside the base. Clifford recognises faces from the party. None of them have out-suits on, and they're watching in wide-eyed horror as the Calliope slides towards them. The wheels gain traction again, and the Calliope narrowly misses the plastic wall of the bubble.

They ride away from the base, in silence, following the rover tracks in the dust. A minute later, the boulders of the border fence appear in the Calliope's headlights, as well as another rover, blocking the gap. It's as old and patched together as the one that the sheriff was driving, but instead of a harpoon, it has a spotlight mounted on its roof. The light tracks them as they get closer. The scratches on the Calliope's windows glow in the spotlight, making it difficult to see ahead.

'Can you make out any weapons on that thing?' Clifford says.

Ward leans forward and shields her eyes with her hand.

'Nothing big,' she says.

'Then drive.'

Dylan steers the Calliope towards the other rover, and slows down until they're nose to nose with it. There's a clink as their front bars collide, and she gives power to the Calliope's wheels. The other rover slides backwards slowly, out of the gap in the boulder fence. The Calliope may be old, but she's got muscle.

A metallic boom shakes the floor below them, and a loud hiss comes from the rear. The Calliope is pulled backwards, away from the other rover.

'What the hell's that?' he says.

Dylan brings up the rear-view camera on the control desk. A second rover is behind them, with a cable stretching from its roof into the back of the Calliope.

'We've been harpooned.'

Clifford climbs back down, skipping the last few rungs of the ladder and floating down to the lower level. At the far end of the corridor, a three-finned spike about the size of his hand is sticking through the rear hatch, with air whistling out around it. The Calliope lurches again, and Clifford rebounds off the wall as he runs down the corridor.

He grabs the tip of the harpoon. It's burningly cold from the outside, and his fingertips stick to it.

'Shit,' he mutters.

He pulls his hand free, losing some skin, and looks around the corridor. A fire extinguisher hangs on the wall next to the door of the chemical toilet. He unhooks it and hammers it on the spines of the harpoon. On the fifth blow the harpoon detaches. The tip disappears from the hole, leaving a black void and a roar of rushing air. The Calliope lurches again as it accelerates forward. Clifford looks around in desperation for something to plug the hole. He pulls the netting off one of the out-suits and grabs an abdominal section, detaching it and holding the fabric against the hole. The roar stops instantly. The white fabric bulges, and for a moment Clifford thinks that it will be blown out of the rover, but the pressure holds it in place.

He climbs back up to the cockpit.

'Hold on,' says Ward grimly. 'We aren't done yet.'

Through the side of the cockpit window Clifford sees the rover with the spotlight driving closer, trying to block their path. Its bumper narrowly misses them, and Ward aims for the rock fence. The Calliope skids and slides through the gap, jolting as they clip the boulders on both sides. The wheels regain traction, and Ward straightens them out.

Clifford checks the rear-view monitor. With the night-vision, he sees the two Pavonis rovers following them out of the fence. But the Calliope is quicker and better maintained. They shrink as he watches, until they're nothing more than blocky pixels, glowing infrared.

Ward switches back to self-driving mode, and leans back in the driver's seat. She takes a deep breath.

'We're free,' she says.

Clifford looks down at his trembling hands, and holds them

under his armpits so Dylan doesn't see. He keeps his jaw clenched. If he lets himself feel relief too quickly then it might overwhelm him, and he can't afford to lose Dylan's trust. Not just yet.

He checks his pocket, and pulls out the letter from Unwin. He got it. It nearly killed them both, but he got it.

# Chapter Twenty

Dear Mr Clifford,

I'm sorry that I have to communicate with you like this. Mayor Kohler told me that the Company network isn't secure, and that I mustn't risk leaking anything that might be classified as top secret. He said that if I write you a physical letter, he'll deliver it to you personally. I hope you get it soon. I'll always do whatever the Company expects me to do, but this matter is far beyond my usual skill set or security clearance, and I'll try to wrap it up quickly so I can return to the census as soon as possible.

Here's the situation. Three days ago, I was in my private room in the Pavonis transient quarters going through their export records, when someone started hammering on my door.

I ignored it and kept entering data into my spreadsheet. I've been harassed like this many times on many different bases, and I expected the troublemaker to get bored and move on. But the hammering was persistent, and after a while I heard my name being called. I reluctantly unlocked the door and slid it open. One of the mayor's private guards was in the corridor outside, and he demanded that I follow him. I had no idea what he wanted, but I didn't dare disobey.

Out on the concourse, I felt the eyes of the Pavonis citizens on me, sizing me up. I was sure I'd be mobbed at any second. I seriously considered running, but I didn't think I would make it far.

He took me up to the repair bay on the surface level, where red-suited workers were clambering over half-assembled vehicles, riveting and drilling and grinding metal. After a week alone in my room, the activity was disorienting and the noise was unbearable.

The guard led me to the far end of the bay, where a rover was standing alone. It was one of our new ones, an FA Marathon 3E, with a big blue Fuller Aerospace launching-rocket logo on the front. It was beaten up, with huge gashes down its side, and two of its six wheels were gone. A cleaning crew was hosing off the dust on its sides, and a pair of medics on top were lowering a stretcher through a hole in its roof.

Mayor Kohler was watching from the edge of the bay. The guard brought me to him, and he told me that his men had found the rover crawling through Pavonis territory, seemingly without a driver. They towed it back to the docking bay to salvage it, but when they cracked it open, they found a survivor.

I watched as a boy in a Company out-suit was lifted out on the stretcher. The side of his face was purple and swollen, and he was bleeding from his abdomen. As the medics lowered him to the ground he screamed incoherently, and his eyes slid off me when I asked him his name.

I followed as they carried him down to the medical bay. They put him in a small private room with subdued lighting. The medics were all overworked, so I had to help them clean and bandage his wounds. He kept mumbling the whole time, but after they gave him some water he quietened down, and eventually passed out.

I stayed at his bedside. The next morning he woke before five. He was shivering, and said that he was in terrible pain, but at least I could finally understand his words.

He said his name was Sam Beatty, nineteen years old, a Security Services guard posted at Chapman Outpost on the northern border of the Free Settlements. Two weeks earlier his team had received orders from your office, instructing them to go on an expedition into Outlier Territory as part of something called Project Granite. They were ordered to locate a hidden base that the Outliers call the Wintergarden, somewhere to the north-east of Olympus Mons.

They set out in three rovers, winding their way across the dangerous landscape and searching for settlements. On the third day they saw an Outlier patrol in the distance: skeletal-looking rovers, moving the way that the Outliers do: crawling slowly to scout the landscape, then accelerating to terrifying speeds as they move to their next lookout spot. Fortunately, the Outliers didn't detect the team. They stayed hidden among the boulders, and after a few hours, the Outliers moved on.

The next day, the scouting team spotted a base in the distance, and went to investigate. Sam Beatty guarded the rovers while the rest of the team went out with circular saws to cut their way in. They called up to Beatty over the radio, saying that they'd found something incredible below ground. They said that the place was full of life. They sounded hysterical. He asked them what they meant, but they didn't reply. A few seconds later he heard the first half of a scream, and the connection cut out.

He put on his suit, hoping to rescue his team, but as he climbed down from the rover, two Outliers attacked. They had been waiting, crouched down beside the rover wearing out-suits daubed with blood. He had a bolt gun, but before he could raise it, the Outliers knocked him to the ground. One swung a club on his hand, crushing his fingers, the other stabbed him through the abdomen with a spear.

When he came around, he was skewered to the ground, and had vomited in his helmet. The Outliers were nowhere to be seen, so, in tremendous pain, he pulled the spear out and got to his feet. His suit had lost a lot of air. The rovers were already partially stripped for parts, and sheets of outer plating were stacked on the ground next to him. He still couldn't see the Outliers, but boot tracks led off towards the base entrance. With tremendous difficulty, he climbed back into his rover. The controls still worked, but the navigation system was gone. He steered around until he was facing south, and set the speed to a constant thirty kilometres an hour. Looking back through his open hatch, he saw one of the other rovers chasing after him, matching his speed. Horror gripped him, until he realised that the second rover's self-driving system was set to automatically follow him. There was no one in the cockpit. He was safe.

He passed in and out of consciousness as he drove south. Without a navigation system he couldn't locate any of the Company outposts, or even a Free Settlement. He kept driving, hoping to make it all the way back into Company Territory. After the first day, the rover following him broke down. He left it where it had failed, at the bottom of a gully, and kept travelling south. He passed out from the pain one last time, and when he woke up, he was in Pavonis Base.

Beatty told me that it was vital for the Company to find that base. He said you, personally, had given the orders to capture it. Unfortunately, without the rover's navigation system, he couldn't tell me it's exact location. But the second rover that made it out of Outlier Territory did have a functioning nav computer, and the location of the Wintergarden should be recorded in it. He told me that, judging by the landscape, the rover was somewhere close to the Twins when it broke down. So as long as Hunter or Tharsis haven't captured the rover and erased its computer, the map to your hidden base will still be on board.

I can't tell you how reluctant I am to leave my census work, but Beatty insisted that relocating the Wintergarden was critical for you. The mayor tells me that I should take the initiative, so I'm going to head north tomorrow morning on the rover train. If I manage to retrieve that map from the Twins' territory then I'll send it back to Fuller Aerospace, so you can send another expedition to capture the Wintergarden. I'm going to have to use the ingots that the Company gave me as a per diem to pay for the journey, but the mayor assures me that you'll compensate me.

I'll write to you again soon, when I have the map and I'm safely back in a Fuller Aerospace outpost. And I'm sorry to have to inform you that Sam Beatty passed away this morning, as I was writing this letter. Please communicate my sympathy to his family, and the families of the rest of his team.

Sincerely,

Chris Unwin

FA - 112 019

# Part 2.5

---

# The Little Green Man

# Chapter Twenty-One

FOR IMMEDIATE RELEASE

ALEXANDER FULLER: OBITUARY
<u>1993 to 2055</u>

The death of Alexander Fuller is an unexpected and painful loss, not just for his family and for the company he founded, Fuller Aerospace, but for humanity. He will be remembered as one of the most historically important people who ever lived. Thanks to his imagination, inventiveness, and willpower, humanity has not just set foot on Mars, but made it a home.

Alexander Fuller studied at Caltech, designing machine-learning algorithms that would become the backbone for his first successful business, FullWell Artificial Intelligence. In 2015 he sold his company and used the proceeds to fund a risky space venture that he called Fuller Aerospace. The company's first four attempted launches (The FX1 to FX4) were failures, but the fifth and final test launch, the FX5, successfully achieved low Earth orbit, and secured the nascent company its first military contract.

Over the next three decades Alexander Fuller continued to lead the Fuller Aerospace team as they iterated their rocket designs, from 2017's Cumulus satellite launch system all the way to 2033's Thunderhead passenger liners. Fuller's hands-on approach to his business and his deep understanding of technology allowed Fuller Aerospace to launch payloads into space more frequently and cheaply than any competing space start-up, and it quickly became the number-one launch provider for both NASA and the United States military.

Like many of his tech-billionaire contemporaries he was prone to making bold promises, and, like them, he was accused of empty showmanship. Unlike his contemporaries, however, his vision was vindicated. When mission commander Sunita Johnson became the first human to set foot on another planet in 2030, she and her crew were carried by a Fuller Aerospace rocket, the Odyssey. Four years later, in 2034, Alexander Fuller and his wife Kelly took the same journey on Fuller Aerospace's first passenger liner, the Hyperion. Three months after they landed, Kelly Fuller gave birth to Alexander Fuller's children Rosemary and Archimedes, the first human beings born on Mars.

In the last nine years, hundreds of engineers and scientists working for Fuller Aerospace have settled on the planet permanently, building the infrastructure to make Mars self-sufficient, and many hundreds more tourists have come to join them on the adventure of a lifetime. But tragically, Fuller did not live to see his greatest hope come true: an independent Mars, free from political control by Earth. At Fuller Aerospace, we pledge to do everything in our power to make Fuller's final dream a reality.

Until then, Mars is waiting, and tickets for the next launch window are on sale from the Fuller Aerospace website. Anyone who wishes to emigrate to a whole new world, or to experience the greatest tourist destination in human history, can thank Alexander Fuller for the new vistas of opportunity that he has unlocked.

Fuller's death is a tragedy, but few people can claim to have done so much with their lives, or made such an impact on history. For that, the human race is grateful. Thank you, Alexander Fuller. We will remember you for all time.

– Fuller Aerospace Press Team

# Chapter Twenty-Two

Rose sat on the end of her bed. Her travel case was on her lap, packed and ready. She checked her watch. Ten minutes to go. She had to time this precisely. If she left too early then her mother might discover that she'd gone, and force her to come back. If she left too late, then the rover train would depart without her.

Outside the window, a huge machine was building a new section of the base. It has been working all day and night, in total silence: a dull metal block fed by a bundle of wires and pipes. It slid slowly and smoothly along a gantry, pouring a strip of finely crushed rock dust out of a hopper. Behind it, a robot arm scooped a long thin trench in the dust, shaping and sintering its sides with lasers bright enough to leave dark spots in Rose's vision. Once the trench was complete, the block slid the other way, pouring molten rock from a furnace into the newly made mould. Layer after layer, it was printing the outer wall of a new building, using nothing but the naturally available regolith and an insane amount of fusion energy. Printing with lava. It was exactly the kind of thing that made her dad famous: showy, seemingly ridiculous, but somehow, it was happening.

He was gone now, but the machine kept on going.

The glow from the long mould faded to a dim red. When the countdown hit five minutes, Rose couldn't keep herself still any longer. She stood, hooked her case's strap up onto her shoulder, and slid the door open as quietly as she could.

The corridor outside was dark. The only light came from the elevator buttons, glinting off all the 'Mars-chic' decor that her mother had chosen. Every surface was either stainless steel, white-coated carbon fibre, or polished Mars rock. The walls were shaped to look like the early settlements, when every structure had to be a dome or a tube to contain the air-pressure inside, and the hard curved surfaces magnified the sound of Rose's steps.

The elevator would be too loud, so she carried her bag down the spiral stairs, and past the glass-fronted display of fire opals excavated in the Fuller mines. She was extra careful as she passed the door to her mother's office. It was close to the extra minutes of the night, and her mother was almost certainly in bed, but Kelly's work hours had been erratic lately, and Rose wasn't taking chances.

The corridor opened into the lounge: a wide dome with an artificial fireplace in the centre. The exit to the rest of the base was on the far side. As Rose crossed the polished stone floor she heard distant laughter, and froze. Her mother was sitting at the bar counter at the side of the lounge, half in darkness, staring at her pad, with an empty wine glass in front of her. It sounded like she was watching something from the daily data package from Earth, some kind of late-night talk show, full of forced cheerfulness and contrived spontaneity. Kelly glanced up and saw her daughter, and the travel bag.

'Rose? What are you—?'

Rose ran.

Kelly drew a breath. 'Rose Fuller! Stop right there!'

Rose touched the pad at the side of the entrance, and slipped out of the door before it could fully iris open. The base outside was dark and quiet. Her feet clattered as she ran towards the rover docks. Her cheeks burned, but she couldn't change her mind now.

She ran into the departure hall: a wide half-dome filled with rows of empty seats. Posters of Rose were up on all the walls, posing in an out-suit, looking up at the sky. Between the benches were terrariums filled with fungi that glowed under UV lights, presumably because they looked alien enough to impress the tourists from Earth. The hall was empty. There was no sign of any other passengers, and Rose's heart sank.

On the curved far wall of the hall she spotted a row of closed hatches. She ran to them, past a tank holding hundreds of tiny robot fish whose shoal formed the shape of the Fuller Aerospace logo. As she got closer, she was relieved to see that one of the hatches was still open, and a man in a blue uniform was standing at its side. He smiled at her

'Miss Fuller! It's an honour. I'm Charles, and I'll be your rover pilot this evening.'

He offered her his hand. He was young, and had the same expression that all strangers seemed to have around her lately: the cautious, sincere look of someone who just wanted to make sure that she was all right. Rose tried to hide her panic.

'Thanks,' she said, giving her best attempt at a smile as they shook hands. 'I'm ready to go.'

'This rover train is operated by United Mars, under license from Fuller Aerospace. The journey to Pavonis Base will take a little over thirty hours.'

Rose screamed inwardly. *Don't make me be polite.*

'Which rover will I be in?' she asked.

'Right this way,' said Charles, gesturing to the open hatch behind him. 'Elite class, up at the front.'

'And when do we depart?' said Rose, hauling her luggage past him.

'Right now. All the other passengers and the cargo are loaded and ready to go. They arrived an hour before departure, but we weren't going to leave without you.'

'Great,' she said, and realised that probably wasn't enough. 'Thank you. It's appreciated.'

'You're most welcome.'

The rover cabin was spacious. It had four wide, blue, soft-looking passenger seats with fold-out tray tables, display screens for en-route entertainment, and a shelf laden with drinks and snacks. At the front was a plastic privacy door leading into the cockpit. As Charles loaded Rose's case into a storage compartment at the back of the cabin, she sat down in the furthest seat from the hatch and stared out into the departure lounge, tapping her fingers on the armrest.

Charles turned to her and clasped his hands together.

'Thank you so much for choosing United Mars, and may I say what an honour it is to be driving you this evening.'

Rose forced a smile. 'Thanks, I'm looking forward to starting.'

'Is there anything at all I can do to make your journey more comfortable?' he asked.

'No thank you. It's been a long day.'

She said it firmly, and he finally seemed to understand. He looked serious, and nodded.

'No problem. Let's hit the trail.'

He pressed a button to close and seal the hatch, and disappeared into the cockpit, sliding the cabin door closed behind him. After an agonising minute, Rose felt her seat shake as the rover train crawled away from Aries Base.

She leaned back into the soft blue cushions of her seat and tried to relax. She should have known better. Almost immediately, Charles was tapping on the dividing door.

'Miss Fuller?' he said. 'May I come through?'

The door slid open a crack, and Charles looked in nervously, with a furrowed brow.

'Miss Fuller, your mother is ordering us to turn back,' he said.

Rose stayed calm. 'I'm a paying customer and I'm over eighteen. I don't need her permission to be here. She can't make me do anything.'

Charles looked pained. 'Yes, ma'am. The thing is, Mars United has a business relationship with Fuller Aerospace, and my bosses...' He left it hanging, and looked at her pleadingly.

'Is there any way I can call her from in the rover?' she asked him.

'Yes, ma'am. She's waiting for you on the cockpit radio.'

Rose got to her feet and squeezed past Charles into the rover cockpit. It had a single driver's seat and an angled screen that showed an infrared view of the landscape ahead.

As Rose took the driver's seat, Charles leaned over and tapped on the screen to bring up the communications console. After a few seconds, Kelly Fuller's voice came through the cockpit speakers.

'Did you get her? Is she there?' Her voice cracked a little, even though the line was clear.

'Hi Mom,' Rose said through gritted teeth.

'Rose. Get back this instant. This is ridiculous.'

Charles took a step back towards the cockpit door. 'I'll give you two your privacy.'

'No,' said Kelly over the radio. 'Stay. I need you to turn the rover train around. Rose, what do you think you're doing? We have a commercial shoot tomorrow morning.'

Charles reached out for the controls. Rose grabbed his wrist.

'No Mom. I'm not doing any more photoshoots. I'm out of fake smiles.'

'What are you trying to prove? Do you need to go to a shrink again? I can find you another one.'

'I'm fine, Mom.'

'Of course you aren't. It's been seven months, and you're still acting out. I'll get you a shrink.'

'I don't need to talk to anyone! I need to get out!'

'You know how the news sites are going to take this,' said Kelly's disembodied voice. 'They'll say that the family is falling apart without Alex at the helm. We have to be united. Where do you even think you're going?'

'Mariner.'

'You're going to the festival? You want to do drugs and dance like an idiot? You're the first human born on another planet, Rose! The things you do matter!'

Rose's cheeks burned. 'I just want to see Archie. I'm going stir-crazy.'

But Kelly was talking over her. 'Then call him! And don't tell me about stir-crazy. I've been stuck on this planet for twenty years, Rose. For this family. And you try to sneak out on me in the middle of the night?'

Charles was wide-eyed. Rose looked down, and realised she was digging her fingernails into his wrist. She let him go.

'Mom,' she said. 'I'm not abandoning you. We're not having a fight. What's happening is, I'm taking some time off to see Mars, and you're letting me go.'

'Like hell I am!'

'Of course you are,' said Rose. 'Because you know what the alternative is? That you're so controlling that you drove your own daughter away. That your whole First Mom On Mars image is a sham.'

Kelly exploded. 'You don't *dare threaten me!* You manipulative ...'

'What, Mom? What do you want to call me?'

There was silence from the other end of the line, then a quiet sob. Rose felt a cold sickness in her stomach, and her eyes prickled.

'No, Mom! No! Don't pull that! You can't just cry when you don't get your way!'

'I just want us to be a happy family.'

'I can't do this now. I'll call when I get to Mariner. We'll talk, okay? Because that's what a normal family would do. Get some sleep.'

Kelly started crying again, in deep, throaty sobs, but Rose cut her off with the disconnect button. She felt warm tears run down her own cheeks.

'Fuck!' she said, slapping a wall panel next to the seat.

Charles raised a hand. 'Please don't do that.'

'Sorry you had to hear that,' said Rose, wiping her face.

'It's okay,' said Charles. 'It's confidential.'

'Thank you. And don't worry about your job. She'll back off, now that she can play the victim.'

Rose stood. In the cramped cockpit, her body was right next to his.

'Is there anything else I can do for you?' he asked, concerned.

His brow was slightly furrowed, but his lips were full, and his uniform had a faint floral scent. Rose's emotions twisted inside her, searching for an outlet.

'What are you offering?' she said, touching his arm.

He took a step back from her, and slid the door to the cabin open. 'I'll give you space,' he said. 'I won't disturb you again.'

He didn't meet her eyes, and stood up straight at the side of the door. Rose felt her face flushing again.

'Of course.'

She slunk back into the cabin, feeling stupid. Charles slid the cockpit door closed behind her. She collapsed back into her seat, alone and at the mercy of her own emotions. She lifted her feet up off the ground and hugged her legs.

The conversation with her mother replayed in her head, over and over. Had she been too forceful, or not forceful enough? Was she a brat or a pushover? And Charles? What the fuck had she been thinking? What was he going to tell people?

'Shit, shit, shit,' she said to herself quietly, rocking her body back and forward. So this is what it felt like to be free.

# Chapter Twenty-Three

ARCHIE FULLER CLAIMS HIS BIRTHRIGHT

Interview with Apoapsis Magazine, 3 November 2055

Archimedes Escher Fuller (Archie to his friends and fans) doesn't just look like a younger, fitter version of his father, he shares the same adventurous spirit. At ten, he famously became the youngest person to own his own custom out-suit. At sixteen, he hosted the first season of his travel series Open Space, in which he explored the extreme-sports possibilities of the red planet. The series gathered a huge audience, partly thanks to Archie's fame and easy-going charm, but mainly for his on-camera antics, and his lavish and largely consequence-free lifestyle.

The filming of season four was tragically cut short by the death of Alex Fuller. But now, Archie Fuller is back to record the show's fifth season, which promises to be the most jaw-dropping yet. Apoapsis caught up with him during his shoot at the Little Green Man Festival.

**APOAPSIS MAGAZINE: The first time we interviewed you was right after the first season. Do you remember? You said you were the new king of Mars.**

ARCHIE FULLER: Did I? [Laughs] I guess I was high on that first wave of fame. I didn't expect the show to become such a cultural touchstone. With all the trouble back on Earth, you know, the riots and the shutdowns, I thought that a show about me having an amazing time would be a bit out of touch. But people love it. I guess they like the fact that I'm not hoarding my wealth, you know? I use my money to show them something mind-blowing. And my fans are the best. They want what I've got, not the wealth, but the attitude. The show lets them ride along, and hang out with me.

**AM: You're getting a reputation for wild stunts, like when you bungee jumped down a lava tube in the third season. How are you topping yourself this time?**

AF: No spoilers, but there's a couple of things I can tell you. For the first episode I got to mess around on the surface of Phobos, totally untethered. You know me, I love zero G, but Phobos is better because it's got, like, ultra-low gravity, so you can jump hundreds of metres. I literally leapt into orbit in a space suit. You'll see for yourself, it was amazing.

**AM: Open Space has been renewed for another three seasons, and there's rumours that you won't always limit yourself to Mars. Any hints about where you'll be going next?**

AF: I've always wanted to visit the Vega research post in Venus's upper atmosphere. I have this idea about skydiving through the sulphuric acid clouds with a Teflon parachute. But I won't be able to do that for a while. Travelling to Venus takes time, and there's plenty more for me to explore on Mars. This planet is a playground, especially with the festival coming up.

**AM: Oh, yes! Tell us about the festival. How did you get the idea?**

AF: I was travelling from base to base with my crew, scouting locations for season four, and we saw this giant empty dome that they've inflated just outside Mariner, four hundred metres across, which will be holding a new section of the base. Construction only just started, and there's this bare rocky ground inside. And I thought, hold on, there's a lot you can do with an empty space like that.

I said, let's have a party like Burning Man. The planet's already a desert, isn't it? We've got a whole lot of really smart scientists and engineers living on Mars who need an outlet for their creativity, so they can make art, and there's gifting and self-expression and participation and everything like that. We can't burn a giant effigy, obviously, because fire's too dangerous on Mars, so we're calling it the Little Green Man Festival instead.

And I think that this is going to be better than Burning Man. No one has to worry about the heat or the dust, because we're all in the dome. No one's going to be hungry or thirsty, everything's provided. And the vibe is going to be incredible. This is a once-in-a-lifetime event, like, once in a hundred generations.

**AM: There's a growing impression that Fuller Aerospace is lacking direction without your father at the helm. The new CEO and board of directors are based on Earth, and they seem more concerned with navigating their own planet's current economic troubles than developing Mars. Would that still be the case if you were in charge? Have you considered taking a more active role in the Company?**

AF: Some day, but I'm not ready to fill a suit just yet!

**AM: Did your father enjoy the TV show? What did he think of it?**

AF: He loved it! He wanted more people on Mars, and I let everyone see what's possible here.

Critics call my series frivolous, but the truth is, I show audiences that space travel is better than they imagined. Open Space has brought thousands of tourists and billions of dollars in business to Mars. Sometimes I get accused of downplaying the downside of space tourism, like the long travel times and the cramped habitats. Well, let me tell you, I *love* the long travel times and the close quarters. There's nothing more fun than six months in zero gravity, especially if you've got companions who are willing to get experimental. Yeah, people complain, and maybe space isn't for those people. But if you're bold, and you want a good time, Mars is the only place to be. Book a ticket and get out here! This is the greatest planet in the universe!

# Chapter Twenty-Four

The next morning, the rover train arrived at the Mariner Base terminal. Rose was relieved to hear the hatch to her cabin hissing open automatically. She grabbed her travelling case and climbed out before Charles the driver could leave the cockpit. She didn't want to have to look him in the eyes.

The Mariner arrival hall was a dome sticking out from the side of the base. Morning light shone down from the geodesic windows above onto her fellow passengers as they spilled out into the hall. Most of them were around her age, wearing the kind of angular skirts, jackets and hairstyles that Rose didn't normally see outside TV shows from Earth, with high-contrast patterns that could be easily recognised by computer vision. Anyone looking at them through AR glasses would immediately know who the designer was, how much the garment cost, and how exclusive and unique it was. Rose had never bothered with that kind of attention-seeking fashion. She had the opposite problem. One of the girls coming from the train saw her, and grabbed a friend's arm.

'Look! Rose Fuller!'

The other passengers stared at her. Some giggled excitedly, and others looked irritated that she existed. The ones who remembered her recent family history watched her with a kind of dull, invasive pity. One boy started jeering, and was elbowed into silence by his friends. Rose lifted the hood of her sweater and searched for an exit. There was an arrow on the floor pointing out of the arrival hall, and she followed it without looking back.

Just outside the hall was a row of open-mouthed storage compartments where previous passengers had dropped off their bags, cases, and jackets. Dylan found an open compartment, and slid her travel case into it. She wasn't worried that anyone would steal it. There was no crime on Mars.

Rose followed the signs for the festival down a tube-shaped corridor. Apparently, Mariner Base had embraced the spirit of the festival, and the walls on either side of her were covered in artworks that didn't seem to have any consistent theme or quality. There were giant line-drawings of skulls printed with the precision of architectural diagrams, finger-painted smiling faces, and calligraphic renditions of famous social media poems. One long series of images showed distorted human forms walking through a forest, with animal-like shapes half-glimpsed through the trees. It was captioned *Pictures reconstructed from the visual cortex of a 7-year-old during REM sleep*. Rose couldn't work out if it was genuine, or if the caption was part of the art.

The sound of voices, music and laughter built up ahead. She rounded a corner into a wide transparent tunnel leading away from Mariner Base. It stretched out a few hundred metres across the floor of the Valles Marineris. In the distance to the right were the northern slopes of the giant canyon, just visible on the horizon. Up ahead the tunnel connected to a huge inflated biopolymer dome that stood alone in the empty landscape, and inside it, she could make out blurry flags, parade floats, streamers, kinetic sculptures, and hundreds of dark shapes that were unmistakably people, moving to the rhythm of the music in the festival dome.

The tunnel ahead was packed. A long line of people was waiting, talking, laughing, and passing bottles. Unlike the tourists from the rover train, most of them were wearing muted greys and browns: practical colours that marked them as employees of the Company. Rose joined the back of the line. The woman in front of her, an older lady in a beige jacket, glanced back. Rose saw the recognition in her eyes, and felt a brief surge of panic. She raised a finger to her lips, and thankfully, the lady understood. She gave Rose a smile and nod, and went back to talking to a couple in overalls ahead of her.

The tourists from the rover train arrived behind Rose. When they saw the length of the queue, one of them groaned.

'Oh, come on! We didn't travel a gazillion miles to wait in line!'

Up ahead, a woman in a light-blue Fuller Aerospace tracksuit was walking along the side of the queue, talking to people and checking a pad in her hand. When she saw the tourists, she hurried over to them.

'Hi!' she said cheerfully. 'Are you all from Earth?'

'Yeah. Take us to your leader.'

'Tourists can join the accelerated security queue. This way please.'

She led the colourful group down the tunnel, past the waiting line.

'That's more like it,' one of the tourists muttered. He waved at the queue. 'Later, y'all!'

His friends snickered, and one of them gave him a playful shove. He shoved back, harder.

'Assholes,' muttered the woman ahead of Rose.

Truthfully, though, no one else in the line seemed particularly troubled. Rose could hear some lively conversation ahead, interspersed with raucous laughter. After a few minutes, a man with an accordion started playing an upbeat shanty.

> I've travelled through the blackest skies
> To lands dead as can be
> And years go by
> Without blue skies
> Without a roaring sea,
>
> But we still dance in the maintenance bay
> Underground in the maintenance bay
> I'll be back in the arms of my love someday,
> But tonight we'll dance in the maintenance bay

He sang it with a sly grin, matching his rhythm to the deep thumping beats coming from the festival dome ahead. The crowd around him whooped and danced, and a bottle of wine and some paper cups were passed down the line. The woman ahead passed one back to Rose, and she took it gratefully. It was full-bodied and complex, a miracle of Martian chemical engineering.

The woman shook Rose's hand.

'I'm Seetha,' she said with an English accent.

'Hi, Seetha. I'm Rose.'

'"Rose", did you say?' Seetha said with a wicked grin. 'I had no idea. Well, it's lovely to meet you, Most Famous Person in History.'

Rose wasn't used to being teased by strangers, but Seetha's smile was infectious, and Rose found herself laughing.

'Why aren't you jumping the queue?' Seetha asked.

'Because I'm local.'

Seetha lowered her head and looked at Rose sceptically.

'You think the rules apply to you?'

Rose watched the dancers ahead, laughing and almost falling over as they spun with hooked arms to the rhythm of the music.

'This is all part of the festival experience, isn't it?' said Rose.

Seetha took another sip of wine. 'Fair enough,' she said. 'I know the event is only really meant for the tourists, and the rest of us are just bodies to fill up space, we aren't saying no. Most of us have been stuck underground for a while. We're ready for a party.'

The line crawled onward. Seetha told Rose about her work, adapting crops to their new environment.

'If you're looking at an individual plant then you're missing half the picture. Plants are part of a network of life. Every species competes and co-operates with a hundred other species, and they just don't work as well when they aren't part of that ecosystem. We even had to add a few mildly harmful bugs. If the plants don't have something to fight against, they don't develop properly. It's like all of us. We all think we're so self-contained, but when you get down to it we need other people, even people we don't like.'

Seetha was clearly passionate about her work, and Rose listened, fascinated. When asked about her own life, Rose talked about the Company's new opal-marketing sideline, and told Seetha that she had handled some of the business side of it herself. Seetha nodded politely, but she didn't have any follow-up questions, and after Rose finished speaking, there was an uncomfortable silence.

They approached the security checks, and one of the blue-tracksuited marshals beckoned Rose out of the line.

'This way please, Miss Fuller.'

Rose glanced at Seetha.

'Go,' the scientist said with a tight smile. 'It was nice to meet you. Have fun.'

The marshal ushered her to a separate entrance into the dome, away from the body scanners and the security checks.

'It's an honour to have you here, Miss Fuller,' he said as he pulled the door open. 'If you need anything, speak to one of the other marshals and we'll organise it for you. Enjoy the festival.'

Rose stepped into the dome, and was met by an overwhelming barrage of noise, motion, light and colour. The biopolymer above was tinted blue, like the skies of Earth. The ground below her feet was raw Martian rock, blown clean of dust. Ahead of her, a rocky path led away between primary-coloured tents and gazebos. Some were conical, some were rectangular, and some were the size of her quarters back in Aries Base. There was a bar inside the nearest one, with a rowdy crowd gathered around it holding bioplastic pint mugs. A pair of young festival-goers rode past Rose on 3D-printed bicycles. They must have been Mars natives who had never been on a bike before, because they were wobbling and laughing hysterically.

The scent of vat protein hot-dogs and burger patties wafted in the air, mingling with incense and spices. Music echoed through the dome in hypnotic polyrhythms, and kinetic sculptures swung overhead: interlocking hinges and gleaming metal poles that spun slowly in the air currents. Rose was startled by the sight of a giant owl, seven metres tall, staring down at her through black almond-shaped eyes. The scale of it was breathtaking, and Rose couldn't suppress a nervous chuckle. She had been prepared for the festival to be overhyped, but Seetha had been right. For the people of Mars, this was more than just a party. She grinned from ear to ear.

Rather than following the main path to the centre of the dome, Rose took a side route under the wing of the owl and through a bright tunnel of red, green and blue flags that ran along the edge of the dome. On the far side of the tunnel was a quieter, sparser area, where small stone circles and henges had been set up on the rocky ground. One of them held a group doing slow, silent tai chi. In another, a wild-haired astrologer in yellow robes sat cross-legged on a carpet, giving a reading to an earnest-looking young couple. Rose eavesdropped as she walked past.

'From here, the Earth is just another planet in the sky, with its own point of influence, sharp and clear. Its power used to be overwhelming, but now we can comprehend it for what it is, a maternal influence. It's Mother Earth, separate from the feminine spirit associated with Venus or the moon. It has completely re-written our understanding of astrology. Mars's combative influence, although closer, is spread out, diluted and dissipated...'

Something flew over Rose's head, and she instinctively ducked. A young man in a wing-suit and a helmet was gliding through the air towards an inflatable landing pad on the far side of the dome. He dropped onto it safely, and a group of people on a platform above Rose cheered. The next of them stood forward in their wing-suit, ready to jump.

As Rose's path curved in towards the centre of the dome, the volume of the music increased. She saw her first naked couple – a man and women in their forties wearing nothing but sunglasses and smiles. No one else gave them a second glance, so she kept moving, past a juggling unicyclist with his long white hair in a braid. At the side of the path, two-metre-high metal letters spelled out *I AM APART*. The sentence was split in half at different depths, and as she walked past, the parallax separated them until they spelled *I AM A PART*. Rose rolled her eyes, but she smiled at the earnestness.

Some children were climbing up a giant word *WHY* made out of tangled rope on a metal frame. A drunk-looking girl was mumbling into a pay phone painted with the words: 'Call God! Or ET! Whoever's closest!'

It wasn't all puns and gags, though. Rose was taken by a realistic sculpture of a leaping fawn, and a pair of giant angel wings at shoulder height that anyone could lean in to. Opposite the wings, a vast spirograph hung down from the dome, tracing ever-changing flower-petal shapes in the sand, and mechanical arms on either side of the path juggled a slow, graceful rainbow arc of coloured balls overhead.

A young girl ran down the path towards Rose. Before she could object, the girl slipped a soft yellow band onto her wrist.

'Oh, hey! What's this?' said Rose.

'Firefly bracelet,' said the girl. 'It flashes in time to your pulse.'

'Uh, cool,' said Rose. 'Do you know if there's a VIP area or something around here? I'm looking for someone.'

The girl scrunched her face in thought, and pointed back the way she came.

'There's a place back there that we can't go into. My sister said it's where all the rich people are.'

'That sounds right,' said Rose. 'Thank you.'

The girl narrowed her eyes at Rose. 'Are you rich?'

Rose was caught off guard by the question.

'I suppose I am,' she said. For the first time in her life, it didn't seem like such a good thing to be.

# Chapter Twenty-Five

Rose found the VIP area at the back of the dome, nestled away behind some khaki-coloured privacy screens printed with the Fuller Aerospace logo. When a blue-tracksuited marshal saw her coming, he ushered her in with a broad smile.

On the other side of the screens was an excavation site. A half buried Easter Island stone head with almond-shaped eyes rose out of the ground at its centre, surrounded by wooden crates, barrels, ladders and coils of rope. A shallow pit behind it revealed more archaeological discoveries: a fallen marble column and a stone tablet inscribed with mysterious triangular writing. It all looked reasonably convincing, but Rose spotted a couple of slip-ups, like the polystyrene pattern on the tablet and the thin gap between the base of the Easter Island statue and the ground.

Distant laughter came from the far side of the pit. She followed the sound, through a stone archway marked with alien hieroglyphs. Behind it was a dirt ramp leading down to a luxury campsite, set up in the ruins of a palace, with more sculptures of alien astronauts designed to look eroded by time. A semicircle of khaki tents with raised sun-shields surrounded a central cooking area, where three chefs were frying tank-bred prawns on a table-sized grill. Opposite the tents, the VIPs were lounging around a swimming pool, under heat lamps hanging down from the dome above.

Rose walked down the ramp. The distant music from the main stage didn't quite mask the gasps of sex coming from one of the tents, and Rose caught a glimpse of entwined legs through a half-open canvas flap. In the temple's cooking area, the chefs moved swiftly and professionally between the ovens, counters, stove tops, and cooler boxes. They avoided eye contact with Rose as she walked past them towards the pool, where tanned bodies sprawled on loungers and under beach umbrellas. A few of the VIPs were floating in the water, incurious and sedate, like sea lions with their fat cells gene-edited away. Rose recognised some faces from the Aries Base galas and fundraisers organised by her mother. One or two influencers, and some astropreneurs. No one she knew properly. Their sunglasses followed her as she walked around the pool, searching among the bodies for her brother. She spotted him at the side of the temple ruins, leaning back against the stump of a column. He was wearing headphones, and staring up at the sky through white plastic goggles.

'Archie!'

He stirred, and took off his headgear. When he saw her, he gave her a big goofy grin. He stood up out of the shadow of the column, and his mop of hair glowed in the sunlight. It looked like he was dyeing it to make it even more ginger than usual. After all, he had a brand to maintain.

'Rose!'

He ran over, and gave her an unnecessary bear hug.

'Oooof! Easy!'

'Sorry, I forgot that you're the fragile one. How're you doing? Mom called. She's super pissed.'

'Not just at me. You disappeared.'

'I told her I'd be home when we're wrapped. The shooting schedule is super tight.'

He pointed towards the sun. Rose shielded her eyes, and saw the drone lurking overhead.

'You're filming us right now?'

'Just B-roll,' he smiled. 'Come on. Let's get food and some privacy. It's good to see you again, Princess.'

'Don't call me that.'

They went to sit at a long dining table under a gazebo just past the pool. The tabletop was scattered with fake exploration gear – yellowing maps, a brass telescope, a compass – and a tray of canapés. Archie put the white goggles down, and helped himself to a handful of local vat-farmed shrimp.

'What's that?' said Rose, pointing to Archie's goggles. 'VR?'

'Nope,' he said, sliding them across the table to her. She turned them over in her hands. They were translucent white plastic. Form-fitting and stylish, but ultimately just plastic.

'They induce the Ganzfeld effect,' said Archie. 'You heard about it?'

Rose shook her head. Archie smiled broadly, delighted that he knew something that his sister didn't.

'When you're wearing them, all you see is pure white across your whole field of vision,' he said. 'It's sensory deprivation. Simulated snow blindness. You start hallucinating after about fifteen minutes.'

'Really?'

'Oh, yeah. With the help of some mushrooms, obviously.'

He grinned at his own lame joke.

'Are you tripping now?' said Rose.

'Nah, this is all business. I'm looking for ways to entertain travellers during the Mars trip. We could make an amazing sensory deprivation chamber in zero gravity. Like an immersion tank, but floating in the air. Imagine it! "Explore inner space in outer space." The ultimate meditation retreat, out in the cosmos, a hundred million miles from planet Earth. Nothing to distract the customers from their sacred journey. We could hand out DMT, ketamine, MDMA, whatever they need to have a deep experience. Top-tier shrinks to talk people through their hang-ups. Make our guests feel like they're really pushing the limits of human experience. Turn the boring six-month trip to Mars into a unique selling point.'

Rose admired how confidently her brother talked. He had been saying the first thing that came into his head for so long that his bullshit was honed like a knife. He didn't overthink, he never stammered, and he never, ever doubted himself.

He flashed her another bright smile. 'So, why did you run away from home? You want to join my circus?'

Rose rested her elbows on the table.

'I can't stay with Mom, Archie. She's booked constant photo shoots and interviews. It's like, if we don't keep projecting the perfect image then we'll have to deal with what we're feeling. We don't talk. We don't go anywhere. I want to do something real.'

Archie looked amused. 'Real? Like what?'

'Like Dad. Pushing humanity forward. Finishing his work. Making Mars self-sufficient.'

Archie barked out a laugh. Rose felt warm blood flowing to her cheeks.

'What?' she said. 'You think I can't be useful?'

His smile faded.

'Rose, are you serious?'

'Of course. Dad wanted us to be an interplanetary species. And what am I doing with my life? I spent the whole of last week smiling into a lens.'

Archie gave her a pitying half-smile, which was worse than being laughed at.

'Do you really think that's what Dad cared about?'

'Of course!'

He shook his head.

'You're putting too much pressure on yourself,' he said. 'Look at how the Company works. We sell package holidays. Dad never really cared about the future, it was all marketing.'

'He got us to Mars!' she said. 'He did something real with his life!'

She didn't know why she was talking so loudly. She didn't even know what they were really arguing about. Archie had a way of taking the self-control from her, the way he took toys from her hands as a kid.

'Nothing's real here, Rose. Look.'

He pick up one of the maps from the table in front of them. It showed canals and pyramids and crashed UFOs.

'When people book their tickets to Mars, this is what they think they're getting. A wild frontier with aliens and treasure! You know what Mars really is? A cold, dead rock. We have to make up reasons for people to keep coming, and Dad knew it. That's why he was always talking about his grand visions of the future. He was a showman.'

'That's not true,' said Rose. 'Mars is almost self-sufficient. We've got manufacturing capability. We've got mines. Opals...'

Archie tossed the map aside. 'There are tons of opals on the Earth. There are tons of *everything* on Earth. The only thing that makes our opals valuable is the *idea* that they're valuable. *Mars Fire Opals. Jewels From Another Planet. From the Private Collection of Rose Fuller, the First Human Born on Mars!* Branding is all we have. If we stop playing make-believe then people will stop coming, and if they stop coming then they won't bring all the things that we need to survive.'

Rose tilted her head back and stared up at the canvas roof so she wouldn't have to look at Archie. But he was on a run, and he wasn't going to shut up now.

'If you really wanted to finish Dad's work,' he said, 'you would go back to Mom and put on that fake smile, get interviewed, and say that everything's amazing. Lie like the future of Mars depends on it, because it really does.'

# Chapter Twenty-Six

Rose wandered aimlessly through the festival. She couldn't handle any more of the VIP area – the lizard-like stares of the sunbathers gnawed at her nerves – but now she had nowhere to go. She wandered through the crowd, lost.

Sweat dripped down her face, and her hair felt matted. Why was it so hot? Were desert conditions really the selling point of the festival? Or was Archie just trying to get more people to take off their clothes?

Under a blue and white striped sun-shield at the side of the path, she found a display stand holding rows of masks. They were all caricatures of famous people: TV stars, soccer players, politicians, streamers. A young man in a top hat lay back in the shade next to it, drawing a sketch of the president of China on a pad. When he saw Rose he jolted upright.

'Oh! Hey!' he said, like a guilty child.

'Hi. How much for a mask?'

'Nothing! Everything's free at the festival.'

'I'd like that one.'

She pointed to a mask at the top of the display stand. It was a girl with bright red hair, high cheeks and a vacant smile, wedged between the faces of two US presidents.

The mask maker winced. 'Sorry. It wasn't my best work. I can redraw it quick and 3D-print you a new one.'

'No, I love it,' said Rose.

She put on the caricature of her own face and adjusted the strap behind her head. The painted bioplastic was thin and chitinous, but it fit comfortably. She took off her sweater, balled it up and threw it in a bin, and felt the heat rising off her in a wave.

She let herself flow with the revellers as they laughed and shouted and made happy fools of themselves, until the sun began to set in the west of the valley. As the sky darkened, thousands of multicoloured LEDs lit up on people's wrists. There was a subtle synchronisation to the lights, as their heart rates aligned to the tempo of the music thudding in the central plaza. Throughout the festival dome, people gravitated inwards to dance around the statue of the Little Green Man.

The statue looked like a classical alien figure from the 1950s, with a round head, large eyes and a tiny mouth, constructed out of angled scaffolding and enclosed by a green metal grille. Steps zigzagged inside the legs and through the torso, up to the out-stretched arms holding up a long viewing balcony packed with people whooping and waving at the crowd below. It was five storeys high, and it stood on a circular pedestal made of display screens live-streaming a three-hundred-and-sixty-degree panorama from a desert on Earth. A UFO hung down from the apex of the dome above the statue, shining multicoloured lights onto the joyous crowd. A musical group on the main stage, sweating and shirtless, simulated electronica with physical instruments, hammer-ing on hollow poles and steels drums with mining equipment to make pounding polyrhythms.

A group of partiers stumbled in front of Rose. When they saw her mask, they pointed and grinned. One of them put on a fake English accent.

'The Kwehn! The Kwehn of Mahrs! Yoh Highness!'

He bowed elaborately, spinning his wrist like a courtier, and his friends all laughed as they disappeared into the jostling crowd.

The drumming came to an end with a machine-gun flourish, and the crowd roared. As the band stepped down from the stage and towelled the sweat from their bodies, the display screens in the base of the statue lit up with the word *Remember*.

A montage of videos of Rose's father began to play, showing him as a young man, seated in front of his computer and smiling, and then older, wearing sunglasses and standing in front of a rocket on a launch pad, then even older, looking out of a spacecraft window, down at the surface of Mars below. The footage cross-faded as stirring orchestral music played. The crowd around the statue didn't pay much attention. They shouted to each other and swarmed towards the bar tents, but Rose was frozen to the spot.

Another title card came up. 'I have given you Mars. Now make the future.'

A close-up of Alex Fuller's face smiled benevolently out of the screens, and the blue Fuller Aerospace logo faded up to replace it.

Rose looked down at her wrist. Her bracelet was pulsing too fast. Her palms tingled, and her chest tightened so much that it hurt. Her vision blurred. She tried to control her breathing, but couldn't slow it down.

The thudding music started again, and an airhorn sounded above. She looked up, and saw the statue of the Little Green Man, lit up by the strings of green and blue lights along its skeleton. People were dancing inside the statue's arms and on the viewing platform, stamping their feet to the music, and making the structure bend and shake with resonant motion. It could collapse at any second, but everyone was laughing.

She fled through the neon darkness, tearing off her mask so that she could breathe. Lights streaked across her vision. Every direction looked the same, filled with bright lights and manic faces. Up ahead, at an intersection of two paths, she saw a hand-painted map of the festival dome. She ran to it, desperate to find somewhere to escape the people's gaze. Near to the *You are here* dot, she spotted a large round structure marked *Temple*. Under it, it said *For Quiet Contemplation Only. Silence Please.*

She looked around and located the building, on the other side of a high trapeze hanging down from the roof of the dome. The temple was constructed from hardened epoxy beams in the shape of an inverted whirlpool, with a wide base that curled upwards into a central spire. The whole structure was painted black, but a warm, gentle glow came out of an entrance at ground level. Rose steadied herself, took a deep breath, and ran towards it.

# Chapter Twenty-Seven

A man in a loose beige gown stood at the side of the temple entrance. He smiled at Rose as she approached.

'Welcome!' he said, over the roar of the music and the crowd. He saw her expression. 'Is everything all right?'

'Fine, fine,' said Rose. 'What's this a temple to?'

'It's non-denominational,' the man said. 'Come in. It's easier to talk inside.'

He led her into the antechamber, which was only a few paces deep. The walls and ceiling were covered in foam acoustic-dampening spikes, and the thud of the outside music was muted.

'Thanks for coming,' the man said, spreading his hands. He was tall and muscular, but had a friendly smile. 'The temple is set up for quiet contemplation. I'm just here to make sure that the environment stays calm, so visitors to the space can have meaningful experiences.'

'So you're a spiritual bouncer?'

He grinned back at her.

'I ... encourage the drunks to go outside. There's a chill-out tent across the way, and they'll probably enjoy it more there. This place is more ... thoughtful. Before you go in, please remove your shoes.' He looked uncomfortable giving her orders. 'You can leave them on this rack, here. It's more of an experience if your bare feet are touching the surface of Mars.'

Rose slipped off her soft base-shoes. The stone beneath her feet was cold and smooth, with all the irregularities polished away. The temple guardian took her shoes and put them on the rack, next to half a dozen other pairs.

'Thank you, Miss Fuller. It's an honour to have you here. I know

I don't have to say this to you, but please respect the experience of the other temple guests.'

'Okay, sure.'

A passage led off to the right, curving along the inside of the outer wall. She followed it in a spiral, curling inwards, deeper and deeper into the temple. Three figures came into view ahead, barely visible in the subdued LED lighting. At first Rose thought they were real people, but as she got closer she saw they were sculptures, held up by thin wires to make it seem as if they were floating in microgravity. A water bottle hung casually next to one of their hands. They were all wearing flight suits, and it looked like they were frozen in the middle of a conversation.

Next to them on the curved wall were three bronze plaques.

**MITCHELL JANKOWSKI – 1978 – 2032**
**SOFIA O. IVANOV – 2001 – 2032**
**LIU JUNXIAN – 1997 – 2032**

They were the first people to die on Mars. The hydraulics on their landing craft failed two years before Rose and Archie were born. The first death had preceded the first life.

The sculptures were beautiful, though. Their faces were stylised and simplified, like a good sketch. Mission Commander Jankowski had his hands spread, as if he was in the middle of telling an amusing story, and the other two had smiles of wry amusement. It was heartbreakingly human.

Rose kept following the passage. Every few metres after the sculpture, a thin metal strip crossed the floor of the passageway. They were engraved with years: 2033, 2034, 2035. Between these year markers were smooth, soft patches on the wall, covered with photographs and news clippings, commemorating the people who had died on Mars in that year. The further Rose walked, the more memorials there were: as the living population grew, so did the dead. Rose looked away from the clippings, scared that she might see her father's face again.

A gap appeared in the upper corner of the passageway, between the ceiling and inner wall. The further she walked, the lower the wall dropped, until she could see over it into the temple's inner chamber.

It was a circular space. The roof was supported by a frame of interlocked beams that spiralled up to a central point, where light shone down from lamps in the spire. The soundproofing here wasn't as effective as in the passageway, and the music and roar from the crowd thrummed faintly through the open space.

In the centre of the chamber was a black tree. It had to be a sculpture: there weren't any living trees that size on Mars. It rose up out of a pool of water in the middle of the room, its trunk twisting, following the curves in the ceiling, its limbs splitting, and splitting again, in fractal branches that hung down to the edges of the pool.

The inner wall of the corridor got lower and lower, until it became a ridge on the floor. It kept spiralling inwards until it entered the shallow water, and disappeared below the surface.

Rose wasn't alone in the chamber. A group of kids were sitting with their backs against the spiral wall, looking up at the tree through AR glasses. An older couple were kneeling on the opposite side, chanting low, resonant *Aums*, and a pair of temple guardians stood to the side, watching silently. Rose became self-conscious about her flashing bracelet and tucked it into her sleeve.

Pieces of white paper hung from the ends of the branches. She walked closer to read them.

*It's been seven years. I wish you could have seen the sun rising here*
*Everyone in Sinai misses you*
*Thank you, Dad*

She walked around the tree slowly, reading more messages, until she found one that gave her a second gut-punch. It was a printout of an online obituary. All the text had been blacked out by a marker pen, but the face was familiar, and smiling. Over the thick black lines, someone had written a message in silver ink:

*No words will do.*
*They could never capture you.*
*I miss you forever, Amai.*

The face was Grace Chiwasa. Rose was flooded with memories of her childhood, of fear and anxiety, and the woman who had showed her understanding. The paper was held by a small hook at the end of the branch. Rose reached up, and pulled it down from the tree.

'Hey!'

She turned to see a young black woman striding towards her from the far side of the temple. Her hair was braided and she was wearing standard base gear: a light-grey top and nylon shorts. An OLED pin on her lapel said 'she / her' against a cycling backdrop of album covers.

'What the hell are you doing? Put that back!'

The other visitors to the temple looked up at the disturbance. The woman strode closer, and when she saw Rose's face, her expression lit up with recognition, and anger.

'Who do you think you are? You can't steal things!'

The temple guardians ran up from the side of the chamber. They had their palms raised, trying to calm the woman down.

'Please. This is a peaceful place.'

She turned on them with a look of fury. 'Don't silence me. She's taking my mother's picture!'

'I'm sorry,' said Rose, hooking the printout back onto the end of the branch. 'I knew her, and I wanted to look ... I wasn't thinking.'

'Maybe you'd prefer to be outside the temple,' one of the guardians said to the woman.

'You can't kick me out!' said Grace's daughter. 'I'm not the one—'

Rose raised her hands.

'She's right. It's my fault. I'll go.'

She turned and walked back towards the spiral corridor quickly, so they couldn't see her eyes filling with tears.

'Hey!' Grace's daughter called, her voice echoing through the chamber. Rose walked faster, but she heard bare feet on the rock floor behind her.

'Miss! Stop!' one of the guardians shouted.

Rose glanced back. Grace's daughter was running towards her, with the two guardians close behind. They caught up and stood between Rose and the young woman, keeping them separated.

'Oh, for fuck's sake!' said Grace's daughter. 'I'm not attacking her. I'm trying to leave!'

Rose wiped her eyes. 'It's okay,' she said.

The two guardians hesitated, looking uncertain.

'You hear that?' said Grace's daughter. 'Rose Fuller and I both want you to fuck off.'

'Is that all right, Miss Fuller?' said one of the guardians.

'It's fine,' said Rose, exhausted. 'Please, leave us alone.'

The guardian raised his palms. 'Okay.'

The two guardians stepped back, but they didn't stop watching Grace's daughter.

'For fuck's sake,' she repeated.

She strode out of the chamber into the spiral corridor. Rose followed a few paces behind her.

'I'm sorry,' she said. 'I didn't have the right to touch it. I missed your mother, that's all.'

'It's fine,' Grace's daughter said. 'I overreacted. I thought you were vandalising the tree for the hell of it. Were you one of her patients?'

'Yes,' Rose said, and hesitated. It wasn't enough. 'She was special.'

The young woman stopped under a passage light, and looked Rose up and down.

'I know. She had compassion for people I wouldn't save from a base fire.' Grace's daughter sighed. 'She loved all her patients. She would have been proud that you turned out okay.'

Rose couldn't hold back a sob. She closed her eyes, and when she opened them, she saw the sympathy in the woman's face.

'Sorry,' said Rose.

Grace's daughter reached out, and put an empathetic hand on Rose's arm. Rose wasn't used to physical contact. Other than her mother, hardly anyone ever dared to touch her. Her instinct was to flinch away, but she needed contact with another human, any human.

She couldn't help herself. She leaned in to Grace's daughter, who flinched back slightly. But before Rose could apologise and pull away, the girl sighed and opened her arms, drawing Rose in for a hug. Rose felt foolish looking for sympathy from someone who so clearly had their own problems. She felt doubly foolish for breaking down in front of a stranger. But as more tears welled in her eyes, Grace's daughter held her steady. Rose rested her head on the girl's shoulder, and cried with all her heart.

# Chapter Twenty-Eight

The festival was spilling over into the corridors of Mariner Base. A red, green and blue Mars flag hung on the wall, next to seismograph printouts that had been watercoloured to look like mountainous landscapes.

'I'm Netsai,' said Grace Chiwasa's daughter, as she led Rose deeper into the base.

'It's great to meet you,' said Rose. 'Again, I'm so sorry.'

'You can stop saying that.'

As they made their way through the base, Rose was flooded with childhood memories. She remembered walking along the concourse for the first time with Archie and her mother. She had been overwhelmed by the sheer size of it. There was so much air and light, and so many people, and Rose had grabbed onto her mother's leg in panic. Even now, she was unnerved to be surrounded by strangers. It was like she was in some overcrowded city on Earth.

Netsai led her past a water fountain on the main concourse that was shooting precisely aimed jets of water in slow, graceful arcs; a hypnotic dance that was only possible in the low gravity. Rose remembered being entranced by it as a child. She had a memory of lying on the ground and watching the water curve over her, and realising that someone had planned its path perfectly, and that it would never change course, and she would never be splashed by a single drop of water.

The old playground was gone, replaced by an extension of a massive food court. With the festival underway, it was almost empty except for some bored-looking workers behind the tills.

Netsai led Rose to an empty booth in the corner of a coffee

shop. The table top was clean white plastic, and the soft furnishings muffled the noise echoing through the court.

'Wait here.'

She came back a minute later holding a tray with two paper cups and two takeaway cartons.

'Here you go. I don't know what you wanted to eat, so I brought options.'

'You didn't have to get me anything,' Rose protested. As a teen, she had been accustomed to leaving restaurants without paying. Her wealth, and the free gifts that people constantly showered her with, had blinded her to the idea that anyone would care. When her publicist called her out on it, it felt like she had been slapped, and now she consciously forced herself to pay for everything.

Netsai sat down opposite her, and slid her one of the cups. Rose sniffed the steam coming off it. It was some kind of herbal tea.

'Rooibos, grown in the local greenhouse,' said Netsai. 'I was going to get you a coffee, but I think we both need to chill the hell out.'

Rose sipped it. It tasted faintly metallic.

'So,' she said. 'You're a therapist too?'

'No,' said Netsai, and took a sip from her own cup. 'I was an electrical engineer for a few months, but right now ...'

She put her cup down in front of her, and looked Rose in the eyes.

'...If you must know, I'm being transported,' she said. 'Your company's going to send me to Earth.'

'It's not my company,' Rose said.

'There's too many people being born on Mars, and not enough jobs. They said my mother's contract allowed them to transport her or her family if we stopped being useful,' said Netsai.

'I'm sorry.'

'You don't need to say it again.'

Netsai pressed her fingers against her temples. After a few seconds, she spoke more calmly.

'I'm not trying to ambush you. It's not your fault. I'm just trying to explain why I acted like I did.' She took the two food cartons off the tray, and slid them both in front of Rose.

'Options,' she said, and lifted the lid off the first container. 'A croissant. Hard to make on Mars, but they did it anyway. The flour is dwarf wheat, and the butter is churned by hand from synthetic milk. Years of experimentation, days of work. Or ...' she lifted the lid on the second container, 'Something called blek. New from the local labs. Crunchy, slightly sweet and tangy, high in protein. Unlike anything on Earth.'

Rose tried a spoonful of blek. It was unfamiliar, but not unpleasant: warm, spicy and nutty, with hints of cardamom in its soft centre.

'It's good,' she said. 'Did I pass the test?'

Netsai slid the croissant over to her side of the table, and broke off both of its wings.

'Yep. They say these are the best croissants in one hundred and forty million miles, but that doesn't make them good. The sooner we all stop exhausting ourselves pretending we're on Earth, the better.'

Rose examined the pebbled texture of the blek. 'What's it made from?'

'That's a dangerous question,' Netsai said with a lopsided smile. 'Just accept that it's delicious and healthy, and never look up "black soldier flies".'

Rose ran her tongue around the inside of her mouth, and took another bite.

'I think I can help,' Rose said. 'I can stop them transporting you. I don't have any control over the Company, but people still listen to me. I can pull some strings.'

'I appreciate it,' said Netsai. 'It's not just me, though. Everyone living on a Fuller base is at risk. If they can't find a job, or if they don't grovel enough to the billionaire tourists, they're shipped away to a pollution-ravaged planet, where they'll spend the rest of their lives paying off the ticket.'

'There's got to be some way around it.'

Netsai shrugged, and pushed the remains of the croissant to the middle of the table.

'Nope. Some people try to find a place on one of the bases built by the Earth governments, but they're all overcapacity and underfunded. Everyone knows that as soon as the governments dump their Mars bases as a bad investment, the Company will swoop in and buy them for cheap. Then everyone there will be in the same shit that we're in now.'

Rose looked down into her container. She didn't know what to say.

'Don't look so embarrassed,' said Netsai. 'I said I don't blame you. Hey, how long are you in Mariner for? I'd love to show you around.'

'Thanks,' said Rose hesitantly. She wasn't quite sure what she was getting herself into, but she wasn't ready to return to her mother's wrath just yet.

'I'll introduce you to my friends. They've been discussing ways to protect the people of Mars. If you're serious about wanting to help then they'd love to meet you. I think they'll be surprised to find out that you're actually a human being.'

'Oh, okay,' Rose said, with a shiver in her chest. It sounded intense, but she'd come this far. She wanted to make a real difference, didn't she? If this is what it took, then she couldn't back out now.

# *Part 3.0*

---

# The Twins

# Chapter Twenty-Nine

This isn't going so well. I tried to take the rover train directly to Hunter or Tharsis Base, but train operators aren't stopping at either of the Twins. Apparently they were recently at war, and though the situation has quietened down, the trains don't risk going back. I was forced to get off at a small base called New Gusev, about a hundred kilometres south-east of the Twins, and hire a trading rover to take me the rest of the way.

New Gusev has a population of just under five hundred. It's a quiet place with an interesting architectural quirk – the drinking halls all have deliberately low ceilings, making it impossible for the drinkers to stand up to fight. The locals are proud of the innovation, saying they've almost entirely eradicated violence from the base, although they say that they've traded loose teeth for concussion.

I did some information-gathering in one of those drinking halls while I was waiting for my rover to arrive. The old residents I spoke to told me that the Twins were once a single base called Hunter, named after its founder Uriah Hunter, who sounds like he was a full-on cult leader. They say he built the base shortly after the Collapse. When Uriah Hunter died there was a power vacuum and a schism, and half of his followers split off into a temporary inflatable base nearby, but which soon dug itself out and became permanent. It called itself Tharsis because it wanted to be the capital of the whole Tharsis region. Since then, the two bases have been locked in a constant, vicious feud.

I'm currently on board the trading rover, which departed this morning. It's being driven by a woman called Prowse. I can't quite tell how old she is, but she has thinning hair and a wicked laugh. After she found out I work for the Company, she hasn't stopped teasing me. When I ask her for anything she tells me to send her a memo. When I annoy her, she says it's going on my performance review. And she keeps trying to force me to drink her dangerous-smelling rover-distilled rum.

I'm the only passenger, and Prowse has stuck me in her cargo bay, sitting on some webbing between two large containers of magnesium.

We'll drive through the Twins' territory tomorrow, and with a little luck we'll locate the missing rover and recover the map data. But there's a good chance that one or the other of the Twins has already found it, and they might not want to give the map to an outsider. If that's the situation then I'll do what I can, but I really hope it doesn't come to it. Negotiation is very far outside my area of expertise.

# Chapter Thirty

'How was Pavonis?' Frank asks cheerfully.

Dylan's lying in her cabin on Rudolf's lower deck, calling him on a tiny screen mounted over her berth. Morning light shines in through the small cabin window, making the LCD screen hard to see. She reaches up a hand to block some of the light. It looks like Frank's also lying in bed, on his bunk in the maintenance workers' quarters.

'Fine. Same as it ever was.'

She doesn't want to worry him, or give him the chance to say 'I told you so' about Clifford.

'Did you find your man?'

'Not yet. He went to somewhere called the Twins.'

'Hunter and Tharsis? I've been there. Crazy places. All the Free Settlements are a little crazy, but those two are like a parrot fighting a mirror.'

'What's a parrot?'

'The talking bird? From Earth? I really failed at educating you, didn't I?' he sighs. 'If you want to understand Hunter and Tharsis, look up *the narcissism of small differences*. Where's your boss?'

'Outside my cabin,' says Dylan. 'He's fixing a problem with the hatch.'

'You know what he is?' says Frank, with a grin.

'Don't say anything.'

'A vac-sac.'

'I don't want to know.'

'It's someone with one foot on Mars, and one foot on the Earth, and their sack dangling in the vacuum of space.'

Dylan covers her face with her hand.

'He can probably hear you. You know that, right?'

'What a tragedy.'

'Are you drunk again?'

'Nope. Just lightheaded from all the candy.'

'Dad!'

'I'm kidding!' he says. 'I've been hitting the cauliflower rice hard. You'd be proud of me.'

'Good,' says Dylan. 'And you're staying safe?'

'Of course. Oh! That reminds me, I got the weirdest visit. That security manager of yours, he wanted to know—'

The call cuts out, with a black screen and three beeps. Dylan tries reconnecting, but the call doesn't go through.

She rolls off the bed, and slides her cabin door open. Clifford isn't in the corridor, but there's a fresh patch of metal over the puncture hole in the hatch, and the out-suit is hanging safely in its webbing.

She goes up the ladder to the cockpit. Clifford is down on his knees, looking under the control desk.

'What is it?' she asks.

'I don't know. I heard a pop. That escape really messed us up.'

He crawls back out and pulls himself to his feet on the edge of the desk.

Dylan checks the console. The data link is offline.

'Zero bits per second,' she says. 'We're cut off from the Company.'

'Damn,' says Clifford, and sighs. 'Well, we're still breathing. We can fix the radio when we get to the Twins. Assuming nothing else goes pop.'

# Chapter Thirty-One

Sealgair's buggy bounds across the rocky terrain. To the east, the sun is rising up over the southern slope of Pavonis Mons, the vast extinct volcano. On the horizon behind him are the dust plumes of Heron and the rest of his entourage. They're far enough away to let him enjoy his solitude of the hunt, but close enough to give him back-up if the hunt stops going his way.

His navigation computer chimes, alerting him that he's two kilometres from his destination, and a few seconds later the radio sounds with a low, repetitive beep.

He checks the buggy's console. It's an incoming call from the Fuller Aerospace headquarters in Mariner Base. He taps the screen to accept the connection.

'Sir,' comes a familiar voice through his helmet speaker. 'It's Baikonur.'

'Any news?'

'Yes sir. Clifford's bodyguard contacted her father on a video call.'

'And?'

'She mentioned the Twins as their possible destination. Then the call cut out, and the rover disappeared from the Company radio network.'

Sealgair nods to himself.

'Clifford knows we're on to him,' he says. 'Put the father under room arrest. We'll use him as a bargaining chip. How's the investigation going in Mariner? Have you had any luck with Clifford's computers?'

'No sir,' Baikonur says. 'The backups were wiped clean. Forty years of data deleted. But we checked in with the finance

department, because he has no authority there. It still has records
of his budget allocations.'

'Oh?' says Sealgair. 'Anything interesting?'

'Just one thing. He's been consistently channelling a small
amount of his budget into something called Project Granite.'

Sealgair breathes in sharply.

'Sir? Do you know what it is? We can't find any trace of it
online.'

'It was a classified criminal investigation,' says Sealgair. 'It didn't
come to anything. I shut it down myself, twenty years ago.'

'Well, Clifford reopened it, sir. He's been running it quietly
ever since.'

Sealgair drums his fingers on the buggy's accelerator. *Why would
Clifford be interested in Project Granite?*

A line of boulders comes into view ahead, crossing the horizon.
In front of it, a cluster of polished metal shapes reflects the morning sunlight.

'Something's happening here,' says Sealgair. 'Call back if you
find anything new.'

He disconnects the call, and looks out through the glass hood of
his buggy. A group of rovers is gathered outside the Pavonis boulder fence, milling about and kicking up dust like a herd of agitated
bison. They're two-deck Campbell Mk5 transports, gleaming silver,
emblazoned with the Fuller Aerospace logo. Sealgair approaches
them from the south, riding slowly so he doesn't spook them.

As he gets close to the herd, his radio warbles again. One of the
rovers peels off from the others and faces him. It has a rail gun
mounted on its side.

'Unidentified buggy, keep your distance,' comes a stern voice.
'This is a Fuller Aerospace patrol.'

'And this is Karl Sealgair.'

The rover rolls to a stop.

'Mr Sealgair, sir,' says the voice, deferential. 'Sorry. I should have
known. This is ensign Wu, code FA-101-046.'

'What's happening here, Wu?' Sealgair asks as he approaches. The
rest of the rovers pull into formation, as if Sealgair's herding them.

'We were trying to get up to the outposts in the north, but rovers from Pavonis blocked our way. They told us to leave their territory, and come talk to the new sheriff if we don't like it. Our patrol leader is negotiating with him now.'

'Let me talk to them.'

'Yes sir.'

The Company rovers part, clearing a path to the boulder fence. Up ahead, Sealgair can see a single Pavonis rover blocking the way through the boulders. It's ancient and red with dust, but it's armed with a large harpoon gun. There's a five-pointed star welded to the front, and one of the Company rovers is facing it.

Sealgair drives his buggy closer, and pulls to a stop between the opposing rovers. He looks up into the cockpit of the Pavonis sheriff's rover. The driver is a middle-aged man with brown hair and a thick moustache. His lips are moving silently as he talks to the driver of the Company rover. Sealgair tunes his radio until he finds the conversation.

'—doesn't matter what the treaty says,' the Pavonis sheriff is saying. 'Our former mayor's authority was illegitimate. The people of Pavonis will renegotiate all his agreements.'

'We're sending rovers north to fight the Outliers!' a voice says. Sealgair twists his head to look up at the cockpit of the other rover. A grey-uniformed woman with a blond crew cut is standing at the front window, looking agitated. 'If we can't go through Pavonis territory, it'll add hundreds of kilometres to the journey.'

'That's as may be, but the free passage treaty is over. Everywhere from here to Plymouth and Indis is off-limits to Fuller Aerospace employees.'

'I'll take over from here, Patrol Leader,' says Sealgair.

She leans forward and looks down at him from the cockpit. When she sees his buggy below her, her eyes widen.

'Yes sir.'

'Who's this now?' says the moustached sheriff.

Sealgair looks up at him.

'Karl Sealgair. C.E.O. of Fuller Aerospace.'

The sheriff is caught off-guard. His mouth opens.

'What caused this change of heart?' says Sealgair. 'I thought we had an understanding with Pavonis.'

'We've got a new mayor,' says the sheriff. 'Laurie Ravine, my predecessor. She has strong issues with the Company stepping into our territory.'

'Any particular reason?'

The sheriff squares his jaw.

'We know how the last mayor got elected. We want you to stay the hell out of the Free Settlements.'

Sealgair looks down at the dust around the gap on the boulder fence. There's about a dozen rover tracks going in and out of it, all overlapping and running over each other. The Company rovers have obliterated the tracks on the outside of the fence, but Sealgair spots a stretch of tread marks on the inside that have the distinctive cross-hatch pattern of an old-model rover, a Fuller Aerospace Muse, the type that James Clifford drives.

'Are you listening to me, sir?' says the sheriff.

Sealgair looks up at him.

'I can see we won't be having a reasonable discussion,' he says. 'We'll leave your territory. But your new mayor might want to talk to your allies in the north. They're quite happy to let us fight the Outliers for them.'

The sheriff snorts.

'We've seen what happens to bases that let you defend them. They become you. Red Rose killed and died to give us freedom. We won't go back.'

'Really?' says Sealgair. 'Your mayor should discuss that with your northern neighbours. I'm sure they'll be contacting her shortly.'

He flicks the radio off, and drives out from between the two rovers, and away from the gap in the fence. As he goes, he connects to the Company's digital radio channel.

'Patrol leader?' he says.

He hears her voice again. 'Yes, sir.'

'Return to headquarters, and reroute our supply chains to avoid Pavonis territory, for now.'

The patrol leader hesitates. 'Yes sir,' she says.

'It won't be for long. When we've finished fortifying the north, there'll be nothing to stop us taking the south as well.'

'Sir.'

The patrol leader's rover reverses away from the gap in the boulder fence. It turns, and the rest of the rovers fall into line behind it for the long drive back to Company Territory.

Sealgair drives forward slowly, until the rover tracks on the dusty ground are spread out enough to be recognisable. He checks them carefully, one by one, until he finds the tread marks of the rover he's looking for, curving towards the north-west. Baikonur's intel was accurate, it seems. Clifford is heading for The Twins.

'Project Granite,' Sealgair murmurs. 'What are you up to, Clifford?'

He grips the handle at the side of his seat and pushes it forward. The buggy accelerates along the tracks, deeper into the Settlements.

# Chapter Thirty-Two

Rudolf rumbles along a track winding up the side of a low hill, past a loose cairn of stones that marks the start of the Twins' shared territory. As Dylan and Clifford reach the top of the hill, they spot dust clouds on the horizon ahead. A few minutes later, a pair of large white rovers come up the track towards them. They both have small metal platforms bolted to their sides, where out-suited figures are standing, holding the handles of rover-mounted cannons.

Dylan brings Rudolf to a stop, and the two rovers circle around them. One of the suited figures lets go of the cannon's handles and taps the side of its helmet.

'They're trying to radio us,' says Dylan.

'Well, good luck to them,' says Clifford from the second cockpit seat. After a few minutes, the rovers give up. They flash their lights at Rudolf, and start crawling slowly back the way they came.

'We should follow,' Clifford says.

Dylan drives after them, matching their pace as they wind down the slope. Another base comes into view at the bottom of the shallow valley, a cluster of eight dusty buildings. The largest of them is a stainless steel tube, lying half buried in the ground, tapered at one end and gleaming metallically under the patina of dust.

'What's that?' says Dylan, craning forward.

Clifford stares at it for a while, then breaks into a grin.

'It's a passenger liner. One of the originals.'

The rovers drive past its curved wall, and Dylan gets a close look. It's a giant fallen spacecraft, hundreds of metres long, with a honeycomb of windows facing up to the sky. The word EURASIA is written down the side of it in bold red letters, half buried under the ground. The shell of the ship has become the core of the base, and towers and domes have grown out of it, sprouting like mushrooms from a carcass.

'I came to Mars in a ship just like that one,' Clifford says. 'Sad to see it like this.'

Dylan has seen pictures of the passenger liners, but she never realised how big they were. Even on its side, the ship dwarfs Rudolf and the two other rovers. It's unbelievable that something this large could have flown through the sky.

They drive slowly past domes, solar heaters, radiators, protective barriers and watchtowers. As they circle around the outside of the base, Dylan catches a glimpse of jagged white on the far horizon.

'Is that the other Twin?' she says. 'I didn't realise they were this close.'

Clifford nods grimly. 'Yep. They barely bothered to move apart. It's like they wanted to fight.'

The rovers lead them to a long docking port attached to the side of the fallen ship. Parked at the far end of it is a newer-model Company rover, with a gun turret on top and a blue stripe down its back. It's the same rough shape as Rudolf, but with a higher centre of gravity and far more rigid suspension. It's missing some of its outer panels.

'That's a Marathon-class rover,' says Clifford.

'Is it the one Unwin was searching for?'

'I'll bet.'

The two rovers ahead of them dock at the port, and flash their lights again. Dylan reverses Rudolf to the nearest available hatch. She's worried that Rudolf's docking loops were damaged in the escape from Pavonis, but the clamps lock onto them with a satis-fying click.

They step out of the hatch and into the docking bay, and Dylan takes a deep breath of the air. Every base she's ever been to has its own distinct smell, and this one is halfway between engine grease and boiled vegetables. The docking bay is tall and long, with wide windows looking out at the rovers. The high ceiling is held up by Vs of diagonal girders every five metres.

A woman in a tea-coloured gown and a white headscarf is waiting in the bay. She's in her mid-twenties, with a round-face and pale cheeks, and she greets them with an anxious smile.

'Welcome to Hunter,' she says politely, as Clifford and Dylan climb through the hatch. 'I'm Kin Francisca, and I'm the liaison in the base. If you need anything during your stay, please let me know.'

This isn't the reception Dylan was expecting. She watches warily as Clifford offers the woman his hand.

'Thank you. We're sorry we entered your territory without warning, our communications systems are out of commission. I'm Reckling, and this is Shay. Kin, is it?'

The woman winces slightly. '"Kin" is my title. I'm a member of the Hunter Kinship. Unfortunately, I can't shake your hand. We have strict rules about physical contact with people from outside the base.'

'Ah,' says Clifford, taking his hand back and wiping it down his shirt. Dylan can't help noticing how uncomfortable he is in new situations. 'Well, I hope we don't have to trouble you for long. If possible, we'd like to retrieve some data from that Fuller Aerospace rover outside.'

Francisca's face lights up with recognition.

'Yes,' she says. 'The maps. I'm sorry to say we already gave them to a visitor called Mr Unwin yesterday. He paid three titanium ingots for them. He asked us to wipe the computer afterwards.'

'Why?' asks Dylan.

'Confidential information,' Clifford mutters. He taps his finger-tips together, deep in thought, and turns to Francisca. 'Do you know which way he went? We'd like to catch up to him, as quickly as possible.'

Francisca smiles. 'Of course. But you've only just arrived. Please, come inside and share a meal with us. I'm sure Avunculus Peter would love to meet you. He's one of the most respected followers of Hunter's Path.'

'Thank you,' says Clifford. 'But we're only really here so we can find that map.'

Francisca is firm. 'This is our custom. Food and discussion first. Then we will get to your business, I promise.'

'All right,' says Clifford, tugging at the wrist of his shirt to straighten the sleeve. 'We accept your hospitality.'

He doesn't hide the annoyance in his voice, and Francisca doesn't comment on it.

'This way, please,' she says, and leads them out of the rover docking bay.

Clifford hangs back a little, until he's walking next to Dylan.

'Hold on to your wits,' he mutters quietly. 'They're going to try to convert us.'

# Chapter Thirty-Three

Francisca guides them through a series of strange rooms with irregular floors and ceilings. There are hatches that are wider than they are tall, and walls with black rubberised surfaces, crosshatched with a grid of shallow almond-shaped bumps. It takes a moment for Dylan to understand. They're inside the body of the giant spaceship, and the rooms are at ninety degrees to their intended orientation.

'When did you find that rover?' Clifford asks, making conversation.

'Last week. It was lying at the bottom of a gully.'

'Lucky for us that Tharsis didn't find it first.'

Francisca's lips purse at the name of the enemy.

'There's no luck there. We've managed to destroy most of their rover fleet. We're the only ones patrolling. They're the weakest they've been in years.'

They come to a long horizontal tunnel through the core of the fallen ship, and follow it out onto a walkway hanging over a brightly lit open chamber filled with warm, humid air. Dylan looks over the metal railing. Down below is another giant greenhouse, but totally unlike the one in Syria. Sunlight shines from the hexagonal windows above onto a multi-level garden with cobbled pathways, trees, bushes, and lawns of untamed grass. Shrubs are growing between scattered boulders. Water spills down from the upper levels into a wide, central paddy, where residents in tea-coloured robes hitched up to their waists are wading and picking rice. Large, lazy insects buzz through the blossoms on the trees.

Francisca turns to face them, framed by the light.

'Welcome to the Grove,' she says.

Dylan grips the railing. She isn't used to heights, and it feels like the walkway is shifting under her, but she can't look away. More robed residents are scattering seeds in a small field below her. Others are plucking broad green leaves from plants growing along the edges of the chamber. After a lifetime of constructed environments, seeing plants growing freely and organically is overwhelming.

'Incredible.'

Francisca smiles at Dylan's reaction.

'This is Hunter's purpose,' she says. 'We're bringing nature to Mars.'

Next to Dylan, Clifford's eyes dart around, absorbing the scene. Francisca gives them a few more seconds to admire the view, then walks off down the walkway, towards some stairs at the far end.

'Huh,' says Clifford, straightening up. He scratches his chin thoughtfully, and follows Francisca at a distance. Dylan catches up with him.

'You aren't impressed?' she says quietly.

'No,' he mutters back. 'It's all standard greenhouse plants, but grown less efficiently.'

'But look at it! It's like … the Garden of Eden.'

Clifford leans over the railing again, and points down at different parts of the chamber.

'Dwarf wheat,' he says. 'Kale. Rice. Soya. Algae for bioplastics. All standard base staples. Planted idiosyncratically, sure, but cultivated and harvested like on any other base. This is just another factory.'

A big black insect buzzes over, and lands on the back of his hand. He raises it to show Dylan.

'See? Sugar flies, to turn food waste into protein. It's all carefully constructed to look unconstructed. They're growing vegetables the Willy Wonka way.'

Dylan can tell he's making a reference, but she doesn't get it.

'But … Why?' she asks.

'Because they're batshit crazy?' Clifford mutters.

They get to the end of the walkway, and descend the black metal stairs into the Grove. They step off it onto a cobblestone path. Trees and bushes grow on either side, and the path makes a tunnel through the greenery.

Dylan and Clifford follow Francisca. Through the branches, they see small groups of people in muted grey and brown robes, gathered in twos and threes, walking, exercising, and washing clothes in the river. Up ahead, a larger group of about twenty is gathered near the waterfall. They're listening to an elderly man, who is standing on a flat-topped rock and reciting from a handwritten book. Dylan catches some words.

' ... *The world is a reflection of our minds, and its impurity is a reflection of our impurity ...*'

The path becomes gravel, and it crunches underfoot. Dylan feels the rocks digging into the soles of her soft indoor shoes.

As they approach the crowd, the old man finishes reading from the book. He looks up at them, and snaps it shut with a smile. He's balding, with a fluffy fringe of white hair around the back of his head. He wears the same type of flowing robe as the people around him, in a deep burgundy. As the crowd disperses, Kin Francisca climbs up onto the old man's rock and talks to him quietly for a few minutes, then holds his hand to steady him as he drops down to the ground. He falls slowly, and his robe billows in the warm air.

With Francisca still holding his hand, he walks over to Dylan and Clifford. His face is scored with deep lines as he smiles.

'Welcome, strangers!'

'This is Avunculus Peter,' Kin Francisca says with reverence. 'He's the interpreter of the Hunter Kinship.'

Peter chuckles.

'I'm just an old man who's learned a few things. Please, join me, I'll be having a small picnic.'

They go to a patch of uncut grass nearby, lit by a hexagon of sunlight from the windows above. Avunculus Peter leans his weight on Francisca as he sits, and rests his back against the trunk of a small apple tree. 'Ah,' he says. 'That's better. My leg has been giving me considerable trouble lately. I don't recommend getting old. Do something better with your time.'

Clifford finds a medium-sized rock near to Peter, and perches on it unhappily. The lack of dignity doesn't suit him. Francisca walks off to talk to some residents in brown and grey. Dylan stays standing, keeping her distance from the two men.

Avunculus Peter looks up at her. 'Come closer.'

'I'd rather stay out of the sunlight,' she says. 'Radiation.'

Peter looks amused. 'Ah, yes, that old thing. Well, I'm not going to make you do anything you don't want to do. Sit in the shade if you wish.'

She does, as far from Avunculus Peter as she feels she can politely go.

The residents that Francisca spoke to bring three small bowls and hand them out to Dylan, Clifford and Peter, being careful not to touch Dylan or Clifford's hands. Each bowl comes with its own ceramic spoon, flattened and polished. Dylan examines her food. It looks like rice, seasoned with soy sauce, and a dressing of strips of carrot, onion and celery.

Avunculus Peter eats a spoonful of the salad, and turns to Clifford.

'So, tell me, Mr…'

'Reckling,' says Clifford.

'Mr Reckling. What do you think of this place?'

Clifford's leg bounces in agitation. 'It seems impractical.'

Peter laughs. 'I thought you'd say that. There's more to this world than practicality. Fuller Aerospace would do well to consider that.'

'What makes you think we're from Fuller Aerospace?'

'Am I wrong?' Avunculus Peter says. 'Please, eat! You're our guests!'

Dylan takes a spoonful from the bowl. The vegetables are crisp and fresh, but strangely flavourless.

'What do you think?' says Avunculus Peter. 'Delicious?'

The vegetables crunch in Clifford's mouth. He looks thoughtful.

'You've done something to them.'

Avunculus Peter smiles proudly.

'Quite the opposite. We've reversed something done to them.

We put them all back to their original state. These are the only natural crops on Mars, one hundred per cent pure, all the genetic modifications reversed. No added nutrition or flavour, no chemical pathways to filter out perchlorates. We have to be very careful about the kind of soil they grow in, but it's worth the extra care.'

Clifford puts his spoon down. 'You made your food less nutritious?' he says. 'Why?'

'For the same reason that we're doing all this,' Peter says, spreading his arms to embrace the whole Grove. 'To return to a natural state.'

'What does natural mean?' says Clifford. 'It's natural for a human on Mars to suffocate.'

Dylan feels a touch of admiration at how antagonistic Clifford can be. For the first time, she sees a crack in the Avunculus's welcoming disposition.

'Mr Reckling. I'm not trying to trick you or sell you anything. All I want to do is build an understanding between us. As Kin Francisca said, I'm the Interpreter. I'm trying to interpret the path of Hunter for you, in a way that you will appreciate.'

'All right then,' says Clifford, putting his half-finished bowl of rice down at his side. 'If we want to come to an understanding. I don't think that this set-up is efficient enough to feed a whole base. I'm prepared to bet that you have more greenhouses and grow-rooms where you're growing food properly, and I think you hide them from newcomers, because they're proof that your philosophy is flawed.'

Avunculus Peter purses his lips, and looks over to Dylan. 'What about you, silent one? I see you watching from the shadows. You can think for yourself. You have to feel the rightness of this place. This is about more than just protein and carbohydrates. This is a space for humans, where you can be your fullest, truest, healthiest self. Can't you see yourself living in a place like this?'

Dylan looks around the Grove. She absorbs the rush of the waterfall, and the dappled sunlight through the leaves. Some children are playing down by the river bank, chasing a big black sugar fly as it darts over the vegetable beds. And she looks at Clifford, who is watching her fixedly. She can feel his judgement.

'Thanks,' she says to Avunculus Peter. 'I'm still on my journey.'

Avunculus Peter sighs. He beckons Kin Francisca over, and she helps him back up to his feet.

'Well,' he says. 'I did my best.'

Dylan and Clifford stand, too.

'Okay. Now that it's clear that we aren't your newest recruits, can we get down to business?' says Clifford.

'As you wish,' Peter says. 'Kin Francisca says you're looking for your friend who passed through here, is that right?'

'It is.'

'We know which base he was heading for, and what rover he was travelling in. We'll give you the information for ...' the Avunculus looks thoughtful, '...five titanium ingots.'

Dylan frowns. 'You sold the maps to our friend for three.'

'Five is the price,' says Avunculus Peter. The twinkle in his eyes has gone. 'We don't haggle with outsiders.'

Clifford folds his arms. 'We don't have any ingots. We lost them in a riot in Pavonis. Is there anything else you'll accept?'

Avunculus Peter looks sidelong at Dylan, and raises his eyebrows.

'We do accept work for trade. Stay with us for three days, and do the jobs that need doing – cooking and cleaning and whatever else comes up, and we'll tell you which way your friend went.'

'Three days?' says Clifford. 'There must be something physical you need. Reserve oxygen. Water. Energy.'

'Three days' work,' says Avunculus Peter, calm but firm. 'Take it or leave it.'

Dylan goes to Clifford's side, and talks quietly.

'If Unwin has the map he'll be trying to contact you. We can go back to Company Territory and wait for him there.'

Clifford closes his eyes and pinches the bridge of his nose.

'No. I need to get that map from him before he gets back to the Company.'

'Why?'

He doesn't answer. Instead, he turns on his heels and faces Avunculus Peter.

'We'll do it.'

'Wonderful!' The Avunculus's jovial smile has returned. 'Thank you for being more open-minded. Maybe with a bit of time here, you'll start to understand your true place in nature.'

# Chapter Thirty-Four

Dylan sits on the corner of the bed in her cell, peeling white, unnutritious potatoes for the Hunter mess hall. She's locked up once again, only this time, there's nothing to stop her escaping. There are no bars on the cell, just an open doorway. The only thing keeping her here is Clifford. And come to think of it, he was the reason they were in the bubbles, too.

His cell is on other side of the corridor. She cranes over to look through both their doorways, and sees him sitting at his desk, copying out pamphlets by hand for Hunter Base to distribute at the nearby commercial hubs.

'We're free to go any time,' she says.

'No, we aren't,' Clifford replies grimly.

Dylan wipes her brow, and gets back to work. Her skin is sticky. She's in the same clothes she wore at the mayor's party in Pavonis, and all her personal hygiene items are gone – toothbrush, sanitary pads, even her deodorant, which is considered vital on enclosed bases. The Hunter Kinship offered her one of the brown robes that the residents wear, but Dylan isn't quite ready for that. Not yet.

Clifford calls back to her. 'How's the peeling?'

'Slow,' says Dylan. 'This knife is terrible.'

'Don't be a perfectionist. They won't mind a bit of potato skin. It's organic.'

'And you, sir? How are you doing with the pamphlets?' she calls back.

'Listen to this one: "Be part of the natural world. Don't let Mars corrupt you. Join the Hunter Kinship, the last bastion of natural humanity." I wonder what they'll get me to do next. Maybe some lines on a chalkboard. "I will not use life-support, I will not use life-support," a thousand times.'

*Schtick, shtick, shtick.* Dylan's knife blade skims the surface of the sickly potatoes.

'Sir?' she says. 'Why do you hate them so much? Is it so bad to try to live naturally?'

'Of course not,' he says. 'I understand the draw. We're all part of a network of life. We want to be part of a living system, but we've cut ourselves off from it and we live in little boxes underground. I know all of that, and I understand wanting to belong to a movement that's pure and real and good. But this place isn't offering nature, just a surface-level approximation of it to lure in new fanatics. They didn't even use real rocks. It's sculpted Marscrete. It's as inauthentic and inorganic as any other base. I don't hate nature, I hate false promises.'

*Schtick, shtick, shtick.*

'Did you imagine being back in the Free Settlements would be like this, Ward?'

'No sir.'

'Do you have any family out here?'

'No sir.'

'Your mother?'

'She died when I was one.'

'I'm sorry to hear that. No one else? No cousins? Uncles? Grandparents?'

'No sir,' she says guardedly. 'Why do you ask?'

'Just something in the way you've been since we got out here,' he says. 'The way you look around new bases. Like you're hoping to see something, or someone.'

*Schtick, shtick, shtick.*

'Something on your mind, Ward?'

'No sir.'

'You sigh when you've got something on your mind.'

Dylan wasn't aware of it.

'What's the problem?' he asks.

'Sir … why are we doing all this?'

'I need to find the census taker.'

'But why?' she says.

He leans one arm over the back of his chair, and looks at her across the corridor.

'I've been a high-level Fuller Aerospace employee for over thirty years. I've got a million secrets, so don't think I'm withholding this one thing from you specifically. All you need to know is that we need to find the census taker.'

Dylan looks down into the bucket of potatoes. Half full. Another two and a half buckets to go.

'Will all of this be worth it?'

'Oh yes,' says Clifford without hesitation. 'It's worth it.'

# Chapter Thirty-Five

Dylan wakes up to the tinny noise of a chant playing through a speaker in an upper corner of her cell. It's a peppy little ditty, halfway between a hymn and a breakfast cereal jingle.

> *Sweep the path with sharpened mind,*
> *Brain and body now aligned,*
> *Clear our eyes and break our bread,*
> *Ready for the day ahead ...*

It's nonsense, but Dylan catches herself humming along as she gets up and stretches. There's no sign of Clifford in the cell opposite hers, but his chair is pushed in, and the pamphlets he was copying the night before are neatly stacked on the desk.

Dylan walks down the corridor to the ablution block. She has a shower, using half her water ration, then spends a few minutes sponging a wide grease stain off her pocket. There's a dozen more patches of grime and gunk on her top and trousers, and she does her best to scrub them away. Her underwear is beyond saving, and she bins them. Whenever Frank got to this stage of a journey he would dump all his clothes in a hot shower, wring them out and wear them wet for the rest of the day. Dylan used to laugh at him, especially when he muttered about chaffing.

'No one can accuse me of not making an effort,' he would say. 'It's better than smelling like the inside of a garbage chute.'

She puts her clothes back on. Her trousers and jacket are still spotted with damp patches, and the cheap bathroom mirror distorts her face.

'Fuck it,' she says under her breath, and sighs.

There's still no sign of Clifford when she gets back to her cell. Francisca hasn't arrived to brief them on the new day's tasks, either. With nothing else to do, Dylan pushes her chair in under her desk and heads out to explore the rest of the base.

Clifford was right. The other sections of Hunter Base aren't nearly as organic as the Grove. Dylan walks through a buried maze of white rooms and corridors, just like in any other base on Mars. The only major thing that sets Hunter apart is its lack of privacy. There are very few doors, and as Dylan walks down the corridors, she sees rooms full of school-aged children at desks, squadrons of fighters exercising, and robed figures reading in quiet contemplation. Life on Hunter seems to happen in public. Everyone exists under everyone else's watchful eyes.

She walks the stairs back up to the Grove, and steps out into the morning sunlight. The gravel path leads her through the orchard, and back to the stairs up to the overhead walkway. Some Hunter residents are standing at the side of the river, hands and eyes raised to the roof in a morning chant.

*Ahm Nee Faa Sho...*
*Ahm Nee Faa Sho...*

The residents intone the syllables with reverence. Kin Francisca is among them, and when she sees Dylan coming past, she splits off from the group.

'Good morning,' she says, walking alongside her. 'Are you looking for your companion? We sent him down to sort through the old texts in the archives.'

'That's okay,' says Dylan. 'I don't need him right now.'

'Where are you heading?'

Her voice is cheerful enough to almost hide the pointedness of the question.

'The radio in our rover's broken,' says Dylan. 'I wanted to see if there's anything I can do.'

It's been a few days since she's spoken to Frank, and she's starting to feel adrift.

'There's no need,' says Kin Francisca. 'I'll ask our engineers to look at it this afternoon. Go back to your room, I'll bring you your tasks now.'

'Would you prefer it if I didn't go to my rover?'

Kin Francisca looks back at the group at the riverside. They're still chanting, but one or two of them are watching curiously.

'Not at all,' Francisca says, running her tongue along her upper lip. 'You have the freedom of the base.'

'All right then,' says Dylan.

She leaves Francisca and goes back up the steps and over the walkway, being careful not to look over the edge. She finds her way through the sideways rooms of the fallen ship, all the way to the docking bay.

The hatch to Rudolf is standing open. As Dylan approaches, she hears a clink from inside, so quiet she might have imagined it, like the sound of someone putting down a tool on a metal surface.

'Hello? Clifford?'

There's silence from inside.

Dylan steps through the hatch cautiously, into Rudolf. She walks slowly down the lower deck corridor, past the out-suits hanging on the wall and the hatches into the two cabins. Both rooms are empty, and the berths are neatly made.

She keeps going, deeper into the rover, one step at a time. As she approaches the ladder at the end of the corridor, she sees a subtle shift in the sunlight coming down from the upper deck, and feels a faint tremble in Rudolf's suspension.

'Hey!' she calls up. 'Who's up there?'

Again, there's no answer.

'This rover is private property.'

A man drops down from the hatch. His dark-grey robes billow around him as he falls, and Dylan catches a glimpse of a tangled beard and wild, panicked eyes. In the low gravity he doesn't have much speed, and as his feet drop down towards her, she jumps to the side.

'Hey!'

He shoves past her, kicking off the bottom of the ladder and running down the corridor.

'Stop!' Dylan yells. She lunges to grab him, but misses his trailing robe as he leaps out of the hatch. She chases after him, and sees him running to the far wall of the docking bay, and disappearing into an open panel.

Francisca runs in through the docking bay entrance.

'What's wrong? I heard shouting.'

'Someone was in my rover,' Dylan says. 'Did you know about this?'

'No. What did he look like? Was it an engineer?'

Dylan looks into the hole in the docking bay wall. Behind it is a long dark chamber that stinks of chlorine. She can see life-support machinery: tanks of pressurised gas, water cisterns, pumps and condensers. The ceiling is low, and every surface is covered in a tangle of cables and piping.

'How deep does this go?'

'All the way around the base,' says Francisca. 'It's access to the air and water circulation systems.'

'I think you have a stowaway in your base.'

Francisca's eyes are wide. 'Are you sure?'

'He didn't look like anyone I've seen here.'

A gurgle in the heating pipes gives way to a gentle hiss, and a shape moves in the darkness.

'There!' Dylan says, pointing ahead.

A man steps out from behind a water tank. He's wearing dark-grey robes, and has an unkempt beard and a greasy sheen to his hair. He stares at Dylan, unblinking.

She feels pressure against her side, and looks down. A knife blade is pressed against her kidney.

'Don't make a sound, and don't move,' Francisca says quietly.

# Part 3.5

—

# Michael

# Chapter Thirty-Six

ROSEFULLER.MARS
Monthly update

Hey everyone, and thanks again to all of you for being my followers. If you didn't realise it, up until now, these posts were written by a bot that aggregates all the news stories about me, but I think it's time for me to take off the mask and tell you about what's going on in person. In this post, I'm not talking about the latest Martian couture or the hottest venues. I'm talking about transportation.

Over the last few months, I've been doing whatever I can to help all the people on Mars who are threatened with transportation to Earth. Fuller Aerospace is using transportation as a way to silence dissent, so I'm offering free legal representation to anyone fighting it, and I'm using all my contacts and authority in the Company to try to stop it.

Every day, more and more people are being born on Mars. They're the children of Fuller Aerospace employees, but they never signed a contract with the Company. They never agreed that if the Company doesn't like them it can force them onto a spacecraft, at their own cost, so they can live the rest of their lives in poverty on a planet they have no allegiance to.

This is unacceptable. This is only legal because Mars is governed by a tangled mess of laws, contracts and treaties all written on Earth. But just because something's legal, it doesn't mean it's fair. It doesn't make sense for the Mars-born to be second-class citizens on the planet of their birth. Everyone should get a say in the laws they live under, and challenge them when they're unjust.

That's why I'm starting an organisation to protect the rights of the people of Mars. We need to start imagining the kind of future we really want to live in. We need to raise our voices, and demand that this unjust system ends.

# Chapter Thirty-Seven

## INTERPLANETARY SPACE, 2058
## THE YEAR OF THE FIRST MURDER

Michael Agee was his new name. Michael, twenty-four years old, tall, skinny, smiling, non-threatening. *Hi, I'm Mike. Pleased to meet you.*

The name was given to him by his employer, a company called Connect Image, which presented itself as a public relations firm specialising in private targeted engagements. The company, and the things it did, weren't widely known outside its small circle of clients. Its name was never mentioned on the news, although its specialty was deciding what the news would be.

Michael had the whole seven-month flight on the passenger liner to get used to his name. For the first two weeks after the launch he was holed up in a tiny coffin-like cabin, being violently space-sick. Every time he moved his head he felt the lack of a 'down' he could rely on, and was overcome by nausea. But as the disorientation wore off, he tentatively ventured out into the rest of the liner and began the job of meeting the other travellers. He connected with them one at a time, as chance allowed: first the ship's nurse, then a geologist heading out to join a mining operation, then a machine-learning tycoon from Estonia. He worked through the list of all hundred passengers, chatting with them by the exercise machines or under the honeycomb windows of the viewing deck where they watched the Earth shrink, day by day, into a tiny point of blue.

He got used to them calling him by his new name. *Michael. Mike. Mikey. Hey, Mike!* He listened attentively, and laughed with them, and paid close attention to everything they said about themselves. In his cabin in the evenings he wrote down what they had said, making particular note of their hobbies, their jobs, and their families. Anything they were interested in, he got interested in too, so he would never be at a loss for something to talk about. He never let a birthday pass him by. By the time they were in orbit around Mars, his new social media contact list was filled with real people, and they would all swear that he was their friend. If that didn't make him a real person too, nothing would.

On the last evening of the flight, as the ship swung close to Mars in its elliptical orbit, they all squeezed into the viewing deck together to watch the mountains and deserts of their new home slide by below them, and shared a moment of wonder, hope, and a tremendous camaraderie. They had started out as strangers, but over the last seven months they had become more than just travel companions. They were a family, and nothing was going to break their connection. Anything he needed, they would happily provide.

# Chapter Thirty-Eight

Fuller Aerospace made the arrival on Mars as polished as any piece of consumer electronics. The nuts and bolts of bureaucracy were all carefully hidden. Minutes after the passenger liner touched down, Michael was handed his identification card, reunited with his luggage, and whisked by rover to his new residence in Mariner Base. His rooms were fully furnished. He had a lounge, a bedroom, a kitchenette and an en-suite bathroom. His bedsheets were scented like freshly cut grass. A meal was waiting for him on the table, prepared according to the dietary preferences that he had logged on board the ship. His wardrobe was filled with clothes that matched his size and fictitious tastes. After the chaos of Earth, the organisation that had gone into every detail of the room was astonishing.

Not everything about being on Mars was comfortable: standing upright was still a challenge, for one, and he had to forcefully remind himself not to leave objects in the air around him and expecting them to float. Back on the ship, microgravity had given him a smooth, cherubic face, and he looked a decade older in the mirror. At least he could eat proper food again, and he didn't have to worry about chunks coming up every time he burped. And he never thought he would be so happy to see a real toilet, without any vacuum attachments. The next few months would be difficult, but he had a good feeling for his future on Mars.

His first assignment began the next morning. He boarded a rover train heading to Aries Base, just to the north of the Valles Marineris. After the fountains and restaurants and underground public gardens in Mariner, travelling to Aries was like stepping back in time. It was one of the first colonies, a cluster of rusty-coloured domes of various sizes, like a spider's eyes poking up out of the ground. In the hallways, the light coming down from the skylights was dim and red from accumulated dust. He asked for directions to the Fuller residence, and the inhabitants pointed the way with the bare minimum of enthusiasm.

The entrance to the residence was a circular hatch three metres high, which opened out from the centre like a mechanical iris. A servant with a pencil skirt and 1960s hair showed him into the cavernous lounge. Kelly Fuller was lying back on a black Bauhaus sofa, talking on her pad.

'Then forget it,' she said. Michael heard a faint warble as the pad tracked Kelly's face and focused the audio to her ears.

'No. They're getting free publicity from their association with our brand, so if anything, they owe me.' She glanced up at Michael. 'I need to go. Someone's here.'

She hung up the call and dropped the pad on the sofa next to her.

'Yes?' she said impatiently.

'I'm Michael Agee, ma'am. Connect Image said you want to see me before I start my job.'

Recognition crossed her face. 'Oh, right. The spy.'

Michael took a deep breath. 'I work in public relations and brand management—'

'Relax. I keep this room swept for bugs, and we can trust Candice. What are you wearing?'

He looked down at his clothes: a simple T-shirt with a slow-moving abstract pattern of black-and-white e-ink, knee-length beige shorts and some Mariner-made thin-soled base shoes.

'I'm trying to fit in.'

Kelly looked Michael up and down. 'Yeah. You look just like the little bastards brainwashing my daughter.'

She leaned back and stared at Michael through her arched fingers. Michael fought the urge to break the silence. He held his hands behind his back, and stood quietly.

After a minute, Kelly said, 'What's your plan?'

'I made some contacts on the flight over. A few of the workers have ties to Rose's inner circle. They'll introduce me—'

'No,' Kelly said, irritated. 'I mean, what's your plan after you get into her group? Are you going to destroy it from the inside?'

'I'm going to collect detailed information about them, so we know their pressure points and can steer them the way we want. Destroying them isn't in Fuller Aerospace interest.'

'They're questioning the treaties and contracts that are the basis of all law and order on Mars, and they're getting my daughter to attack the Company. How's that in our interest?'

'A toothless enemy is more valuable than no enemy,' said Michael. 'If we make this anti-transport movement seem naive and hysterical, Fuller Aerospace's gets more support.'

Kelly frowned. She swiped and tapped on her pad, and flipped the screen over to reveal a video of a man in mining overalls. He was middle-aged, with yellow-grey hair and red cheeks, standing in front of the slowly rotating cutterhead of a tunnel-boring machine.

'These kids that grew up here,' said the man in the video. 'They're like this little hive mind. They all grew up together, and they look down on everyone on Earth. All this talk of human rights … if you dig a little deeper, you'll see it's a power-grab. They want to declare independence, dissolve the Company, and seize its assets. They want to take everything that Earth paid for. And you know who's going to suffer? Everyone who's ever sweated to build anything here. Everyone who relies on Earth for technology, or medicine, or trade. Rose Fuller's just a lightning conductor for their Star Trek futurist communist nonsense. We've all got a responsibility to stamp it out, for the sake of everything we've built. Talk to your friends, talk to your co-workers. Let them know that we aren't going to let Red Rose take our planet!'

Kelly snapped the pad closed and tossed it aside.

'Is he one of yours?'

'No,' said Michael. 'Those are our talking points, though. They must be resonating.'

Kelly Fuller's lips tightened. 'A bit too well. I don't like my daughter being targeted. Change the message. Say she's been kidnapped, and she doesn't know what she's getting into. Say she's like ... what's her name? Patty Hearst.'

'I'm sorry,' said Michael. 'I don't handle the messaging. Connect Image was briefed by the Fuller Aerospace board ...'

'And you're just following orders. Fine. Then I'm going to ask you this as a human being and not an employee, okay?'

Michael nodded, hesitantly.

'Look after my daughter,' said Kelly Fuller. 'Make sure she's safe. Don't let her get too tarnished, and don't let an angry mob take her. When this all blows over, I want you to bring her back to me older and wiser, okay? I want you to bring her home.'

# Chapter Thirty-Nine

The aircraft skimmed over the rippling dunes, flying north. Its wings were smooth, white and rounded. It had arrived on Mars the week before, packed away in a single crate in the hold of the passenger liner. The Fuller Aerospace engineers had assembled it, inflated its wings and body, and hardened its outer coating of soft resin by exposing it to ultraviolet light. It was the first aircraft on Mars capable of carrying people, and this was its third flight since it had arrived.

The aircraft flew low, catching the denser air near ground level. Dunes and boulders streaked past, ten metres below. The flight was computer-controlled and incredibly smooth, with barely any turbulence in the thin Martian air.

Karl sat in the back seat, behind his father and Mr Hunter. The sound of the engine was a quiet roar at his back. If he looked carefully, he imagined he could see the fusilage flexing. He had never heard of an inflatable aeroplane before, and it didn't sound like a very good idea. He knew that the air of Mars was thin, and he knew that aeroplanes needed air to fly. He pushed himself backwards into the cushions, and tried not to look out of the windows on either side.

The aircraft skimmed along the edge of some low cliffs, narrowly missing a jutting escarpment. In the seat ahead of him, Mr Hunter whooped.

'Quite something, isn't it?' he said. 'Is your boy enjoying it?'

Karl's father turned back and looked at him through dark-brown sunglasses.

'Are you enjoying yourself, Karl?'

'Yes sir.'

'Damn straight he is,' said Hunter. 'How old is he? Twelve? This is a memory that'll last him forever.'

Karl didn't know if he liked Mr Hunter. His father said he was as rich as them, maybe richer, but he wasn't clean-shaven like his father. His cheeks were patched with red under the stubble, and his suit was rumpled. He wore too much aftershave, and he wouldn't stop talking.

'You're riding in the future,' said Mr Hunter. 'Fuller Aerospace will have hundreds of these things on Mars in the next five years. They'll open up the economy in a big way. Travelling by rover will be a thing of the past.'

Gold light shone in through the cockpit window. Through it, Karl saw a cluster of blocky grey shapes rising up on the horizon.

'Ah! There it is,' said Mr Hunter. 'My baby, the Tycho Mine. We've got enough hydrazine in the tanks, let's see if we can get this thing to extend our flight and get us a better view.'

He tapped a touch-screen in front of him, and selected an option from a menu. The aircraft curved into a wide orbit around the mine, and Karl looked out at it through the transparent plastic side window. All he could see was three grey rectangular buildings with conveyor belts leading into them, and an empty square pit. Black smoke was rising out of a vent in the roof of one of the buildings, and a yellow rover with a mechanical scoop at the front was driving down a ramp into the pit. Other than that, the mine looked dead.

'Look at her,' said Mr Hunter proudly. 'She isn't much from the surface, but nothing on Mars is. We've got a three-level habitat down there, and a fully kitted processing plant. We're mining magnesium for Fuller Aerospace. They can't get enough of it. They use it to convert carbon dioxide into methane and methanol, and in their foundries to get the sulphur out of the iron. Useful stuff.'

'And it's making you money?' Karl's father asked.

'Absolutely. I'll show you the books.'

'So, why sell?'

Mr Hunter chuckled.

'I'm just concentrating on my core business,' he said. 'I'm in the lifestyle game. People here are getting pretty tired of artificiality. They aren't comfortable with all this stale air and plastic food. Folks will pay a premium for tradition, freshness, cleanness, and simplicity, and I'm offering products and experiences that deliver that. But the mine's doing fine. And magnesium prices can only go up, with Fuller Aerospace expanding the way it is.'

Karl looked down at the mine. Until this flight, he hadn't known that his father was thinking of settling on Mars.

'Business on Mars is different,' Mr Hunter said, as they began their second orbit of the grey mine buildings. 'Here, it's all about making your legacy. That's what Alex Fuller told me when I first arrived. There's an infinite future for those who claim it.'

Karl's father turned in is seat, and looked back at him.

'What do you think, Karl? You want to make a fresh start of it here?'

Karl knew what was expected of him.

'Yes, sir.'

Mr Hunter chuckled, and looked ahead into the golden light. 'Polite kid,' he said.

Karl's father nodded. 'The Sealgairs raise their children right.'

Mr Hunter leaned back in his seat, and put his hands behind his head.

'You won't regret this,' he said. 'And I'll tell you what. The labour here is dirt cheap. Ex-Fuller Aerospace employees are desperate not to get transported. They'll work for practically nothing.'

'I heard Fuller's kid was causing trouble about that.'

Mr Hunter snorted.

'No one takes Rose Fuller seriously. She's like Minnie Mouse spouting Karl Marx. There's been a couple of protests, but it's nothing. Don't worry about your investment. Fuller Aerospace isn't going to let her dent the Martian economy without a fight.'

# Chapter Forty

'You need to say something, Rose,' said Netsai from across the table.

Rose winced, trying to block out the noise in their new headquarters. They were set up inside the only available space that they could find on Mariner Base: an open-plan office that had once been a gym, back when the base had been contained to a single dome. One wall was still a giant mirror, which made the room seem much bigger and more impressive than it really was. The other walls were lined with standing workstations operated by volunteers. Netsai said it looked like the bridge of a retro sci-fi starship.

Rose scrolled through her social news feed, and tried to wrap her head around the crisis of the day. It looked like a Fuller Aerospace server was down. It was part of the central administration system, tracking the taxes people owed to all their various governments back on Earth. It was wonderful news. It was terrible. It was a hack. It was an explosion. People were dead. No one was dead. Hundreds of people could die. It was terrorism. It was justified retribution. It was Red Rose's fault.

Rose put down her pad. 'What actually happened?'

Netsai was sitting opposite her, on the other side of a round table in the middle of the room.

'Someone wiped out the local Fuller Aerospace file server. Probably just an accident, or some random hacker.'

'I got that, Nets. But what does it mean? Why are they dragging me into it?'

Netsai shook her head. She was in full business mode, with her glasses on and her braids tied back.

'Last week you were talking about how ridiculous it is for us to pay taxes to Earth, and now someone wipes out the server that the Fuller Corporation uses to automate the process. In real terms, it doesn't make any difference. People still have to pay their taxes, it's just going to be a little harder. From a rational point of view, it's a non-issue.'

'But from a political point of view?'

'It's Armageddon.'

Rose ran her hand down her face.

'This isn't right,' she said. 'I need to make a call.'

She picked up her white AR goggles, and called her brother. A few seconds later the room in front of her was overlaid with a depth map of a cave lit up with spotlights. The carved rock walls were damp and glistening. A semi-transparent film crew was milling about inside it, adjusting microphone stands and camera drones. The ground ahead sloped down, way below the still-visible floor of the headquarters. Archie appeared, standing next to Netsai, with half of his leg intersecting the office table. He was in a puffy blue jacket, and was adjusting his own pair of AR goggles on his face.

'Princess!' he said with a smile. 'I wasn't expecting to see you! How's it going? Still pretending to be a pauper?'

'That's not what I'm doing. Where are you?'

Archie looked around at the cave.

'Oh, yeah, welcome to Clarke Base. It's going to be huge, with a whole network of tunnels for electric cars. They're still melting out the underground ice layer, so I asked them to put work on hold for a few days so I can show the viewers what snowboarding on Mars looks like. The tricks you can do in low gravity … Anyway. Why are you calling? Because of the hack?'

'Was it really a hack, Archie?'

Netsai could only hear Rose's side of the conversation, but she raised her eyebrows.

'What else would it be?' said Archie.

'I don't know. Are you sure someone isn't trying to frame me?'

The corner of his ghostly lip twisted up in amusement. 'When's your return trip from planet paranoia?'

'You think the Company isn't trying to shut me up? Come on!'

She realised she was talking too loud. A few of the volunteers looked up from their workstations.

'I don't know about any of that stuff, Princess,' said Archie. 'I'm just a shareholder. I'm all for democracy and equality and human rights.'

'Really? Then why aren't you helping me?'

'Seriously?' He pointed to the volunteers around Rose's headquarters. 'These people don't want me there. Remember all the posts and comments about you when you started this? Calling you a parasite, latching onto a cause to make yourself look good? And that's just the people on your own side! Forget it.'

Rose took a deep breath. 'I'm trying to fix things. I don't care what they call me.'

'Yeah you do. You're like Dad. Remember when he gave billions to global health initiatives? Everyone hated him for it. Half the world said he was trying to whitewash his image, the other half said it was all part of some conspiracy to control them through, I don't know, mind-control malaria medicine. If he'd just left people to die, they wouldn't have given him a second thought.' Netsai was leaning one elbow on the table and staring at Rose, waiting for the call to end. Archie looked at her, and waved a hand through her head.

'Is this the one?' he said. 'The girl who's making you do her dirty work?'

'She isn't making me do anything,' said Rose. 'It's my decision.'

'Really? I heard that she was calling the shots.'

'She knows the situation better than me. I'm not going to try to swoop in and fix things from a point of ignorance. I'm not going to play saviour.'

'You sure?' said Archie, raising his transparent eyebrows. 'You want to be one of these people, but they'll never give you that. They'll take your money and they'll use you for publicity, and they'll resent you every step of the way.'

Rose shook her head.

'Thanks Archie,' she said. 'Great chat.'

'Don't get me wrong,' said Archie. 'I respect what you're doing. You're trying to make the world a better place. I hope these people appreciate you shooting yourself in the foot for them. See you around, Red Rose.'

Rose tore off the goggles, and Archie disappeared along with the rest of the ghostly cave.

'So Archie was as cooperative as ever?' said Netsai.

'I don't like this.' Rose dropped the goggles on the table and rubbed her temples. 'It feels like we're being set up. I don't know what to do.'

'I told you. Make a statement denouncing whoever did this. We're finally getting solidarity with the Chinese and Russian and Indian bases. We're going to lose it if they think we're fanatics.'

'Maybe our supporters did do it,' said Rose. 'They have every right to be angry at Fuller Aerospace.'

'You think I'm not?' said Netsai. 'But what can we do? When we get angry then they say we're overreacting. Emotional honesty is one of the many luxuries that we can't afford.'

'Excuse me.'

Rose and Netsai looked up. One of the volunteers was standing at the side of their table. He was tall, a year or two older than Rose and Netsai, in a tight red T-shirt. He was holding a pad across his chest, and the other volunteers in the room were watching him.

'From what we've seen online, we don't think it's a good idea for Rose to denounce the hack.'

'Why not?' said Netsai.

He glanced at Rose.

'Your name is too tightly associated with Fuller Aerospace. It's good for us when you attack the Company, because if even Alex Fuller's daughter is saying that the Company is evil, it must be true. But if you say anything to defend the Company, our core supporters will turn on us. They'll say you're showing your true colours.'

Rose closed her eyes, leaned back in her chair, and put her hands on the sides of her head.

'Okay. If I'm the problem then I'll stay out of it. Netsai, you can denounce the hack without me.'

'No,' said Netsai, tapping her fingernails on the table, deep in thought. 'Then it would look like you're distancing yourself from us, and that's no good either.'

'So, what do you want me to do?' said Rose.

Netsai stared down at the tabletop.

'We have a suggestion,' said the boy in the red shirt, looking around at the other volunteers in the room. 'In the past hour, we got two hundred new supporters. There's a rumour going around that the server was tracking more than taxes. They're saying that it had a list of people flagged for transport, and we took it down.'

'But it's not true,' said Netsai.

'We know,' said the volunteer. 'But there's no way to prove it one way or the other, and the theory doesn't hurt us. We think that Rose should keep quiet and ride it out.'

'I don't like it,' said Netsai. 'It's disinformation by omission.'

Rose shrugged. 'So? We've taken our share of ugly rumours. Let the Company find out how it feels for once.'

'Fine,' said Netsai, pressing her palms together. 'Stay silent.'

'Good,' said Rose, and looked up at the volunteer. 'Thank you. Sorry, what's your name?'

'Michael Agee, ma'am.'

Rose winced slightly, and smiled at him. 'Please don't call me that. It's Rose. Just Rose.'

# Part 4.0

## Romeo And Juliet

# Chapter Forty-One

The blade is 3D-printed ceramic. If it goes into Dylan's side then there's a good chance that the tip will snap off, and she doubts that any base within a hundred kilometres has the medical facilities to handle that kind of injury.

The man ahead of her in the dark chamber takes out a blade of his own. It's ugly serrated metal, and it glints in the light coming from the docking bay behind Dylan.

'Get her in here,' he says.

Francisca pushes Dylan into the chamber, and the man holds the blade up to Dylan's neck while Francisca pulls the panel closed behind her. The chamber darkens, until the only light comes from the orange and red indicators on the heating subsystem.

'We can't let her tell anyone,' the man says in the darkness.

'She arrived with an old man,' says Francisca. 'He'll know she's gone.'

'We could remove him, too.'

Even in the heat of the chamber, Dylan feels ice crawling outwards from her spine.

'Then what?' says Francisca. Dylan sees the outline of her, walking around until she's next to the man. 'Their rover will still be here. The Kinship will search the base for their bodies, and they'll find you.'

Francisca puts a hand on the man's arm, and hugs it to her chest.

'Hey,' says Dylan, quietly.

The man holds his knife up, and Dylan sees the glint of the blade in front of her face.

'She told you not to speak.'

He puts one arm around Francisca's waist, and pulls her closer. Dylan can make out their faces now, and sees their wide eyes.

'Please,' she says quietly. 'You need a way off the base, right? That's what you were doing in the rover? Trying to start it?'

Francisca looks up at the man's face. He nods.

'Right.'

'What's happening here?' says Dylan. 'Between you?'

'Anil is from Tharsis,' says Francisca.

'We met on Mendeleev Base,' says the man. 'I was there on a recruiting mission, and Francisca was out scouting for supplies. We fought, at first, but Francisca thought she could convert me, and...'

'We were in Mendeleev for three months, together,' says Francisca. Dylan sees her fingertips slide, very slightly, under the lip of his robe. 'But I was called back to Hunter.'

'I get it,' says Dylan. 'I think. How'd he get here?'

'I stowed away with some traders,' Anil says. 'They brought me here. To her.'

'Okay,' says Dylan. 'I can help you.'

Dylan hears a rustle in the darkness as Francisca shakes her head. 'How can we trust someone from Fuller Aerospace?'

'Because I know what it's like,' Dylan says, putting all her confidence into her voice. 'I was born in the Free Settlements, but I've been forced to live in Company Territory. I know what it's like to hide, and to pretend to be something I'm not.'

Tiny glints of red from the control systems reflect in their eyes.

'I want to help you,' Dylan says. 'Let me help.'

'How?' says Anil.

'You need a security code to start the rover. Clifford has it. The four of us can leave together.'

It isn't the whole truth. Dylan knows how to start the rover, but she can't let them leave without her.

Anil slowly lowers his knife, and Dylan exhales. The adrenaline washes away, leaving prickles in her fingertips.

'Thank you,' she says.

'She'll tell the Kinship,' Francisca hisses. She still has a grip on her own knife. 'As soon as we let her go, she'll warn them.'

'I won't,' Dylan insists. 'I don't want to see anyone die.'

Anil looks to Francisca.

'If we don't trust them then what else can we do?' he says.

'Wait,' Francisca says. 'I know what to do.'

She turns back to Dylan.

'If you get us off this base without warning the Kinship, I'll give you something you need. The map from the rover's memory.'

Dylan doesn't understand. 'You erased it.'

'We wiped the rover like your friend requested, but the Avunculus made a copy of the data first. As far as he's concerned, Hunter Base salvaged that vehicle so any data on board is his, especially data that the Company thinks is valuable. I can get it for you in exchange for passage off this base.'

'Done,' Dylan says quickly. She wasn't expecting a deal this good. She gets the map, and she gets to live, too.

'That's how we get trust,' Francisca says to Anil. 'If she betrays us, it'll be bad for both of us.'

He nods in the darkness. 'Okay.'

Francisca circles Dylan again, and light floods the chamber as she pulls the panel back open. Dylan steps out, and looks back at the two of them. They're standing, half in shadow, with their arms around each other.

'Thank you,' says Anil. 'We're trusting you.'

# Chapter Forty-Two

'Absolutely not,' Clifford hisses. 'What the hell are you thinking?'

The two of them are back in their cells, facing each other across the corridor. Clifford returned before lunch, but some Hunter engineers were busy repairing a carbon filter in the corridor. They've only just completed the job, and gone off to join the rest of the Kinship in the Grove for another session of chanting. Dylan can hear it through the dusty speakers up in the corner of her cell. It's rhythmic and atonal, and between each verse there is a call and response of furious shouting, like a war-cry.

'What else was I going to tell them?' Dylan says. 'They had me at knifepoint.'

Clifford runs his fingers through his white hair in frustration.

'It doesn't matter what you said. I'm not letting strangers on my rover.'

'Listen,' said Dylan. 'Avunculus Peter copied the map. If we help them escape, Francisca will get it for us.'

Clifford stares down at the tiled floor of his cell.

Dylan presses on. 'You won't need to find the census taker. We can get the map and be heading home tonight.'

'Shh,' he says. 'I'm thinking.'

After a minute he stands up straight, adjusts his shirt, and walks out into the corridor. Dylan runs after him.

'What are you doing?'

'I'm going to warn Avunculus Peter.'

'What! Why?'

He turns and glares at her.

'Because what you're doing is incredibly stupid. You've put us in the crossfire between a stowaway and a whole base. When you're

194

choosing who to betray, don't piss off the side that can murder you.'

Dylan runs ahead of Clifford to block his way, but he doesn't stop, and she walks backwards ahead of him.

'If we take Anil and Francisca out of here then we get out early with the map. It's win–win.'

'No it isn't. There are too many ways for them to screw us over. And even if we somehow get off the base with them on board, what exactly do you think will happen when we drive away? The Calliope is fast, but not fast enough to outrun Hunter's rovers.'

'Just stop!' says Dylan.

Clifford stares right through her.

'If we turn them in, Avunculus Peter can give us that map in return. That's what I call win–win.'

She spreads her arms and stands firm, forcing him to stop. Fortunately, no one's around to hear the argument. From the chanting, it sounds like the whole Hunter Kinship is up in the Grove.

'I told Anil and Francisca we'd help them. If we don't, they'll die.'

'You think it's immoral?'

'Yes!'

'Morality is a rationalisation of tribal instincts, Dylan,' says Clifford. 'And Francisca and Anil are not your tribe. I never agreed to put my life on the line for them. Hunter Base won't hesitate to kill us if we help those two, and I'm not going to risk our lives when we're so close to getting what we need. I'm ending this now.'

# Chapter Forty-Three

Avunculus Peter stands at the front of the crowd and leads the Kinship in chant. On the rock platform before him are the seven newest warriors of the Kinship, only recently freed from their initiation and ready to defend Hunter Base, looking both self-conscious and proud. The song for them has been building in intensity and complexity for half an hour, and a dozen different layers of voices weave in and out of the underlying rhythm, washing through the crowd, filling their minds and bodies with focus and energy and burning certainty.

*Lo Ra Ra Ki Pe Ro Ro Ka.*
*Lo Ra Ra Ki Pe Ro Ro Ka.*

The chants are part of Hunter life. Uriah Hunter called them his proudest invention, a social technology to bond the people of a base into a single mind, a single organism. Most of the chants are for the daily rituals of focus, gratitude, work and rest, but there are longer, more potent chants to enhance significant life moments, like births and deaths and weddings. The longest and most powerful chant of them all is this one: the chant of war.

*Lo Ra Ra Ki Pe Ro Ro Ka.*
*Lo Ra Ra Ki Pe Ro Ro Ka.*

After this, the seven warriors will be going out of the base to join the blockade around Tharsis Base. They will sever its supply lines, and strangle the enemy. And when the last believer in the False Path is crushed, then, finally, Hunter Base will be safe and free.

*Lo Ra Ra Ki Pe Ro Ro Ka.*

The crowd around the Avunculus are arm in arm. This is what the taboo of touch is for − to keep the connections within the Kinship sacred and powerful. All the faces around him glow with pride. He sees it in everyone: Kin Jeremiah of The Hand, Kin Angela the Pathkeeper, Kin Constance of The Word, and so many others, all reflecting his expression of conviction and joy. He would die for the people in the Grove, without question. He would kill for them. He swells with love and pride, and all his secret doubts and fears are drowned by the chant. He has become pure.

*Lo Ra Ra Ki Pe Ro Ro Ka.*
*Lo Ra Ra Ki Pe Ro Ro Ka.*

Avunculus Peter knows with certainty that Uriah Hunter's words are true. He hears it in the voices all around him, and feels it in his core. They are on the true path. They are the torchbearers of the natural order, and the corrupted who stand against them will be cleansed.

It's so simple.

*Lo Ra Ra Ki Pe Ro Ro Ka...*

There's a slight irregularity in the chant, at the edge of Avunculus Peter's hearing. Some of the Kinship at the fringe are talking in forced whispers. He wants to ignore them, but a shout from the back of the Grove cuts over the song.

'Avunculus!'

Peter looks up, and his eyes focus. He is irritated to see the outsider, the arrogant man from the Company in his crumpled suit, approaching the group with his hands raised. Behind him is his travelling companion, the one he had higher hopes for. Her arms are folded and her head is lowered like she's trying to hide from the world.

At the Avunculus's side, Kin Francisca gasps and takes her hand off his shoulder. The chanting continues, but more and more of the crowd are looking over at the disruption. Some of them step towards the outsider with their hands raised, trying to intercept him.

'No, no, no,' one of the Kin calls out. 'This is a sacred ceremony. You must not be here.'

The outsider locks eyes with Avunculus Peter.

'There's an infiltrator on your base,' he calls out.

Kin Francisca grips Avunculus Peter's arm.

'It's a trick,' she whispers. Her face is crumpling, and her voice is desperate.

The chant has broken down completely. The seven soldiers on the stone platform are charged up by the war chant, and their bewilderment quickly turns to fury. Two of the young men leap down and charge at the outsider. They grab him by the arms and start dragging him back the way he came. The outsider screams in pain, far louder than necessary for such restrained treatment.

'No!' the outsider shouts. 'Listen! There's an infiltrator on the base! He's from Tharsis!'

Avunculus Peter has no patience for the outsiders, but he hasn't survived this long by ignoring paranoia. He looks around the Grove for anything out of place, and sees only the rightfully angry crowd, churning and bristling. He beckons to Kin Damascus, the head of the warrior caste.

'Find out what the outsider is talking about,' he says quietly. 'If he thinks he can cause trouble, correct him.'

Kin Damascus puts a beefy hand on Avunculus Peter's shoulder.

'It will be a pleasure.'

'And send patrols through the base. Make sure there's nothing to worry about.'

Damascus raises a doubtful eyebrow, but he nods.

'Yes, Avunculus. If it's necessary.'

Damascus turns and calls over a few of the red-robed warriors from the edge of the crowd. As he gives them their orders, Avunculus Peter climbs, with some difficulty, up onto the stone platform. Now that Damascus's warriors have control of the outsiders, the new initiates return to the platform. Peter stands in front of them, and raises his arms to silence the crowd.

'My Kin, the interruption is over. Now don't disrespect these fine new warriors by holding back! *Lo Ra Ra Ki Pe Ro Ro Ka!'*

The chant begins anew, but Avunculus Peter can still hear the agitation in the voices. The Kinship is out of its trance, and so is he. Even when he closes his eyes, he can't block all the little sounds that the chant previously drowned out – the hiss of the air system, the roar of the waterfall, a cough in the crowd, the footfalls of the patrol on the metal walkway above.

*Lo Ra Ra . . .*

A siren whines, high-pitched and loud, and he feels a spike of fury in his chest. *What now?* When he opens his eyes he sees the crowd looking around in confusion. Some of them point up.

He cranes his head back. Three of Damascus's warriors are running along the walkway. Ahead of them, at the exit to the rest of the base, the thick pressure door is sliding down. They reach it too late, and it hisses closed in front of them. One of them pulls the emergency release handle at the side. It flips down with a dull thud, but the door stays shut.

Someone in the crowd coughs. Kin Barnabas, standing at the back, is struggling to clear his throat.

Avunculus Peter takes a deep breath, tightens his jaw, and tries not to let the crowd see his concern.

'Don't worry. The engineers will have it fixed in no time.'

The sun lamps hanging down over the Grove cut out simultaneously. The only remaining light is the glow of dusk coming through the hexagonal windows overhead, and it paints the crowd in dark blue and grey. The murmuring builds into shouts of panic.

'What's happening? Engineers!' Avunculus Peter calls out over the noise. 'Summon the engineers!'

# Chapter Forty-Four

Kin Damascus and three of his red-robed warriors push Dylan and Clifford down a long corridor, away from the Grove and back towards their cells. They're halfway along it when the lights cut out, leaving them in pure darkness.

'Keep hold of the outsiders!' Kin Damascus shouts, his voice reverberating in the corridor.

'No,' Clifford murmurs to himself, so quietly that Dylan barely hears it. 'I'm such a fool.'

A flashlight snaps on, shining directly into Dylan's face. She shields her eyes with her hand. It swings over to Clifford, who is ashen-faced and clutching his broken rib.

'You,' Kin Damascus's voice comes out of the dark. 'What did you do?'

'Nothing. This wasn't us,' says Clifford.

Damascus steps into the light.

'Kin Jerome. Go back to the Grove. Find out what's happening.'

'Yes, Kin.'

The warrior holding the flashlight runs back down the corridor. After a minute he returns, out of breath. His eyes are wide.

'The pressure doors into the Grove are shut,' he says. 'I couldn't get in. I heard them hammering on the other side.'

Kin Damascus waves his warriors onwards down the corridor. 'Quick. We'll go up through the base and activate the reserve power.'

'What about these two?' asks Kin Jerome, shining the light in Clifford and Dylan's faces. Dylan winces.

'We need to watch them. Take them with us.'

Kin Damascus and Kin Jerome take the lead, and the other two red-robes push Dylan and Clifford forward. Dylan feels Clifford's hand on her upper arm, and she clenches her jaw at his touch. He talks quietly by her ear.

'I've made a terrible mistake,' he says, almost inaudible over the footsteps echoing in the corridor. 'I shouldn't have said anything.'

'I told you we should have trusted them,' she hisses back.

'That's not—'

Kin Jerome turns the flashlight back on them.

'What are you two whispering about?'

One of the warriors behind Clifford gives him a shove, and he stumbles forward, clinging on to Dylan's arm to stay upright. When the flashlight is off them again, he talks more quietly.

'Dylan, do you understand what's happening?'

'A power outage.'

'Anil did this,' he says. 'Do you think he just came here to mope about and pine for his lover, while he was hiding in the life-support systems of his mortal enemies? With full control over their air and water and energy? This isn't Romeo and Juliet. It doesn't matter if he loves Francisca or not. He heard me warning the Kinship. He knows that he's not getting off the base alive. He has access to every system on Hunter Base, and right now, he has absolutely nothing left to lose.'

# Chapter Forty-Five

A voice starts coughing in the darkness of the Grove, then another, and another. Avunculus Peter catches a scent, halfway between pepper and pineapples, and feels a burning at the back of his throat. In the blue light he sees people wiping their eyes and covering their mouths. His eyes sting, and he blinks away the tears.

'Chlorine!' a voice cries, between coughs. 'Chlorine gas!'

'Get up to high ground!' Avunculus Peter shouts. Kin Anthea, one of the newly appointed warriors, grabs him by the elbow.

'This way, Avunculus.'

She leads him to the edge of the platform. As they drop down to ground level together, there's a surge in the crowd. Avunculus Peter is knocked free from the young warrior's grip. He falls to the ground, and yelps in pain. In the low light, all he can see is a frenzy of shadows above him. People are running, stumbling, shoving into each other as they try to find the steps to walkway. Panicked feet come down all around him, kicking his ribs and crushing his fingers. He tries to call out, but a heel comes down on his solar plexus. His lungs fail him, and all he can manage is a braying moan.

Tears flood his eyes, He doesn't know if they're from the gas, the pain, or despair. The people that he loves are trampling him like panicking animals.

'Sto—' he calls out.

A hand comes down in front of his face, and he looks up to see the silhouette of Kin Francisca. He grabs at her, and she pulls him to his feet.

Through the blur of tears, they stumble through the crowd

towards the metal stairway. There's a mass of bodies around it, shoving into each other as they try to escape the gas.

'Stand back!' Avunculus Peter shouts through a coughing fit. 'One at a time!'

Kin Francisca pulls him through the throng. People press against him on all sides, squeezing the air out of him. When he gasps for breath, his lungs sting. But Francisca keeps pulling, and his sandalled toes hit the edge of the lowest step of the stairs. He climbs upwards, pushed from behind by the panicking swarm.

The air gets clearer the higher they climb, but bodies still crush him from every side. Francisca pulls him up onto the walkway, which is solidly packed with coughing, gasping people. The walkway was never designed to hold this load, and it sways alarmingly under his feet. There's a metallic bang from behind him, and he turns to see a railing breaking free. Bodies spill off the walkway, tumbling down onto the rocks at the side of the waterfall.

'By the Path, no,' he says.

And then, there's light. The security door at the end of the walkway is rising. It goes up in starts, painfully slowly, but Avunculus Peter sees a flashlight shining out from under it, and hears Kin Damascus's booming voice.

'Quickly! Come through!'

As the door gets to waist height the frontmost Kin duck under it, and a mass of bodies pushes forward to take their space. The walkway creaks below Avunculus Peter, and he feels dread in his stomach, but the door keeps rising, and more and more people get free. Kin Francisca keeps pulling him along. The crowd around him jostles forward, and he barely stays on his feet. They get closer and closer to the door, and the crowd squeezes tighter and tighter, until purple spots are dancing across his vision. And then he's through, and Kin Damascus and a squadron of warriors are waving flashlights and calling to the people behind him. Some yellow-robed engineers are turning a manual crank at the side of the door, and the warriors are taking the injured aside, and directing everyone else in the tunnel that leads through the heart

of the Eurasia. As the flood of bodies slows to a trickle, warriors
in orange out-suits walk down into the Grove to rescue any more
injured members of the Kinship.

Avunculus Peter takes a deep breath of clean air. His eyes and
throat still sting, but his world is no longer collapsing. He pushes
his way to Kin Damascus's side, with Kin Francisca close behind.

'What happened?'

Damascus points to the two outsiders behind him, still being
guarded by warriors.

'They were right. We had an infiltrator on board trying to
sabotage us.'

'Where's the infiltrator now?'

Damascus points to the tunnel through the core of the fallen
ship. Two of his warriors are dragging a body between them, a
young bearded man. His head is hanging limp, and his eyes are
open and unblinking.

Avunculus Peter looks at the outsiders, gauging their reaction.
The old man is stone-faced. The young woman looks visibly
shaken. Kin Francisca gasps, and covers her face. Avunculus Peter
sees tears from the gas are still streaming from her eyes.

'It's all right,' says Kin Damascus. 'He isn't a danger to anyone
now.'

'Where was he?' Avunculus Peter asks.

'My warriors found him in the air processing unit by the rover
bay. He had a transmitter, and some supplies pilfered from our
stores. Looks like he tapped into our base controls and security
cameras. He was already dead when they found him. Cyanide.'

A yellow-robed engineer runs past with a roll of cable under
her arm. Damascus stops her.

'How much longer before we get power back?' he asks her.

'We're almost there, Kin.'

A minute later the lights in the chamber flick back on, accom-
panied by the piercing sound of a siren.

Avunculus Peter winces. 'Can we turn that off?'

Kin Damascus freezes and stares up at a speaker grille in the
corner of the chamber.

'That's a proximity alarm from the watchtower,' he says. 'We couldn't hear it without the power. This isn't just sabotage, Avunculus. The base is under attack.'

# Chapter Forty-Six

Kin Damascus runs out of the Grove antechamber, leaving Dylan and Clifford under the guard of the red-robed warriors. Francisca stares at the two of them with hate in her eyes. Dylan feels her cheeks burn, but Clifford meets Francisca's gaze, cold and unblinking. After a few seconds she turns away from him, and strides away into the base.

'Are you going to tell the Avunculus about her part in this?' says Dylan quietly.

'Not yet. It's good to have leverage on someone.'

Dylan's fingernails dig into her palm. Clifford's exactly the psychopath that Frank said he was.

The siren is replaced by Damascus's voice barking over the speakers. 'Three rovers approaching from the south-east. Unassigned Equestrians to the rover bays. All other ranks to safety and security positions.'

Avunculus Peter's face is wooden. He beckons the warriors to follow him.

'Come. To the rover bays.'

The warriors shove Clifford and Dylan down the central tunnel and through the maze of sideways rooms to the rover bay. The chamber is swarming with young men and women of fighting age, climbing through open hatches into the Hunter rovers. The back of their robes are stitched with stylised horse heads.

'Equestrians,' Clifford mutters. 'Cute.'

Pushing between the Equestrian rank are the yellow-robed engineers. They run between the hatches and storage lockers, carrying replacement batteries and actuators and spools of orange cable. A crowd of other ranks in blue, green and brown robes are clustered around the long windows between the hatches.

The warriors lead Dylan and Clifford to the nearest window, where the Avunculus is staring out into the night. The ground outside the base is lit with floodlights. Scattered across it are the broken remains of a dozen rovers, all torn open and burned out. The nearest one is nothing more than a twisted, wheelless chassis. Half the destroyed rovers that Dylan can see are white, like the ones that led Clifford and Dylan to Hunter Base. The rest are dark grey. A war just happened here, and no one inside heard it.

'Our fleet,' Avunculus Peter murmurs. 'The whole rover fleet.'

On the horizon, silhouetted against the last of the evening glow, a cloud of black dust is rising up with three dark-grey shapes below it. A deep thud shakes the walls of the rover bay, and a glowing projectile shoots away overhead. It arcs down towards the Tharsis rovers, and they steer to avoid it. The innermost rover collides with the left one and briefly rides up onto two wheels, then drops and bounces on its suspension. The projectile disappears into the dust behind them, and the three rovers keep coming. They've barely slowed down.

More projectiles launch from the roof of the base. One hits the ground in front of a rover, detonating and spraying up a cone of dust, but the rover doesn't slow down or change course. It rides through the flying debris, and rocks bounce off its dull grey surface. It's less than a hundred metres from the window now, and Dylan sees a suited figure inside, lit up by the floodlights.

A hatch slams closed in the docking bay, and a few seconds later one of Hunter's cargo rovers, twice the size of Rudolf, disconnects from the bay and rumbles forward. It steers towards one of the incoming rovers, throwing up a dust cloud behind it.

'I don't see any weapons on that thing,' Clifford mutters.

The incoming rover adjusts its course, so that the two rovers are aiming directly at each other. Dylan puts a hand to her temple.

'Oh God,' she says. 'They're playing chicken.'

The gap between the two rovers closes. At the last possible moment, the cargo rover turns hard left and skids sideways on the dust, with three wheels lifting up off the ground. Its rear clips the side of the Tharsis rover, and shards of ceramic plating scatter across the rocky ground. The Hunter rover flips onto its roof, and a white cloud of vapour erupts from a cracked window.

The Tharsis rover slides to a stop about a hundred metres in front of it, with its suspension mangled. It's a sitting target, and the artillery on the roof of Hunter Base fires again. Two projectiles fly down, and slam into the side of the Tharsis rover.

The flash of the explosion lights up the landscape and leaves a dark spot in Dylan's vision. The shockwave rocks the base, and the windows shake. Dylan falls backwards against one of the warrior guards. When she looks out of the window again all she can see is a dust storm, and rock debris hailing down on the window.

For a moment, the docking bay is silent.

'What the hell was that?' she whispers.

'A base-burster,' Clifford says, staring into the dust cloud from the explosion. For the first time since Dylan met him, she hears a tremble in his voice.

As the dust thins, Dylan sees the crater from the bomb blast, and the grey shadows of the two remaining Tharsis rovers driving around it. They're heading away, towards the rear of the giant fallen rocket.

Avunculus Peter shouts out.

'Foot Soldiers! Get out there! We can't let another base-burster get near us!'

At the far end of the docking bay is a door marked *Airlock 01*, with a row of out-suits hanging on the wall next to it. Four Hunter warriors run to it and start suiting up. Their orange out-suits are newer and cruder than the ones Dylan and Clifford have on board Rudolf, and it takes time for the warriors to put them on. A pair of engineers hurry between them, tightening and adjusting the arm and leg attachments and hooking up all the necessary cables and tubes.

'Hurry!' Avunculus Peter calls desperately.

More engineers run over to them carrying bolt guns and metal spears. They aren't sophisticated weapons, but all they need to do is damage an enemy's suit, and the Martian atmosphere will do the rest.

The last helmet clicks into place.

'Go!' Avunculus Peter shouts. 'Go! Go! Go!'

One of the engineers looks up from adjusting a warrior's shoulder strap. 'But the safety checks …'

The Avunculus explodes with fury. 'Tharsis is at our walls! We need foot soldiers out there now!'

The warriors grab their spears and bolt guns and climb into the airlock. The inner door slides closed, and an engineer flips a switch on a control desk. The lights in the airlock turn red, a siren sounds briefly, and the outer door whips open.

The four soldiers sway as the air blows out, and one of them stumbles and falls against the others. They catch him, and hold him up by the chests straps. There's a rasping sound over the speakers, mixed with the voices of the other soldiers in the airlock.

'Kin Jarrod? Kin Jarrod!'

'He's depressurising!'

The rasping sound from the soldier's suit fades away, but his body keeps convulsing silently. There's no air in his lungs to allow him to scream. He pulls himself free from his friends and throws himself at the inner airlock window, hammering at it with a fist. The man's helmet mists up as the tears boil in the vacuum. The docking bay crowd watches in horror.

'Open the door!' shouts one of the other soldiers.

The suffocating warrior slides down the glass, tilting his head back like a drowning man. Another soldier catches his limp body.

'Leave him!' an engineer shouts. 'Get out of there! We need to repressurise the airlock!'

Reluctantly, the warriors leave their unconscious companion and run out of the airlock. As soon as they're gone, the engineer flips more switches on the control desk and the outer door slams shut. Air *whomps* into the chamber, and the inner door slides open. The engineers drag the soldier's body out of the airlock and frantically begin the process of removing his misted helmet.

Dylan presses the side of her face against the window, and looks as far as she can down the side of the base. The three Hunter warriors bound away across the floodlit ground with their spears and bolt guns raised. One of the attacking rovers has parked next to the giant skeletal landing strut of the fallen passenger liner. Its hatch is open, and suited figures are carrying a metal cylinder towards the outer wall of Hunter Base.

'Base-burster!' Avunculus Peter shouts. 'It's too close. Stop the artillery. Don't shoot it. Seal the security doors!'

'This might be a good time to consider evacuation,' Clifford suggests.

'Shut up!' the Avunculus snaps. 'No one leaves. Our warriors will stop them. They have to!'

Dylan feels a rumble beneath her feet as one of the Tharsis rovers rolls past outside, chasing the three Hunter warriors on foot. The warriors look back and see it coming. Two of them run towards the side of the base, but the third stops to fling a spear at the rover's cockpit window. It misses, and bounces off the front plating. The rover accelerates, and the warrior's orange out-suit disappears beneath its steel-stripped wheels.

The whole event is completely silent. The rover curves around to chase the other two warriors, leaving the body in the red-brown dust.

The two remaining Hunter warriors keep running towards the Tharsis foot soldiers and the bomb. They stay close to the wall of the base to keep the rover from running them down. When they're within twenty metres of the Tharsis soldiers, one of them flings a spear.

The aim is flawless. A Tharsis out-suit drops to the ground, clutching the spear in its side, but the others keep carrying the bomb towards the base. They drop it against the outer wall and turn to face the Hunter warriors, guarding it with their own bodies.

The Hunter warriors can't use their bolt guns for fear of detonating the base-burster, but the Tharsis soldiers have no such restrictions. They draw their bolt guns, and Dylan hears faint pops, like distant bubble wrap.

One of the Hunter warriors goes down. The other flings the last spear, but it flies wide. He's outnumbered, and he has no cover. He gets within five metres of the attackers before their bolts bring him down. The last of Hunter's defenders stumbles forward, and drops dead in the dust.

# Chapter Forty-Seven

A piercing siren sounds in the rover docking bay, and Kin Damascus's voice comes over the speakers.

'All Kinship to the rover bay. Evacuate the base.'

Dylan sees Avunculus Peter's hands tremble.

'It can't be,' he mumbles. 'It isn't possible.'

Clifford steps forward and stands in front of the Avunculus. He plants his feet and looks him in the eye.

'I need the map,' he says.

Avunculus Peter looks up at Clifford, and through him. 'Map?'

'The map from the rover,' says Clifford. 'I'll help with the evacuation, but I need the map.'

There's no hint of understanding in Avunculus Peter's face. One of the red-robes grabs Clifford's shoulder and pulls him away.

Through the windows, Dylan can see four rovers still docked at the bay: Rudolf, the Fuller Aerospace rover, and two large transports that would be too slow for combat. The three red-robes escort the dazed Avunculus towards the hatch to the nearest transport. Dylan and Clifford are left unguarded.

'Wait!' Clifford calls out. 'We can't leave without the map!'

'Yes we can,' says Dylan, pulling him towards Rudolf's hatch. As they run for it, more terrified members of the Kinship race into the bay ahead of them. Dylan can see people of all ages, from original colonists down to babes in arms. The red-robed warriors shepherd them into an orderly line, and start ushering them through the hatch.

'Hey! What are you doing? That's my rover,' Clifford says.

A red-robe points a metal baton at him.

'Back of the line. Kinship first.'

'It can't carry this many people. Get them out,' says Clifford.

'I said get back!'

The red-robe puts a hand on Clifford's chest, and shoves. Clifford stumbles backwards holding a hand to his rib, face contorted with pain.

Dylan pulls him back to his feet. As they straighten up, she sees Kin Francisca squeezing out of Rudolf's hatch. She comes to them and leans in close to Clifford. Her mouth is twisted in contempt.

'You. Come with me.'

She grabs him by the shoulder and pulls him back towards the hatch. Dylan follows behind. The red-robe blocks their way again.

'I need this one,' says Francisca. 'He's the only one who can start the rover.'

The red-robe looks irritated. 'Are you sure?'

'Unfortunately.'

'I won't leave without her,' says Clifford, pointing at Dylan.

'Fine. Get in.' The red-robe stands aside, and the three of them squeeze into the back of Rudolf.

The lower-deck passage is blocked by a solid mass of bodies, all shouting and crying and making far too much noise for the enclosed space.

'Listen up!' Francisca calls from next to Dylan. The voices briefly die down. Francisca puts a hand on Clifford's shoulder. 'This is the driver! He needs to get to the cockpit now!'

People squeeze aside to let Clifford through. He steps over a man protecting a fallen child on the floor, and hauls himself up the metal ladder.

Behind Dylan, the red-robe pushes the outer hatch closed. Dylan seals the inner hatch, and looks at Kin Francisca.

'Thank you.'

Francisca shakes her head. She looks far older than she did this morning. Her cheeks are less round, and the skin under her eyes is darker.

'I'm just trying to save these people,' she says.

Dylan follows after Clifford. The upper deck is just as packed as down below. Evacuees, old and young, are clinging to the railing to stop themselves falling through the floor hatch. Clifford is still pushing his way to the cockpit. He drops into the driver's seat, and enters his code into the controls. Rudolf powers up, and the clamps holding it in place detach.

'Hold tight!' Clifford shouts.

The wheel motors strain under the extra weight of the passengers. Dylan looks out of the cockpit window at the battlefield. She sees the bodies lying on the ground, and the silver bomb leaning against the wall of the base. The grey Tharsis rovers are disappearing into the dark. To the right of Rudolf, one of Hunter's large transport rovers is slowly pulling away from the base, with more evacuees pressed against its windows. A few seconds later the second big transport breaks free, followed by the small captured Fuller rover.

There's a flash, and another shockwave. Even in the thin Martian air it sounds like a mallet hitting Rudolf's outer shell. The ground falls away below them, and rocks and shrapnel pepper their side.

For a moment, everything is still. Dylan sees a crater in the side of Hunter Base and an expanding cloud of dust, but the bulk of the base is still standing.

Then a blinding plume of flame shoots out from the fallen spacecraft.

'What's that?' says Dylan.

'A fuel line. It's going to blow. Hold on.'

Clifford accelerates, and some of the evacuees in the cockpit lose their footing and fall against each other.

There's a third flash, so bright that it registers on Rudolf's rear monitor as black. The rear half of the giant fallen ship shatters, throwing chunks of metal into the dark sky, and launching the whole front half out of the ground. It flies through the air, impossibly large and impossibly fast, spinning and crumpling like foil. There's no time for Clifford to steer clear of it. One second the front of the ship is behind them, and the next it's overhead, raining down chunks of rock and metal and plastic that churn up clouds of dust as they slam into the ground around them.

A chunk of hull crashes down in front of Rudolf, and Clifford skids to a halt. For the first time since Dylan entered Rudolf, the interior is quiet. Even the children are shocked into silence. There are flashes of distant light through the falling dust, and the faint rumble of secondary explosions. The debris hails down, and slows, and stops.

A piercing wail fills the cabin, and an acidic smell hangs in the air. One of the infants has vomited, but the mother just stares ahead at the remains of her base.

Clifford crawls the rover forward through the parting dust. The bare bones of the great ship loom ahead, a skeleton of steel and carbon fibre that once contained the Grove. Littered around it are the twisted guts of the base, walls and floors and whole prefabricated corridors, torn out and scattered across the land.

Dylan presses forward until she's behind Clifford's seat.

'Should we go back?' she asks quietly.

'Why? No one survived that.'

'There were people underground…' she says. And she realises what she's saying. The survivors would be trapped. There's no possible way to dig them out without suffocating them.

'They all died, Dylan,' says Clifford, easing Rudolf forward through the debris-strewn landscape. 'It was painless.'

'How do you know?'

He stares ahead into the darkness.

'Because the alternative is unthinkable.'

# Chapter Forty-Eight

AUDIO LOG - CHRISTOPHER UNWIN, FA-112-019 - DAY 213, 2103

Once in a while, things go easier than I could have hoped. As soon as Prowse's trading rover drove into the Twins' territory, we were stopped by a rover from Hunter Base. I connected with them over the radio, and told them that I was searching for a missing Company rover. They said they had found it, and invited us to dock with their base.

I can't explain how amazing the inside of Hunter Base is. They've created a giant Earth-like habitat, with fruit trees, small fields, a river and even a waterfall! The inhabitants were surprisingly welcoming, too. Unlike most Free Settlements that I've visited, they didn't especially mind that I worked for the Company. For historical reasons, they don't seem to worship Red Rose like most other settlements, and this definitely worked in my favour.

They sold me the data from the rover without any trouble. They even invited me and Prowse to join them permanently, although I suspect they make that offer to everyone who comes through. Of course Prowse refused, and so did I. I have to admit though, I might be tempted to go back there if it ever comes time for me to retire. It seems like a safe and comfortable place to live, especially now they've won their war against Tharsis. It really is a special place.

Because my stop-off was so quick, I was able to get another lift with Prowse out of Hunter Base. I'm currently squeezed back into the storage area of her trading rover as we drive north-west towards Marcus. When we get there, I'll rejoin the rover train and head further north to Loyola Base, where Prowse says I'll be able to hire a private rover that can take me all the way back down to Company Territory.

I have to admit that the route sounds frustratingly inefficient, but

Prowse tells me that this is just the way of the Free Settlements. Life here is all about embracing chaos, and she laughs at my attempts to plan ahead.

I looked at the map from the rover to make sure that it has what Mr Clifford is looking for. The Outlier base is right there, up in the far north. I'll be able to give it to him soon, if this next leg of my journey goes as smoothly as the visit to Hunter. I was out of there in less than a day. It's great when things are that easy.

# Part 4.5

---

# Red Rose

# Chapter Forty-Nine

'Volkov!' Karl's father called as he strode through the mine's processing bay, along the side of a conveyor belt leading from the outer doors to the dead electrolysis furnace. Karl half-ran to keep up. His new yellow Sealgair Mining Industries T-shirt was too thin, and he hugged his arms for warmth.

Workers called to each other ahead, their headlamps bobbing in the darkness. The sound of grinding metal filled the bay, and showers of sparks sprayed out from unseen tools. In a pool of light at the end of the conveyor belt, the mine foreman, Volkov, was huddled in quiet discussion with two of the workers. One of them was holding a metal cylinder with a shaft running through its centre. Karl was proud that he could recognise it as an actuator from one of the processing plant's robot arms.

Volkov looked up, and faced them as they approached.

'Mr Sealgair?' he said, wiping grease from his hands on a cloth that was hanging casually over his shoulder. He was a big man, gutted but muscular.

'What's the delay? You promised we'd make the next shipment.'

'It's unavoidable. Three of our rover operators quit in the last week. We can't cover their shifts. We're using the free time to do some much needed maintenance.'

Without warning, the worker with the actuator bent down, and leapt up from the walkway. He flew through the air, grabbing a diagonal support beam with one hand and swinging from it, up to a robot arm next to the electrolysis chamber. In a businesslike manner, he began to screw the actuator into place.

'Don't we have ladders?' said Karl's father.

Volkov nodded. 'Yessir. But in this gravity, it's quicker to jump.'

'That has to stop.' Karl's father was firm. 'This isn't a playground. Equipment could get damaged. People could get hurt.'

'Yes sir.'

'I'll hire new workers, but you need to wrap up this maintenance before the end of the week.'

'You're the boss,' said Volkov.

Karl's father turned back the way he came, and Karl followed him along the walkway.

'They didn't look happy,' Karl said as he caught up.

Karl's father smiled, and patted him on the back.

'I know, son. I don't like being a tyrant, but Mars isn't like Earth. Everything's fragile here. People can't just do what they want. If someone loses control and breaks a window, or if they get lazy and forget to replace a carbon filter, then everyone in the base could die. I know they don't like being told what to do, but they need to get used to it. I keep the order around here for everyone's sake.'

At the end of the walkway ahead, light and warmth was spilling in from the open door to the living quarters. They went through it together, and Karl felt relieved when it slid closed behind them, cutting off murmurs of the workers in the darkness.'

# Chapter Fifty

Michael lay in bed and stared up at the ceiling. It was his normal position in the evenings, after he had finished his volunteer work, written his reports on Rose and her associates, and read through the barrage of briefing documents from the Company. He could have watched TV, but nothing from Earth gripped him any more. He could have gone out to meet new people, but his handler discouraged it. Fuller Aerospace made alcohol, MDMA and THC freely available, but Michael couldn't risk getting intoxicated and blowing his cover. All that was left for him to do was lie still and stare up at the acoustic-dampening tiles in the ceiling, trying to sooth his itching mind. He knew every indentation in those tiles. He had run his fingertip along every scratch in his white plastic table. His honeymoon with Mars was well and truly over.

He rolled over, and was surprised to see the screen lit up on his black pad. He normally only got calls on his other pad, the red one, that he hid in a wall safe behind the air vent. The black pad was for people who thought Michael was Michael.

He picked it up, and it unobtrusively scanned his retinas. The screen unlocked to reveal one message.

**ROSEMARY FULLER**
**Are you busy**

Michael sat up straight. His thumbs skittered across the screen.

**Nope. What's up?**

**Come up to the dome. Room 301. Central tower. Third floor**

**What for?**

Three dots bounced at the bottom of the screen. He took the pad through to his little en-suite bathroom and brushed his teeth, keeping one eye on the pad. He rinsed his mouth, went back to the bedroom, and pulled off the red T-shirt that he had worn while volunteering that morning. He threw it in the laundry tube. His pad chimed again.

**Just come**

He took a button-up shirt out of his thin bedroom cupboard. It was maroon with a stylised black skull print pattern, his only vaguely stylish item of clothing. He put it on, locked his red pad in the safe behind the vent, and replied to Rose on the black pad.

**I'll be there in 20**

He put the pad in his pocket and left his quarters, making certain that the door was locked behind him.

Just before the escalators, he passed a blue-tracksuited Fuller Aerospace guard standing over a tourist lying on the carpeted floor of the habitat hub. The tourist was shouting and swearing incoherently.

'Don't fucking patronise me!' he slurred at the guard.

The guard bent down closer, and spoke quietly and calmly.

'I'm just here to help you, sir. Would you like me to take you back to your rooms?'

'No! Go away! Get me another fucking vodka!'

Some workers came down the escalators, laughing among themselves. One young woman saw the drunk tourist, and pulled out her pad. The guard held up his hands ineffectually.

'Please! No recording. Give this man his privacy.'

Michael took the escalators to the surface level, past light-field displays of the sun setting over a tropical beach and speakers playing calypso-inspired electronica. He followed signs to a long transparent tube leading into what had once been the festival dome. The recently completed apartment buildings inside were floodlit and sparkling in the dark. With their art deco spires and their interconnecting walkways, they looked like a cross between the Magic Castle and the Chrysler building. Around them were lawns, lamplit pathways, and manicured fruit trees. The impracticality of it was the whole point. Michael walked under a glass walkway between two spires and into the entrance of the central tower. A virtual assistant on a wall screen confirmed his invitation and waved him through to the elevator, which carried him to the top floor.

The door opened directly into a penthouse. The outer walls were glass, looking out over all the other gleaming spires. Rose was standing next to a dining room table made from what looked like real Earth wood, and Netsai was leaning against a baby grand piano in the corner. They were both in the same work clothes that he'd seen them in that morning in the organisation headquarters: Rose in her black-and-grey flight suit, Netsai in her red dungarees with ultraviolet buttons designed to flare out the images on security cameras. As Michael stepped out of the elevator, Netsai raised a palm.

'We won't pat you down,' she said. 'But do you have a pad on you? Or AR glasses? Anything with a microphone?'

Michael handed her his black pad. She took it through a door into a curved-walled bedroom enclosure at the centre of the apartment, leaving him alone with Rose.

She was watching him. It was unsettling to be stared at by someone so famous. It was as if the eyes on a billboard had started tracking him.

'Hey,' she said.

Netsai came back out of the enclosure, and closed the door behind her.

'I made a Faraday cage to put our devices in, so no one can record us. I'll give your pad back after we're done.'

'Done with what?' said Michael.

'The sacrifice, obviously,' said Rose. 'You're a virgin, right?'

Michael was taken off-guard. In all his time studying Rose, he hadn't considered that she might have a sense of humour.

'Nope,' he said. 'Sorry to disappoint, but I've had sex at least once. Not to brag.'

Rose shrugged casually. 'Damn. I hope we can get our deposit back on all the candles and daggers.'

Netsai folded her arms.

'What's wrong?' Rose asked her.

'Nothing.'

Rose looked at Michael.

'Are you going to run to the media and tell them about my bad comedy routines? No? Okay then. Let's get to business.'

She sat on a red sofa with its back to the windows, and gestured to a high-backed wooden chair opposite. Michael took the seat.

'We want to talk about the future,' she said. 'The bases run by Earth governments don't want to get bought out by the Company. They're planning to declare independence on their own terms, and provide each other with all the goods and materials that they need to survive. And if the workers in the Fuller Aerospace bases want an equal society, we need to seriously consider joining them.'

Netsai leaned forward over the chair back behind him. 'The problem is that most Company employees are terrified of what that means. They don't want to risk their jobs for the chance of a better future.'

Rose nodded curtly to acknowledge Netsai's point.

'Any Company bases that declare themselves independent are going to need material support of the international bases. The Indian bases are willing, but the EU bases are concerned about alienating the Company, and the Russians and Chinese are worried that they'll have their resources drained if they support a lot of smaller bases.'

'We need clear and consistent messaging if we want the bases to do this together,' Netsai said. 'We need to sell a vision of a united, independent Mars, and we need the Fuller employees to know that declaring their bases independent is the only way to guarantee democracy, equality and human rights. It's a hard message to get across. We know you already volunteer a lot of your free time, but you seem pretty handy crafting a sound bite ...'

'You should be flattered,' Rose mock-whispered, with a hand to the side of her mouth. 'Netsai doesn't usually trust people.'

Netsai rolled her eyes.

'So, are you on board?' Rose said to Michael. 'The three of us will be running the campaign. I'll be honest, things could get ugly, but if we don't act now then the people of Mars won't have a future.'

Michael gave her a very genuine smile. All his years of preparation were finally paying off.

'I'm in,' he said. 'When do we start?'

# Chapter Fifty-One

'No,' said Netsai. 'Cut this bit.'

She was sitting on the sofa, arm outstretched on the armrest, reading the draft of Rose's speech on her pad. Rose lay with her head in Netsai's lap and her own pad resting on her chest. Over the last month, Rose's apartment had changed. Research printouts and draft speeches were strewn across the wooden dining table and the lid of the baby grand.

'Which bit?' said Michael, pushing back his chair from the table. He couldn't hide his annoyance. It was late, and they'd been refining the speech for days.

'This, here. "We need to protect the cultural identities of each base, but at the same time, everyone should be able to participate in society without barriers. Therefore, we need to develop a new *lingua franca* for public discourse, so everyone is on an equal footing…"'

'What's wrong with that?' said Rose, tilting her head back to look up at Netsai's face. 'We want the minority bases to know that their cultures will be respected, don't we?'

Netsai sighed. She took off her glasses and massaged her eyes.

'You can't force people to learn a new language. Remember when we first got here, when some people wanted to call days "sols", and there was "yestersol" and "Monsol" and "Wednessol" and all that nonsense? People couldn't even handle that! Or what about when they tried to make "Mars years" a thing, when all we really need to know is what year it is on Earth? It's a waste of energy. Don't go French-Revolutioning this.'

Rose sat upright. 'But we want people to know that independence will make a difference to their lives. We want them to get excited. Right?'

'Right,' said Michael. 'We need to have a positive message. This isn't just about protecting people against future exploitation, it's a chance to break free from the cycles of the past.'

'Keep it simple,' Netsai said. 'The wilder the ideas, the less they'll listen. No grand visions, okay? Just democracy and human rights. Full stop.'

She shut off her pad, got to her feet, and stretched.

'I'm going to Eli's quarters. Maybe I can get a few hours of sleep.'

'Enjoy,' said Rose.

Netsai went into the elevator. Before the doors closed, she gave Michael a stern look.

'Rose has got a big day tomorrow. Don't keep her up too late, okay?'

'Got it.'

She pressed the button, and the doors slid closed in front of her.

'Let's go through it again,' said Rose, patting the empty space on the sofa.

Michael came to sit down next to her. She handed him her pad, and leaned in close to read it over his shoulder. After a few minutes, she yawned. She put her feet up onto the sofa, and her head in his lap.

Michael froze for a moment, then kept reading.

'You don't mind, do you?' Rose asked.

'Of course not.'

She closed her eyes. Michael tried to read, but his attention kept slipping.

'Why is Netsai sleeping in Eli's room?' he said eventually.

Eli was one of the most recent volunteers. Michael had only seen him once or twice. He was buff, with an easy-going smile.

Rose didn't even open her eyes. 'Why do you think?'

'I didn't know they were into each other.'

'Not just each other.'

'What?' he said. 'Polyamory?'

Rose snort-chuckled, and used a hand to cover her smile.

'What's so funny?'

'You sound so shocked. It's sweet,' said Rose. 'It's like you're from the past.'

Michael flipped back to the start of the speech.

'Netsai's seeing Eli and Mustafa,' Rose said. 'Sometimes she's with Cait, too. Ruth and Hanna and Cait are inseparable. Eli and Hanna used to have a thing. Eli and Mark as well. It's complicated. I could draw you a diagram.'

Michael stared down at the screen.

'What's wrong?' she said. 'Aren't people poly where you're from?'

'No. We have antibiotic-resistant gonorrhoea.'

'Yeah, well, Mars has a natural six-month quarantine, both ways.'

Michael sighed. 'You must think I'm pretty ... square.'

She laughed, up into his face.

'"Square"?' she said. 'Okay, Daddy-o.'

Michael felt Rose's hair tickling his wrist as he flicked through the document.

'Don't worry. We're all a bit stuck in the past,' said Rose. 'The old rules don't make sense here, so we can't keep clinging to them. It's a different planet. We need to adapt.'

He smiled down at her. 'That's a good sound bite.'

'I know. Write it down.'

Michael obeyed, then turned off the screen and rested the pad against his chest.

'So ...' he said. 'Are you ...?'

'I'm not in the polycule.'

'Oh,' he said. His ears burned. 'Okay. I didn't want to pry.'

'Sure you did,' said Rose. 'It's fine. I've tried, but ... you know. Power dynamics. They keep their distance. And most of them grew up with each other, so I'm not really part of the tribe.'

'I thought you and Netsai had a thing.'

Fine wrinkles appeared at the sides of Rose's closed eyes.

'It might have happened. But I had hang-ups, and, you know ... then all this started ...'

'I get it.' Michael ran his fingers down the edges of the pad thoughtfully. 'How mad will she get if you go off-script tomorrow? You know what you really want to say.'

'You think I should?'

'It's your speech. She's not your boss.'

'She's my friend.'

'Then she won't mind.'

Rose shifted her weight.

'I'll think about it,' she said. 'Stay there for a bit. I need a nap. We can finish the speech in a couple of hours.'

'Okay.'

He put the pad on the coffee table and lay back into the sofa with Rose's head resting on his chest. The lights sensed their new position, and automatically started to dim.

'Set timer for two hours,' Rose said. The room speakers gave a quiet chime of acknowledgement.

'Juggling relationships sounds hard,' said Michael. 'Isn't there jealousy?'

'Sometimes,' Rose said. 'That's why honesty is so important.'

He let his eyes close. After a while, Rose chuckled.

'What is it?'

'Nothing,' she said. 'I can hear your heart beating. That's all.'

# Chapter Fifty-Two

ROSE FULLER'S ADDRESS

MARINER BASE AUDITORIUM,
DAY (SOL) 201, 2058

I was literally born in the heavens. For most of human history, my existence would have been called a dream. So when people call independence a dream, remember that the impossible has a precedent.

When Fuller Aerospace has bought every last base on Mars, it will be the *de facto* ruler of the planet. That will be independence, in a way. But the tourists will still be the first priority of the Company, and everyone born on Mars will still be a second-class citizen. Nothing will change. It isn't enough.

This evening, across Mars, dozens of bases formerly controlled by China, India, Russia and the EU are unilaterally declaring independence. These include major industrial centres like Olympus, Titov and Huoxing Cheng. They have realised the obvious: that the treaties and contracts that we treat as law are meaningless, created decades ago and a hundred million kilometres away by people who did not have our interests in mind. Not even the Earth governments take those treaties seriously. The people of Mars never agreed to them, and nothing on Mars can force us to obey them.

If you are currently in a Fuller Aerospace base, and you don't trust the Fuller Aerospace board on Earth to meet the needs of your inhabitants, I urge you to declare independence, and join the united Free Settlements. You won't be threatened with transportation. You won't need your Company salary to survive. And you will not be alone.

This is my vision: everyone in the new Free Settlements will have an absolute right to air, food, water, security, health. These essentials of life will be manufactured for free. Once we jettison the exorbitant patent costs that the Earth demands for medicine, AI, GM plants and life support, every base will have the machinery to provide these necessities automatically. And when we are freed from the struggle to survive, we will turn our minds to the real business of life: discovery, development, and unity.

The Free Settlements will each have their own founding culture and ethos. Once their own needs are met, they will be able to share their surplus resources, and build a greater community. This kind of trust between cultures is unthinkable to people from Earth, who are mired in the mindset of isolationism and the grievances of the past. But Mars has no past. We are starting fresh, as a unified people, and we know that we are stronger together than apart.

This is an opportunity unlike any other in history. We're so used to Earth's despair that we don't see how close we are to utopia. We just need to recognise that it could be ours, and seize it.

# Part 5.0

---

# On The Run

# Chapter Fifty-Three

AUDIO LOG – CHRISTOPHER UNWIN, FA-112-019 – DAY 214, 2103

This mission has been eye-opening. I can see how much I have been missing out on in the Free Settlements by hiding and keeping myself isolated. Travelling from base to base under my own initiative like this has been challenging, but satisfying. I've been forced to talk with base inhabitants, try the local food, and haggle for my transport and lodgings. It hasn't been easy, and every base seems to have its own unique bacteria breeding in its water systems, that wrecks the guts of outsiders. Still, after I deliver this map, I'll approach the census with a bit more enthusiasm. I'm looking forward to all the new bases that I'll visit, and I'll eat more than the dry peanut-flavoured protein bars I brought with me from Company Territory. It feels faintly ridiculous to say that I'm on an adventure, but the word fits.

After Hunter, Prowse and I drove to Marcus Base, which was originally a Canadian settlement. Its community is organised around an altruistic hierarchy, where everyone is assigned a rank depending on how much food, medical care, or maintenance they provide for the rest of the base. I thought it was an interesting idea, but Prowse says it's a scam. The highest-ranking members of the hierarchy determine the value of everyone's labour, and, by chance, their own labour is always the most valuable.

I'll admit, I was sad to say goodbye to Prowse. I even got a little teary-eyed, and she mocked me about it, but she promised to pour some more vat-rum down my throat the next time she sees me out on the road.

From Marcus I caught the rover train heading north. We seem to be docking at every small base we pass, but even so, we're making good progress. First stop was Ben-Gurion, a Jewish base with about three hundred inhabitants. The train driver was allowed to trade, but none of the passengers were allowed inside, so we all waited in the cargo hold, sitting on crates of refined insect protein. I passed around a container of rum that Prowse had left me with, and the brutal strength of it won me a little respect from my fellow passengers.

Twenty kilometres north of Ben-Gurion we stopped again at Binan Suo, and we were allowed to get out and stretch our legs. It's one of the few bases I have visited that manages to maintain order without any written laws. The resident I spoke to, who was selling warm, soft buns, said that it's a deliberate decision on the part of the community. Without written laws, there's no arguing over definitions or specific wording, and no legal loopholes to abuse. And since crime is harshly punished, even though it isn't always clear what's considered a crime, the residents and visitors all play it very, very safe. The docking bay of the base was clean, quiet and peaceful, but after the loading and unloading was complete, the driver ushered us back onto the train as quickly as possible. We moved on swiftly towards the slopes of Olympus Mons.

It used to amaze me that all these bases have such distinct cultures, but I guess it makes sense. Their biggest threat is sabotage from outsiders, so they lean heavily into internal unity. Every inhabitant of every base I visit seems to be actively trying to act the same and believe the same things as their base-mates, because friction could get them banished, and that would be fatal. Accommodating the beliefs of any other base would mean betraying their own internal cultures, so all these little bases are in a state of constant distrust and barely contained hostility with each other.

The only thing most of them seem to have in common is Rose Fuller. There are reminders of her everywhere, all over the Free Settlements. Some are simple, like posters stuck up in an airlock, or iron busts of her head tucked into nooks, but I've seen a full stained-glass window of her, lining the inside of a dome in the Ruby Palace. Some bases respect her for her vision of a free Mars. Some respect her for shedding her family blood to protect it. Even in Binan Suo, I saw a small shrine to her in the corner of the docking bay. It was a 3D-printed model of her face surrounded by lit candles, which is amazing, considering how dangerous naked flames can be. The only base I visited that didn't venerate her was Hunter, but getting all the Free Settlements to agree on anything would be impossible.

This afternoon the train docked at Olympus Base, and we're stopping here for the night. I've booked a private room, and I'm currently recording this at my desk. The data-card holding the map is on a string around my neck. Tomorrow morning we depart for Loyola, and we should reach it by midday. From there, I'll hire a rover down to Company Territory.

I have to admit, I'm dying to find out what the final result of this mission is, and what the Outliers are hiding in the Wintergarden. It's way outside my security clearance, of course, and I'll probably never know. Still, as I turn this data card over in my hands, I can't stop thinking about it. I hope that, someday, I earn a clearance level high enough to find out.

# Chapter Fifty-Four

Clifford stares straight ahead. His knuckles on the control stick are white. The rover is still silent, except for some quiet sobbing from the back of the galley. Out of the side of the cockpit, Dylan sees the two large Hunter rovers and the small Company rover driving parallel to Rudolf away from the wreckage. Next to her, Kin Francisca leans over the back of Clifford's seat.

'We need to talk to the other rovers,' she says. 'We need orders from Avunculus Peter.'

'The radio's dead,' Clifford says flatly, still staring ahead. Francisca's lips tighten to thin lines.

'Sorry,' says Dylan.

The other three rovers change direction, heading towards the north-west.

'Follow them,' says Francisca.

Clifford turns the rover, and draws parallel with them again.

'Where are they going?' Dylan asks.

'I don't know,' says Francisca.

Dylan reaches into a pouch by the driver's seat and pulls out her dad's paper map. Francisca takes it from her, and nudges aside some of the evacuees. She unfolds it piece by piece, until she finds their location and direction.

'Olympus,' she says. 'We're heading there. It's the only base big enough to take all of us.'

'They'll never let us in,' Clifford says. 'We should split off and find somewhere smaller.'

'No,' says Kin Francisca firmly. 'We can't split up.'

Francisca refolds the map and pushes it into Dylan's chest. Dylan takes it. All the evacuees in the upper deck are watching her and

Clifford, and their bodies are taut with adrenaline. She feels ice in her spine, and hopes that Clifford has realised that he isn't in charge.

To Clifford's great credit, he keeps Rudolf in line with the other rovers.

'Then we're going to Olympus,' he says calmly, staring ahead.

Dylan does a rough calculation. Water and food can be rationed, so they aren't a big problem. The real dangers are oxygen and electricity. With this many people on board, the air and power will be depleted in a day, or a day and a half at most.

'Will we make it to Olympus?' Dylan says to Clifford quietly, over his shoulder.

'Does it matter?' He keeps driving Rudolf forward in the darkness.

Francisca pushes her way back through the crowd. In the dim light of the galley, Dylan sees her talking to a group of the evacuees, who listen and nod seriously. A few minutes later, she raises her voice.

'It's time to chant "Oh Happy Departed". Spread the word to the lower deck.'

The evacuees nod sombrely, and Dylan hears the message spread through the rover. Some more evacuees push their way up the ladder, and hold hands with the people squeezed into the cockpit and the galley. Dylan is standing between two young women, and they look at her uncertainly before reluctantly taking her hands. The chant begins with Francisca, her voice half buried under Rudolf's rumble. Slowly, more voices join in harmony. Unlike the chants that Dylan heard on Hunter, this one is complex, haunting, and horrifying.

> Oh happy departed, you're gone from a world,
> Where the pain tears the heart, and the joy stains the soul,
> No more to suffer and no more to sin,
> No fruit to unripen, oh happy taken

*Oh happy departed, Now for you I sing,*
*Though you're free from all tears, and mourn for nothing,*
*The hole you have left is a suff'ring to me,*
*Until I pass through it, then happy I'll be*

*Oh let us not dig ourselves into this world,*
*Pull roots from the soil when our time is told,*
*We'll join you in joy when we're finally free,*
*Of the cold world we cling to, oh happy deceased.*

Dylan's breath catches in her throat. She doesn't know if the song is genuinely ancient or if it was just meant to sound that way, but something wells up inside her that she can't dismiss. These people are in pain, but they are together in a way that Dylan has never been. All around her, the singers are a single organism, suffering but unified.

When the chant has scoured their tribal wound, and the last note has faded away, there is silence.

And then, the war chant begins.

*Lo Ra Ra Ki Pe Ro Ro Ka.*
*Lo Ra Ra Ki Pe Ro Ro Ka.*

The chant is slower than it was in the Grove. Tears still stream, but as the chant builds, Dylan sees the pain disappear from the evacuees' faces. The hands she is holding squeeze tight, and the song sours in her soul.

*You're not part of this group. The tighter they embrace each other, the more you're constricted.*

The last repetition of the chant ends with a shout of fury, and Dylan lets the hands go. As the group breaks apart, she pushes her way to the ladder and climbs down to the lower deck, hoping to find a quiet place for herself. There's nowhere to go. The corridor and the cabins are packed with furious, bristling bodies.

She hears a voice, and looks around. Kin Francisca is at the foot of the ladder, talking to another group of survivors.

'We'll sleep in shifts. We'll need places to stand, places to sleep, and places for the children. Some of us are going to need more rest than others, so if you don't need special treatment then be ready to make a sacrifice.'

The survivors bob their heads, and spread out throughout the rover to organise the sleeping arrangements for the evening. When they're gone, Dylan comes to her side and talks quietly.

'I'm sorry,' she says. 'I tried to stop Clifford.'

'Don't talk about it,' Francisca says through gritted teeth. She glances around at the other evacuees, and pulls Dylan to the end of the corridor, by the hatch. It isn't exactly private, but with the rumble of the rover, they can talk without being overheard.

'We aren't going to talk about what you two did,' Francisca hisses. 'We aren't going to talk about what I did, either. We're going to get these people to safety. They're the only thing that matters. Do you understand?'

'Perfectly.'

Francisca takes a deep, trembling breath.

'When it's over I'll tell them,' she says. 'And I will die. But not before it's over. Not unless you cross me again.'

'Understood.'

'Good,' Francisca says coldly.

Dylan helps her to shepherd the evacuees to their allocated sleeping areas. The children are packed in Dylan and Clifford's small berths, three per mattress. The benches and tabletop in the galley become sleeping spaces for the adults, and so does the space under the table. The rear of the corridor by the hatch is secluded enough to be a sleeping area too. A mother with a six-month-old gets the spare cockpit seat. Everyone else will have to stand for the first four hours of the night, before trading places with the sleepers.

'Take the first shift,' Dylan says. 'I'll stand watch.'

For a moment Francisca's face flashes with visceral anger at the suggestion. But there are rings under her eyes, and her shoulders slump. She nods wearily, and disappears into the rear of the cor-ridor by the hatch, where the light doesn't reach.

Dylan goes back up to the cockpit to check on Clifford. He hasn't given up the driver's seat to any of the evacuees.

'Do you want a rest?' she says.

He shakes his head grimly. 'No. I'm going to push on through the night.'

He beckons her closer with a wave of his finger. She leans in close.

'Francisca's going to turn on us,' he says quietly.

'I know. But right now we're allies by default.'

She finds a place to stand near the hatch down to the lower deck, and leans against the wall with her arms folded, trying to ignore the cries of the babies and the quiet tears of the adults. Her legs and the soles of her feet ache, but there's nowhere to sit. The survivors leaning on the wall on the other side of the hatch stare back at her, stone-faced. No one wants to talk. Dylan closes her eyes, and blocks them all out.

After four hours the sleepers wake, and Dylan is given a tiny patch of floor space at the rear of the rover. She curls up between the hatches and the out-suits. As soon as she closes her eyes she feels someone's body pressing against her side. She doesn't bother looking to see who it is. At this point, it doesn't matter.

Faces from the day flash across her vision, expressions of hate and fear and despair. The destruction plays on repeat in her mind. Then a hand on her shoulder shakes her, and she finds herself swimming back to consciousness. Her brain feels like lead. She looks up at Francisca, silhouetted in the first light of dawn.

'On your feet,' she says. 'We're there.'

# Chapter Fifty-Five

Olympus Mons is the largest mountain in the solar system, a volcano the size of France. Like most things on Mars, it's much more impressive in theory than in reality. It's far wider than it is high, and now that Rudolf has climbed the initial slope, it almost feels like they're on level ground. When Dylan gets back to the upper deck and looks out of the cockpit window, the landscape all around them is the same as everywhere else on the planet: bare, lifeless and endless.

Dylan's leans in behind Clifford's seat.

'Morning,' she says.

He grunts in response, and stares unblinkingly ahead. He's still gripping the control stick, and the tendons on the back of his hand are taut.

Olympus Base is a bump on the horizon ahead. The outer shell is a vast ceramic shamrock, almost a kilometre wide. From this distance it looks like an unusually smooth rock outcrop dotted with metre-wide openings. From her visits to similar bases, Dylan knows that it's protecting three inflatable domes inside. It's the essence of Martian architecture: a temporary structure that's been forced to become permanent.

The rovers from Hunter Base approach Olympus slowly and unthreateningly. Clifford matches their pace, driving alongside them to avoid their dust. The four of them slow down when they get within fifty metres of the base, and roll up to a stop facing the pitted ceramic wall. There's a rectangular entrance gate in it, about ten metres wide, but the metal door is down. There's no sign of life from inside.

Dylan's leans closer over Clifford's shoulder. 'Do you think they know we're out here?'

'Of course,' he says grimly.

Dylan frowns, and drums her fingers on his headrest.

'Stop that,' says Clifford.

'Hold on. I've had an idea.'

Dylan climbs back down the ladder to the lower deck, and pushes her way through the evacuees to the back of the vehicle. There's a queue of people lined up outside the door of the chemical toilet. She squeezes past them to the out-suits, which are still hanging behind their netting next to the rear hatch. She powers up one of the suit's backpacks and plugs in the helmet, still hanging on the wall. She pulls out the suit's sleeve and clicks a button on it, searching through the channels on the suit's short-range radio. It can't connect to distant bases, but there's a chance it will find the frequency that the other rovers are using. Sure enough, after a few seconds of static, a tinny voice comes out of the speakers in the empty helmet.

'—survivors of the Hunter Kinship requesting emergency assistance,' says a desperate voice. 'Olympus, please respond.'

The plea is met with silence. Dylan clicks through the other frequencies, but they're all quiet. She returns to the voice from the other rover.

'Olympus, we have dozens of evacuees here, and we're getting low on air and energy. Unless you want a new graveyard outside your gates, please respond.'

Francisca comes to Dylan's side, and looks into the empty helmet.

'Don't they hear us?'

Dylan feels her chest tighten.

'Yes,' she says. 'They know we're here. They just don't care.'

More evacuees gather around to listen to the faint static hiss.

'Why aren't they answering?' a child asks. An adult shushes them. Dylan looks at the survivors' faces, and sees clenched jaws and fists. She leaves the suit radio on for them, and climbs back up the ladder.

'We need to drive closer,' she says to Clifford quietly. 'Get right up to one of their windows.'

'What for?'

'So they can see us. Show them we're real human beings.'

Clifford shakes his head sceptically, but he uses the control stick to ease Rudolf forward until the cockpit window is almost touching the wall of the base. Straight ahead is a gap in the ceramic wall, and through it, in the shadows, Dylan can see the soft white plastic of the inflatable base. A window is set in it, aligned with the opening in the shell. It's tinted black, and no light is coming from inside. Still, when Dylan stares into it, she can feel eyes watching her back.

'Turn on the cabin lights,' says Dylan. 'Make us more visible.'

'If you want to waste batteries,' Clifford mutters, flipping on the lights in Rudolf's cockpit.

Francisca comes to Dylan's side and stares though the hole at the black window. After a minute, she calls out to the evacuees behind her.

'Get the children.'

The children are pushed through the crowd, and the infants are passed hand-to-hand, until all of them are in the cockpit. There are seven in total. The six-month old squalls in a stranger's arms, and all the others are silent and wide-eyed.

Francisca lifts a young girl with tangled hair, and holds her up to the glass of the cockpit window.

'You see that hole there?' she says. 'With the dark glass inside?'

The girl nods silently.

Francisca talks to her with a slight sing-song lilt.

'Inside there are people who can save our lives, but they don't want to right now. So we have to show them that we're good people. Are you a good girl?'

The child looks around desperately.

'Are you?'

'Yes,' the child squeaks.

'Good,' says Francisca, and hoists the terrified girl up higher. 'Then lift up your face. Show them how good you are.'

The evacuees in the cockpit lift the other children to the glass, too, and the baby cries louder. Dylan takes a clipboard from the pouch next to Clifford's seat. She writes on it in big black letters, and holds it up to the window, so that Olympus Base can see.

TAKE THE CHILDREN

'Come on, you bastards,' she says under her breath.

They all stare into the darkness.

'I think I saw something,' says Francisca.

Clifford shakes his head. 'It's our reflection.'

The baby is still crying, and the other children are starting to squirm.

'Look happier,' Francisca says desperately to the girl she's holding. The girl forces a terrified grimace. All around her, the survivors start commanding the other children.

'You can do it! Show them how pretty you are!' one woman says.

'Tilt your head. Show them your dimples.'

'Make them want to save you! Come on!'

Tears are running down the little girl's face.

'No!' a woman says. 'Smile properly! Wave to them!'

Dylan feels nausea rising her throat, and lowers her sign. She glances at Clifford, who nods. He slams Rudolf into reverse, and the survivors stumble at the sudden movement. The rover pulls back from the dark window, and sunlight shines into the cockpit.

'What are you doing?' Francisca snaps at him. 'Go back! We've got to keep trying!'

'This was a mistake,' says Clifford firmly. He rolls Rudolf back towards the other two rovers.

'It's our only chance to survive,' says Francisca. 'You don't decide when we give up!'

'We're trying to convince them that we're worth saving,' Clifford says. 'Child abuse isn't a great advert for our humanity.'

Clifford brings the rover to a stop a hundred metres back from the base, and folds his arms. Dylan spots a man in the galley clutching a length of metal pipe like a truncheon. She squares her feet and raises her fists, but Francisca speaks again.

'The outsiders are right. We need another plan.'

The evacuees by the window lower the children back down to the ground, and pass the crying infant back to its mother. It finally stops wailing. The cockpit is quiet.

'Can we attack the base?' says a man wearing a red sash over his robe. Dylan guesses it's some kind of mark of office.

'Perhaps. Those windows looked vulnerable,' says the man with the metal pipe. 'We need to get some warriors out there. Does this rover have an airlock?'

'No,' says the man with the sash. 'But we can dock with the other rovers and clear everyone out of here, and then use this whole rover as an airlock.'

Clifford turns in his driver's seat to face the survivors.

'Are you seriously considering bursting Olympus Base?'

'Enough from you, outsider!' the sash man shouts.

'I know more about the defences of Olympus Base than any of you,' says Clifford calmly. 'It's one of the best-guarded bases in the north. There are a dozen vacuum doors in each section, with internal guard posts and a defence squadron on permanent alert. How exactly are you planning on attacking them?'

'We'll take them by surprise,' the sash man sneers.

'No you won't.' Clifford points out of the cockpit window at some stacked tubes on the top of the Olympus shell. 'You see that artillery? You see how it's pointing at us? At the first hint of a threat they'll burst all four of our rovers. In fact, they're prob-ably applauding themselves for being so civilised that they haven't done it already. Now, I know what you're thinking: you're out of options, so you might as well ignore me, take control of this rover, and attack Olympus anyway. Is that right? Well, lucky for everyone, I have an actual solution.'

The room shifts uncomfortably. The sash man glances at Francisca, and runs a nervous tongue over his upper lip.

'So tell us,' he says.

Clifford pulls Dylan's map out of the pouch by his seat, and unfolds it across the console.

'Part of my job is knowing the trade routes in this area. I know who transports what to where, when it comes through, and most importantly, how well it's guarded.'

He takes a pen and draws a line on the map, from the centre of the Tharsis plain up through the western side of Olympus Mons. Dylan cranes in to see.

'This is the major autopilot route for trading vehicles in this area. There's a supply train coming north every two days, passing by a few kilometres from here. It's loaded with everything you need to survive: air tanks, energy stacks, standard rations, bubble tents. The point is, it's much easier to ambush a rover train than a base.'

Francisca and the sash man examine the map, taking it all in.

'How far is it?' says Francisca.

'Ten kilometres. Fifteen at most.'

'And how long will we have to wait before the train comes past?' she says.

'If the schedule hasn't changed, a few hours, maybe.'

The sash man's lip curls. 'So we just go there and say "stick 'em up, we're taking your air and power"?'

'No,' says Clifford. 'If you want to rob a rover train then you're going to have to fight like hell, and your chances aren't good. But you'll have a chance, which is more than you have here. If you succeed, you'll have air and power and something to trade, but make no mistake about it, that train is going to have guards, and they're going to be well trained, and well armed.'

'But we'll still have the advantage,' says Kin Francisca.

Clifford raises his eyebrows.

'How so?'

'They'll be fighting for their cargo,' she says, and smiles mirthlessly at the survivors around her. 'We'll be fighting for our lives.'

# Chapter Fifty-Six

Dylan squeezes in next to Kin Francisca, and listens to her talking into the empty helmet of the out-suit. She has explained the plan to the evacuees in the other three rovers, and now there's a painful back-and-forth as the Kinship tries to think of every reason not to do it.

'We don't have enough initiated soldiers,' a scratchy voice resonates in the helmet. 'Can we trust the uninitiated to pull off a military procedure?'

Dylan wants to help Francisca make the case, but she stays silent. The Hunter survivors don't trust her, and the more she defends the plan, the more suspicious they'll be of it.

Avunculus Peter's voice cuts in over the radio. He sounds anxious and short of breath.

'Oh, for goodness sakes. We aren't getting into Olympus, and we don't have enough air to get all of us to another large base. Unless we're willing to split up, we don't have another choice. We're going with the outsiders.'

Kin Francisca looks over her shoulder at Dylan, and nods. Dylan climbs back up the ladder to give the word to Clifford.

'Finally,' he says.

He powers up the motors and steers east, away from the red hive of Olympus Base. The three other rovers follow behind them on either side to avoid their dust cloud. After ten kilometres, they come to a light-brown streak of recently disturbed dust running from north to south, perfectly straight. It's a track made by rovers on autopilot, all following the same optimised path.

Clifford powers Rudolf down and joins Dylan on the lower deck. Francisca holds up a bedsheet to shield the end of the corridor, and the two of them strip off their clothes to put on their out-suits. There are other, younger, fitter people on board who would be better suited to battle, but Rudolf's out-suits are custom-fitted to him and Dylan, and Clifford has insisted that he should be part of the team that captures the train.

'Do we really need the sheet?' Dylan calls out to Francisca as she strips off her grey top. 'It seems a bit prudish, with our lives at stake.'

'There are children here,' Francisca calls back from the other side of the fabric.

Clifford faces away from Dylan as he undresses. As he pulls on his out-suit's undergarments, she catches a glimpse of his naked back, all ribs and spine and mottled skin. She hadn't realised how thin he was. The chain of the locket is around his neck, and he keeps it on as he pulls on his suit's underlayer.

She strips out of the rest of her own clothes, and pulls on her out-suit section by section: first the underlayer, then the chest and pack, then the legs, then the arms. As she tightens her arm straps, Francisca lowers the sheet to check on both of them, and hands them two half-filled paper cups of coffee from the galley above. Dylan accepts hers gratefully.

'What's next?' Francisca asks, as Dylan takes a sip of coffee. It's very different from what she's used to. The coffee in the Syria Base canteen is little more than caffeine tablets dissolved in brown water, but the stuff Clifford carries with him in Rudolf is a complex construct of bitter volatile chemicals. She guesses he's trying to match some flavour from the distant past that she's never experienced.

'There's a blind rise a few hundred metres south,' says Clifford. 'We can set up an ambush. We'll transfer the civilians out of this rover and let your warriors from the other vehicles into here, then use this whole rover as an airlock. Once we're out, we set up a boulder trap and hope the next train comes past on schedule.'

'Great,' says Francisca. 'Oh, and if you think of crossing us ...'

She reaches into the collar of her robe, and pulls out a memory card hanging on the end of a soft red string.

'I got the map. And I'll crush it. Happily.' She tucks it back into her collar. 'But I might change my mind when you get back.'

Dylan hands Francisca the empty cup and locks her helmet into place. The murmuring of the survivors is muffled. She's still surrounded by bodies, but she feels alone again.

Clifford climbs back up to the cockpit in his out-suit, and Rudolf starts bouncing on its suspension. After a few seconds it comes to a stop with a dull metallic clunk, and an LED above the hatch turns green.

Dylan pulls it open to reveal the bright interior of another rover. Sunlight streams in from wide windows along the side,. There aren't crowds of bodies inside to block it. The few evacuees on the other side of the hatch are sitting on long benches with their backs against the outer walls.

Dylan steps aside, and the evacuees on Rudolf's lower deck squeeze past her suit, and through the hatch into the larger rover. When the lower deck is evacuated, two fully suited warriors come out of the Hunter rover into Rudolf. They're carrying weapons even cruder than the spears that the warriors were armed with in the battle outside Hunter. One is holding a pair of bolt-cutters, and the other has a steel pipe hammered flat and angle-ground into something like a machete.

Dylan closes the hatch after them, and with a thud and a hiss the Hunter rover detaches. A few minutes later the second rover clunks into place, and Dylan repeats the process of ushering the evacuees from the upper deck out of Rudolf, and letting in two more suited-up Hunter warriors. After that, they connect to the captured Company rover and Kin Damascus comes through, ducking his head to get through the hatch. His face is invisible behind his golden visor, but there's a strip of red cloth tied around his upper arm to show his rank. He's holding a crude machete, too, as well as the group's only bolt gun.

The remaining evacuees in Rudolf come down from the cockpit and squeeze out of the hatch. Francisca is the last to leave. She gives Dylan a curt nod, and Dylan nods back. It's the best they're going to get out of each other. The hatch locks closed again, and Clifford's voice comes down from the upper deck.

'Are all the warriors on board? Everyone's suits sealed?'

Dylan looks around at the five warriors in the passage with her. Other than Kin Damascus, they all seem far too young for this.

'We're ready.'

There's a clunk as the air system shuts down, and a hiss as air blows out of Rudolf into the thin Martian atmosphere. An alarm sounds, getting quieter as the air thins, until the only noise that Dylan can hear is the familiar thrum of her suit's life-support.

Clifford's voice clicks on again.

'We've agreed on a radio frequency to talk to the soldiers,' he says. 'Twenty-nine point eight. Use the digital channel when you need to talk to me privately.'

'Got it.'

Dylan taps the radio controls on the forearm of her suit until she hears the voices of the warriors around her.

'—make a barricade,' Kin Damascus is saying.

'Yes Kin.'

'And then we stay out of sight until the ambush—'

'All right, everyone,' Clifford's voice cuts in. 'We're down to Mars atmospheric pressure. Let's continue the discussion outdoors.'

Dylan opens the rear hatch again. It swings inwards, letting sunlight shine into the corridor. She jumps down to the rocky ground, followed by Kin Damascus and his warriors. The sun is high overhead, and the landscape glows through the greasy hand-prints on her helmet. Ahead of them, the dusty track crosses the landscape, with the blind rise to the right. The Hunter rovers are on the horizon already, driving silently away to protect the civilians during the attack. They'll need to be out of sight before the train arrives.

Kin Damascus waves a stiff arm, and Dylan and Clifford follow the soldiers as they lumber onto the track.

'We'll set up a barricade here,' Damascus says. 'We'll need a line of boulders across the track, extending out as wide as possible. We have to make sure the train doesn't see it until it's over the blind rise. At that point, it should be too late for the self-driving system to drive around it, and it'll be forced to stop. Any questions?'

'Yes, Kin,' says one of the warriors. 'What countermeasures are we expecting?'

Damascus doesn't answer, but turns his gleaming helmet towards Clifford, who steps forward.

'This is a cargo train, so most of the rovers won't be pressurised. All the guards are going to be in the driver's rover up front. It's a long trip, which means that they probably won't be suited up, so we'll have a few minutes before they can get out and fight back. They'll have roof-mounted artillery, but that's only dangerous at a distance. Once you get close enough, you'll be safe from its arc of fire.'

'You heard the outsider,' says Damascus. 'Once the train's stopped, get in close, do some damage to the front rover, and try not to get yourselves run over. Now, come on, let's haul some boulders.'

Damascus leads them to the first rock, a few dozen metres away. It's just over a metre high, and even with Martian gravity and six people, it's a struggle to lift. The suits aren't helping. Dylan can barely bend her arms and legs, and her backpack weighs her down. Clifford stands to the side, and doesn't even try. To his credit, Damascus keeps the men from hurrying. None of them can afford a torn suit, or even a sprained ankle.

Dylan lowers her sun visor to hide her straining face. The warriors do the same, but she can tell from their breath on the radio that they're suffering. She checks the oxygen use readout on her forearm, and sees the needle hovering over orange. There's nothing she can do about it. There are plenty of rocks to move, and time isn't on their side.

They're halfway through moving their fifth boulder when Clifford's voice comes through her earpiece.

'I don't want to alarm anyone, but we have visual contact.'

He points over the low rise, where a plume of dust is rising up in the distance.

The warriors pick up the pace, and the boulder lurches in

Dylan's hands. They carry it to the side of the track, and drop it next to the others.

Clifford takes a step back, out of breath, to look at the boulder barricade. 'Five rocks. The train's going to have no trouble steering around this.'

Damascus turns to his warriors. 'More boulders! Now!'

'There's no time,' says Dylan.

'Then what?'

Dylan looks at the warriors around her.

'We use our own bodies,' she says.

Damascus is facing into the sunlight, and Dylan can't see his expression through the reflection on his visor, but she feels the weight of his silence.

'Dylan's right,' says Clifford. 'An unmodified autopilot won't run over a human. Problem is, as soon as the train starts slowing down then the driver will switch over to manual, and humans have no problem killing other humans.'

Dylan looks back at the dust cloud. She doesn't know if she's imagining it, but she feels a faint shaking through the soles of her boots.

'Okay,' she says. 'If you all stop the autopilot, I can use our rover to stop the driver.'

Damascus nods, and Dylan runs back towards Rudolf. As she bounds over the rocky ground, she hears Damascus giving orders in her ear.

'Okay, warriors. Spread out at the sides of the boulders, and get down. The lower we are, the less time the train will have to see us and react. Crouch down, and be ready to move if the train comes for you.'

She glances over to the blind rise. The dust cloud is billowing closer, and the top of the frontmost rover of the train is coming into view. She sees roof-mounted artillery, just as Clifford predicted: a double-barrelled cannon set on a rotating base.

She drags her attention back to the uneven ground. Rudolf is ahead, with its rear hatch open. She jumps up, and hauls herself through the hatch into the lower deck. With her out-suit on there's no reason to close the hatch behind her, so it stays swinging open as she clambers up the ladder to the cockpit. The out-suit pack is on her back, so she perches on the front of the driver's seat as she taps in the access code and grabs the control stick. Rudolf lurches forward, and she swings its nose around to face the blockade.

She gets her first good look at the train as it comes over the rise. It's a line of twelve rovers, twice what she was expecting, and all of them are taller than Rudolf. Eleven of the rovers are little more than motorised bases stacked high with crates held in place by tight black plastic nets. The rover at the front is white at the top, shading to dusty brown at the ground, and Dylan can see lights through its cockpit window. It's cruising towards the line of boulders, eerily quiet for something so large.

Clifford and the warriors are on the ground, crouched down on either side of the boulders. The train hurtles towards them, but it doesn't turn. As the front rover gets to within fifteen metres of them, its brakes kick in with an anti-lock shudder that makes the train look like a stop-motion model. It slows, and stops a meter from the warriors. The eleven cargo rovers all stop with equal precision, and the gaps between them squeeze closed.

The warriors pull themselves to their feet. Damascus recovers first.

'Outsider, keep blocking the autopilot until your rover arrives. We'll take out the train guards.'

'Will do,' says Clifford.

As Dylan drives Rudolf closer, the warriors swarm around the front rover of the train, finding conduits and gaps in the plating to pull themselves up onto its sides. Clifford stands in front of the train with his arms raised.

'Dylan?' he says.

'Almost there. You'd better get out the way when I get close.'

Clifford glances at her over his shoulder, and raises a hand to acknowledge her. In front of him, the front rover of the train lurches forward. He sees it just in time and leaps, tripping and falling onto the rocky ground. The wire mesh wheel of the rover rolls towards his legs, and he pulls them up just in time.

'Shit!' he shouts in Dylan's ears.

Only the front rover is moving. The cargo rovers behind it remain still, in a long line. As Dylan drives head-first towards the front rover, trying to block its path, the cannon on its roof turns towards her.

There is nowhere for her to hide. The landscape is bare. Her only hope is to get under the cannon's firing line, but that means driving straight towards it.

Rudolf's cockpit window shatters. The seat lurches under Dylan, and glass hails down on her out-suit. She looks back and sees fist-sized holes in the rear wall of the galley. The cannon fired too fast for her to see the projectiles. She skims past the other rover, narrowly avoiding two of the Hunter warriors climbing up its sides. The cannon swings around to follow her, and Rudolf lurches again. A new hole bursts open in the cabin wall next to her, wide enough for her to see the speeding landscape through it.

She rides alongside the line of stationary cargo rovers, hugging them as close as she can. In Rudolf's rear view screen she sees the roof-mounted cannon turning to follow her, but it isn't fast enough. She reaches the end of the line and steers around the back of the rovers, using them as a wall between herself and the cannon. When she's out of range, she slams on the brakes.

'Change of plan,' she says over the radio. 'Stop that gun.'

Through the gaps between the cargo rovers, she can see the front rover curving around towards her. The Hunter warriors are still clambering slowly up its exterior, holding on to conduits and the edges of its armoured plating. One warrior is between two huge wheels on the rover's right side. As the rover turns, the wheels twist inwards, and the climber is caught between them. The treads grind against his suit, kicking him upwards. His arms flail as he struggles to keep his grip, and his legs swing sideways into the rear wheel. Dylan hears his scream as the treads tear through his suit. For a second she thinks he'll be pulled under the rover, but he catches hold of a gap in the plating, and holds on for his life. Dylan sees blood running down from his leg, mixing with green temperature-control fluid from his suit.

The wall of cargo rovers springs to life. The ones at the rear reverse, and the ones at the front accelerate forward.

'They're switched to remote control,' says Clifford.

The gaps in the wall of rovers open up, and the cannon fires again, narrowly missing Dylan as she accelerates forward. She drives parallel to the nearest cargo rover, matching its speed and keeping it between her and the cannon. The cargo rover reverses unexpectedly, and at the same time, one ahead of her breaks out of the line and charges back towards her. She steers to the side, losing cover again, and the cannon opens fire. Rudolf jolts as more metal slugs hit its side.

'Get the cannon!'

'Almost there,' says Damascus's calm voice.

Dylan glances between the moving cargo rovers at the front rover. The warrior with the injured leg has a foothold now, and is climbing up the side of the vehicle. He reaches the front and hammers on the side window of the cockpit with his wrench, trying to break the glass. On the other side of the vehicle, another warrior is using a bolt cutter on some piping. A plume of gas shoots up into the air.

'What are you doing?' says Damascus.

'Killing the pneumatics.'

'We need the drive systems intact! Destroy the weapons and life-support!'

The cargo rovers scatter in all directions, steering erratically. Dylan reverses, doing whatever she can to keep them between herself and the cannon. Red lights flash on the desk in front of her. She pulls the control stick left and right, but the wheels stay straight. She's lost all steering.

'Shit!' she shouts into her microphone.

She drives Rudolf straight ahead, trying to match pace with the nearest cargo rover, but it curves into her and she pulls back to avoid a collision. She has nowhere left to hide. The front rover slows down, and Dylan sees the cannon swing towards her, and an out-suit with a red armband climbs up over the lip of the roof behind it. Damascus grabs onto the back of the cannon, and clamps down on a bundle of exposed wires with his bolt cutters. The cannon freezes, and Damascus turns his visor to Dylan.

'Got it.' She lets Rudolf roll to a stop, and powers down the motors. But they aren't done yet. She allows herself one deep breath, then pulls herself up out of the driver's seat and unsheathes a Company-issue knife from her leg pouch. She climbs back down the ladder, and out the open hatch.

The battle is in full swing as she jumps down to the rough ground. The front rover of the train is lurching forward and backward, still trying to shake off the warriors clinging to its outsides. All around it the cargo rovers are stampeding, changing speed and direction unpredictably and kicking up a dust storm. Through the side of her helmet she sees one of them coming for her, fast and silent. She leaps backwards, and it blurs in front of her. Pebbles from its treads pepper the side of her suit.

Ahead, the front rover slams on its brakes. On its roof, Kin Damascus loses his balance and grabs the barrel of the cannon to stop himself falling. The warrior with the bleeding leg swings loose under the cockpit window. He keeps a grip with one hand, his body twisting until he's facing outwards.

All around, the cargo rovers roll to a stop, and the dust hangs in the thin air.

'What are they doing?' says one of the warriors.

'The guards will be coming out,' says Clifford's voice. 'They don't want to run themselves over.'

'Cover the hatch!' says Damascus.

He jumps off the roof of the rover. It's a long fall, even in Martian gravity, but he sticks the landing with bent legs, and runs to the rear of the vehicle. Two of his warriors drop down behind him and join him at the rear hatch, while the one with an injured leg twists around, searching for a way down.

Dylan can't see Clifford. She looks back, and spots him running towards one of the stationary cargo rovers. She flips over to the private channel.

'What are you doing?' she asks.

'Cutting the cargo free. You go help the warriors.'

He gets to the cargo rover, and slices through the black plastic netting with his knife. He tugs at a stack of dusty crates, and four of them tumble off the rover platform onto the ground.

Dylan flips back to the warriors' channel as she approaches the front rover. Damascus raises his crude machete, waiting for the hatch to open, but the rover stays lifeless.

'Kin Aaron?' Damascus calls up to the injured soldier. 'What can you see in there?'

The warrior with the injured leg is breathing raggedly, but he pulls himself up to the cockpit glass and presses his helmet against it.

'It's dark,' he says. 'I can't make out ... Wait. There's something movi—'

The window explodes, and Kin Aaron falls outwards from the side of the rover. His radio crackles in Dylan's ear as his body hits the ground. His helmet is a mess of cracked glass.

'Aaron!' Damascus runs towards the front of the vehicle. Dylan looks up and sees a figure in a white-and-black out-suit looking out through the broken glass, holding a blocky yellow bolt gun. The helmet turns in her direction, and the barrel rises.

'Look out!' Damascus cries.

Dylan runs forward and presses against the side of the front rover, staying out of the suit's line of sight. Aaron's crumpled body is five metres in front of her. Damascus slides to her side, with his pack pressed against the vehicle.

'They blew out their own window.'

'Smart,' says Clifford's voice. 'Now they have a sniper's nest.'

Dylan looks up, and sees the back of another black-and-white figure dropping down from the broken cockpit window, holding a second bolt gun.

'Pull back!' says Damascus to the warriors. 'Flank them!'

Dylan runs for the nearest cargo rover, fifteen metres away. She grabs onto its black netting to slow herself down, and looks out from behind it. Damascus and the warriors have scattered out, and are hiding behind the cargo rovers opposite her. Between them, the sniper swings the yellow bolt gun around, searching for a target.

Dylan catches movement out of the side of her eye. The edge of the shadow of the cargo rover that she's hiding behind shifts slightly. When she turns to it, all she sees is the boundary between light and dark, cast across the stones and dust. There's stillness. And then, very slowly, the shadow moves again.

Dylan does a quick mental tally. She knows where Damascus and his warriors are, and where Clifford should be, and none of them are close. She raises her knife, and edges towards the side of the cargo rover. As a black-and-white figure steps into sight Dylan swings her blade upwards, into the soft neck fabric just below the helmet. The suit stumbles back, and bolts fire silently into the ground next to Dylan, kicking up spurts of dust. Dylan pulls the knife out, and with all her strength she slams her knife's solid metal handle into the helmet's visor, and feels the glass crack.

The suit stumbles to its knees, and drops its gun. It claws at its broken helmet, desperate to stop the escaping air. Dylan glimpses a female face, eyes closed and mouth open, as the body slumps and falls.

Dylan catches her breath, and resheathes her knife. A shard of golden glass is sticking out of her glove, just under her thumb. She pinches it, and grits her teeth as she tugs it out. The fabric around the tear flutters lightly as air escapes, but right now, a hole in her out-suit isn't her biggest problem.

The bolt gun is lying in the sunlight, a metre away from the cargo rover. As Dylan leans out of cover to reach for it, puffs of dust erupt around her. She pulls back quickly.

'Watch out for the sniper,' Clifford calls.

Kin Damascus's voice cuts in urgently. 'Incoming!'

Dylan looks around. A few dozen metres behind the hauler, a third white-and-black-suited figure is running straight at her. She doesn't know where it came from: she didn't see it dropping down from the sniper's nest. She ducks between the rover's large wheels, and unsheathes her knife again.

'I'm pinned down,' she says.

There's no response. She swears under her breath, and drops down under the cargo rover. She can still see the bolt gun lying in the dust in front of it. She crawls forwards on her hands and knees, out of cover, and grabs the gun. She puts a finger on the trigger and rolls onto her side, aiming it towards the sniper. She expects another hail of bolts, but when she looks up, she sees the sniper's body hanging limp out of the broken window, and Damascus and his warriors running back towards the front rover.

A suit steps out of the shadow of the cargo rover, and Dylan whips her bolt gun to it.

'Woah! Hey!' says Clifford over the radio, and the suit raises its hands.

'Where's the third guard?' she asks.

Clifford points back the way he came.

'I took care of it.'

The warriors are climbing up the front of the armed rover. They reach the cockpit window, and pull out the sniper's body. It falls to the rocky ground next to Aaron, and the warriors climb in to the cockpit, stepping over the fringe of broken glass at the edge of the window.

'We won,' says Clifford. 'It's over. You mind pointing that somewhere else?'

Dylan lowers the bolt gun, and gets to her feet. The front rover lurches forward a few metres, slowly, then stops. One at a time, the cargo rovers come back to life under remote control, and fall into place behind it.

When the train is rebuilt, the hatch at the back of the front rover opens. One of the warriors drops out of it, and looks up and down the length of the train.

'All good?' asks Clifford, as he and Dylan walk over.

'Yep. Looks like we've got full control. It's a shame the window's broken, but with all this cargo to trade, Kin Damascus reckons—'

The back of his helmet shatters, and he falls forward. Behind him, another black-and-white-suited figure ducks behind one of the cargo crates that Clifford cut loose.

'You said you took care it!' says Dylan, ducking behind the train.

'I did,' Clifford says. 'There's a fourth guard.'

'What's happening out there?' comes Damascus's voice, crackling on the radio.

'Warrior down,' Clifford replies. 'We were ambushed. There's another guard out here.'

Dylan looks out from her cover, and sees the fourth black-and-white suit running closer with its bolt gun raised. The muzzle flashes, and Dylan pulls her head back.

The cargo rovers that they're hiding between start to move, pushing them both forward. Dylan's boots slide along the ground.

'Damascus!' she calls out. 'Stop!'

'Drop down!' says Clifford.

They both fall to the ground, and the cargo rovers rumble over them, huge wheels rolling on either side. Dylan lies still and aims her gun between her feet, towards the back of the train. As the last rover rolls over them, the sunlight shines down into her face. Through the glare she sees the black-and-white suit running towards her, twenty metres away. She squeezes the trigger, and the bolt gun lurches in her hands. The fourth suit staggers forward, and falls to the ground.

She pulls herself to her feet and looks back. The train is departing without them. Clifford is already running after it.

'Damascus,' says Dylan. 'The last one's dead. We're safe. Stop the train.'

The radio crackles. The train curves around until it's facing west, and accelerates.

'Shit,' says Dylan.

She drops her gun, and chases them. Ahead of her, Clifford catches up with the last rover of the train and grabs hold of its black netting. His boots throw up a cloud of dust as they drag on the ground.

'Stop, Damascus!' Dylan says.

She sprints over the rocky ground. The sweat soaks into her suit's underlayer, and her legs and chest burn.

Clifford reaches a hand back for her, but she's still ten metres away, and the gap is growing. A rock slips under her boot, and she stumbles. When she regains her footing, the train is twice as far.

'Damascus!'

'Damn it,' Clifford mutters. He lets go of the netting, and tumbles to a stop on the rocks. He swears to himself as Dylan runs to his side.

'Are you crazy?' she says, giving him a hand and pulling him upright. He holds his side and sucks in air through his teeth.

'My fucking ribs.'

They look out towards the rover train as it heads away into the west.

'They aren't coming back,' says Dylan.

'Why would they?' Clifford turns to look at her. 'We aren't friends. We just needed the same things for a while.'

The dust cloud billows outwards in the still air as the train rides out to the horizon.

# Chapter Fifty-Seven

Dylan and Clifford stand together outside Rudolf, looking up at the shattered cockpit window and the fist-sized holes puncturing its sides.

'What did you do to her?'

'I stopped the train,' says Dylan.

Clifford holds a hand to the side of his helmet.

'Okay,' he says. 'I'm going to see if anything's still working in there. Check the crates that I cut loose from the train, and find out if there's anything we can use.'

Rudolf rocks on its suspension slightly as he climbs back inside. For a moment, Dylan lets herself be still. When she blinks, she sees a face of the train guard suffocating through a cracked helmet. She lets out her breath, slowly. The landscape around her is vast and lifeless and disconnected from humanity, and for a moment, she takes comfort in that. She breathes in and out, and when she's ready, she walks out across the battlefield.

On the far side of the criss-crossing rover tracks and scattered bodies is the pile of dust-covered plastic crates that Clifford pulled out of the train. One of them is cracked open and spilling out spools of black 3D printer filament. She kicks some of the spools aside, and pulls the lid off the second crate. It's filled with squares of soft grey plastic flooring.

A third crate has a dozen orange fabric cylinders with the word *Emergency* written on the sides in five languages. At the sight of them, Dylan feels all the air squeeze out of her lungs. She doesn't know whether to laugh or sob in relief. It's a crate of ballents: single-person balloon tents that can be inflated into survival shelters.

She grabs one of the cylinders and tugs it out of the crate. It's heavy, and about half her height. Through her gloves she can feel some metal components inside it, beneath the soft outer casing. She turns it over and sees a list of instructions. A Fuller Corporation logo is printed underneath.

*Shit.*

Dylan pries the lid off a fourth crate. It's full of prepacked meals, also marked with the Fuller logo. She bends down to pick up one of the spools of printer filament. On the side is a small Fuller logo, next to the words *50m, 0.5mm diameter.*

She tosses the spool away, and rests her weight on the side of the crate.

'How are you doing out there, Dylan?' Clifford says in her ear. 'Find anything?'

Breathe in, breathe out.

'Yep,' she says. 'I'm coming back now.'

She lifts the ballent tube again, and carries it back to Rudolf under her arm. On the way, she spots the bolt gun that she dropped earlier, and picks it up, too, strapping it to the leg of her suit. She hauls the ballent through Rudolf's rear hatch and climbs the ladder to the upper deck. Clifford's facing away from her, standing over the control desk and running his finger down an on-screen readout.

'Look at this,' she says, holding up the ballent.

He glances back at her.

'That'll be handy.'

'No. Here.'

She points the Fuller Aerospace's blue diagonal launching-rocket logo. He looks again, squinting back at it through the glass of his helmet.

'What's the matter?' he says. He doesn't sound concerned.

'Was that a Company train?' she asks.

'Why do you think that? Because it was hauling ballents?' He looks back at the control desk. 'We sell them all over the Free Settlements. They're very common.'

Dylan doesn't say anything.

'What's the matter?' he says, glancing back again. 'Do you think I made you attack a Company train? Why would I do that? If it belonged to the Company I could have just ordered them to stop. They were traders. We did what we had to do.'

Dylan lowers the ballent slowly, and leans it against one of the benches in the galley.

He steps back from the console. 'If you need some good news, I got the radio back online.'

'That's great.'

'And now the bad news.'

He holds up a bulky Mars-made circuit board with a crack down the middle.

'This was the decoder that connected the radio to the computer. Without it, we can't access the Fuller network or the long-range channels.'

Dylan frowns. 'Our suits have digital radio, so they must have a decoder like that built into them, right?'

'Maybe, but I'm not going to disassemble my suit to find out,' he says. 'Luckily, we don't need a digital channel. We can still communicate on AM, like the Free Settlements, but...'

'But?'

'But it means we'll only have about a twenty-kilometre range.'

Dylan presses her gloves against her helmet's faceplate, and wishes she could run her hands down her face.

'Okay,' she says. 'It's better than nothing. If we transmit a Fuller Aerospace emergency code, there's a chance that someone from the Company will pick us up.'

'Sure,' Clifford nods his helmet. 'Of course, as soon as we start transmitting, we'll be a target for Free Settlement raiders, and maybe the Outliers.'

Dylan comes to his side and pulls her father's map from the pouch next to the driver's seat. She takes it to the galley table, and slides her finger right from Olympus Mons until she finds their current position.

'The closest Company outpost is Vanguard.' She estimates the distance in gloved finger-widths. 'About fifty kilometres away.'

Clifford leans in over her shoulder and pores over the map.

'That's too far. Anything else?'

'Just some Free Settlements.' She leans in to decipher the base names, written by her father. 'Jayan Depot, Loyola, Wellington.'

'Then we'll have to count on other rover drivers. Let's hope someone from Fuller Aerospace is wandering past.'

He sits in the driver's seat, and plugs a cable from the control desk into the chest plate of his out-suit.

'What are you doing?'

'Listening for digital carrier signals,' he says. 'There's only a handful of frequencies that the Company uses. If I hear one of ours, then I'll know it's safe to send out a distress call on AM.'

'Okay.'

Dylan folds the map and stows it again. She raises the galley table and it concertinas against the wall, leaving a wide empty space in the middle of the upper deck. She removes the protective wrapping from the ballent, revealing a pleated cylinder of orange plastic. When she pulls on a tab, compressed gas from a small silver canister on the ballent's side begins to inflate the rib-like struts running through it. The ballent unfolds itself into a dome-like tent, slightly too small for the upper deck. Its outer edges squeeze against the galley benches. Dylan pushes it down, straightens it out, and uses its universal umbilical dock to hook it into Rudolf's power system.

She checks on Clifford. He's still in the driver's seat, listening to frequencies that only he can hear. For a moment his eyes flicker like he's heard something, then he shakes his head in disappointment, and turns the dial on the console radio.

'The ballent's ready,' says Dylan.

'Great,' he says, nodding distractedly. He turns the radio dial again.

'There isn't much else I can do right now,' Dylan says. 'I'm going to go into it and get some rest, okay?'

'Sure.'

As she turns, he reaches out and grabs her wrist.

'Hey!' She looks into his helmet, and she sees that he's gazing off into the distance. 'What is it? Are you hearing something?'

He breaks into a big, genuine smile.

'You're not going to believe this,' he says.

He flips a switch on the side of the radio, and takes a cable from a drawer under the control desk. He plugs one end into a socket under the radio, and the other into the chest piece of Dylan's suit. A warbling hum comes through her helmet speakers.

'What is this?'

'Just a second.'

He flips another switch, and the hum becomes a crackle. Clifford talks slowly and clearly.

'F A one one two zero one niner, come in. This is F A zero zero one zero zero three. Do you copy?'

The crackle continues.

'F A one one two zero one niner, come in,' Clifford repeats.

A rising whine builds up under the crackle, and a faint, distorted voice replies.

'Hello? This is F A one one two zero one niner. Who is this?'

Clifford tilts his head back in his helmet, and whoops.

'This is James Clifford, Company code F A zero zero one zero zero three,' he says. 'I can't tell you how happy I am to hear your voice. You're a hard man to track down, Chris Unwin.'

# Part 5.5

---

# This Is Not A Love Story

# Chapter Fifty-Eight

Rose sat on the corner of Netsai's bed, hugging her knees.

'What do you mean "out"?' she said.

'I mean I can't keep doing this any more,' said Netsai, swivelling to face Rose on her desk chair. 'I told you, keep the speech simple. Human rights! No one can argue with human rights. What the hell were you thinking, talking about utopia? Are you high?'

'Now hold on,' said Rose. 'You said we needed a speech that would get people's attention.'

'And you sure know how to get it, don't you?' said Netsai. 'You alienated the former Earth Government bases. It sounded like you were taking credit for them declaring independence. All the Fuller Science bases that were about to join them are pulling out, because they think we haven't thought things through. Hundreds of people did the real work, and risked their livelihoods, and you just swept in like it was all your idea and screwed up everything!'

Rose folded her arms.

'I'm trying to help! I don't have to be doing this!'

'Why are you here, Rose? Really? What are you trying to get out of this?'

Rose pressed her knees together, and held her hands around them.

'I want to help. I didn't want all this attention, but if I keep getting it then I shouldn't waste it. I need to make things better. Whether you like my dad or not, he achieved something, and I've done nothing. I just want to live up to expectations.'

'No one has expectations for you, Rose,' said Netsai. 'Not a single person.'

Rose opened and closed her mouth. Anger and shame robbed her of speech. Netsai saw what she'd done, and sighed.

'I'm making tea,' she said. 'You want?'

Before Rose could answer, Netsai got up from her swivel chair and picked up a kettle from her desk.

'I don't have a faucet. I fill this in the communal washroom.'

She walked out of her room, leaving the door open behind her. Rose sat where she was, and looked around Netsai's small room. She'd never been down here before. The built-in desk was scattered with printouts and D.I.Y. electrical components. On the room's single shelf was a soldering iron and a row of 3D-printed figurines from the games and TV shows of the previous decade. The wall above the bed was plastered with dozens of hand-drawn sketches of faces, hands, dancing bodies, growing plants, and Martian landscapes. And that was it. That was the whole of Netsai's life.

Netsai came back in with the sloshing kettle, and plugged it into the wall socket. She sat back down on the desk chair, and spun it around to face Rose. Neither of them spoke. The kettle reached a rolling boil and clicked off, and Netsai slid open her desk drawer, and took out two mugs and a can of granulated green tea. She scooped a spoon of it into each mug, and poured boiling water. Rose took one of the mugs and cupped it in her hands, letting the heat burn her.

Netsai crossed her legs on the chair.

'Listen,' she said, looking at Rose over the rim of her mug. 'You need to understand. This independence thing might be exciting for you, but you're playing with a lot of other people's lives. I know the Company doesn't have an army, but that doesn't mean they won't retaliate. A lot of people will lose their jobs, and maybe worse. It's true, people listen to you, and we value the fact that you speak up for us. We need you. But if you don't listen to us, and if you say the wrong thing, then we could lose everything. So all I'm asking is that you listen. Is that fair?'

Rose rested her chin on the top of her tea cup, and nodded. 'Fair.'

Netsai looked at Rose with her head tilted to the side.

'What is it?' said Rose.

'Look at us. Expressing our feelings and resolving conflict. My mom would be so proud.'

Rose stifled a laugh. Warm relief washed over her hunched shoulders.

'When we've finished we should get back up to the HQ,' said Netsai. 'A lot of people are wondering how the hell we're going to deliver on what you promised.'

Rose sighed.

'Sure,' she said. 'Okay. Let's get this future started.'

# Chapter Fifty-Nine

Michael sat in a corner booth of the Caliente Marte and thumbed through the menu. The restaurant was tucked away on the lowest level of E wing, and even though it was 12 p.m., he was the only customer. Colourful paper flags and star-shaped lampshades hung from the ceiling above, and the seats were upholstered with striped fabric. The shelves on the walls held ceramic pots and sculptures moulded from clay ground from the local iron-rich regolith.

The door of the restaurant chimed and a middle-aged man strode in, and acknowledged Michael with a small wave. He had thinning hair, and was wearing a T-shirt a few sizes too tight, printed with an image of a martini glass with a slice of Mars hanging on the rim. Even in the temperature-controlled environment, he was out of breath and sweaty. He sat down opposite Michael, and smiled.

'Nice to finally meet you,' he said, offering his hand over the table. 'Dene.'

'Michael,' said Michael, shaking it.

Dene was Michael's handler. They had exchanged hundreds of messages in the last few months, but Michael still knew absolutely nothing about him. Dene hadn't revealed his surname, or any hint of his personality under his business-friendly tone. Somehow, being on a first-name basis made their relationship even more impersonal.

'Really well done on Rose's speech,' said Dene. 'The regular Company employees are freaked out. We've started an online movement attacking any Company base that tries to declare independence. They call themselves the Vanguard. Volunteers for Company guard positions have shot through the roof.'

'So we're stirring up a bunch of online fanatics, then giving them weapons?'

Dene shrugged.

'We need the recruits. We barely have any law enforcement. All we've got right now is a bunch of butlers in blue tracksuits. How are Rose and Netsai doing, by the way? Still fighting?'

'They seemed to have patched it up,' said Michael.

'Shame,' said Dene. 'Well, at least you spread some distrust. I don't think they'll stay together for long.'

He leaned back in his seat, and looked around at the decor.

'You know this is the first Mexican restaurant on Mars? Open for fifteen years.'

'I never heard of it,' said Michael.

Dene leaned in, cheerfully conspiratorial. 'Yeah, it isn't the best. The owner tries, but she can only get so close to an authentic taste with the local ingredients. Have you ever tried vat-grown chilli? Even the tortillas don't taste right. No one comes here any more.'

'How does it stay open?'

'We subsidise the place,' said Dene. 'Secretly. People need to think that small businesses can survive on Mars. The good news is, we can meet here without calling attention to ourselves. The doors are locked. Don't expect to order, by the way. The owner knows not to disturb us.'

Michael put the menu down, and glanced across the restaurant. A sad-looking, dark-haired woman was leaning on a counter next to the door, scrolling on her pad, paying them no attention.

'So,' said Dene. 'Why did you want to meet? What's so important that it couldn't leave a paper trail?'

Michael leaned in over the table.

'I have a situation with Rose,' he said quietly.

'What kind of situation?'

'A situation.'

All the smile evaporated from Dene. His eyes darted over Michael's face.

'From your side or hers?'

'Hers.'

'Have you acted on it?'

'No. But she's made her intentions pretty clear.'

'And you turned her down?'

'Not exactly. Not yet. I've been playing up the fact that I come from Earth, and that I have a different playbook. I've bought myself time.'

Dene nodded slowly. He put his elbows on the table and his chin on his fist, and stared down, deep in thought.

'I want to make this very clear,' said Dene. 'Neither Connect Image nor Fuller Aerospace can expect you to engage in sexual relations, particularly with a target like Rose Fuller. It would be a complete violation of our code of conduct. Do you understand me?'

'I do.'

'But...we can't control your private relationships. What you do in your free time, and who you do it with, is none of our business. Are you still following me?'

Michael nodded cautiously. 'I am.'

'We brought you out from Earth at tremendous expense, specifically to win Rose's trust. Your entire job relies on how deeply you can embed yourself in her group. You can't be standoffish or aloof in any way. Still with me?'

'Yes.'

'So if you turn Red Rose down, what are the consequences? Will she feel rejected? Will she be embarrassed that she's overstepped the bounds of your friendship, and give you space? The question is, will she sideline you?'

'Possibly.'

Dene tugged at the front of his T-shirt, to let air in through the collar.

'Okay. Then listen. If you engaged in relations with someone like Rose Fuller, and it became public knowledge that we planted you in her organisation, then the fallout would be disastrous, and it would be on you. We would have to denounce you as a rogue player, and transport you back to Earth. So, I am telling you, clearly, right now, that I advise you against it. If anyone asks me, that is exactly what I'll be telling them.'

Dene leaned back in the booth, and spread his hands on the table in front of him. He looked Michael in the eyes.

'Are we still on the same page?'

Michael nodded, and felt a gnawing emptiness in his chest.

'Yes,' he said. 'We are.'

# Chapter Sixty

POST 24,361 on MarsChat/Social/Politics. Day (Sol) 212, 2058

JOIN THE VANGUARD!

The Free Settlements want to seize control of our bases. They want to take control of everything that Fuller Aerospace and its employees have built. Our economy and our way of life are at risk, and we need to defend ourselves.

   Decades without crime have left us without proper law enforcement. There are no armed forces to deter the ideologically driven insurgents on our bases.

WE DEMAND:

   – Fuller Aerospace must appoint a local CEO, and give them the authority to co-ordinate its defences on Mars, without any bureaucratic delay.
   – Fuller Aerospace must upgrade its law enforcement, training real guards and supplying them with the necessary weaponry to tackle insurgents and saboteurs, so we can defend our bases from the Free Settlement threat.

The Vanguard stands ready to sign up to the new guard forces, as soon as positions are available.

Until then, we need YOU to be vigilant.

WATCH for signs of rebellion, or attempts to take control of your base.

REPORT any seditious behaviour, or any signs of possible sabotage.

CHALLENGE the extremist views of the Independents.

And, when the time comes, be ready to FIGHT.

WE ARE HOLDING A RALLY ON MARINER BASE TO SHOW OUR STRENGTH OF NUMBERS
10 A.M., DAY (SOL) 215, 2058, MAIN MARINER CONCOURSE

# Chapter Sixty-One

Karl sat the desk in his father's office, kicking his heels against the wheels of his chair as he read up about the chemistry of magnesium extraction. He didn't understand much of it yet, but earlier that evening his father had patted him on the back, and told him that it was important.

'This is our life's work,' he had said. 'One day, you'll be making the decisions, so you need to know more about this than anyone else.'

*...The hydroxide is converted into a partial hydrate of magnesium chloride.* $Mg(OH)_{2(s)} + 2\ HCl \rightarrow MgCl_{2(aq)} + 2H_2O_{(l)}$ ...

The office was on the upper level of the Tycho Mining Base's living habitat. Three of the walls were printed to look like oak panelling, and the fourth was half-frosted glass looking out onto the rest of the administration offices. Right now all the lights were down low, and the desks outside his father's office were empty.

*...The salt is electrolysed in the molten state. At the cathode the* $Mg^{2+}$ *ion is reduced by two electrons to magnesium metal. The formula is* $Mg^{2+} + 2\ e- \rightarrow Mg$ ...

'What do you mean, "I can't"?' he heard his father say.

Karl looked up over the frosted portion of the glass wall, and saw his father storm into the administrators' office. The foreman Volkov followed him, and closed the door behind them. He spoke in a forced whisper, and his voice rasped.

'Victor's our best driver. You want to miss the quota?'

'He's openly talking about joining the Free Settlements.'

Karl sat where he was, and kept his head down. He couldn't interrupt them now.

'It's just talk,' said Volkov.

'But it's more than that, isn't it?' said Karl's father. 'Remember the cut wires? And the mining rover? Someone's trying to stop us from making the delivery to the Company.'

Karl looked up over the frosted glass again, and saw Mozorov facing away from his father, running his fingers over his scalp.

'Those were accidents,' he said. 'But even so, why are we killing ourselves trying to meet the demand of the Company? We can trade with Olympus, they're desperate for magnesium.'

'No. I'm not supporting the Free Settlements. The more bases declare independence, the more precarious Mars becomes. Can you imagine what would happen if the economy collapsed?'

Volkov stared down at the threadbare carpeted floor, and shook his head slowly.

'The Company heard about the sabotage,' said Karl's father. 'They're sending some of their new guards to make sure we make the next delivery on time.'

'You can't be serious. The crew won't accept a bunch of Vanguard goons breathing down their necks. They'll resist.'

Karl's father spoke with a dangerous calm.

'Then they can find employment somewhere else. Like Victor.'

He strode out of the office, and the door slid closed behind him.

When Karl risked looking over the frosted glass again, Volkov was standing at the administrator's desks and clawing at his scalp. He met eyes with Karl, and for a moment his face was a mask of contempt. He swung around and left the office, and Karl stared back down at his training manual with a cold, sick feeling growing in his stomach.

# Chapter Sixty-Two

Rose's apartment's AI chimed. Rose held a pillow against the side of her head and hoped that it would give up, but the noise didn't stop. After a minute, the pad on her bedside table pinged, too. She groaned, and rolled over in bed.

'What is it?' she called up at the ceiling.

'Sorry to disturb you,' the apartment replied, in a calm voice with an intonation that was trained to match her own. 'There's a visitor downstairs for you, and you have nine new messages.'

Rose reached over, and slid her pad off the bedside table. The screen lit up, and she blinked as she tried to focus on it.

**Today**

**MICHAEL (EARTHLING)**
**You need to leave the base**

**11.04**

**Netsai has booked a rover to Kepler for you**
**You can stay there for a while, it's safe**
**She'll get your stuff sent there**
**I'm coming to get you now**
**Are you awake?**

**11.12**

**I'm outside.**
**Hello?**
**Rose?**

**Now**

'Let him up,' she said to the ceiling. She slid out of bed, and pulled on a robe from her walk-in closet. As she stepped out of her

284

bedroom's privacy enclosure, the doors to the elevator next to it slid open and Michael came out, looking agitated.

Her breath caught in her throat at the sight of him, with his thin cheeks and tousled hair. He was wearing a tight jacket and colour-blocked pants, the most basic Martian fashion choice possible, but like Netsai, whatever he chose to wear just seemed to work. Rose caught herself staring, and she looked away. Since he had turned her down, she didn't know where to put her eyes.

'Did you just wake up?' he asked.

'It was a busy night,' she said. She had been up until three reading people's opinions of her online, which was stupid and vain, as Netsai kept telling her, but she couldn't seem to stop.

Michael walked to a glass wall of the apartment and looked down, and Rose came to his side to see. Below them, a scattering of tourists and wealthy locals were wandering the paths, admiring the multilayered flower gardens that made the most of the free vertical space. Rain fell gently from a grid of sprinklers on the dome above, tracking the positions of the pedestrians below and making sure that no water touched them. A group of children ran across a lawn, trying to reach the edge of the rain, but the sensors predicted their movements and the sprinklers stayed ahead of them. Rose looked around the scene, but couldn't spot anything out of place. She clutched at her robe, making sure the front of it was closed.

'What's going on?' she asked.

Michael looked sideways at her. His blue eyes were hard and sharp.

'It's the protests on the main concourse. The Vanguard are telling people that the aluminium mines were shut down because of a lack of confidence in Mars's economy. They're blaming us.'

'So? No one takes the Vanguard seriously.'

'People who just lost their jobs do.'

He unfolded his pad and showed her a video of a crowd in the main Mariner concourse, chanting and yelling. Rose couldn't make out any words, just inarticulate roars of anger. A shaven-headed man with grey skin was standing on a plastic crate at the front of the crowd. He didn't look healthy, but when he spoke it was with the intensity of a firebrand preacher, and the crowd fell silent.

'These Free Settlements want control of the planet!' he said. 'Wrecking our jobs, so they can take the ruins of Mars! We're going to show them what happens when they try to take what's ours. Raise a fist! Raise a fist!'

The crowd howled, and waved their fists in the air.

'Rose Fuller says that she's just trying to give the people of Mars a voice,' the man said. 'Well, you're the people of Mars, aren't you? If you have something to say to her, say it! Apartment 301, Central Tower!'

Michael stopped the video, and Rose groaned. 'Shit.'

'Yep,' said Michael, turning away from the window. He folded up the pad and slipping it into his pocket. 'You're doxxed.'

Rose ran back into her bedroom enclosure. She dressed quickly, pulling on her best hoodie, the one she called the anonymiser. She stuffed a few more comfortable clothes and her essential hygiene products into her gym bag, and slung it over her shoulder. When she came back out, Michael was still at her window, looking down. He glanced at her.

'Ready?'

'Ready.'

They took the elevator down to the gold-trimmed lobby of the Central Tower, and walked out of the entrance in lockstep. The rain had stopped, and drones hovered along on the path, blowing it dry. Some residents passed Michael and Rose, heading to the Maritime Restaurant in the west tower. They were caught up in their own conversation, and didn't even glance in Rose's direction. Neither did the underdressed tourists following behind them, wearing primary-coloured swimsuits. It looked like they were heading to the pool at the north end of the dome. It was built above ground, with glass-acrylic composite walls so that the swimmers could show off to the passers-by. Rose had been there once or twice, but that kind of attention always felt more like her brother's domain.

As they approached the exit of the dome, two men in dark

glasses stepped out from behind the vine-covered public toilets, and strode towards them. The tiny hairs on Rose's arms stood on end.

She stopped dead, and pulled back her hood. As scared as she felt, she knew how to project her voice.

'Hi,' she said, with forced cheerfulness. 'Can we help you?'

'Yeah. We need to talk,' the taller man said.

'We're big fans,' said the other, with a smirk. The two of them came to a stop in the middle of the path ahead.

'Another time, maybe,' said Michael. 'Rose is in a hurry.'

He stepped forward, putting himself between her and the two men. He wasn't short by any stretch of the imagination, but the taller men still towered over him.

'This won't take a second,' said the shorter one.

He stepped around Michael. Michael grabbed at his jacket, and the man's fist shot out, hitting his face. Michael stumbled backwards. The back of his head hit the corner of the toilet block, and he crumpled to the ground.

'Hey!' a voice shouted from behind Rose. She looked back, and saw a group of five young people running up the path. It was the half-naked tourists in their swimming costumes, carrying towels and crates of locally brewed sake. A young man at the front of the group, all tattoos and crafted muscle, faced down the men in sunglasses.

'What the hell are you doing?'

'Stay out of this,' said the man who had assaulted Michael. But the other grabbed his shoulder.

'Forget it,' he muttered. 'It's too late.'

The shorter man glared at Rose. 'She'll destroy Mars! She'll take us all down!'

The taller one pulled him away. After a few paces, the shorter one gave up, and ran with his companion towards the exit.

'Raise a fist!' he shouted over his shoulder.

'Yeah, yeah,' said Tattoos. 'Keep moving.'

Michael was still on the ground, with his back against the vine-covered wall of the toilet block. His eyes were wandering randomly, but when Rose kneeled down at his side, they settled on her and his face lit up.

'Oh, hey,' he said.

One of Tattoo's friends ran over to help Rose pull Michael to his feet. She had a yellow bikini, and her hair was tied up in a knot of braids.

'You okay?' said the girl.

'I'm fine.'

'You should go to a medic. It might be concussion.'

Michael shook his head.

'No, no, no, it was just a few sparks. It's fine. I'm okay.'

Now the excitement was over, Tattoo's other friends were gathering around him, slapping him on the back.

'You saw that?' said one of the boys, laughing. 'Ferdie saved Red Rose!'

The one with tattoos grinned, lapping up the praise. He called out to the girl in the yellow bikini.

'Hey, Dee! Is she okay?'

'Yeah,' the girl called back, and gave them a V-for-victory hand sign.

That seemed to be good enough for the group, who didn't stay and chat. They bounded back towards the habitat's pool, smirking over their shoulders at Rose as they went.

'We don't agree with your politics,' said the girl in the yellow bikini. 'But there's no need for violence, right?'

She gave Rose a worried grin, and scurried off after her friends.

'Right,' Michael muttered under his breath, rubbing the back of his head. 'We wouldn't want to ruin their holiday.'

'Come on,' said Rose, taking Michael by the arm.

She led him out of the dome, and through the tube into Mariner. He was more steady on his feet now, but his head kept turning to the tourism videos playing on the walls. He stared at the images of buggies trailing dust in the air as they launched over the dunes in the Dejnev Rally, and of a couple nestled together on a bed with silk sheets, alone in an empty landscape, looking up at stars through a glass dome.

'Hey,' muttered Rose. 'Stay with me.'

'I'm fine.'

'I've never seen violence like that in my life.'

'It's okay. I'm used to it. I'm from Earth.'

A host greeted them at the far end of the docking bay. She was wearing a tight blue uniform obviously modelled on a 1960s flight attendant, and her blonde hair was bunned up tightly at the back. She welcomed them with a smile and some polished patter.

'Welcome to the Cavalier Triple-Decker Luxury Liner, Miss Fuller. The route to Kepler Base is just over one thousand four hundred kilometres, and the travel time is twenty-five hours. We hope you get a chance to explore all our on-board leisure options, including the spa, buffet, arcade, and the live entertainment in the main hall. Please, follow me.'

She led them inside. Rose's private cabin had two soft reclining seats with their own tables, two wall screens, a wardrobe for the luggage, and an en-suite bathroom.

'Your lunch menus are on your tables,' said the host with a smile. 'I'll be back to take your orders in a few minutes.'

She went back out into the hallway, sliding the door closed behind her. Rose clicked the lock button, and breathed out, long and slow. It was just her and Michael now.

He collapsed into one of the seats, and Rose put her bag down and sat next to him. The room started to vibrate as the rover rolled out over the uneven ground. Now they were on the road, Rose unfolded her pad and made a call.

The screen lit up with Netsai's face. She was wearing her glasses, and sitting in their headquarters. Rose could see the red and blue threads in her braids reflected in the mirrored wall behind her.

'Hey!' Netsai said. 'Are you on the rover? Are you safe?'

'I am now,' Rose said, stretching back in the soft, puffy rover seat. Just the sight of Netsai's confident face made everything manageable again. 'We had a run-in with a couple of the Vanguard chuds.'

'Shit. What happened?'

'They assaulted Michael. He'll be fine, though. They didn't touch me.'

Netsai frowned, and pressed on the bridge of her glasses.

'I'm glad you're okay. You won't be able to meet with the Indian delegation this evening, though. If the Company wants to sabotage us then they couldn't have timed it better.'

There was some movement in the reflection behind Netsai. The red-shirted volunteers were picking up the touch-screen monitors and carrying them out of the headquarters.

'What's going on over there?' Rose asked. 'Are you evacuating?'

'We're going to set up a new headquarters in Kepler with you.'

'Have you also been getting harassed?'

Netsai smiled, and shook her head.

'Don't worry about me. This is my home turf. I've got backup. Besides, you're the real hate-magnet. With you around, the bastards forget I exist.'

'You want to swap?' Rose said.

'Next revolution, maybe. How's the Earthling doing?'

Rose looked over at Michael, who was rubbing the back of his head.

'He'll be fine. I'll look after him.'

Netsai pursed her lips for a moment. 'Okay. Good. See you in Kepler.'

The call disconnected. Rose folded up her pad, and dropped it into her bag. She could see Michael out of the side of her eye, looking ahead with his hands clasped in front of him. The silence between them stretched on until Rose couldn't bear it.

'I'm sorry,' she said. 'About the other night. I shouldn't have hit on you.'

Michael's eyes widened.

'What?' he said. 'No, it's fine.'

'It wasn't great of me,' said Rose. 'I just wanted things to be straightforward. People are mostly weird around me so I wanted to make my intentions clear, but I came on too strong.'

'How are people weird?'

Rose pushed her head into the seat cushion, and looked up at the lights embedded in the plastic ceiling.

'I don't know. My fame breaks people's brains. They think that I'm, like, a different species. Or maybe they don't want to make the first move because they're scared to make fools of themselves. I was tired of all the second-guessing, but I don't want to pressure you. If you're not into it, or you think the power dynamic is messed up, I'll back off. It's just...' she hesitated, but she had to say it. 'I like you, and I don't want you to think you have to say no because of who you think I am.'

Michael reached out over his armrest, and gently took her hand. At the touch of his fingertips, Rose felt a shudder in her chest.

'It's okay,' he said. 'You did the right thing. The problem is all on my side, believe me.'

He turned his blue eyes away from her.

'What is it?' said Rose.

'I know everything about you, Rose,' he said. 'But you don't know anything about me. If you got to know the real me, maybe you wouldn't be so keen.'

Rose laughed, but Michael didn't smile.

'You're serious?'

'Absolutely.'

'That's very considerate,' said Rose, leaning in closer and squeezing his hand. After years of rejection and confusion and complication, this could finally be something with substance. 'That's the reason you were holding back?'

'The main reason, yes. I like to take things slow.'

'We've got twenty-five hours,' Rose said. She smiled as she leaned back in her soft recliner. 'So. Tell me about the real Michael.'

# Chapter Sixty-Three

'I think I've got it,' said Rose, frowning down at the manual. Michael stood next to her with her suitcase at his side. Rose's new room on Kepler was smaller than her glass-walled apartment in Mariner, but it wasn't as intimate as their rover cabin. He already missed the cabin. It had been a relief to spend time with Rose in a hermetically sealed environment, where no one was listening and he didn't have to worry about what the Company expected of him. He told Rose about his whole life up to his late teens, glossing over the rest. After that, she thought she knew him, and he had been able to relax. In the evening, the two of them had watched an Earth movie about a couple falling in love while working together in an internet troll farm, and they had held hands. Rose had swirled her thumb in his palm during the sex scene. And at the end of the movie, they kissed. Michael had been relieved that Rose broke it off first. With a blushing smile, she had muttered something about the cabin walls being too thin. They each curled up on their own seat, and slept hand in hand.

But now they were in Kepler, things were complicated again.

This was the first European base to declare independence, and five different administrators had met with Rose on arrival. Their hospitality had a tight-smiled anxiety to it. No one would quite say if Rose was welcome here, or if her presence was a diplomatic nightmare. Navigating the politics of a fledgeling Free Settlement was going to be tricky. But, right now, the biggest, most complex problem that Michael and Rose were facing was the mystery of Rose's room.

It was an empty rectangle, five metres by eight, with white walls and a black floor. Light came down from a grid of square light-emitting panels above. There was no furniture, just a thick ring-bound manual that the base manager had handed Rose on arrival.

'Okay,' Rose said. She closed the manual, but kept a finger wedged in it like a bookmark. 'It should be straightforward. It's voice activated, and the room should already know that I'm its owner. Hey, Room, sofa.'

A wall panel folded down, and a fluffy white sofa slid forward quietly. Rose grinned.

'What's the point of that?' said Michael. 'You could have folded it down yourself.'

'It's all part of the futuristic experience,' said Rose. 'The Europeans were trying to out-Fuller the Company. Hey, Room, TV.'

A screen appeared on the wall opposite the sofa, showing rows of icons for different genres of shows, games, and social experiences. It had been there the whole time, set to the exact same shade of white as the room's plastic wall.

'See? Magic.'

Michael looked around.

'So what else is hidden in the walls?' he said.

She tossed the manual onto the sofa. 'Let's guess. You go first.'

Michael shrugged. 'Uh. Sink.'

A door slid open, revealing a small en-suite bathroom.

'That was too easy,' said Rose. 'Stove.'

A counter-top with hot plates folded down from the wall next to the bathroom door.

'Whoa!' said Michael.

'I was cheating, I saw it in the manual,' said Rose. 'You go again.'

'I don't know. A hot tub.'

There was no reaction from the room.

'Okay,' said Rose. 'Pool table.'

Again, there was no reaction.

'A live capybara,' said Michael, looking around expectantly.

'A one-quarter scale model of the Statue of Liberty,' said Rose.

'Three muffins and an anvil.'

'The Green Bay Packers.'

'A coat rack.'

A coat rack folded out of the wall next to the sofa. Rose cheered.

'Well done, Room! Okay. How about a bed?'

The sofa folded down, and sheets unrolled from the wall panel, pulling themselves tight over the bed.

'Hey,' said Michael. 'Would you look at that.'

He stepped in closer to Rose, until he could feel her breath on his neck, but she put a hand on his chest.

'Cool it, George Jetson,' she said. 'I've got to unpack and talk to Netsai. We've got a lot to catch up on. Work now, play later.'

'Sure,' said Michael. 'Just say "Earthling" and I'll unfold from the wall.'

Rose giggled, and pushed him away.

'Door,' she said.

Michael walked out into the corridor, and used his pad to find his own room. It was on the level below Rose's, and about half its size. His bed was folded away just like hers, but it took a bit of manual effort to pull down.

He rubbed his cheek, and the back of his head. He was bruised and scratched from the fall the day before, and a few drips of blood had dried and clumped in his hair. The attack had genuinely taken him by surprise. The Company was happy to work the public up into a fury over Rose and the Free Settlements, but when it was all over, did they really think that the Vanguard would just stop? Or would it become the new face of the Company?

But, as Dene would remind him, questions like this weren't his responsibility. He explored the seams in the walls until he found a small lever marked *DESK*, and pulled at it. With a click, a desk and built-in chair unfolded in front of him.

He sat down and began planning the rest of his day. He needed to order new clothes, and other basic supplies that he hadn't had time to pack back in Mariner. First, though, he needed to keep track of Netsai. He took out his private red pad, and logged into

the back end of Netsai's messenger app. The data rolled up his
screen, scraped and decrypted from the servers on Mariner Base.

> Netsai Chiwasa (13:33:16) : Anything in his room?
> Eli North (13:34:04) : Nothing. Just books and dirty clothes
> Eli North (13:34:41) : Hold on
> Eli North (13:36:02) : I found a hidden safe. It's behind the
> panel of an air vent

'Shit!' said Michael, standing quickly. He held his hands over his
mouth, and kept reading.

> Netsai Chiwasa (13:36:51) : Can you open it?
> Eli North (13:37:35) : It's already open. Nothing inside
> Eli North (13:37:58) : Why would Michael need a safe? Did he
> say anything about it?
> Netsai Chiwasa (13:38:06) : No
> Eli North (13:39:14) : Maybe it came from whoever had the
> room before him
> Eli North (13:39:29) : Like some tourist or something
> Netsai Chiwasa (13:40:13) : You really believe that?
> Eli North (13:40:38) : We should tell Rose
> Netsai Chiwasa (13:40:51) : Wait, need to check something
> first

'Shit,' Michael repeated. He sat back down and opened another
window on his pad. From Netsai's online activity, he could see that
she was going through all his social media and running reverse
image searches on his pictures. A year before, she would have
caught him immediately. There had been thousands of snapshots
online proving he wasn't who he said he was. There had been
family photographs and videos on cloud servers all across Earth.
Connect Image had scrubbed all of it, even the pictures taken in
public by strangers that happened to have him in the background.
Some of his distant family members had complained about the

missing pictures, and had been met with a shrug from the hosting companies. An unfortunate server error. What can you do?

But if Netsai was looking, then it was only a matter of time before she found something that Connect Image had missed. There was still twenty-six years' worth of evidence out there that he wasn't who he said he was. All she needed to do was take a random thread in Michael's life, and pull.

He paced around the room, frowning and biting the side of his thumb. He could do nothing. It was a valid option. He would be caught, and kicked out of Rose's organisation, and shipped back to Earth. He would have wasted the millions of dollars it had cost the Company to bring him to Mars, and Connect Image would never hire him again.

Or.

He tapped on the screen, pairing the red pad with the room's printer. It unfolded from the wall – a sleek grey rectangle with an opening at the bottom for the printed pages.

He went through the pad, selecting the most incendiary documents and sending them to the printer. He printed out his dossiers on Rose, Netsai, and the rest of the volunteers. He printed out the results of the agent-based simulation of the newly independent Free Settlements. He printed out the Company's strategies to turn them against each other, and the plans to send in guards to 'bring back order'. He printed out the misinformation used to stir up resentment in the Vanguard, and the memos of the plan to force Rose out of Mariner Base, and to turn Rose and Netsai against each other.

As the pages printed one by one, he prepared his speech to Rose.

'You want to know why I'm doing this?' he said to the slot in the printer. 'It's because I'm not who Fuller Aerospace thinks I am. They ran a lot of psychological tests on me back on Earth, which is why they trust me. But I'm not the same person I was back then. Utopia feels a lot less far-fetched up close. I want to stay with you, Rose. I want you to win. But I'm taking a hell of a risk, and I need you to help me, too.'

He turned on the pad's front-facing camera and checked him-self, making sure his hair was neat and his shirt was clean.

'I just want to be the person you think I am,' he said.

His door chimed. He turned the pad off.

'Who's there?' He called.

'Rosemary Fuller,' the room's speakers said calmly.

He slid the door open for her. She was standing in the corridor, smiling, and her cheeks were flushed.

'Hey,' she said.

'Hey,' he said. 'I was just about to come up. I need to tell you something important.'

'Me too,' said Rose. 'Can I come in?'

'Of course.'

He stood aside for her. She walked in, and gave the room a cursory glance.

'I decided not to wait,' she said, turning to face him and running her hands up and down her sides anxiously. 'I've been taking things slowly just as an excuse not to move forward. I can't keep doing it. I'm not going to blow this by keeping one eye on the exit.'

Michael looked at the wall-mounted printer. Rose followed his glance, and saw the pages in the slot.

'What's that? Work?'

'Yes,' said Michael.

Rose put a hand to his cheek. 'Important work?'

Her eyes darted around his face, and her fingertips dropped down to his chest. He felt them through the fabric of the base jacket that he wore to make her trust him. They swirled, searching for a way in.

'I'm only asking once,' she said. 'And if the answer's no, I'll leave. Do you want this?'

Michael kept his face still, and locked eyes with her.

'Yes,' he replied.

# Part 6.0

---

# Outlaws

# Chapter Sixty-Four

*What are the odds?*

Dylan leans forward in the passenger seat of the cockpit, and listens in as Clifford explains their situation to the census taker. The same census taker they had been searching for all along, who just happened to be the first person in the whole Free Settlements that Clifford managed to contact. Purely by luck. How about that.

'I didn't realise how badly you wanted this map,' Unwin chuckles nervously.

'So you do have it?' says Clifford. 'Where are you right now?'

'Loyola Base. I've hired a rover to take me down to Company Territory, but we'll change the route and come and pick you up.'

'How long?' Clifford looks over at Dylan. 'The clock's ticking here.'

'A few hours,' Unwin says on the crackling line. 'The driver I hired is just prepping the rover. As soon as we're ready I'll come down to get you. I've got your location. Hold tight, sir.'

'Thank you.'

Clifford disconnects the radio connection, and unplugs the cable from his chest panel. Without the hissing whine in Dylan's helmet, the rover is eerily quiet.

'Well,' says Clifford, rubbing his gloves together. 'That's what I call a reversal of fortune.'

'Yeah, big relief.' Dylan nods.

Clifford pulls himself up from his driver's seat.

'We've got a couple of hours to kill,' he says. 'What's the plan? Do you still want to get into the ballent?'

Dylan looks at the inflated black-and-orange dome.

'You know what, sir, you should take it,' she says. 'You were

301

driving all night. You need it more than me. I'll keep a lookout in case the Outliers caught our transmission.'

Clifford nods. 'Thanks. I won't say no to an hour's rest. The adrenaline's wearing off. But keep your eyes open. We aren't out of danger yet.'

He unzips the outer layer of the ballent and pulls open an adhesive seal. As he kneels down, preparing to crawl inside, Dylan turns to him.

'Mr Clifford,' she says. 'Why's that map so important? What's in the Wintergarden?'

He pauses in mouth of the ballent.

'The answer to a question that's been plaguing me for a very long time,' he says, and crawls inside. A few minutes later, the interior of the ballent pressurises, and the loose orange plastic between the black ribs expands outwards. Dylan watches, and waits. When she's sure Clifford isn't coming out again, she turns off her connection to his suit. She faces the cockpit control desk again, and reconnects the radio.

It crackles in her ears. Eventually, Unwin answers.

'Mr Clifford! Great news, We're fully stocked and ready to depart. We'll be there within the hour.'

'This isn't Clifford,' says Dylan. 'My name's Ward, I'm his body-guard. Unwin, how much do you trust Clifford?'

'Completely,' says the census taker without any hesitation. 'He's on the board. He runs the whole of Internal Affairs.'

'Have you ever heard of the Company giving away or selling ballents in the Free Settlements?'

'Ballents? No. Fuller Aerospace keeps them for itself. If anyone else had them, we wouldn't be able to easily locate Company employees in an emergency.'

'That's what I thought,' Dylan says. 'Clifford made us ambush a train loaded with ballents. We killed the crew.'

There's a long crackle on the line.

'Maybe...' says Unwin. 'Maybe it was a train of stolen goods? That must be it, right?'

'When was the last time you called back to headquarters?' asks Dylan.

'Back in Pavonis. Sam Beatty said that Clifford told him to stay off all the digital channels...'

His words hang in the air, and the radio hisses.

'I think we've been played,' says Dylan.

'No, it's got to be a mistake,' says Unwin. Even through the crackling radio connection, Dylan can hear the desperation in his voice. 'Listen, I'll hop onto the Company network now, and call in to the census office. I won't tell them anything about the map, I'll just check in. That should be fine, right? Assuming this is all above-board. If there's any kind of problem with Clifford, the census office will let me know.'

He disconnects. Dylan keeps the cable from her suit to the radio plugged in, and looks back at the ballent. The plastic is still safely bulging. She waits, tapping the heel of her Mars boot against the base of the cockpit seat.

'Be wrong,' she mutters to herself.

She hears a buzz in her ear, and Unwin reconnects. His voice is wobbling. She can't tell if it's from the stress or the connection.

'Stay on this line,' he says. 'I'm going to hold my pad up to the radio, okay? They're saying that there's someone who needs to speak to me. I think you'll want to listen in.'

Dylan feels the weight of dread in her chest.

'Who is it?' she says.

'Karl Sealgair.'

# Chapter Sixty-Five

Sealgair searches the ground in the remains of Hunter Base. Dust and debris blanket the landscape in every direction. All around are twisted girders, scattered pieces of silica ceramic, and the open-topped shells of cracked domes.

He walks slowly away from his buggy though the ruins, studying the barely visible rover tracks under the dust. The guards of his entourage are spread out around him, twenty metres away.

'Sir.'

Sealgair looks up. The radio gives him no indication of where the voice comes from, but he spots Heron off to his left. The large man is waving Sealgair closer, and one of his men is kneeling in front of him, examining something in the dust.

'It this what we're looking for?'

Sealgair strides over to them. Between the debris is a stretch of rover track, with the distinctive cross-hatch wire tread of the Calliope. He follows it for a dozen paces, until he finds a groove cut into it, two metres long.

'Here,' he says. 'This was made by a stone that was kicked up by their treads...'

He picks up the rounded pebble.

'It was thrown south, so they were heading away to the north. They were accelerating.'

As Heron and his men follow the curved path of the track, a chime plays in Sealgair's headphones. He frowns, and taps a button on his suit's forearm to answer the call.

'Yes?' he says.

'Sir,' says a voice in his helmet's speakers. 'It's Baikonur. You said I should call if there was any update on James Clifford.'

Sealgair straightens up, and looks out at the horizon. In the distance, the rovers of the rest of his entourage are waiting patiently for him to finish his investigation.

'And?'

'The census bureau just called us. A missing census taker just came back into contact. Apparently he's been doing some kind of job for Clifford.'

Sealgair starts walking back to his buggy, which is waiting by the ruins of a docking bay fifty metres away.

'Is he still on the line?'

'Yes sir, that's why we called. I thought you'd want to question him personally.'

'Put him on.'

Sealgair's earphones click.

'Hello?' says a hesitant voice, clearly audible on the digital channel.

'This is Karl Sealgair. Who am I talking to?'

'Chris Unwin, sir. F A one one two zero one niner.'

'Where are you? Where's Clifford?'

'He's about twenty kilometres south of me, sir,' says the census taker. 'Ten K east of Olympus. His rover is shot up and disabled.'

'All right. What were you doing for him? What were his orders?'

'I wasn't following his orders, sir. Not directly. It's hard to explain. I was getting a map for him, for a location up in the north—'

Sealgair cuts him off.

'Unwin, listen to me. James Clifford has been stripped of his position and red-listed. He has no authority in the Company. Get to him as fast as you can, and make sure he doesn't escape. I'm coming to deal with the matter myself. Clear?'

The census taker doesn't reply.

'I said clear?'

'I … yes, sir.'

'And be extremely careful,' says Sealgair. 'James Clifford is a wanted criminal. Don't listen to him, don't trust him. Do you understand?'

'Yes sir.'

'Good. I'm on my way.'

He presses the button to terminate the connection, and the static cuts out.

Heron and his man are looking his way, waiting patiently. Sealgair waves a hand, summoning them back to him.

'What is it, sir?' says Heron. His low voice rumbles in Sealgair's headphones.

'We've got him.'

Heron breaks into a grin, visible through the glare on the glass of his helmet.

'All right boys,' he says. 'Let's finish this.'

Heron leads his men back towards their rovers. Sealgair strides to his buggy, which stands apart from the other vehicles, and pulls his rifle up out of the mount next to his seat. He checks that the auto-aim is still engaged, and that he has a full clip of ammunition. Satisfied, he hooks the rifle back into its cradle, next to his knives and a packet of plastic explosive. He won't be needing the full clip. Three rounds will be enough. He nods to himself, and climbs back into the buggy.

# Chapter Sixty-Six

Dylan disconnects the cable from her suit to the console, and looks back into the galley. The ballent is still inflated, and she relaxes slightly. If Clifford is still resting then she still has some time to prepare. She just needs to make sure that he doesn't get out of the ballent.

As she stands up she feels a slight jolt through her feet, a small but noticeable shift in the weight on the suspension, and she freezes. After a moment she feels it again. Someone else is moving on board Rudolf.

She approaches the ballent, and takes hold of one of the inflated ribs. She pulls it upwards, so gently that anyone inside wouldn't know. The whole ballent lifts up off the ground without any resistance. It's empty.

She flips the switch on her forearm, and turns on her digital radio.

'Clifford?' she says.

She reaches down to unstrap the bolt gun from her leg, and edges towards the hatch down to the lower deck.

'Hello Dylan,' he replies through her helmet. His voice is calm and measured. 'I saw you were busy. I didn't want to disturb you.'

She wants to check the passage below, but she can't just drop down. There's every chance that he's waiting for her, armed with a pipe or a machete. She kneels down next to the floor hatch with the bolt gun in one hand, and unstraps her knife with the other. The side of the blade is reflective, and she angles it until she can see down into the passage below. The lower deck is dark, and she can't see any sign of Clifford's out-suit.

'You didn't want to rest, then?' she says.

'It doesn't look like you're giving me much opportunity. Who were you talking to? Unwin?'

'Yes.'

'You didn't trust me.'

She resheathes her knife and drops down to the lower deck, landing on her haunches, and pointing the bolt gun down the corridor. There's no sign of him. She reaches down and spreads her free hand on the floor, feeling for motion. Nothing.

'We could have called for help. You destroyed the radio circuit board,' she says.

He doesn't answer.

'You made us attack a Fuller train,' she says. 'You made me kill Company guards.'

'If we hadn't given the Hunter survivors what they needed then they would have killed us.'

She swings the muzzle of the bolt gun into Clifford's cabin, then her own, then the toilet booth. All are empty.

'You could have ordered the train to stop.'

The rear hatch is closed, blocking her view of the outside world. She edges towards it.

'They wouldn't have listened. I've been taking an unscheduled sabbatical, and I doubt that Karl Sealgair is happy about it. He's coming for us, isn't he?'

Dylan pulls the hatch open and stands back, pointing the barrel of the bolt gun into the light. As her eyes adjust she sees Clifford fifty metres away, kneeling next to the body of one of the train guards. He stands up and faces her, holding a bolt gun.

'I'm not your enemy, Dylan,' he says. 'You have bigger problems than me.'

She reaches for the switch on her forearm, and flips the radio off. There's no sound except the hiss of air in Dylan's helmet. If he can't cajole or manipulate her then he's just an injured old man.

She walks towards him over the rocks, slowly, keeping her bolt gun trained on him. Bolt guns are just modified riveters, jury-rigged into weapons after the Collapse. They have notoriously bad aim. If Dylan wants her bolts to count then she'll need to get close.

Clifford's mouth moves, but he makes no sound. He raises his own bolt gun and aims it at her.

She keeps creeping closer, holding her aim on him steady. Twenty metres. Fifteen. Ten...

Clifford's trigger finger tightens. Dylan freezes, but there's no recoil from the gun in his hand.

She starts walking again. *Nine, eight, seven, six, five...*

Now that she's close, she can see the crack down the side of Clifford's barrel. One of the cargo rovers must have rolled over his bolt gun. It's useless.

She keeps her own bolt gun level, aimed at his face. Clifford's mouth is still moving, so she fires a warning bolt past his helmet. He purses his lips as he glares at her, and opens his hands to show her the palms of his gloves. His bolt gun falls to the ground.

She tilts the barrel of her bolt gun back towards Rudolf. He walks ahead of her, slower than she'd like, towards the rear hatch. She nudges him down the corridor with the muzzle of her gun, and up the ladder. When they're both on the upper deck, she points to the seat on the left. Clifford sits slowly. Dylan keeps the gun pointed at him as she takes a thick black cable tie out of the supply pouch on her hip, and binds his wrists together. She secures his ankles with a second cable tie, then goes to the lower deck to collect her bed sheet. She tears it into strips and ties him to the seat, with his arms tight against his sides. When she straightens up, she sees him staring up at her, unblinking. He mouths something slowly to her. She can't make out the words, and she doesn't care. She fastens the bolt gun to her leg, and plugs the chest piece of her suit back into the radio to let Unwin know that Clifford is secure.

# Part 6.5

---

# The Traitor

# Chapter Sixty-Seven

Michael and Rose sat side by side on the fold-out bed in Michael's room. The pages from Michael's printer were spread out on the sheets in front on them, all marked 'confidential' and 'highly classified'. Rose picked up each page in turn, skimming through them and stacking them at her side. Her fingers were tight, and so was her jaw. Out of the corner of her eye she could see Michael watching her intently, studying her face. He was still naked, and so was she.

Rose picked up the next page, and read through it silently. It was a transcript of a private conversation she'd had with a potential union organiser from one of the Russian bases, three weeks before. Just one of dozens of transcripts of everything Rose had said in the last five months. And even now, Michael was still watching her. When she lowered the page he reached out a hand towards her leg. She moved over, putting some space between them, and pulled the sheet up to cover her body.

'How did you get all this?' she asked.

Michael looked down at the piles of papers.

'The Company shared it with me,' he said.

'Why?' she said.

'Because I was working for them.'

Rose looked him in the eyes, but she couldn't read a trace of emotion.

'Doing what, Michael?' said Rose.

'Rose,' he said. 'Stay calm. I'm on your side.'

'When were you working for them?'

'Since the beginning.'

'Fuck!' Rose swung her feet off the bed. She stood up quickly and pulled the sheet around her. The printed pages fell to the floor. Rose picked up her clothes from the corner of the room, and started pulling them on.

'Stop, Rose,' said Michael. 'Calm down. It's going to be okay.'

'You could have told me any time, Michael,' she said, her shame curdling into fury. 'The first words out of your mouth when I met you could have been "I work for the Company." Why did you wait until now? Until after we had sex? Did you think you could fuck me so well that I'd lose my rational mind?'

'Rose, please, listen,' Michael said, pulling on his pants on the side of a bed. He sounded like a robot.

'Then why, Michael? Why wait until now?'

Michael opened and closed his mouth.

'What?' she said. 'No clever words to win me over?'

'I hoped that if we had ... if we had a connection, then you wouldn't discard me when you learned the truth.'

Rose pulled on her shirt, and slipped on her shoes.

'You're unbelievable, Michael. How did you think this was going to go?'

She started gathering up all the scattered pages.

'Please, Rose. I'm sacrificing everything for you.'

'Yeah, well, sacrifices are meant to hurt.'

He pointed at the documents in her hands.

'Look at what I'm giving you! This is proof of how low the Company is willing to go. It'll ruin them. You win!'

Rose stood up, holding the documents like a barrier between them.

'That's not the point, Michael.'

'Then what is the point?'

She closed her eyes and breathed in deeply. When she opened them again, she felt calm. 'If I knew who you really were then I would never have had sex with you. So think about what hiding it from me means. Think about what that makes you.'

She walked to his door, and pressed the switch at its side. It slid open in front of her.

'Wait!' he said, pulling his shirt on over his head. 'This isn't an act. Yes, I worked for them, but I'm not that person any more.'

'Really? So you woke up this morning and decided to betray the Company?'

'I just want to be the person you thought I was.' he said.

'Why?'

Michael looked her in the eyes. 'Because of you.' he said. When Rose saw the yearning on his face, she had to laugh.

'You think that's going to work?' she said. 'You're unreal. I'm done. Goodbye, Michael.'

She walked out of the room with the documents in her hand, and let the door slide closed behind her.

# Chapter Sixty-Eight

Netsai sat opposite Rose in a window booth of Kepler's above-ground cafeteria, flicking through the printouts from Michael. Rose didn't watch. She held her head in her hands to block out the world and the eyes of the other Kepler cafeteria patrons, but she could still hear the pages rustling.

Dim orange sunlight shone through the window onto the table between them. Over the last few weeks a dust storm had been spreading across Mars and darkening the sky. The atmospheric scientists had been warning about the possibility for years, saying that it would interrupt transport and communication. The predictions had finally come true.

'So this is why,' Netsai muttered under her breath. A light flickered on a plastic pendant around her neck: a voice blocker, emitting sound frequencies outside the range of normal human hearing that would interfere with any microphones attempting to record them.

'Why what?' said Rose, keeping her head down. All she wanted to do was crawl back to her own room and hide forever, but Netsai had insisted that they meet up here. Rose had never been to this cafeteria before, and normally it was the kind of place she loved. Most of the tables were occupied by engineers and scientists in blue ESA flight suits, sharing food and coffee as they pored over their spreadsheets and quietly discussed the problems of self-sustainability. Everyone had important work to get on with, and very few of them had time to stare at a celebrity.

'This is why we never caught a break,' said Netsai. Rose heard her shaking the stack of pages. 'It wasn't bad luck. It was planned.'

Rose put her fingers on her forehead, and covered her eyes

with her palms. She heard Netsai leaning forward, and felt a hand on her shoulder.

'How are you feeling?'

'I'm such a fool,' Rose said, removing her hands. She looked up at Netsai through the waterfall of hair over her face. 'I should've seen through him. I shouldn't have let him get so close.'

Netsai nodded, and kept reading the documents.

'We all underestimated what bastards the Company can be.'

Rose turned away from her, and looked out of the round cafeteria window. In the area immediately outside their dome, five out-suited figures were unfolding a huge circle of transparent plastic from a crate, and holding its edges down so it wouldn't blow away in the wind. As Rose watched, one of them walked around the perimeter of the plastic circle, using a yellow gun-shaped device to fire metal bolts into flaps on its rim, and pinning it to the ground. Another suited figure came out of the base, carrying a coiled air tube. It hooked it up to a port on the plastic circle, which began to inflate into a giant transparent bubble. The suits all around it raised their arms in a silent cheer.

'What are they doing?'

Netsai looked up from the stack of papers.

'They're working out how to make cheap new bases. It's going to be important when we expand the Settlements.'

Rose admired the engineers outside. Everyone was working together to solve a problem. It seemed like an alien world.

'Where's Michael now?' Netsai asked.

'In his room,' said Rose, turning back to her. 'He promised not to have any contact with the Company until we decide our next steps. I think he's pining for me, or pretending to. I said we'd bring him food.'

Netsai didn't say anything. She was staring down at a page halfway through the stack.

'Holy shit,' she said quietly.

'What is it?' said Rose, leaning forward.

'Did you read this?' said Netsai.

'I skimmed most of it. What is it?'

'The strategy for what to do if one of their bases declares independence. This is a technical description of a software intrusion into a base's life-support system.'

'Does that mean ...'

'...Hacking into a Free Settlement to shut off its oxygen? Yes.'

Rose's mouth dropped open.

Netsai flipped through the documents one more time, then stacked them neatly on the table in front of her.

'Okay. We need to get word out immediately, and warn the other Settlements what the Company's capable of.'

Rose frowned down at her half-eaten blek.

'We should contact Archie, too,' she said.

Netsai tilted her head. 'Your brother? Why?'

'Because he won't want to be associated with the Company if they're seriously considering murder. And if he turns on them then his fans will follow. They're immature edge-lords, but we need them on our side, don't we? Besides, he deserves to know.'

'He's done everything he can to trip us up.'

'Archie's a jerk, but he's my brother.'

Netsai sighed, and pushed her glasses up the bridge of her nose.

'Okay,' she said. 'He gets one chance to get on board, but one way or the other, I'm getting this news out. The Free Settlements need to start getting a lot more paranoid about their data networks. And what about Michael? Fuller Aerospace will be coming for him as soon as they find out he gave us this. Are you going to protect him?'

Rose shook her head.

'No. He made his own choices,' she said.

# Chapter Sixty-Nine

Michael sat at his desk, completely still. From the outside, he knew, he looked calm. Only the tight tendons on the back of his hands gave away his fury. The foil container of blek that Netsai had brought through to him lay on his desk, untouched. He stared down at it. He had given up his life for Rose, and she had thrown it back in his face. She had used him, and discarded him. But he wasn't done with her yet.

He stood, and pulled open the waste chute. From the thin gap in the wall behind it, and fished out his red pad.

A dozen messages from Dene were waiting for him, asking where he was, and why he hadn't signed in. His thumbs skittered across the screen's keyboard.

**Emergency**

Immediately, three bouncing dots appeared to show Dene was typing.

**What is it?**

**Someone leaked info on our campaign and FA's contingency plans for the Free Settlements**

Michael paused, waiting for Dene's reaction. There was no response. He pressed on.

**R and N plan to capitalise on the leak
They want to recruit Archie to support the Free Settlements**

Finally, the three dots reappeared.

**That can't happen**
**Archie can't turn on the Company**
**Stop them at all costs**

                                              **I can't**
                                **They don't trust me**
                      **They put me under room arrest**

**Are you safe?**

Michael hesitated, genuinely surprised at Dene's concern.

                                              **For now**

**Okay. Well keep watch**
**And make sure they don't get close to him**

                              **What are my orders**

**Send a full report and wait for instructions**
**Don't worry**
**We've got this**
**The new recruits are armed and ready**

Michael closed the messaging app, and created a blank document.
He stared at the white screen, imagining what would have happened if he had done nothing wrong, if someone else had leaked
the documents. If he had been taken by surprise, and if Rose and
Netsai had grown suspicious of him, and held him captive. He
played the fiction through in his head, imagining every moment
of it. And when he had enough details to make it feel true, he
began to write.

# Chapter Seventy

There were nine other kids on the Tycho mining base, aged from eight to sixteen, but Karl had barely spoken to any of them. They all played together, swinging like apes from the railings of the stairwell, but they never invited him to join in. They spoke to each other in their weird made-up language, like they were deliberately trying to cut him out of their conversation. And they were vandals, too. The faucets and light fittings were broken on the second level, and 'RR' and 'INDEPENDENCE' had been melted into the plastic walls of the corridors with a soldering iron.

And then there was the bolt. Karl had been sitting and reading a book about mining on a bench in the lower habitat, when a metal bolt flew down from the walkway and hit him on the scalp, just above the hairline. He touched the wound, and when he pulled his fingers away, they were red with blood. He heard laughter from the children above, but they were cut off by a yell from one of the new Company guards. He charged at them, his shiny black boots clattering on the metal, and the children scattered. When they were gone, the guard looked over the edge of the walkway at Karl, and raised his fist. Karl felt a thrill of recognition. He'd seen the gesture in the news reports about the Vanguards, the group that was going to save Mars. He raised his fist back to the guard solemnly.

That evening, Karl logged onto Fuller Aerospace's social network. He'd been avoiding it before that. Every time he said anything negative about the independence movement he was targeted by a hundred angry strangers, hounding and insulting him. This time, he stayed off his regular channels where people talked about games and movies and TV. He found a private channel for the Vanguards, and after sending an access request, he was thrilled to be allowed in.

By the end of the evening, he knew this was his new home. The people on the group accepted him. They encouraged him to say what he really thought about Rose and the Independents. It felt fun, and a little dangerous. It was more fun than any of the games he was playing.

**TRIAGE**
**I wish all the shit Red Rose spews was literal shit. Liquid sewage pouring out her mouth, filling her out-suit till she drowns. Ha ha**

**IRON GATE**
**Not painful enough**

**TRIAGE**
**I'd still love it, tho**

**IRON GATE**
**I heard the Free Settlements are deliberately trying to take down the passenger liners, to stop anyone new coming from Earth**

Karl nodded to himself. It was the kind of thing the Settlements would do.

**TRIAGE**
**I don't understand why Fuller Aerospace are letting them get away with it**

Karl took the opportunity to throw in his own opinion.

**KS**
**The Company's weak. They need a strong local leader**

**TRIAGE**
It's true. They need a local CEO. Without Alex Fuller around, no one else is strong enough to stand up to the Free Settlements

**KS**
What about Archie?

**TRIAGE**
Yeah. Archie could do it, if he stops messing around. He'll get Mars back on track

**IRON GATE**
Let me show you something

A photograph appeared on Karl's screen. It showed a line of six bulky black weapons laid out on the grey bedsheet, and twenty packs of ammunition.

**KS**
Where did you get that?

**TRIAGE**
Fake

**IRON GATE**
Not fake. We got an alert. The Free Settlements are going to try to get Archie Fuller. Me and the new recruits are ready for them

Karl chimed in excitedly.

**KS**
If they get near Archie, blow their heads off

**IRON GATE**
We'll do more than that, kid. We'll burst their bases. Take their mines. No Free Settlement will survive

**TRIAGE**
**Can't wait for them to try it**

**IRON GATE**
**Me too. Watch the news. Get ready for fireworks**

Karl smiled to himself as he folded up his pad. He turned out the lights, and stared up at the dark plastic ceiling. It was all getting real. It was exciting. The Vanguard was finally going to show Mars what it was capable of, and he was part of it.

# Part 7.0

---

# Scarecrows

# Chapter Seventy-One

Dylan sits on the front edge of the driver's seat, and flips the radio back on.

'Hello, Unwin?'

'Ward!' Comes the reply over the roar of the radio. 'Where did you disappear to? I've been trying to call you.'

'I had a bit of trouble with Clifford. Don't worry, he's tied up and muted now.'

From the seat next to Dylan, Clifford glares at her silently.

'That's good,' says Unwin, relieved. 'We've just departed Loyola. I'm in the back of a single-deck rover. You can't miss it, it has a red stripe and a Jesuit crest on the front. It's a picture of some wolves jumping up at a cauldron. It's all very medieval. I'm your knight in shining armour.'

Dylan only knows what a few of those words mean, but she gets the gist.

'We'll be there in less than an hour,' Unwin says. 'What are your plans?'

'I'm not sure. I'd love to crawl into the ballent and get some rest, but I should probably keep an eye on this guy. Oh, listen. Can you call up Company Territory again?'

'Sure,' says Unwin. Through the radio noise, she hears him unfolding his pad. 'Who do you want to talk to?'

'Try my dad. His name's Frank Ward, in Syria Base. He should be easy to find.'

She hears Unwin's fingers tapping on his screen. After a few minutes, he snorts in annoyance.

'He's not there.'

'Maybe he's left his pad turned off,' says Dylan. 'He does that.'

'That's not it. I'm getting an error from the system. It says there's no one of that name on the base. Are you sure I got it right? Frank Ward?'

Dylan frowns, trying to hold back the anxiety that always kicks in when Frank doesn't pick up her calls.

'Okay, let's try someone else. Security Manager Merrick, also in Syria.'

'Cool,' says Unwin. 'Give me a second.'

She hears three long beeps from Unwin's pad before a video call connects, and her former boss answers.

'Hi?' comes Merrick's voice, annoyed. 'Who is this?'

'Sorry to disturb you, Security Manager,' Unwin says. 'This is Unwin from the census bureau. I have an audio connection here with one of your guards.'

Dylan steadies her voice.

'Sir? This is Dylan Ward.'

'Ward?' he barks. 'Where are you? We've been trying to contact you for days!'

'Yes sir,' she says. 'I just heard.'

'I shouldn't even be talking to you until you're brought in. Karl Sealgair was looking for you.'

'I know sir. Where's my father? Is he all right?'

She hears Merrick draw a breath. 'I'm sorry about your father, Ward. I truly am.'

'What happened to my dad? ... Sir? ... Sir!'

Merrick doesn't answer. With a quiet chime, she hears the video call disconnect.

'Okay,' says Unwin. 'What was that about?'

Dylan feels a weight in her chest. She drums her gloved fingers silently on the edge of the cockpit controls.

'You're on all the Company's social channels, right?' she asks.

'Of course,' says Unwin.

'Can you do a search for my dad's name? See if there's any news about him.'

'Will do.'

He goes silent, and Dylan listens to the quiet roar of the static. After a few minutes, he clears his throat.

'Anything?'

'Yes,' he says. 'Ward ... I'm so, so sorry.'

# Chapter Seventy-Two

Frank Ward wakes up to see a huge armed guard with a black knife-proof jacket standing at the foot of his bed, staring down at him with all the charm and personality of a concrete post.

'Whoa, shit. Morning, Vinnie,' Frank says. That isn't the guard's real name, but Frank is determined to piss him off, so he's taken to calling him Vinnie 'Quicklime' Romano.

In the last three days Frank has only succeeded in pushing Vinnie too far once, by suggesting that he took a little too much radiation in the womb. He got a crack across the cheek with a nightstick for his trouble. Today, he's decided that he's going to monologue at Vinnie. That'll be good. He'll say every thought that comes through his head, and wear Vinnie down through total banality.

'You scared the daylights out of me,' he says, getting up out of his bunk. He lifts the grey fabric of his Company-issue sleeveless vest, and scratches his belly. 'Well done. But you'd probably look a lot scarier if you wore a mask. All good henchmen should wear masks, don't you think? More intimidating. And what do you need a face for? They're for expressing feelings, you know, the things other people have. Plus, when you're wearing a mask, the good guys don't have to feel guilty about mowing you down. Masks are in your future, I'm telling you. Oh, look at Burma munching! Look at him go.'

Frank shuffles to the table in the middle of the room and lifts the almost-hairless guinea pig out of its translucent crate. Burma barely seems to notice, and keeps chewing obsessively on a piece of green pepper from Frank's supper the night before.

'Any word from my daughter yet?' Frank asks.

Vinnie grunts.

'And how much longer are you going to be keeping me company?'

'As long as I have to,' Vinnie says woodenly.

Frank puts Burma back into the crate and gives Vinnie his biggest, least sincere smile.

'This relationship is getting co-dependent. You mustn't feel tied down by me. Why don't we go our separate ways, discover our real selves?'

'It'll be over once your traitor daughter's dead,' Vinnie says leadenly.

Frank keeps the smile on his face. He scratches the back of his head, giving Vinnie a full show of unwashed armpit hair. 'What's all this about "dead", now?'

Vinnie lashes out with his nightstick. He jabs it into Frank's abdomen without warning, and Frank doubles over and retches. Vinnie leans over him, smirking.

'I had the best news this morning. Sealgair's red-listed Clifford, and anyone who assisted him. You know what that means? No more of this wanted-alive bullshit. As soon as your daughter shows her face in Company Territory she's dead on sight. She's going to pay for what she did to Raul and Chen. I can't wait to see you make a joke out of that. One way or the other, I'll be laughing.'

He chuckles his way back to the corner of the bedroom.

Frank leans against the table, clutching at his belly and staring down at the almond-shaped bumps on the floor. He's heard Vinnie lie about a lot of things, like how much money he gets in bribes, and how many women on the base he's slept with, but as far as Frank can tell, he doesn't have the imagination for psychological torture.

Burma hops closer on the tabletop and sniffs Frank's fingertips. Frank picks him up gently and puts him back in the crate. The hairless little creature skitters around, searching for an escape route.

'I need the can,' Frank says, as he puts the lid back on the crate.

'After breakfast.'

'C'mon, Vinnie. You just whacked my bladder. I need to go.'

'I said no. Now shut up.'

Frank finds it surprisingly difficult to wet his own pants. He grew up on Clarke Base, and back when he was far too young to be drinking, he and his friends had a game called 'spotting'. The goal was to piss their own pants just a little, and let a single spot of urine through. When he tried it the first time he ended up with his pants thoroughly drenched. But in the years since then, he's built up a solid habit of not pissing himself in public, and it's a hard habit to break.

He thinks back to documentary footage of waterfalls back on Earth. Thousands of tons of water, falling, cascading, churning and hammering into a cool green pool below. Liquid drums down onto the plastic floor. Vinnie's upper lip rises in disgust, exposing rodent-like teeth.

'Oh Jesus,' says Vinnie. 'What the fuck's wrong with you?'

'I told you I was busting.'

Vinnie raises his nightstick, and steps into the puddle of Frank's piss.

'Shit!' he says, kicking the droplets off his boots. They're thick enough to protect the guards' toes from getting stood on, but they're only designed for indoor use, and they aren't waterproof. Vinnie steps around the rest of the puddle, and grabs Frank by the collar.

'I'm going to mop that up with your face.'

'Careful,' says Frank. 'You're on candid camera.'

Vinnie looks up at the security camera in the corner of the room, and snarls. He gives Frank a hard jab with the nightstick.

'Nobody cares what I do to you.'

Still, he yanks Frank's door open, and drags him out of the puddle of piss and into the corridor.

'You want everyone to see what you've done? Come.'

The bathrooms are on the other side of the cafeteria. At this time of the morning, it's roaring with the voices of the breakfast crowd. There are six long parallel tables filled with locals, eating and mingling and getting ready for the work day. Frank knows many of them, particularly the older ones who like to share a grumble, and when they see Vinnie dragging him into the room, they erupt into a ragged cheer. Frank spots his mates Ali and Hudson at the far table, pointing and laughing at the stain on his trousers. He forces a smile for his audience. He needs to put on a big show; big enough that Dylan will hear about it, no matter where she is.

By the far door on the other side of the cafeteria, a second guard is leaning against the wall and watching the crowd. Frank knows him. He's one of Dylan's friends, a guy called Yang. He isn't a bad guy, he just takes a bad guy's salary. Frank hopes that Yang can keep him alive through the next few minutes.

When they're halfway across the cafeteria, Frank pulls himself free from Vinnie's grip. He runs through a huddle of maintenance, workers knocking their coffees across the floor. The escape catches Vinnie by surprise. By the time he's unhooked the nightstick from his belt, Frank has pushed his way between more of the diners and climbed up onto the long table.

The room roars with laughter and surprise. Vinnie and Yang both yell at him, and one of the maintenance workers claws at his legs to slow him down. Frank runs down the table, back the way he came, stepping on trays and scattering plates. The whole cafeteria's attention is on him, and he sees some people holding up their pads to record him. He waves to them as he runs.

'Dylan!' he calls out to the cameras. 'It's a trap! You're red-listed!'

He reaches the end of the table. Vinnie charges towards him at ground level, pushing aside the people in the way, knocking plates and cutlery out their hands. He's younger and fitter than Frank, but his armour makes him less agile. He clambers up onto the table, but Frank dodges out his way, and Vinnie falls forward and crashes into the diners on the other side. Frank sees Yang circling around the edge of the room, trying to box him in. He climbs down onto the bench and hops over to the next table, dodging the hands of the patrons trying to stop him, keeping his movements unpredictable.

'Don't come back for me! Stay in the Settlements! Hide! Change your name!'

Yang lunges at him through the crowd, and raises a stun gun. Frank drops off the table and runs between the diners. A man next to him seems to sprout coiled wires and falls to the ground, shaking.

'Sorry lad,' Frank calls back to him as he runs. 'You can't trust the Company! What am I saying, this isn't a company! It's a dictatorship with nostalgia! Rise up! Fight the power!'

This is some real capering-jester-level shit, but he has to go big. This has to make the news.

'Come at me, you bastards! You won't pacify me. Dylan, if you come back I'll only embarrass you some more. You're free, so run!'

He darts through the jeering rabble and up onto the furthest table. The crowd is tiring of him now, and more of them are grabbing at him to slow him down. Mugs and plates fly though the air, and he ducks out of their way.

The exit to the rest of the base is up ahead, and Frank makes a break for it. But one of the diners reaches up and grabs the back of his shirt, and he finds himself being tugged backwards. He falls from the table, and rolls off a bench on his way down to the sticky cafeteria floor.

'Corporate lackey!' he shouts. 'Brown-nosing bastard!'

Vinnie wades through the crowd towards him, red-cheeked and shaking with fury, pushing aside everyone in the way. He pulls out his knife.

The diners around Frank scatter, and a metal tray clatters on the floor. Frank grabs it and stands up, whipping it at Vinnie like a frisbee. It flies true, hitting him across the face and gashing the bridge of his nose. The crowd whoops again.

'Holy shit! Did you see that!' says Frank, genuinely impressed with himself.

'I'll kill you!' Vinnie screams, elbowing people aside as he charges at Frank.

There's an explosion from a bolt gun behind him, and Frank feels a hard jolt from the back of his right leg, followed a second later by the kind of pain that robs him of speech. His leg buckles under him and he collapses to the floor. He looks up to see Yang pushing closer through the crowd with his bolt gun raised.

The pain in Frank's leg makes his ears ring. His vision is blurring. He hears his own voice, braying like a donkey. The diners are climbing up on the benches and tables all around to get a better view.

'Medic!' Yang calls into the crowd.

Vinnie comes to Yang's side, and looks down at Frank with a sneer.

'Don't bother the medics,' he says. 'It isn't worth it.'

He gives Frank a kick in the abdomen, and another in the face. Frank's world explodes into sparks. Another three kicks, and all thought is gone. As Frank's consciousness burns away, he hears Vinnie saying, 'Now, *that's* a job for a medic.'

# Chapter Seventy-Three

Frank's voice calls out through the radio static and the roar of a crowd.

'Dylan, if you come back I'll only embarrass you some more. You're free, so run!'

The rest of the audio is barely intelligible, except for the pop of a bolt gun, and Frank screaming. There's the distant sound of someone speaking, and then five stomach-churning thuds. Unwin gasps, and the audio cuts out.

'The video was recorded by someone in the canteen,' says Unwin. 'It's been shared over a thousand times.'

'When did it happen?'

'Yesterday.'

Dylan stares in silence at the switches on the control desk in front of her. A furious guilt is rising inside her, and hot tears well in her eyes. She blinks them away angrily.

'What happened at the end of the clip?' she says. 'Is he still ...?'

'I don't know,' comes Unwin's apologetic voice. Dylan can hear his pad clicking as he types on it. 'I'm checking the news feeds, but no one's saying anything other than he was taken to the medical bay.'

'But what did it look like?'

'It ... wasn't good.'

Dylan grits her teeth, and glares down at the buttons of the control desk.

'Ward?' Unwin says eventually. His voice is strained. 'I'm sorry to ask this right now, but if you've been red-listed ... Am I red-listed too?'

Dylan shakes her head slowly.

'No idea. Maybe. You abandoned your post and followed Clifford's orders, like I did.'

'No,' he mumbles. 'No no no no. Sealgair knows we're trustworthy. We're capturing Clifford for him.'

'You might be okay,' says Dylan. 'I killed Company guards. I don't know if I'm getting out of that one.'

Dylan glances over at Clifford. He can't hear them, but when he sees her looking at him, he raises an eyebrow.

'What have you heard about Sealgair?' Dylan says.

'I know you don't mess with him.'

'You heard about his hunting trips? Where he goes into the Free Settlements to kill enemies of the Company?'

The radio whistles.

'We should call him back,' Unwin says.

'And say what?' asks Dylan, with her eyes still on Clifford. '"Sorry sir, I'd just like you to reassure me that you're not going to execute me"?'

'But what else can you do?' Unwin says desperately. 'You can't side with Clifford over Sealgair!'

From the cockpit seat, Clifford stares at Dylan fixedly.

'Hold on,' she says to Unwin, and unplugs the radio cable from her suit. She uses her forearm controls to reconnect her suit's radio to Clifford.

'Finally,' she hears him say.

'No,' Dylan says firmly, holding up her palm. 'Don't make me regret talking to you. I need some answers, and if I think you're lying to me or leaving out any important details, I'm hitting "mute" and it's never coming off.'

'I'm glad you've found such a deep well of trust.'

Dylan raises her finger and holds it over the control pad on her forearm.

'Fine,' he says. 'What do you want to know?'

'What were we really looking for out here?' she says. 'Why would Sealgair red-list us for it?'

Clifford raises his eyes to the roof of the cockpit, and takes a deep breath.

'Decades ago, there was a criminal investigation called Project Granite. Sealgair closed it. I reopened it.'

'What was it?'

He hesitates before answering.

'It was an investigation into the murder of Archie Fuller.'

Dylan grips the edge of the console in fury. It feels like the walls of the cockpit are moving around her.

'That's what all this is about?' she says through gritted teeth. Her voice rasps. 'Some kind of conspiracy theory?'

'It's not a theory,' Clifford says calmly.

Dylan hangs her head until her forehead touches the cold glass of her helmet, and closes her eyes. Clifford is insane. She should have realised it on the evening they first met. Everything he's put her through, everything that happened to her dad, was all because she hadn't spotted the flicker of insanity in his eyes. She feels nausea rising inside her; a dangerous sensation in an out-suit. She bites the side of her lip, and tears of rage well in her eyes. She has been so, so stupid. She should have seen the signs.

'Large parts of the initial reports were fabricated. Archie Fuller wasn't—'

'Stop!' Dylan barks, snapping open her eyes. 'It doesn't matter what you believe. It's history. You got us killed for history!'

Clifford is unfazed. 'Archie Fuller's murder is where everything started. The Collapse. The Free Settlements. The Outliers. It's the spark that lit the furnace that we're all burning in.'

Dylan raises her hands in claws of frustration.

'Who cares?' she yells. 'Why do you care? Why would Sealgair care?'

Clifford breathed out slowly, making his microphone rumble.

'If you want my guess, he's scared.'

'Why?'

'The Free Settlements have always had more land than us, and more bases, and more weapons. The only reason they haven't crushed the Company yet is because of our reputation. We paint ourselves as the enlightened ones, the defenders of civilisation.

If anything threatens that reputation, if anyone tries to correct history, Sealgair steps in.'

Dylan turns away and stares down at the glass-strewn floor of the cockpit. It takes all her concentration to control her own breathing, until she can talk with measured breaths.

'It doesn't matter one way or the other,' she says. 'All that matters is that we get out of this. Somehow.'

Clifford doesn't speak. He just tilts his head and stares at her like a teacher waiting for a pupil to solve an equation.

Dylan squeezes her eyes closed. The *thud, thud, thud* of the internal pump circulating liquid through her suit sounds like her father being beaten down by the Company guards.

'Wait.'

Her eyes snap open. She mutes Clifford again, and plugs herself in to the AM radio.

'Unwin?'

'I'm here,' comes his voice through the radio's howl.

'You need to help me,' she says. 'I'm pretty sure that there's a place in the Free Settlements that'll take me in. I don't think even Clifford knows about it. I need you to help me escape.'

'You're siding with Clifford?'

'No. I'll leave him here for Sealgair to pick up. If he has his prize, there's a chance that he won't bother following me. I just need you to help me get out of here.'

Out of the side of her eye, she can see that Clifford is still watching her. She hopes he can't read lips.

'You can't run from Sealgair,' Unwin says over the radio.

'I can. Just give me a lift to the nearest Free Settlement.'

'I can't,' Unwin whispers, heartfelt.

'Then I'll go on foot,' says Dylan. 'Just promise you won't chase me. Please.'

'I swore an oath to the Comp—'

The radio connection cuts out.

'Unwin!' says Dylan. She adjusts the volume dial on the radio. The noise of the static rises, but the census taker is silent.

'Unwin!' she shouts, standing up from the driver's seat.

She yanks the radio cable out of her chest-plate in frustration.

Clifford starts rocking his body back and forward. Dylan glares down at him, but he doesn't stop. He's staring out of the cockpit window ahead of them, and he keeps rocking, making his whole seat shake.

Dylan reconnects the audio connection to his suit.

'What's your problem?' she says.

'Look,' says Clifford. His eyes stare fixedly ahead.

Dylan turns to look out of the shattered cockpit window. Rising up over the eastern horizon is a plume of dust.

'How long has that been there?'

'I don't know,' says Clifford. 'I've been a little distracted.'

Dylan stares at the dust cloud. There's no wind outside, so any dust that the vehicle leaves would be hanging in a long trail behind it. To make a dust trail appear this thin, the vehicle would have to be driving straight towards them.

'Is it Sealgair?' says Dylan. 'Or Unwin?'

'No.' Clifford shakes his head in his helmet. 'Wrong direction.'

Dylan catches her first glimpse of the vehicle. It's still over a kilometre away, but already she can see that there's something off about it. It's driving into the evening sunlight, but there are no reflections from any windows. At this distance, it looks like a jagged black cage.

'Check the sides,' Clifford says.

Dylan turns to the plate-sized hole that the cannon punched in the wall of the upper deck. She presses her helmet against the torn plastic and metal, and looks outside. A second cloud of dust is rising straight up in the south.

'There's another one,' she says.

'We're being hunted,' says Clifford. 'It's the Outliers.'

# Chapter Seventy-Four

Dylan leans over the control desk and gives power to the motors. Rudolf lurches forward, and jolts left and right aimlessly as its wheels hit random rocks on the dusty plain. Dylan pulls on the control stick, but gets no response. The steering system is still dead, and they're heading right towards the first dark rover.

She stretches over to the left side of the control desk and flips the switch to channel independent power to each of the wheel motors then cuts off the middle wheel on the left side. The wheels on the right are now more powerful, and Rudolf's nose swings to the left, and straightens out again when she powers the motor back up. They're heading roughly north-west, away from their two pursuers.

Rudolf bounces over the uneven ground, its nose swinging right and left randomly with every bump. Dylan hovers her hand over the control desk, flipping the motor switches on and off to keep them on course. She feels a cold sweat of motion sickness creeping over her.

The rear monitor is dead. Clifford twists in his straps, trying to look behind them through the holes in the hull.

'How far are they?'

Dylan turns to look. Through the cannon hole, she sees a thick plume of dust rising up in the light of the early evening.

'Getting closer.'

She keeps correcting the angle of the wheels. Left. Left. Right. Left again.

'Up ahead,' says Clifford, staring out of the cockpit window. Just under a kilometre away, a third rover is perched at the top of a low rocky hill, about twenty metres up.

He squints into the light of the setting sun.

'Is that the Outliers?'

Dylan stares into the light reflecting off the side of it, and sees a streak of red.

'No,' she says. 'It's Unwin. Hang on.'

She adjusts the power to the wheel motors and swings their nose around again, aiming for the hill. Rudolf bounds over the rocky terrain, and Dylan grips the edge of the desk to keep herself in her seat. As they get near to the gleaming rover, Dylan plugs her radio cable back in.

'Unwin!' she says. 'Forget Sealgair, we need to work together. We've got Outliers!'

There's no response, except the background roar of static.

Dylan cranes her neck, and sees a pair of orange out-suits on the hilltop.

'They're outside the vehicle,' says Clifford.

'What are they doing?' she says. 'If they've had a break-down, we're dead.'

Rudolf grinds up the low hill. Every rock it bounces over sets it off-course, and giving power to the correct motors takes all of Dylan's concentration.

'How far are the Outliers?' says Clifford.

Dylan glances around. She can see the black cage vehicle clearly now, riding around the bottom of the hill. It's welded together from carbon fibre and scrap metal, skeletal and lopsided, and it has no pressure cabin. A driver in an out-suit rides on top of it, pulling control cables by hand. It's a jury-rigged nightmare. Behind it, a similar-looking rover is approaching from the south, with its rider inside an empty roll cage. Both Outlier rovers are slowing down, and the drivers are staring up at them through dark visors.

'Why are they stopping?' Dylan asks.

'Because they've already caught us,' Clifford says quietly, staring ahead. As they approach the top of the hill, Dylan sees Unwin and his driver properly for the first time. They're both standing perfectly still, with their arms outstretched. Their backs are against metal poles driven into the hilltop. Cables come down from the poles, looping around their arms and throats, holding them upright. Their helmets have been removed, and their frost-covered eyes stare blankly at the vast landscape below. They're scarecrows.

'Shit,' Dylan whispers.

She slams Rudolf's motors into reverse, and the wheels shoot dust and stones ahead as they ride backwards.

A third Outlier rides into view from its hiding place behind the shining Loyola rover. Like the others it's barely welded together, but it moves significantly faster than Rudolf.

'Right!' say Clifford.

Dylan twists around and sees that they're rolling backwards towards a boulder. She flips the control switches, but not fast enough, and Rudolf collides with it. Dylan is thrown across the control desk, and Rudolf slides sideways down the hillside.

She pulls herself back to her seat. The two other Outliers are driving around them, blocking their escape.

Weapons are mounted on their tops and sides. Dylan recognises custom-made rail guns and explosive wall-busters. She has one desperate chance to outmanoeuvre them. As the rovers approach, Dylan forces Rudolf's nose around and charges at the gap between them. But they're too fast for her, and the gap closes.

She steers to the right, but the rover coming down from the hilltop rams into Rudolf from behind. Rudolf spins, and Dylan is knocked against Clifford. The sides of their helmets collide, and Dylan falls to the floor by the hatch. She grabs the top of the ladder to pull herself to her feet, and looks out of the broken cockpit window. The impact has spun them fully around to face the hill, and all three Outlier rovers are circling them. Dylan flips the switches to give the motors full power, but there's no response.

'The electrics are dead,' she says flatly. She's surprised at how calm she suddenly feels. She unstraps the bolt gun from her leg, and checks the chamber.

'Two more rounds. You want the easy way out?'

'Cut me loose,' says Clifford.

'What?'

'I'm not going to die tied to a seat. Cut me loose.'

'No.'

'I don't want to trust you either, but we have no choice.'

'Wait,' says Dylan. 'I need to know something. It's important. I know a picture of Red Rose won't save us, but do you think the Outliers still care about her?'

'Probably,' he says. 'Maybe.'

'And how much do you think they remember about her life?'

Clifford hesitates.

'No idea.'

'Then it's worth a try.'

Dylan puts the bolt gun down and scrabbles in the seat-side pouch. She finds the pad of notepaper that she used to communicate with Olympus, and flips over the top page. She takes the lid off the marker, which immediately starts to dry out in the thin atmosphere.

'What are you writing?'

Dylan doesn't answer. She presses the marker hard on the page, forcing the ink onto the paper, and writes a message.

The cockpit fills with flying debris, and her headset crackles with static. Plate-sized bullet holes explode through the wall next to her, and she drops to the ground. The writing pad falls at her side. Metal and plastic shrapnel drums down on her suit and helmet. White gas blows up through the hatch next to her. A gas line on the lower deck is severed, and within seconds Rudolf is filled with a blinding fog.

'Dylan?' says Clifford over the radio. 'Still there?'

'Still here.'

The roar of escaping gas subsides, and the fog in the cabin starts to thin. Rudolf begins to shake slightly on its suspension.

'You feel that?' she says.

'They're on board,' says Clifford.

A helmet comes up through the hatch. It's white, marked with dark-brown streaks of dried blood running down from the top of its dome. The black sun-visor is down. A hand holding a bolt gun rises up next to it, with the barrel pointed at Dylan.

She scrambles for the writing pad on the floor, and holds up the barely readable message. The faceless Outlier's bolt gun stays raised, but doesn't fire. After a few seconds, the gun shakes impatiently. Dylan drops the pad on the cockpit floor and raises her hands. The suited figure climbs the rest of the way up onto the deck, and stands on the other side of the hatch with the weapon aimed at Dylan. She climbs down slowly, with the bolt gun trained on her the whole way.

Another Outlier is waiting for her on the lower deck, also wearing a blood-streaked suit. It holds up a long, curved knife, and points down the corridor towards the rear hatch. Dylan walks, but she isn't fast enough for the Outlier, who shoves her onward.

The sun outside is setting, and the light is getting dim. Dylan drops down from Rudolf's hatch. The three Outlier vehicles are parked around her, looming like mechanical insects. A driver stands on the back of the middle one, with a bolt gun pointed down at Dylan.

Clifford comes out of the hatch behind her, shoved ahead of the Outlier from the corridor. The one from the upper deck follows them out. It points at Dylan, and then holds up the pad, so the other two Outliers can read the almost-illegible message for themselves.

Clifford sees the message, too. Through the reflection in his helmet Dylan can barely see his face, but she hears him draw a breath.

**I AM NET AI CHIW SA'S GRA DDA GHT R**

He stares at her, confounded.

'Dylan,' he says. 'If we live long enough, we're going to need a proper talk.'

# Part 7.5

---

# The First Murder On Mars

# Chapter Seventy-Five

Netsai and Rose stood at the bottom of a giant dune and watched the distant figure of Archie Fuller surfing down towards them. The sun was setting behind him, barely visible through the dust of the storm, and the sky glowed orange.

'We shouldn't have agreed to this,' Netsai said, looking up at the darkened sky. The drifting dust was painting her suit a dirty red.

Rose kept watching Archie.

'Don't worry. The storm isn't dangerous. The Company wouldn't have let Archie off his leash if it was. And I don't know when we're going to get another chance to talk to him privately.'

The dune was the size of a skyscraper, and Archie was riding a sandboard down it, slaloming and jumping over the ripples streaked across its sides. He was making Rose wait. His open-topped dune buggy was driving automatically down the slope a hundred metres away. It reached the bottom of the dune before he did, and rolled to a stop next to Rose's rover, ready to carry Archie back up for another round.

By now, Rose knew Netsai well enough to hear when she was rolling her eyes. She didn't have to sigh aloud any more, but she did anyway.

Archie snaked down to the bottom of the dune and skidded to a halt in front of the two of them, throwing up a shower of sand that whipped away in the wind. Once again, Rose and Netsai had to wait for him as he unclipped the sandboard from his boots. He pressed a button on his arm, and their radios paired with a soft chime.

'How was the ride?' Rose asked.

Archie straightened up. 'Not great. The headwind slowed me

down a bit. But look at this scenery! You don't get anything like this on Earth!'

He waved an arm at the majestic waves of gold and orange sand. Netsai folded her arms.

'Any particular reason why you wanted to meet us all the way out here?' she said.

'What? Isn't it amazing? Just look around you! If Rose wants a private place for a family reunion, I can't do better than this!' He looked Netsai up and down. 'Sorry, what was your name again?'

'Netsai Chiwasa,' said Netsai, shifting her weight uncomfortably.

'Oh yeah. Hi,' he said flatly, and turned back to Rose. 'We need to keep this private. If the Company finds out I'm meeting with you then we'd be crawling with security guards. You know they're calling you terrorists.'

'Did you read those documents I sent you?' said Rose.

'Yeah, I glanced through them,' said Archie.

'Did you know about any of it? The plan to hack the Settlements' life-support?'

'Nah,' said Archie. 'I don't believe that's real. The Company would never go through with it. I wish you well, but I'm not taking sides between the Settlements and the Company.'

'You're going to have to,' said Netsai.

Rose put a gentle hand on her arm, and turned to Archie. She spoke to him calmly.

'You're all about freedom, right? You want the Mars that Dad promised? Because we've got the proof that the Company is blocking that.'

Archie bit his lip. He drummed his fingers on his suit's breast-plate.

Rose pressed on. 'When this news gets out, there's going to be a lot of angry people on Mars. You don't want your name associated with a planned genocide.'

'So what do you want me to do? Start wearing a beret and a red T-shirt?'

'We just want you to support the Settlements,' Netsai said. 'Is that so hard?'

'I told you. I don't do politics.'

'Just sell your shares,' said Rose. 'Show the world that the Fuller family doesn't support the Company any more. They've stolen our name.'

'I'm not giving up my shares.'

'Come on, Archie,' said Rose. 'Do you want to make more money, or do you want respect? Because there's a lot of ways for you to make cash, but if the respect goes, it's gone for good.'

'Rose, we've been through all this,' Archie said, talking down to her. Even though they were twins, he was always playing older brother. 'Mars can't survive an economic crash, and the economy is Fuller Aerospace. I'm trying to protect it.'

Rose could see her brother's face through the tinted glass of his helmet. The muscles around his jaw were tense.

'You're scared,' she said.

'I'm not.'

'We're asking you to show the world who you really are. You're scared.'

Archie choked out a laugh.

'I know what I am! I've done something with my life! Who are you, Rose? The saviour of Mars? Who are you fooling? Dad would be ashamed.'

It was like a gut punch, and it knocked Rose silent. She felt her eyes sting, and had to turn away from him.

'Oh, hey,' said Archie, suddenly sincere. 'I'm sorry. That was low. Rose? I didn't mean that.'

Netsai put a hand on Rose's shoulder.

'You okay?'

Rose nodded silently in her helmet. Netsai faced Archie, who was bowing his head.

'You're both symbols,' she said to him. 'For better or worse, millions of people care what you do. So what are you going to be? Are you going to represent all the rich kids, entertaining themselves at all our expense? Or are you going to be a hero to the people of Mars?'

Rose breathed in deeply through her nose, and out through her mouth. She stared down at the sand in front of her feet until the thud of the heartbeat in her ears died away. When she felt ready, she straightened up, and looked her brother in the eyes.

'We can do what Dad never did,' she said. 'We can make the future real.'

They were level with each other, and she could see herself reflected in the curved glass of Archie's helmet: a tiny figure in the dead centre, surrounded by dust. And above it, high up on the dune behind her, a row of shifting shadows.

'Who's that?' Archie said, pointing over her head. She turned, and saw four rovers snaking their way down the dune.

'Are they with you?'

'Not us,' said Rose.

'Then it must be Company security,' he muttered.

The rovers had the Fuller Aerospace logo printed on their sides, and were fitted with railed platforms on their roofs. Rose could make out black-suited figures standing on the platforms, and each one was holding a long black tool that looked a bit like a drill. Rose had never seen a gun in real life before and she stared in cold horror. She couldn't believe that the Fuller Aerospace security guards now had the power to kill.

The rovers slid to a stop at the bottom of the dune twenty metres from the three of them, and four more black-suited armed guards climbed out. A chime played in Rose's ear as their radios connected.

'You're trespassing in Fuller Aerospace Territory. Back away from Archimedes Fuller,' said a voice. All the guards' visors were down, and she couldn't tell which of them was speaking.

'This isn't necessary,' Archie said, but one of the guards spoke over him.

'I said back away!'

The black-suited guards ran towards Rose and Netsai, with their weapons in their hands.

'Release Archie Fuller now, and place your hands on your helmets.'

'It's a set-up,' Netsai muttered.

'These guards aren't with me,' Archie said. He stepped in the way of the guards, and held up the palms of his gloves to slow them down. 'Hey! Will someone explain what's going on? Who's in charge here?'

The guards reached Archie, and one of them raised his black outer visor. In the dusk light, Rose saw the face of a man with a blond crew cut.

'Sir, we're from Fuller Aerospace Security Services. The Free Settlements have kidnapped an employee of a PR firm we work with, and we know they have a plan to target you. These two are a direct danger.' He pointed past Archie, at Rose and Netsai. 'I said hands on helmets!'

'Where are you getting your intel? This is my sister and her friend. No one's kidnapping anyone.'

'We were invited here,' said Rose.

The guard leader pushed Archie aside easily, and strode towards Rose and Netsai.

'You're on land assigned to Fuller Aerospace for mining exploration. Under agreement with the United States, Russian, Chinese and Indian governments, we have the right to arrest you and transport you to Earth for trial.'

'This is insane,' Rose looked back at Archie, desperately. 'We haven't kidnapped anyone. Archie, tell them.'

'Rose,' he said. 'I don't—'

He was cut short by a tremble in the ground. Rose felt it through her boots, and saw the sand rippling all around them. The guards raised their guns and pointed them at Rose and Netsai.

'Look,' Netsai said, pointing up above their heads. The dune that Archie had surfed down was moving. His stunt had disturbed the sand, and now, in complete silence, an arch-shaped line was crawling up the dune. Above the line the sand was still. Below it, sand was pouring down in a torrent, throwing up dust. Thousands of tonnes of it, sliding towards them.

'Avalanche!' a guard shouted.

There was no time to move before the front of the wave hit. Rose's legs were knocked out from under her, and her body twisted like a doll as the sand churned on all sides, crushing and burying her. It crashed over her helmet, and the world went dark. She felt the weight of it hammering into her, squeezing her from all sides.

'All guards report!' came a voice in her ear.

The sand slowed, and the roar of it against her helmet grew dull, until the world around her locked solid. Her cheek was pressing against her helmet glass. She was buried on her side.

She pushed outwards with her left arm, and her hand burst free of the surface. She clawed at the sand, digging around her helmet until she saw light shining in through it's left side. She twisted herself until half her body was free. The air was murky from dust, and flying sand sizzled against the glass of her helmet.

The avalanche wasn't over yet. A hundred metres away, another wave of sand was coming loose, pouring down into the valley between the dunes.

Rose tugged her right arm free, and pushed the sand off her legs. As she rolled up onto her hands and knees, she saw the second wave of avalanche hit the valley floor and churn outwards towards her. Rose's rover was halfway between her and the avalanche. The torrent of sand hit the rover's side, pushing against it. The rover skated ahead of the roaring sand, sliding towards her, faster and faster. She wanted to jump out of the way, but the rumbling ground below her was soft, and her legs began to sink. She pushed herself up to her feet and waded forward, step by painful step, as the rover accelerated towards her. With one final push she lurched out of its way. The rover coasted past her sideways, pushed by a wave of sand.

'Rose?' came Netsai's voice. 'Where are you?'

Rose looked around, but could barely see anything in the thick red dust.

'Near the rover.'

'Get to it,' Netsai said. 'We need to go.'

The ground trembled again. The sand on the other side of the valley was now coming loose, and pouring down towards them.

The rover came to a stop fifty metres ahead of her. Rose's legs were dead weights as she waded down the valley towards it. Sand crashed down on either side, threatening to bury her. The sun was setting, and the world was getting dark.

She was five metres from the rover when a spotlight shone onto her from behind, casting her shadow on its metal side. And not just one shadow; she turned to see Netsai and Archie's suits trudging closer through the sand. Behind them, the spotlight shone down from the gun platform of one of the Company rovers. Faint shapes were running and stumbling below it. In her radio headset, all the guards were talking at once, swearing and barking orders.

'Don't let them get away! Keep them in the spotlight!'

'I've got a clear shot!'

'Stop them!'

'Get down! Hands where we can see them!'

A flash of gunfire lit up the blurring dust, coming from a guard rover platform. There was a loud crackle in Rose's headset. When it cleared, she heard Netsai's voice.

'They're shooting!'

'Run!' said Archie. 'Get to the rover!'

'Down on the ground!' said the guard captain.

More muzzle flashes came from the darkness around the spotlight, and more static buzzed over the radio.

Archie broke away from Rose and Netsai. He waded towards the spotlight with his hands raised, as high as the arms of his out-suit would let him.

'Stop!' he shouted. 'Don't shoot! They aren't a threat. You're making this worse!'

'Out of the way!' said the voice of a guard. 'You're blocking the shot!'

'I told you to stand down—'

There was another muzzle flash, and Rose saw Archie's body dropping into the boiling sand.

'Archie!'

The sand sucked at Rose's legs as she waded towards him. More guns flashed in the darkness. The ground shook as another wave of sand poured down onto the Company rovers, and the spotlight swung away.

For a long moment, there was nothing. And then Rose heard a whisper, almost too quiet to hear.

'Oh God,' came Netsai's voice. The horror in it was unmistakable. 'Speak to me. Come on.'

Rose stared into the roiling darkness. Netsai was limping towards her, dragging Archie behind her. Rose ran to him. His helmet was cracked open, and through it she could see his pasty face, gashed red.

'Help me,' said Netsai.

Rose grabbed an arm of Archie's suit, and the two of them pulled him to the back of Rose's small rover. The hatch was swinging open, and the dust in the inside was ankle high.

The rover was basic. There was a main cabin that took up most of the space, suit storage and a chemical toilet on the left side, a small sleeping cabin on the right, and a driver's seat and control desk up at the front. The roof wasn't high enough for them to stand up straight. They laid Archie down in the main cabin, and Rose slammed the hatch closed behind them. Netsai climbed to the front, and tapped on the control screen to repressurise the interior. The vents in the roof hissed, and the air filled with dust. It was everywhere: on the console, around the driver's seat, and in the small sleeping cabin on the side.

'We've got to clear out the sand,' said Netsai. 'It's toxic.'

'There's no time. Archie can't breathe!'

Rose knew she was in denial, but she clawed at the clasps of his helmet, swearing under her breath at her clumsy gloves. She tore Archie's helmet off, and his head lolled backwards on the sandy floor of the rover. His eyes were open, and the broken glass had left a deep cut across his cheek and his nose.

She put the balls of her wrists onto his chest-plate and pushed down, trying to start his heart, but the torso of the suit was rigid. In desperation she fumbled at her own clasps, and pulled her helmet off. The cabin was still freezing from the outside air, and the dust made her sputter. She leaned in over Archie, pinched his bleeding nose, and put her lips against his. She blew air into his lungs, then took a deep breath and did it again, and again, hoping he would cough and start breathing. But his face stayed limp, and his lips stayed cold.

'Come on!' she shouted down at him.

The spotlight shone on her through the round window in the rear hatch. The Company rovers were getting close, and another burst of silent machine-gun fire lit the dusty air.

'Drive!' said Rose.

Netsai gave power to the motors. The rover was designed for this kind of terrain. The half buried wheels were wide and deep, and the treads got traction. They jolted up from the sand and pulled away, weaving erratically down the valley between the dunes.

The spotlight followed them, casting their shadow onto the dunes ahead. In front of them, the valley split into two. Netsai aimed towards the left side, and at the last possible moment she switched off their rover's lights, and swung hard right. The spotlight lost them in the dust, and they rode blindly down the right fork.

Behind them, Rose could see the spotlight swinging and searching. After a few minutes, she lost all sight of it in the darkness.

Netsai turned their headlights to the dimmest setting, and they drove forward through the dunes. Rose sat up from Archie's body, and pushed herself away until her backpack pressed against the cabin wall. She put on her helmet again, and sealed it closed.

Netsai kept driving in silence, winding her way through the deep valleys. There was no GPS, and no stars to navigate by. Compasses didn't work on Mars. From here on out, Netsai and Rose were driving blind.

# Chapter Seventy-Six

Netsai chose her way randomly down the branching paths between the dunes. Left. Left. Right. Left again. Rose slid along the
wall of the rover's main cabin to get closer to Netsai, and to keep
herself away from her brother's body.

'What do we do?' she whispered.

'How am I meant to know, Rose?' Netsai snapped. Then she
took a deep breath and said, 'I'm so sorry. I don't know. I wish I
did, but I don't.'

Rose kneeled next to her, and put a hand on the side of the
rover's touch-screen console. It was currently lit up with diagnostic
information about the rover's motors.

'Can I look up something?' she said.

'Go for it.'

Rose touched a button in the upper left corner of the screen,
bringing it back to the main menu. She selected the Company
news portal, and a list of thumbnails came up to illustrate recent
reports. Most of them showed Archie's face. Rose jabbed at one
of them randomly with her gloved finger, and the thumbnail
expanded to fill the screen.

'Fuller Aerospace Security Service guards have just called in to
Mariner Base, reporting that Archimedes "Archie" Fuller, the son
of Alex Fuller, the founder of the Company, is dead.'

The screen cut to dark, grainy footage of the valley between
the dunes. Sand was sliding down on either side, and a group of
armed Fuller guards was running away from the camera in the
foreground. A spotlight swung across the scene, and for a brief
moment, two figures in suits were visible in the distance, dragging
a limp body towards the open back of a half buried rover.

The voice-over came in again.

'This is footage recorded from one of the Company rovers. Details are still coming in, but from the guard team's initial report, Fuller was killed in the dunes thirty kilometres north of Aries Base in what seems to be an ambush by members of the radical Martian independence group led by Archimedes' sister, Rose Fuller.'

The footage cut back to a freeze-frame, and zoomed in. In the enhanced shot, Rose Fuller's blurry face was visible through the glass of her helmet, straining under the weight of Archie's body.

'The Company is severing its diplomatic ties with the Free Settlements. Members of the independence movement on Company bases are being brought in by Security Services for questioning—'

'They're framing us,' said Rose flatly.

Netsai turned off the video, and pulled the rover to a stop. She hung her head, and put both hands on the glass of her helmet.

'They don't even have to try,' she said. 'They just have to suggest we're murderers, and people will believe it.'

Rose put a gloved hand on her shoulder, as gently as she could.

'We need to tell the world what really happened, fast, or this is going to get out of hand,' she said.

'Who?' said Netsai, still covering her face. 'Who could we tell? Who would listen? Who could stop this?'

'My mother.'

Netsai dropped her hands from her helmet. Her eyes darted over Rose's face for a few seconds, and she nodded.

Rose brought up the communication menu, and logged into her profile. After a minute Kelly Fuller's face appeared on the rover's screen. Her eyes were lined with red, and her cheeks were pale. Behind her was the ceiling of their private quarters on Aries Base, with its fire-opal chandelier.

'Rose?' she said. Her voice was shaking. 'What did you do?'

Up until that moment Rose had been able to control herself, but at the sound of her mother's voice cracking with despair, her eyes started to prickle.

'No, Mom. It was Company guards. They shot Archie, Mom.'

'Why were you fighting? Why did you drag him into this? Why—?'

Her voice broke down into sobs.

'Mom!'

But it was too late. The screen blacked out, and returned to the communication menu. Kelly Fuller had disconnected the call.

Rose's eyes were streaming. She pulled off her helmet again, and wiped them on the back of her thick gloves.

'We can go back to Mariner,' she said. 'If they try to arrest us, we can tell everyone what happened.'

Netsai took off her own helmet, and swung herself around on the driver's seat to face Rose. She put her arms around her, and leaned in so that their foreheads were touching.

'Rose,' Netsai said. 'I'm sorry. No one will believe us.'

'But it's the truth!'

Netsai untied the braids from the back of her head, and shook them out.

'You can't rely on that, not when this much is at stake for the Company. This is their chance to bury the Free Settlements. They won't give us a fair trial. You heard those guards. They want us gone.'

Rose felt her mind filling with cold lead.

'What else can we do?' she said. 'We can't hide in any of the Free Settlements. The Company can track us.'

Netsai pulled away from Rose and turned back to the rover's console. She opened up the command tools on the menu, and deactivated the radio connection.

'Not any more.'

'And the survey satellites?'

'They can't see us in the global storm. We'll be safe for another month, at least.'

'They'll find us,' said Rose stubbornly. 'If we run, we'll look guilty.'

'We already look guilty.'

'We've got evidence!' said Rose desperately. 'Archie's body! We can prove that he was shot by the guards' guns!'

360

'The bullet clipped his faceplate and cracked the glass. We have no proof the guards did it. All we have is a shattered helmet.'

In the light shining up from the console, Netsai's face looked far older and sadder than Rose had ever seen it.

'So it's their word against ours,' said Rose.

'No. It's their word against nothing. They wanted a war, and this is how they'll get it.'

Rose buried her face in her hands.

# Chapter Seventy-Seven

Over the next hour the dunes around them grew smaller, until the dusty rover rolled onto harder ground. Netsai kept driving for a few more kilometres in a direction that they hoped was north, until the eroded wall of a low plateau appeared ahead of them. Scattered at the foot of it were hundreds of boulders, worn smooth by millennia of Martian winds.

'We should stop,' said Rose. 'We need to get rid of all this dust.'

They pulled up next to a huge rock, about thirty metres long, eroded into a shape that reminded Rose of a surfacing whale. The two of them put their helmets back on and opened the rear hatch of the vehicle. Rose took Archie under his arms, and Netsai took his legs. They carried his body out slowly, and laid it on the dark ground. When the back of the rover was empty, they took two hand-brushes from the utility kit and started sweeping out all the poisonous dust and sand. It was everywhere, on every surface, wedged in the gaps between the wall panels and the ridges on the floor. They gathered and removed as much of it as they could, and when they couldn't collect any more, the two of them stood over Archie's body. Rose started to pick him up by the arms, but Netsai reached out a hand to stop her.

'Wait. Are you sure you want to put him back in there?'

Rose hadn't thought about it. She wasn't ready to say goodbye to her brother, but she didn't know how much longer their journey would be, or how much longer she could bear being in close confines with his body.

'We'll bury him,' she decided.

She walked to the front of the rover, and searched in the light of the headlights. About twenty metres ahead, between the fallen rocks at the base of the plateau, she found a boulder half her height jutting out of the ground. It was thinner than it was wide, and with a bit of imagination she could call it a headstone.

'Over here.'

Together, Rose and Netsai pulled Archie's body to the base of the boulder, and covered it with helmet-sized stones. When they were done, they stood together at the foot of the simple grave.

'I'll come back for him once we fix all this,' Rose said quietly, to reassure herself.

Netsai put a gentle hand on her shoulder, and led her back to the rover. They climbed inside, and when it was fully repressurised, they began the laborious process of taking off their suits. Slowly, methodically, they removed their helmets, gloves, packs, outer tops, outer legs, and inner linings. They put back on the clothes they had been wearing before, Netsai's stylish customised flight suit, and Rose's neo-paisley frock and sweater. They stowed the pieces of their suits in the correct wall-mounted compartments, and plugged the rover's internal umbilicals into the packs to recharge and re-gas. They flushed away the accumulated urine from their suits in the rover's small chemical toilet. When they were done, they finally looked at each other. Now that Netsai was out of her suit, she seemed suddenly far more vulnerable.

'How are you doing?' Rose asked her.

'Not great.'

Every part of Rose felt heavy. She drew Netsai in for a hug. They hadn't held each other like this since they'd first met in the temple, and it felt like Netsai's body was the only warmth on the planet. After a few seconds, Rose felt Netsai's tears on her shoulder, and her body shook with sobs.

Rose had been holding back. Before this moment, it felt like could never cry, not properly. Like if she felt all her pain, all at once, she would be torn to pieces. But as soon as the tears touched her skin, she couldn't stop herself. She collapsed into Netsai's shoulder, weeping.

She cried, deep and hard, but there was no release. The tears wouldn't stop. She wished she could stay like this forever, but whenever she felt herself melting, Archie's lifeless face flashed across her vision.

Netsai pulled away from her, and wiped her face on her sleeve.

'Let's get some sleep,' she said. 'When the sun comes up, we'll be able to tell which way is north. Then maybe we can find a base that won't turn us over to Security Services.'

Rose looked over at the tiny cabin on the right-hand side of the rover. It was little more than a padded storage locker covered by a white plastic flap, big enough for one person to lie down in.

'Do you want to take that?'

'I'm fine out here,' said Netsai, patting the floor next to her.

Rose felt immense gratitude. As Netsai curled up under a fire blanket in the middle of the rover's main cabin, Rose crawled into the sleeping nook. It was tight, but once she was inside, she had enough space to pull the flap closed behind her and seal it shut. An LED lit up, turning the inside of the tiny cabin a warm amber.

The bottom of the nook was lined with a soft and spongy mattress that was still lightly coated with dust. Rose rolled onto her back and looked up into the bright LED. Through the tears in her half-closed eyes, the light from it stretched out into streaks that looked like solar flares.

She switched off the light, and hugged her legs in the darkness. She didn't want to think about Archie, but the images came anyway. His action-boy hair. His wry little smile. The way he frowned to stop himself from laughing when he teased her. The time they argued for hours over the exact wording of a joke in a movie they'd just seen, until their mother lost her temper and slammed their heads together. The way he drove her crazy, and made her cry and swear at him. All the pain he'd put her through, again and again and again.

Including this, right now.

# Chapter Seventy-Eight

The next morning, Rose felt the sleeping nook lurch around her. Light was shining in around the plastic privacy screen. She pulled it aside and looked out into the rover's main cabin. Sunlight flooded in through the front window, and Netsai was in the driver's seat.

'Hey,' she called back.

Rose got to her feet shakily. Her eyes and mind were blurry. The memory of Archie's death kept forcing itself back to her, bringing as much pain as the night before. She wasn't certain that she had slept. She felt her way to the chemical toilet, and threw up. When she was finished, she rinsed her mouth in the tiny sink above it, and washed her hands and face.

When she felt strong enough, she scouted through the main cabin to check on their supplies. Next to the out-suits she found some netting containing two flares, a medical kit, four containers of water, and four packs of emergency rations.

She wasn't particularly hungry, but she drank from one of the bottles, then brought another bottle up to the front of the vehicle, along with one of the ration packs.

'Thanks,' said Netsai, with her eyes on the ground ahead. 'Let's see what we've got.'

Rose opened the pack. Inside was a container of rice paste, a meat-like substance in a foil wrap, a bar of chocolate, two hard crackers, a sealed tub of pickled vegetables, and a sachet of peanut butter. She gave the chocolate to Netsai, and started spreading the peanut butter on one of the crackers.

'How's the drive?'

Netsai chewed the chocolate, and swallowed.

'All right,' she said. 'I think I've found a rover track. It should lead us to a base eventually.'

'And then?'

'And then we pray they're friendly.'

After another hour, through the haze of dust to their left, they spotted a cluster of white domes and towers built around a wide radio dish. As they steered towards it, Rose squeezed in next to Netsai for a better view.

'Any idea which base this is?' said Netsai.

'I'm not sure. I've only seen dishes like that on bases built by Earth governments. They don't like to rely on the Company for a direct line home.'

Netsai drove slowly around the outside of the base, searching for the docking bay. They found it on the far side, with twenty other rovers lined up in front of it.

'Whoa,' Netsai murmured. 'I've never seen a queue like this before.'

'What are they all doing here?' said Rose, crouching down next to the driver's seat.

'I don't know.'

Netsai drove to the back of the queue, and reactivated the radio. After a few minutes they were met with a chime as the computer initiated a local connection. A dark-skinned woman appeared on the screen. She was wearing a blue blazer, and had straight black hair tied back in a bun.

'This is Mangala docking control. This base is sovereign territory. If you're from Fuller Aerospace, you should know that we do not recognise the authority of your security services, and we won't be intimidated into giving up any of our citizens for questioning.'

'I'm not with the Company. This is Netsai Chiwasa, requesting permission to dock.'

'Chiwasa,' the woman said. She looked down at something off-screen. 'Are you with Rose Fuller?'

Netsai glanced at Rose.

'Would you let me in if I was?'

'I don't think so. Fuller Aerospace is hunting her. They already have rovers surrounding Kepler Base. What's your situation? Are you also asking for asylum?'

'I am.'

'Then I'm sorry,' the docking controller said, shaking her head. 'We're overloaded. Unless you're a citizen, we can't let you in without a docking fee.'

Netsai gritted her teeth.

'Okay,' she said. 'How much will it cost?'

'Forty thousand rupees. It's about five hundred dollars.'

'That's ridiculous!'

'That's what we're charging to cover the costs of overcrowding.'

Rose gripped Netsai's arm.

'You need to get us in,' she whispered urgently.

Netsai glanced down at Rose, and briefly met her eyes.

'Okay,' she nodded to the docking controller. 'Send me the transaction details.'

She ended the call, and tapped on the rover screen, using the Mangala network to connect to her online banking page. After a few minutes, she muttered 'Shit.'

'What is it?' Rose said.

Netsai leaned out of the way, to show Rose the console screen.

ACCOUNT BLOCKED. Contact your Fuller Aerospace customer assistant for more information.

Rose reached over Netsai, and tapped on the screen. 'Let me try.'

She typed in her password, and the same message came up.

'Damn it.'

She leaned back out of sight, and Netsai reconnected with the docking controller.

'I'm sorry,' she said to the woman. 'We don't have any money.'

'Then we can't let you in. I sympathise, I really do, but our first priority is to look after our own people.'

'Are there any other bases taking people seeking asylum?' Netsai asked desperately.

'Try Marcus, or Rayleigh, or Fortune Point. But look out. We heard that Fuller Security Services were sending guards up to, what did they call it, "bring order" to all the bases on the Ulysses Fossae.'

'Thanks for the help,' said Netsai. She disconnected, and slumped back in her seat.

'You weren't lying,' Rose said quietly. 'This is a war.'

# Chapter Seventy-Nine

Tourists were shouting in the lower level of the Astro Departure Lounge of Mariner Base. Kelly Fuller stood at the edge of the balcony with a guard on either side of her, and watched the panic below. The people were pressed up against the window, holding their luggage and bundles of garish clothes under their arms. Stubble was growing out, and cheeks were grey and free from cosmetics. People were clawing at each other to get to the departure gate, screaming and pleading with the Fuller employees to let them onto the ship.

'Sorry, sir,' said one of the young, muscular, impeccably polite men guarding the gate. 'The ship is only arriving now, and it still needs to go through maintenance and refuelling. It'll be weeks before it departs.'

'Then what are they doing there?' said the middle-aged tourist. He pointed up to the viewing balcony, where Kelly Fuller and the other passengers were waiting. His eyes burned into her with a mix of fear and rage. 'They're the ones you're getting off the planet, aren't they?'

'They are the legitimate passengers with tickets for this flight, yes, sir,' the man at the gate said calmly. 'They've been invited to watch the arrival of their ship as a courtesy, nothing more.'

The tourist looked at the man in wide-eyed desperation.

'I own Web Four Bank. If you get me on that ship I'll make it worth your while, I promise you.'

The tourists all around howled in anger at the attempted bribery, but the man guarding the gate stayed admirably calm.

'As I said, sir, the ship won't be departing for two weeks.'

'Then get me on it when it departs!' the tourist spat. 'You can squeeze on one more!'

'The ship only has fuel to take a hundred passengers, sir. It's physics.'

'Fuck you, you smug little prick!'

Kelly stepped back from the balcony railing. Like the other legitimate passengers around her, she looked up at the glass-composite roof of the departure lounge and waited for her salvation to arrive. At this moment, a Thunderhead passenger liner was dropping out of space towards them. Her assistants had told her that it was called the Trinity, and it would be the last flight out. After this, the planets wouldn't be in the right position for a flight back to Earth, and the launch window would be closed for the next two years. And if the rumours of economic collapse were true, the flights might never resume at all.

Kelly Fuller looked up at the empty, dusty sky above, waiting to see her first speck of hope. After decades trapped on this planet by family and pride, she would be leaving everything. Her right hand was bandaged from when she had smashed the glass of the display cases, thrown the fire opals on the floor, and torn the panels off the walls. She had wept, in pain and fury, and howled at Rose, and Alex, and Archie, and herself. She wept until there was nothing left in her, nothing to keep her on this dead planet.

The crowd around Kelly started to chatter, and a man next to her pointed at the sky. Kelly searched, and saw a glint as the passenger ship dropped down through the dust. It quickly grew from a spark into a giant gleaming tower, remaining perfectly upright as it dropped down towards its landing pad. When Kelly was sure it was going to slam into it, the rocket engines fired. The vast ship slowed and hovered impossibly over the pad, billowing dust in all directions. The crowd on the balcony cheered.

Then it started to tilt. One of the engines was sputtering. The others fired harder to keep the ship flying, and the whole structure leaned, flew parallel to the ground, and collapsed on its side. Some of the crowd screamed as the shockwave of the explosion ballooned outwards. The windows of the departure lounge rattled, and the world went grey. When the dust and smoke cleared, the tourists and the passengers alike stared out in silence. There was nothing left to see but gleaming debris, scattered across a barren landscape.

# Chapter Eighty

The message was burned into the wall of the Tycho Mining Base docking bay. They hadn't used a soldering iron this time. The letters were two metres high, melted in place by a welding torch. The plastic of the wall had dripped and hardened into strands of black bubbling rope below the words. Karl stared.

**NO MORE TALK**
**NO MORE COMPROMISE**
**RED ROSE SHOWED THE WAY**

'Hey,' said Karl's father. 'Hey!'

He took Karl's chin gently in his hand, and turned his face away from the words, until their eyes met.

'Don't look there. Look at me.'

Karl stood at the hatch of the Company rover. His father was kneeling in front of him, wearing his work suit. It had become rumpled over the last few days of the riots, but it still gave him the appearance of authority.

'I'll bring this under control. But I need to make sure you're safe first.'

Behind him, four armed Fuller Aerospace guards stood around the docking bay door. It was thick enough to protect against blow-outs, but not against a protracted assault by the rioters. The rumble of a circular saw reverberated through the metal, making the hairs on Karl's arm stand on end. The bay was cramped, and the air was acrid.

'I'm not going without you,' said Karl. 'I'll fight.'

'So brave,' said his father with a tight smile, ruffling his hair.

Karl pulled his head away. 'I mean it!'

'I know you do, Karl. But you have to go now. I mean it. These men will drag you onto the rover if they have to.'

Karl's eyes stung.

'Why? Why can't I stay?'

Karl's father pulled him in for a hug. 'I came to Mars for you, Karl. I bought this mine to give you a future, and I'm going to defend it until my dying breath. But you're more important than any of this. If this goes wrong then the Company will look after you. You're my proudest achievement, you know that? You'll do great things, with or without me. But you can't do them if you stay here.'

The glowing tip of the circular saw blade burst through the door, throwing sparks and screeching. Two of the four guards stood back and aimed their weapons at the door, the other two ran towards the rover's hatch.

'Take him,' said his father.

'Wait!' Karl said, throwing his arms around his father's neck. His father pulled himself away.

'There's no more time,' he said, picking up one of the guards' crowd-control shotguns from the ground at his side.

'No!' Karl cried.

The two guards grabbed Karl under the arms and dragged him backwards. His feet skidded over the lip of the hatch as they pulled him into the rover, and slammed it closed behind him.

Karl threw himself at the hatch, and looked through the glass porthole into the docking bay. The tip of the circular saw had already cut across the top of the door, and was working its way down the other side.

The rover detached from the side of Tycho Base, and Karl's father disappeared from his sight. Karl kept staring out of the porthole as the rover drove away through the storm. The blocky mass of the base shrunk, until all he could see of it was its outline in the blurring dust.

A faint stuttering came through the speakers in the rover's cockpit.

'Gunfire,' the driver said grimly.

Karl pushed his way between the white bucket seats to the front of the rover, and listened to the speakers. The gunshots continued in rapid bursts, then cut out. The driver leaned over the console, and pressed a button.

'Come in, Tycho,' he said.

The silence stretched out. Karl blinked. Tears were filling his eyes.

The driver let go of the button, and sat back in his seat.

'No!' Karl yelled. 'No, no, no!'

He beat his hands on the back of the driver's seat, and kept repeating the word until his throat was hoarse.

'Shut that kid up!'

The other guard kneeled down next to Karl, and slapped him across the face with a gloved hand. The shock silenced Karl. The guard grabbed his shoulders, and looked him in the eyes.

'Hey! You need to be strong now! Okay?'

Karl stared back, numbly.

'We'll protect you. The Company will take care of you. But you need to keep control of yourself.'

'We need to go back,' Karl mumbled.

'We will, kid. They won't get away with this. We'll build an army, and we'll come back. But you've got to be strong until then, okay? You've got to be a man. Are you a man?'

'I'm a man.'

The guard held his fist up.

'Raise a fist.'

Karl Sealgair raised his fist in the air in return.

'Good kid,' the guard said, slapping on the shoulder, and giving him a push towards the back of the rover.

When Karl got back to the porthole, there was no sign of the mining base through the dust of the storm. He turned away from it, completely numb, and sat down in one of the rover's plastic bucket seats. He stared straight ahead as the guards drove him away through the swirling dust.

# Chapter Eighty-One

The rovers from outside Mangala Base drove together into the north-west, forming a loose and reluctant convoy. After two hours of travel, they saw shapes coming towards them through the dust cloud in the south: a second convoy of rovers. The two groups stopped together in the middle of the plains. Netsai turned on the short-range radio and Rose looked out of the windows at the huddle of small, dusty rovers around them, and listened as all the evacuees made their introductions and discussed how they were going to survive.

'I'm Suyin, from Mariner,' said a female voice. 'I'm heading to the mining bases in the north. I've got a cousin up in Moab. They've been preparing for a while, stockpiling life-support equipment and tools they can use as weapons. I thought they were crazy when they started.'

'I'm going to Olympus,' said another voice. 'I heard they're still taking people.'

'We're running out of water,' said a third. 'But we've got plenty of batteries. Anyone willing to trade?'

Rose watched through the cockpit window as pairs of rovers with compatible hatches reversed towards each other and docked, so they could trade for whatever resources they were lacking: air, water, rations, carbon filters.

'Hey,' said a desperate voice on the radio. 'This is rover F3 from Aries Base. We're really running low on oxygen and energy here. We won't make it much further. Can anyone help us out?'

Rose glanced at Netsai.

'Can we?'

'Sure,' said Netsai, fidgeting with a bead at the end of one of her braids. 'We have a couple of days' worth to spare. But we're going to need help ourselves, soon.'

They docked to the back of the rover from Aries, which was even smaller than theirs. When their hatches opened, Rose saw seven people crowded on the other side, with their knees up and their backs pressed against the walls of the vehicle. Their cabin smelled of sweat and disinfectant. When they saw Rose, three of their faces lit up with awe, and the other four turned stony.

'Red Rose!' said a woman in the driver's chair, and looked at Netsai. 'Why didn't you say we had Red Rose in the convoy!'

Netsai raised a hand.

'Don't tell the others unless you want the Company after us.'

'Here,' said Rose, passing them a round-ended cylinder of oxygen. They accepted it, but their thanks weren't wholehearted.

'That was ... strained,' said Rose, after the hatch was closed.

'You're a god,' said Netsai. 'They're angry at you for not doing more.'

Once all the trading was complete and all the rovers were separate, the radio chatter led the caravan to the consensus to head for Titov Base, fifty kilometres away. As it came into view through the fine dust of the global storm, they saw a cluster of half buried tube-shaped habitats, with an improvised barrier surrounding them. The barrier was made from two-metre-high plastic crates, bright yellow and stacked with rocks, and it was being patrolled by three out-suited figures holding guns. As the convoy approached they ran out towards them with their arms raised, telling them to stop.

'Where did they get those weapons?' Rose asked.

Netsai squinted out of the front window.

'They're bolt guns. Like, for riveting. They work in a vacuum. I guess you could shoot someone with them, if you really had to.'

'Are there a lot of bolt guns lying around on Mars?'

'Thousands.'

The rover at the front of the convoy rolled slowly to the barricade. An armed patroller stood in front of it, and after a minute he started waving his arms, like he was engaged in an intense conversation. Netsai reconnected the radio, and they listened in.

'Please, just let one of us in,' said the driver from the front of the convoy. 'We need someone to buy water, air, and power for all of us. We'll pay.'

'With what?' said the patroller at the barrier. 'We can't send money through the Fuller network.'

'Please. We're begging you.'

'Sorry,' said the patroller. 'We can't take any risks. Miranda Base accused us of stealing an oxygen consignment meant for them. They're threatening to take it back by force. This place isn't safe for anyone. You all need to go.'

And so, the convoy continued north. Every base they stopped at had the same story: sorry, not enough supplies. Too dangerous. Keep moving. New Gusev allowed one of the rovers to dock for an hour so the convoy could restock and refuel, and Marcus allowed a Canadian citizen from one of the rovers to enter permanently. But most bases stonewalled them.

At each base, Netsai did her best to subtly let them know who she was travelling with. The news was met with growing excitement and alarm. The Free Settlements were struggling to make sense of the news of the first murder, and rumours had spread.

'We heard she killed Archie to stop the Company from installing him as a local dictator,' said the docking controller in Wellington. 'Is it true?'

But as usual, they loved the idea of Rose more than the person. The bases gave them the supplies they needed for their journey and wished them well, but they weren't going to risk giving sanctuary to Red Rose.

For seven long days, the convoy crawled from base to base. It kept on heading north until the last of the settlements, then struck south-east. When Rose wasn't driving, she spent the time staring out of the window in the rear hatch, watching the retreating landscape. The world was sliding away from her, disappearing into the dust. Every rock and pebble they drove over got smaller and smaller, and shrank down to nothing.

Then, finally, on the seventh day, Netsai whooped. She turned in the driver's seat to look back at Rose, grinning ear to ear.

'We're in!'

Rose clambered to the front of the rover and looked out of the window. They were parked in front of a small base, nothing more than three white domes surrounded by desert.

'Where's this?'

'Rayleigh. Built by the ESA. It isn't much, but they had a vote, and the base administrator is going to let us in. We did it!'

Netsai pulled them out of the convoy and connected to the Rayleigh docking port. Through the front window, Rose watched the rest of the rovers crawling away from them towards the east in search of somewhere to rest.

'So we're abandoning them?' she said.

Netsai rested an arm on her shoulder. 'I'm sorry.'

The docking port door opened for them, and they followed it out into Rayleigh Base. The dome they walked into was smaller than Rose's apartment in Mariner. It had subdued lighting, and a long table set with chairs in the middle. There was a sofa against the curved far wall, under an old, tatty flag of the European Space Agency. On the sides there were two docking hatches, an airlock, a bathroom with a shower, an engineering bay, and a metal staircase going up to a balcony mezzanine where Rose could see a row of small sleeping cabins. Above them was the domed roof. Nine people in matching blue flight suits were waiting for them in front of the docking bay hatch.

'Welcome to Rayleigh,' said a blond man with glasses, shaking their hands nervously. 'I'm Colin, the base admin. We weren't going to take anyone in, but, well ... it's an honour to have you with us.'

He introduced the rest of the residents.

'We're all scientists. This is Léo, Gabin, and Tiago, at the table there is Elise and Mohamed. That's our surgeon, Yan, and that's Andrea there on the sofa.'

Everyone seemed awestruck by her, and a little scared. All Rose wanted was a shower, but she shook their hands, and did her best to memorise all their names, while Netsai stood behind her, quietly watching.

When the greetings were over, Colin led Rose and Netsai up

the metal staircase to the mezzanine, where ten prefabricated sleeping cabins were arranged in a semicircle under the roof of the dome. Each one was an identical cube with cream-coloured carbon-fibre walls and a sliding door on the front. He showed them into the nearest one.

'This is your dorm. You'll have to share it. I'm sorry.'

The walls were padded with a thin layer of brown sound-absorbent foam. There was a double bunk on one side, a countertop and built-in cupboard on the other, and a strip of floor space between them, fifty centimetres wide.

'Thank you,' said Rose. After a week in the rover, it was a relief to just stand upright.

Colin put his hand on the small countertop, which was stacked with goodies.

'We've left a few essentials for you. Clothes, stationery, soap, clean towels, paper cups, two bowls of blek, some water, and rum. We distilled it ourselves in the bio lab. Do you need anything else?'

'Just a chance to get cleaned up,' Rose said. She couldn't hide her exhaustion any longer.

'Of course,' said Colin, pushing his glasses up his nose. 'No problem. The washroom is downstairs on the opposite side of the dome. There's a five-litre limit, and only space for one person at a time. See you soon.'

He left the two of them in their tiny new room.

'You go first,' said Rose. 'You did most of the driving.'

'Thanks.'

Netsai took her towel, soap and new clothes from the counter and left the room, sliding the door closed behind her. Rose sat on the lower bunk and ate her blek. After ten minutes Netsai came back wearing her new ESA flight suit. Her braids were damp and her skin was glowing.

'What do you think?' she said, turning and modelling it for Rose.

'Sci-chic. It suits you.'

'Get to the shower,' said Netsai. 'It's great.'

Rose put down her bowl and gathered her own shower gear

from the counter. When she went back downstairs, the base inhabitants were sitting around the table, talking quietly amongst
themselves. They went silent as she walked across the common
room. She gave the room a small wave with her free hand, but
didn't make eye contact.

The shared washroom held a single toilet, a sink, and a small
corner shower. Rose stripped and showered quickly, scrubbing
away a week's worth of accumulated rover grime. When she was
done, she dried herself and pulled on her new uniform. It hung
on her loosely; she was too small to fill it. She took her dirty
clothes back out, once again avoiding the gaze of the other base
inhabitants, and climbed the stairs back to her chamber. As soon
as the door slid closed, she felt a tremendous sense of relief.

'Hey!' said Netsai from the lower bunk. 'Ready to mingle with
our new base-mates?'

'Can't we just... hide for a bit?' said Rose, putting her clothes
on the counter. 'There'll be plenty of time to get to know them
tomorrow, right?'

Netsai held up the bottle of base-distilled rum and two paper
cups. 'I'm very glad you said that.'

Rose came to sit next to her. Netsai poured for them, and gave
a toast.

'To our new home.'

They downed the rum, which tasted like bitter burned sugar.
It stung Rose's throat, and she coughed. Netsai poured herself
another as soon as the first was done, and lay back in the lower
bunk.

'It's weird to be able to stretch out,' she said.

Rose didn't answer. She stared up at the underside of the top
bunk.

'Tomorrow we'll regroup,' said Netsai. 'We'll make contact with
our allies. Work out how we're going to fight back. I bet a lot of
people will be happy that you're alive.'

'Sure,' said Rose, staring blankly. The world was a mess, and
Netsai still thought they could fix it.

After a few minutes of silent drinking, Rose realised that Netsai was breathing heavily. She looked over, and saw her eyes were closed. She lifted Netsai's legs up off the floor, pulled off her shoes, and rested her legs on the mattress. As she was about to climb the ladder up to the top bunk, she heard a quiet tap on the cabin door.

She slid it open. Colin was outside with his fingers interlocked in front of him. The base lights outside were off for the night, but over the balcony, she could see the other residents were still sitting down below, lit up by the screens of their pads.

'How are you doing?' said Colin. 'Is your room still okay?'

Rose felt the base spinning slowly around her. But a public face was second nature to her, and she smiled politely.

'Wonderful. It's lucky you had a room available.'

'Well, one of our team left for Ferne Stadt, so we had the space...'

He shifted from foot to foot, uncomfortable. The other residents were all looking up at him.

'Is something wrong?' said Rose.

Colin winced, and took off his glasses. He polished them on the sleeve of his flight suit.

'It's not a big thing, but... We've just found out that the Company attacked Mangala Base. There was a rumour that you were there, so they sent in their guards... We thought you should know.'

Rose looked down at the faces glowing in the dark. Their unspoken fear was hard to miss.

'You think they'll come here next?'

'Sorry,' said Colin. He ran his tongue over his lips nervously. 'I shouldn't have said anything. You're our guests. You're welcome.'

Rose's heart sank, and a dark clarity settled in.

'Thank you,' she said. 'You're all very kind.'

She went back into the cabin and slid the door closed behind her, leaving it open a crack. Netsai was still on the bunk, eyes closed, mouth half open. Rose watched her for a while, then went to the countertop. She pushed aside the pile of their old clothes, and found a pad of paper and a pen.

She climbed up onto her bunk, and wrote a letter to Netsai, in the neat cursive that had been drilled into her in childhood. She folded it up, tucking in the corners like a dinner invitation, then lay back down and held it to her chest. She waited there with her eyes open until she heard the rest of the base inhabitants finish their muttered conversations, take their turns in the washroom, and head up to their tiny cabins. Through the thin soundproofing, Rose could hear them bumping around, preparing for sleep. When the base was finally quiet, Rose got back to her feet, and put her letter on Netsai's pillow, beside her sleeping face. She slid out of the cabin and crept down the metal stairs, across the dark living area, and back to the docking bay. She sealed the hatch of the rover closed behind her, and ran the automated safety checks. When the motors were warmed up, she undocked from Rayleigh Base. Tears streamed down her face as she steered the rover away, following the tracks of the departed convoy.

# Chapter Eighty-Two

At 4.15 a.m., a helicopter drone launched from Michigan Base. Its body was cubic, seventy centimetres wide. It was completely black, with no LEDs to give away its position. The drone's blades shrieked in the thin atmosphere as it lifted off from the triangular Marscrete pad built to the east of the base, and accelerated towards the horizon. The night was dark. The only light came from Deimos, the smallest and furthest of Mars's two moons, glowing on the eastern horizon. The drone scanned the terrain ahead with invisible infrared lasers, guiding itself north-east over the ancient caldera of the extinct volcano, Ascraeus Mons.

For an hour, it flew through the darkness. At nineteen minutes past five, its infrared sensors registered a cluster of twelve heat signatures on the horizon, and the navigation system automatically adjusted course. Five minutes later, the onboard AI sent a brief encoded message back to Michigan positively identifying the heat signatures as a rover convoy. There were eleven heat sources driving together in a loose group, and a twelfth a kilometre behind, driving faster to catch up with the others.

The drone slowed down. Its neural network analysed the heat signatures, using their shape and intensity to estimate the size, model, and probable contents of each of the rovers. It selected its target.

As the final rover caught up with the convoy, the weight of probabilities in the drone's neural network reached their necessary threshold. The helicopter blades tilted, and the drone swooped down out of the darkness towards the rear of the convoy.

Five hundred metres.

One hundred.

Fifty.

Ten.

A new calculation ran through the neural network, to find the optimum point to generate maximum damage to twelve rovers in their current configuration. It adjusted course again.

As the drone reached its destination, the AI sent one final instruction to the drone's payload, a block of nitroglycerine manufactured in the Michigan Base chemical processing plant. The detonator triggered, and communication from the drone terminated.

# Chapter Eighty-Three

Dear Netsai,

I'm sorry I'm disappearing on you like this. I know you hate it when I make plans without you, but if I wait for you to wake up before I go then I know you'll talk me out of it.

You're the only person on this planet I truly care about, and you're never going to be safe if you're near me. I can't be responsible for your death, too.

We should have done it differently back at the start. I should have pointed all the attention at you, made you the star. You would have hated it, and maybe we wouldn't have made the news so easily, but if the focus had been on you rather than me then maybe none of this would have happened.

All I wanted to do was be your friend, Netsai. I wanted to do right by the people of Mars. I'm sorry it came to all of this. You'll be able to do more good if I'm not around, using up all the oxygen.

Please give my thanks to everyone on Rayleigh Base. It was generous of them to offer us a place with them, and I'm sorry that I couldn't take it. I hope that they treat you well and take care of you, and I hope that they stick by you when I couldn't.

All the love on Mars,

Rose.

# Chapter Eighty-Four

The next evening, Netsai stood at the window of Dome Two and watched the first team returning, hauling twisted stacks of scrap metal in a trailer behind the base's small buggy. Her head still hurt from the rum the night before, and she still felt the adrenaline-prick of horror from her day, but she hadn't given up hope. Not just yet.

The buggy came to a stop. Colin, Elise and Tiago climbed out of it in their suits. They walked to the trailer and started to unload the salvage from the drone strike: burst oxygen tanks, melted motors, and torn pieces of plastic. Netsai hurried through the underground tunnel to Dome One, and joined the other base-mates waiting expectantly in the shared living space.

Colin was the first back through the airlock. When he took off his helmet, his face was grey.

'We need to get back there,' he said. 'There's a whole lot more we need to collect. The other bases are scavenging, too. A team from Novvy Mir arrived just as we left.'

The other base inhabitants shuffled uncomfortably. One of them, Mohamed, glanced at Netsai.

'I don't like it either,' said Colin. 'But we need to get self-sufficient. Right now, we're alone. Really alone. We don't know how long the supply lines will be down, and none of the other former ESA bases have anything they're willing to share. Every scrap of equipment will help. Who's up to join the second shift?'

'Me,' Netsai said, stepping forward.

Colin put a hand on her shoulder, and shook his head sympathetically.

'Please, don't. Just stay here. It isn't pretty. It's hard enough for us to look at, and we didn't know those people.'

Over the next two days, the nine other residents took shifts going out to the site and searching for salvageable material. Netsai waited at the window, and watched them bringing back frozen food packs and water bottles. When they finally finished picking through the remains, slowly and thoroughly, the last team returned with the bodies in the trailer, wrapped in orange sample-collection plastic sheeting. They carried them from the airlock to the medical bay in Dome Three, and closed the hatch.

Netsai sat on a stool outside the bay, and waited. After an hour Mohamed came to her, bringing a coffee and a bar of chocolate from an ESA rations pack.

'Thanks,' she said.

He leaned against the wall next to her, just to be present.

'Any idea where the drone came from?' she asked, sipping the coffee.

'We don't know yet. The Company denies they're involved. So do all the bases around, Michigan, Leonov, New Prague. But someone must have hoped that all of this would end if Rose was dead.'

'How did they find out where she was?'

Mohamed shrugs. 'Not from any of us. But people talk. It's hard to keep secrets about Red Rose.'

Netsai looked down into her coffee cup.

'How are you?' he asked, quietly.

'I don't know what to feel,' said Netsai. 'Except angry. I know she left to protect me, but … she cut me out. She never made me feel small before. I guess if you grow up with that kind of power then you never realise how self-centred you are, even when you're trying to do the right thing.'

She finished the last of her coffee. The hatch opened and the face of Yan, the base surgeon, appeared around the side of it. She was a willowy woman in her late fifties, with dyed black hair that was growing out grey.

'Are you ready?' she said.

Netsai nodded. Mohamed took her empty coffee cup from her, and put a hand gently on her shoulder.

'You can do it,' he said.

The base's medical bay was a small, neatly organised room. One wall was taken up with a shelf stacked with pill bottles and small white cardboard boxes. Opposite it was a counter top, and a sink for scrubbing up. There was a bin, and a yellow plastic bag hanging from the wall above it with a sign saying *Clinical Contaminated Waste Only*. Most of the floor space was taken up by bundles wrapped in orange plastic sheets, sealed with thick black tape. The smell of alcohol-based disinfectant made Netsai's eyes water.

There was a stretcher next to the hatch, also covered in an orange sheet. The surgeon led Netsai to it.

'I wouldn't ask you to do this, but we don't have a DNA sequencer. There wasn't much left of any of them, so this isn't easy to look at. Are you sure you're okay with this?'

'I'm sure,' said Netsai.

The surgeon pulled back the sheet, and Netsai stared down at the human remains beneath.

'Netsai?' said Yan. Her voice was coming from a long way away.

Netsai clenched her jaw. She nodded.

'Yes,' she said. 'I officially confirm that it's Rose Fuller.'

# Chapter Eighty-Five

When Michael finally left his room in Kepler Base, the world had changed. The corridors were full of hushed conversations. On every wall were posters asking for volunteers to defend the base. In the docking bay, desperate refugees begged him to take their dollars if he would only give them something they could easily trade, like water, air, or metal ingots.

A small private rover operator in the corner of the bay agreed to get him past Kepler security and take him back to Mariner. The fee in dollars was exorbitant, but after a tense wait, the digital transfer went through. The journey south was slow and bumpy.

Back in Mariner, the docking bay was empty. So was the concourse. The fountains were turned off, and the food stalls were boarded up with sheets of carbon fibre. Security Services guards stood at the intersections of the corridors, checking credentials and enforcing the curfew. The news feeds on the silent wall screens kept playing the same scene of Archie Fuller's body being dragged away across the sand, interspersed with a dozen talking heads.

Michael's old room was still open for him. He went inside, closed the door, and sent a simple message back to his handler, Dene, confirming he was still alive. And then, he waited.

And waited.

He couldn't eat or sleep. His mind and body were numb. He lay in his bed, staring up at his old familiar ceiling tiles.

The next morning he woke to find a circular message on his pad, sent to all the residents of Mariner Base. It was an instruction to assemble in the food court on the upper level. By the time he arrived, the line already stretched twenty metres down the concourse. The residents in the queue ahead of him looked subdued and anxious.

'What's this all about?' he said to the man at the back of the line.

'We think they're rounding up the independence sympathisers. They waited long enough, if you ask me.'

The queue continued to grow behind him. Agonisingly slowly, they moved forward, towards the white marble archway into the food court. When he finally got through it, he saw six tables, lined up in two rows. Seated at them were six bureaucrats in Fuller Aerospace uniforms, each interviewing a base resident. Four large Security Services guards stood with their arms folded in front of the boarded-up food stalls. Blocky black stun guns hung from their belts. Their eyes darted around, keeping careful watch over everyone in the chamber.

Michael was beckoned over by one of the bureaucrats.

'Name?'

'Michael Agee.'

'Are you a member of the political group associated with Rosemary Fuller?'

'No.'

'Do you have any casual or work associations with any known members of the independence movement, or with anyone residing in one of the dissident bases that call themselves the Free Settlements?'

'Not currently.'

'Do you have any information about the whereabouts of any members of the independence movement on any Fuller Aerospace base, or any suspicions about people who might be affiliated with the group?'

'No.'

The bureaucrat looked up from his pad, and called one of the guards over.

'This one.'

The guard put a hand on Michael's shoulder, and pushed him out of the court, and through the corridors to the north-east wing of the base. He was shoved through the door of an office, which automatically closed behind him.

A man in a white shirt with the sleeves rolled up was sitting at a desk littered with stacks of forms and loose stationery. He was typing something on his tablet, but when Michael entered, he smiled, and stood, offering his hand.

'Michael!' he said. 'It's a pleasure to see you again!'

'Hi, Dene,' Michael said. He shook his handler's hand.

'Please, sit. Can I get you a coffee?'

'No thanks.'

'Okay. Just a second, I need to send this off. I'll be with you now.'

Michael sat and watched Dene warily. Dene eventually finished typing, and hit return with a flourish.

'I'm so sorry,' he said. 'I got your report yesterday, but things have been utter chaos. With the state of emergency and the special-powers thing there's been a huge shake-up in the Company ... Anyway. The point is, it's time for your debrief.'

Dene poured a coffee for himself and settled back down in front of Michael.

'That was a tough assignment, wasn't it?' he said cheerfully. 'To be honest it was a disaster, but we can't blame you. You were out of your depth. We all underestimated those two.'

He sipped his coffee. Michael kept his composure.

'The first thing you should know is that your contract with Connect Image has been terminated. On the plus side, we no longer have to keep you at arm's length from the Fuller Corporation, so I'm glad to be able to offer you employment in Internal Services. Starting immediately, if you'd like.'

Michael raised his eyebrows. For the first time in weeks, he felt something like a glimmer of hope.

'What will I be doing?'

'Well, two things. The first one is a desk job. We're severely understaffed, but your experience is going to be extremely valuable. We have more and more bases in the north declaring independence. They're going to outnumber us soon, and we need strategists who know how to divide and conquer them. You will need to identify threats, and come up with ways to play them off each other. Is that the kind of thing you think you can do?'

'Absolutely,' said Michael.

'Good. And the second task is a bit more ... confidential.'

He glanced at the door, and ran a hand through his thinning hair.

'We're starting an investigation of an extremely sensitive nature,' said Dene. 'It's called Project Granite. We're searching for an object that could be very damaging, in the wrong hands.'

'What's that?' asked Michael.

'Archie Fuller's out-suit.' Dene leaned in across the desk. 'He was recording a TV series. His suit had a dozen cameras built into it. It's very likely that it captured footage of his own murder.'

Michael nodded.

'You want me to find it?'

'If you can. Archie Fuller's editor says that the footage will be password encrypted. Here's the code.'

He slid a piece of paper across the desk to Michael. He looked down, and memorised the eight characters.

'We have four Company guards who witnessed Archie Fuller's murder,' said Dene, interlocking his fingers on the desk in front of him. 'They're loyal employees, but we suspect that they may have been a little ... overzealous in their duties. We don't know for certain what happened out there, but this is a sensitive situation. The Company needs to build trust as quickly as possible, for the sake of stability on Mars. So if the footage on that suit gets uncovered, and it contradicts the current narrative ... If it proves that we're in any way complicit in the murder ...'

'I understand,' said Michael. 'It'll be better if that suit doesn't exist.'

Dene nodded. 'Exactly. Project Granite. Cold, dead stone.'

'When do I start?'

'As soon as possible. Sorry we can't give you time to readjust after your last assignment, but if you need to talk to a therapist, we'll provide one. It's Company policy. Fully confidential, of course.'

'That won't be necessary,' said Michael.

Dene finished his coffee, and wiped his upper lip with a napkin. 'Oh, that reminds me. Last time we met, you were talking about a relationship with Rose Fuller. Did anything come of that?'

Michael kept himself calm.

'No,' he said. 'Nothing.'

'Good. We found some confidential documents at the scene of Archie Fuller's murder. We don't know who leaked them, and if anyone found out that you had a relationship with Rose Fuller then that would make you a suspect, and that wouldn't be good for either of us. I'm just glad we can put it in the past.'

He let that hang in the air for a moment, and then smiled.

'The good news is, you won't have to use your assumed name any more. I put in a request to adjust all your local records, so I suppose I should officially say, welcome to Mars, James Clifford.'

# Part 7.6

—

# Dylan And Frank

# Chapter Eighty-Six

Dylan pressed her face up against the glass of Frank's rover's cockpit, hoping to get a glimpse of the children in the other rovers of the convoy. The traders had been converging around them for the last few days, and Frank had let Dylan talk to some of the other trader kids though the radio. After months alone in the rover with Frank, she couldn't wait to meet up with her old friends. She knew Stef and Mina from their time together at Lü Bao, and there was another kid called Joachim who she met back in Calico, who did an impression of the nasal accent of the base-kids living there that made Dylan laugh so hard that the sugar water she was drinking came out of her nose.

Rayleigh Base was just ahead. Dylan had been here before, but she had been too young to remember it properly. It was a vast collection of domes, spires and walkways, some white and new, and some dusty with age. Even as they approached, a crane on the top of a rover was lifting girders up to the jagged top of a half-constructed tower.

She hoped that Rayleigh would have a playroom cave with slides carved into the rock, like they did in Woolstonecroft Base. And Mina had promised that after they docked, Dylan could play with the Earth People toys that her dad had 3D-printed, and give her the files so that Frank could make some for her, too.

'How long are we going to be here for, Dad?' she asked, squeezing her way onto his lap. He scooched back in his driver's seat, making some space for her between himself and the console.

'I don't know,' he said. 'It depends on how quickly I can sell these crates of potassium.'

She twisted around to look at his face.

'Can I come and see the trading floor this time? I've always wanted to see it.'

'You want to watch the haggling?' he asked. 'Why? It's just a lot of people swearing and talking fast.'

'Yeah, you said. It sounds awesome.'

The convoy rolled into the shadow of the Rayleigh Base docking port, and slowed down to a crawl. Frank was next to Dylan in the driver's seat, and she could hear the chatter of the other drivers leaking out of his headphones. After a few minutes, he pulled them off and grinned.

'Guess what? They're letting us make a hive!'

'Woohoo!'

Rover hives were Dylan's favourite. A large trading rover with four docking hatches (one at the front, one at the back, one at each side) connected to Rayleigh Base. Once it was in place, three other rovers drove in and docked with its exposed hatches. More rovers came in, connecting to the first available hatch, haphazardly forming an interconnected maze of vehicles. Dylan and Frank's rover had a hatch on either side. Frank drove in, and connected his right side to the hive. After a few minutes, another rover came in and docked on the left. The hatches opened, and soon their rover was a thoroughfare for traders streaming to and from the hub. Everyone who came through shook Frank's hand and hugged Dylan. She met up with Mina and Stef and Joachim, and the three of them ran wild through the rover labyrinth, playing hide and seek and annoying the older traders, while her dad met up with his friends and bartered for equipment and medicine.

In the hub of the hive, the grown-ups passed around the beer and rice wine that they'd been brewing on their trips, and some of them cracked out their plastic guitars and violins and started playing a jig for people to dance to. All around the hive, people were meeting and hugging and sharing dumb jokes and fooling each other with magic tricks that they'd been practicing on their long journeys. When Dylan got back to their rover Frank told everyone gathered there that it was Dylan's ninth birthday, even though it was still two weeks away. An old trader brought her a bowl of noodles. 'It's traditional. Long noodles for a long life.' And after she had finished, another trader brought out sticky rice cakes for everyone to share, and Dylan had two thick slices.

After months stuck in one rover, being able to run free felt wonderful. One place was off-limits, though. When she tried to run out into the Rayleigh Base docking bay with her friends, a local guard blocked her way.

'No. No more traders on the base. Wait your turn.'

The anger in his voice was like a slap. Dylan worked her way back through the hive, and found Frank talking to a dreadlocked friend in one of the outer rovers. They were laughing, but Frank stopped when he saw her face.

'Dad?' she said. 'Why don't they like traders here?'

Frank leaned down to get to her level, and looked her in the eyes. His cheeks and nose were red, and there was a hint of Mars-shine on his breath.

'What's wrong? Did someone hurt you?'

'No. The guard was just … mean.'

'Don't feel bad,' he said. 'It's not you. They don't trust any of us.'

Dylan looked around at all her friends, and their families.

'Why? What did we do?'

Frank put his hands on his knees as he thought about it.

'Well, sometimes a trader comes through a base, and a few days later the locals see that something valuable is missing, or the filling that a travelling dentist gave them falls out, or a new carbon filter gums up. So the next time a trader comes around, they aren't quite as welcoming.'

'We don't steal things though, do we?'

'Never,' Frank said, with a cheeky smile. 'But it doesn't take much to damage a reputation. If one of us does them wrong, they won't trust any of us. Don't worry about it, though. It'll be our turn in the base tomorrow. Let's find a place for you to get some rest.'

She curled up that night in a hammock in an outer rover. Her dad stayed nearby, in the rover's cockpit, drinking and laughing with the same dreadlocked friend. The man told Frank that he remembered Dylan from when she was just a baby, and wouldn't her mom be so proud. She closed her eyes and pretended to sleep, so she could listen in secretly. She didn't understand most of what they were talking about, but it was fun to listen anyway.

Eventually, the dreadlocked man lowered his voice.

'So? Does she know?'

'About my diagnosis? Yes, I explained it to her. She doesn't know that I'll have to move to Company Territory for the insulin pump, though.'

Dylan kept her eyes tight shut, and wondered what that meant.

'How's that coming along?'

'I've started the paperwork. You know the Company. Bureaucracy, right out the gate.'

The man took a puff from a metal tube, and blew out a cloud of rich-smelling vapour.

'And have you taken her to see her grandmother?'

'Not yet,' said Frank. 'We'll be allowed onto the base tomorrow. I don't know if Netsai will want to see me, though. She still blames me for what happened to Maita.'

'Yeah, well,' said Frank's friend. 'You're doing the right thing. Dylan needs to meet her properly, at least once. Netsai's a remarkable woman.'

Frank grumbled under his breath.

'I'm serious,' said the rover driver. 'When Dylan's older, she'll want to remember her grandmother.'

Frank didn't reply, and the rover driver dropped the subject.

'She's been making a lot of good memories today,' he said.

'Thank God,' said Frank. 'I hope they all stick. Whatever happens, I don't want her forgetting all this.'

# Chapter Eighty-Seven

'Do we really have to go and see my grandma?' Dylan asked, letting a little whine slip into her voice.

'Yep Munchkin,' said Frank. 'We really do.'

The two of them walked hand in hand out of the hive into the Rayleigh docking bay.

Dylan looked around the chamber, with all the bustling residents going their own ways, hauling crates, and barrels, and construction tools. Everyone looked busy, and only the guard was paying them any attention. Frank had said that her grandmother would be waiting for them, but Dylan couldn't spot her, at first. She was expecting to see her the way she remembered her, as a strict-looking lady with black braided hair. She didn't recognise the round-faced woman with the greying Afro sitting on a bench at the edge of the bay. But when her grandmother saw her, she stood up and smiled.

'Dylan!' she said, spreading her arms.

Dylan was still scared, after the way she yelled at her dad the last time they were here, but she reluctantly went over for a hug. Her grandmother's sweater was warm and soft, and smelled like coffee.

Frank followed behind, and muttered 'Hello' with his hands in his pockets. He didn't tell any jokes or funny stories, and Dylan was a bit disappointed, because he was good at making people laugh.

'Thank you for seeing us,' he said.

'It's a pleasure. You should have brought her back sooner.'

Her grandmother gave him a stern look for a moment, then smiled at Dylan and led them away through a wide passageway into one of the domes of the base.

'I have something to show you, Dylan. Rayleigh is getting a lot of new residents, so we're melting new rooms for them out of the underground ice sheet. We're pumping air down there, and we're got roof supports in place. There isn't much insulation, so it's very cold.'

Her grandmother led them through some protective plastic sheeting hanging across the middle of the small dome. Behind it was a construction site, and a shaft with a rickety metal staircase leading down. Dylan's grandmother took a scarf from around her own neck, and gave it to her.

'Put it on before we go down,' she said.

Dylan wrapped it around her neck three times. They went down five flights of stairs, and came out in a chasm lit by amber light. The cold hit Dylan's exposed face, and gave her a creeping feeling across her scalp. It felt strange, but also new and kind of fun. When she breathed out, a cloud puffed out of her mouth. People were all around, wearing thick padded clothing, and were chatting to each other as they waited in line at food stalls around the chamber's edge. Dylan couldn't see anyone handing over any coins or ingots, so she guessed this must all be some kind of celebration.

'Come,' said her grandmother, leading them across the ice chamber to one of the exposed walls. It was black and rough, with a glossy sheen. 'Feel this.'

Dylan ran her fingers over the wall, and felt grit mixed in with the slick ice. It was bitingly cold, and the ice tugged at her fingertips. She pulled them free, and shook her hand for warmth.

'It's pykrete,' said her grandmother. 'We mixed plastic fibres in with the ice to make it strong. It melts at a fraction of the normal rate and it's resistant to temperature fluctuations, so we can use these chambers before we've finished construction. Pretty cool, right?'

Dylan agreed, although she didn't fully understand.

Some children ran past, laughing and shouting. Dylan leaned back against the wall, and watched them disappear into the crowd.

'Go play,' said her grandmother.

'Are you sure?' said Dylan.

'Of course. I need to talk to your dad. Go and have some fun. Don't worry, we grow good kids round here.'

Frank and her grandmother sat down on some chairs next to one of the food stands, and Dylan walked off into the crowd. She followed the sound of children laughing, and found them on the other side of the cavern., blowing clouds out of their mouths and trying to make vapour rings. None of them had any problem letting her join in, and even though they laughed at her mistakes, they cheered when she finally blew a ring. She enjoyed herself, but she was annoyed that her friends in the hive weren't allowed to come down and play, too.

Dylan's grandmother came through the crowd, with a paper tub of warm tomato soup for her.

'Where's my dad?'

'He's fine. I just need a bit of time to talk with you, now. Is that okay?'

Dylan said goodbye to the other children, and followed her grandmother back to the chairs by the food stall. Her grandmother sat down, and patted the chair next to her. Dylan sat and clutched the tub of soup to her chest, lifting her legs and huddling around it for warmth.

'Do you like it here?' asked her grandmother.

'I guess.'

'I just had a good chat with your dad. I'm sorry I was so angry at him last time.'

'What did he do?'

Her grandmother put an arm around Dylan's shoulder, and pulled her in close.

'He took my daughter,' she said. 'She went away with him in a little rover, without any radiation shielding, and she never came back. He's irresponsible, sometimes. But he can be a grown-up when it counts, I have to give him that.'

Dylan didn't know what to say to that, so she tried blowing another ring of vapour out of her mouth.

'He needs to move to Company Territory. Do you know what that means?'

'Yes,' Dylan said. 'He told me this morning. We're at war with the Company, kind of, but they're the only people making the special machine that can keep him alive without lots of injections. We can go there, but then we can never come back to the Free Settlements.'

'That's right,' said her grandmother. 'They're the enemy. Once you join Fuller Aerospace, no one in the Settlements will trust you again. That's why he came to me. He wants to know if I'll take you in, so you don't have to grow up in Company Territory.'

Dylan rolled the mug of soup between her hands.

'Does my dad want me to stay here?' she asked.

'Your dad wants to be with you forever, but he knows that isn't what's best for you. He thinks you'll probably have a better life here.'

Her grandmother took her arm off Dylan's shoulder, and turned to give her a long, thoughtful look that made Dylan feel embarrassed. She huddled down, hiding behind her own knees.

'When I was young, I hated it when big decisions were made without me,' said Netsai. 'And your mother did, too. When she wanted to leave this base and go off with your dad, I tried to stop her, and it only drove her away from me. I think you're old enough to make this decision for yourself. I don't think you'd forgive me and your father if we tried to make it for you.'

Dylan sipped her soup. She had to admit, Rayleigh seemed like a fun place to live. It was all a bit of a construction site compared to the other bases, but the kids were okay.

Company Territory sounded exciting, though. Fuller Aerospace was the enemy, but everyone was someone's enemy in the Free Settlements. And all the best technology came from Company Territory. She had heard stories about how the people there were lazy, and used their technology rather than working for a living, but she secretly thought that sounded kinda great. She heard they still had pads there, too. And, most importantly, Frank would be there.

'I think I want to stay with my dad,' she said.

'Are you sure?' her grandmother said. 'Once you decide, there's no coming back. This will be the last time I see you.'

'But it'll be the last time I see my dad if I stay.'

Her grandmother sighed, and nodded.

'All right,' she said. 'I tried. Come on.'

Dylan finished her soup, and left her mug on the chair.

'I'm sorry I didn't get to spend more time with you,' her grandmother said. 'Come on. Give me another hug.'

Once again, Dylan was cocooned by her grandmother's warm arms. She felt comfortable in them, but also a little bit trapped.

Her grandmother let go, and kneeled down in front of her.

'I'm going to have to ask you for something,' she said quietly, so no one around could hear. 'Going into the Company Territory is going to be hard. They're going to ask you a lot of questions about why you want to be there, and about everything in your past, and who your whole family is. They're going to try to scare you into telling them things that you want to keep secret.

'Whatever you do, never tell them about me. If they ever find out that you're my granddaughter, they might want to hurt me, and hurt you. Please, for your own sake, never tell them you're related to Netsai Chiwasa. Just pretend I don't exist. Do you understand?'

# Part 8.0

---

# The Outliers

# Chapter Eighty-Eight

Dylan and Clifford are herded up onto the back of the skeletal rover. The Outliers tie their wrists and ankles to the carbon fibre and metal frame with long strips of black wire. There isn't a seat for either of them, and the only place that Dylan can stand is on an exposed strut sticking out of the rover's side.

The driver takes Dylan's message, and climbs back up to the top of the rover. He tugs on the control cables, and the rover lurches forward, away from the shattered carcass of Rudolf.

'Hey!' says Clifford, shaking his body to get the Outlier's attention. 'We need to talk to you! Give us your frequency!'

'He can't see you,' says Dylan.

'Can you reach the radio controls on my arm?' says Clifford.

Dylan slides her hands along the frame towards Clifford, but her ankles are tied in place.

'I can't get close enough.'

The Outlier driver turns the black visor of his helmet towards them, and waves a hand at her with a forceful downward motion.

'I think he wants you to be a nice quiet captive,' says Clifford.

'Radio!' Dylan says to the Outlier, exaggeratedly mouthing the word, but the driver turns away. The rover accelerates, and steers towards the hills in the north.

Dylan twists her body around, and looks back. One of the other two Outliers is climbing up the sides of Rudolf with a tool belt, and pulling out the valuable coolant pumps. The third is walking up the low hill towards the scarecrows. The last of the evening light gleams off a long knife.

The glow of the sun fades as they drive north across the plain, towards the distant hills of the Cyani Sulci.

SAM WILSON

Dylan's legs begin to ache. She kneels down, wedging her knee pads between the struts of the rover, trying to give her calf muscles some relief.

'So,' says Clifford. 'Netsai's granddaughter. When were you going to tell me?'

'Never.'

'I could have used that information.'

'That's why,' says Dylan. Her feet are getting pins and needles.

'Did you know her?' she asks.

'We were friends once,' says Clifford. 'Of a kind. And you? Did you know your grandmother well?'

'Not really. I know she was a big part of the independence movement. I know she knew Red Rose.'

'What happened to her after the Collapse?'

'Not too much. She kept her head down. She was the mayor of Rayleigh Base while my mother was growing up.'

'Good for her.'

Dylan looks into the darkness.

'I guess we learned one thing,' she says. 'The Outliers care about Red Rose enough to remember my grandmother's name.'

'Assuming your message is why they took us alive.'

The landscape ahead ripples in the rover's spotlight. The driver makes no concessions for the uneven terrain, and Dylan's teeth slam together as they ride over jagged rocks.

'Tell me about the Wintergarden,' she says. 'What were you hoping to find there?'

'Archie Fuller's out-suit. It was covered in cameras. It recorded the first murder.'

'Okay,' says Dylan, thinking it through. 'And from the way the Company's acting, I guess the murder didn't go the way they say it did.'

'Exactly.'

'How do you know the suit's there?'

'I don't,' says Clifford. 'But from the way the Outliers are guarding that place, they're keeping something there that they specifically don't want the Company getting their hands on. I

410

can't think of anything they'd guard like that except for Archie Fuller's suit.'

'Why do you care?' says Dylan. 'Why did you drag us into all this?'

She looks over at him. His body is silhouetted against the headlights on the ground ahead. There's an arched reflection on the side of his helmet, but the inside is dark. When he talks, his voice is tired.

'When you get to my age, Dylan, you'll look back and find that many of the things that gave your life meaning have been taken away from you, through time, or accident, or your own mistakes. All the threads that your life was woven from have snapped, one by one, so slowly that you barely noticed, until all you're left with is emptiness. And if you find a trace of something that you lost, if there's a sliver of a chance to bring it back, then you'll grab that thread with both hands and follow it no matter where it leads.'

The Cyani Sulci rises up ahead of them, blotting out the stars. It's a natural maze of cracked terrain, a network of thin valleys weaving through a wide chain of hills. They drive around its western side and ride parallel to it for several kilometres, past the openings into a dozen different valleys. Eventually, the driver steers into one of the seemingly identical gaps, and they ride up it into the Sulci. After a kilometre they steer into a side valley, then another, weaving deeper into the cracked terrain between dunes of sand and scattered boulders. Every so often a rock barrier rises up out of the darkness ahead, and the driver steers around it into a new valley.

A faint beeping comes over Dylan's radio.

'What's that?'

'My oxygen alarm,' says Clifford. 'I've got about fifteen minutes left.'

He stands as high as his bindings will allow, and shakes his body back and forward hard.

'Driver!' he says. 'Any spare air tanks?'

The driver's back stays turned away from them.

'Come on!' Clifford says, and shakes the rover with all his might.

411

The vehicle's already rattling on its suspension, and his movement make no difference.

'Talk to us!' he shouts. Dylan's speakers buzz in her helmet.

'You're using up your air,' she says.

'I'd rather die from trying than not trying.'

He keeps rocking back and forward, back and forward as far as he can go.

'Come on!' he shouts. 'Look at me!'

'Knock it off!' says Dylan, wincing. 'Are you trying to deafen me?'

'Help me shake this thing.'

'Why?'

'It doesn't matter how much you hate me, Ward. By my reckoning, you've got twenty minutes more air than me, at most. We're up the same creek, so grab a paddle if you don't want to die from spite.'

Dylan takes her time in getting upright. She crouches down and straightens her legs to get the blood flowing again, tightens her wrists against the support bar, and starts shaking the rover.

'Get in sync with me,' he says. 'One, two. One, two.'

They lean back and forward, tugging on the frame. The rover rocks with them, but the driver still doesn't look back. Through the radio, Clifford's beeps become a steady whine.

'Come on,' says Clifford. 'You can do better than that!'

Dylan channels all her anger into the carbon fibre and metal frame. She shakes it until everything disappears except the rhythmic motion of her rage.

Clifford's legs buckle, and his body drops and twists to the side. He's held up by his wrists, and his arms cross in front of him. Dylan stops shaking.

'Hey!' she says. 'Wake up!'

She hears a cough, and he slowly pulls himself up to a crouch.

'Ward...'

'Save your breath,' she says. 'Calm down. Breathe slow.'

His throat is constricted. 'If the suit... if the suit... is... there... tell them... Princess.'

'What?'

Clifford's breathing speeds up.

'All upper-case. Numbers instead of letters. P. R. One. N. C. E. Five. Five. Princess. Oh, God. I can't... I can't...'

He shouts incoherently, and starts to convulse. He tugs repeatedly at his bonds. The front of his helmet slams into the rover frame.

'Hey!' Dylan shouts at him. 'Keep it together!'

His body contorts and arches. He spasms and flails for longer than Dylan thinks is possible. She closes her eyes and keeps shaking the rover frame desperately. When she opens them again, Clifford hangs limply from his wrists against the side of the rover.

'Clifford?'

There's no sound on the radio, except the protracted tone from his oxygen alarm, high-pitched and distant.

Dylan crouches down, letting her helmet hang between her bound arms. She stares ahead, through the skeletal frame of the Outliers rover, to the rocky world on the other side. She breathes slowly, conserving her air. Her own oxygen alarm starts to beep. She keeps breathing, as slowly and shallowly as she can.

Her weight shifts, and the rover slows down. They're rolling down a slope: a ramp down into a huge square pit lit up by spotlights. Below them, armed figures are standing guard around active mining rovers. Like the Outliers that captured her, the tops of all their helmets are daubed with dried blood.

Their rover gets to the bottom of the ramp and drives slowly across the base of the pit. An armed figure raises a hand, bringing them to a stop. The Outlier guard and the driver have a silent conversation, and Dylan watches, feeling helpless. Her helmet beeps incessantly.

'Come on,' she mutters.

The guard waves them forward, and the skeletal rover drives to the other side of the pit, and into a tunnel barely wider than the rover. Yellow lamps light the roof every fifty metres, making the world flip between light and shadow as they ride deeper. The tunnel angles downwards, and opens up into a floodlit cavern.

At the far end of it is a ridged ceramic wall, and parked in front of it are more decrepit rovers. The driver brings them to a stop at the end of the row, next to a metal gateway embedded in the ceramic wall.

It's the end of the line.

# Chapter Eighty-Nine

Dylan yanks the bar that she's tied to with all her strength, pulling and pushing to make the rover shake on its suspension. The driver looks back at her. He raises his black sun-shield, and for the first time, Dylan sees a real human face. He's younger than she expected, in his early twenties, with a high forehead, thin cheeks, and pale blonde hair that's almost as white as his skin. He snaps his fingers at her silently, then frowns at Clifford's collapsed body, and clambers over the top of the rover towards them.

The Outlier doesn't unbind Clifford's hands. He stands over the body, and his lips move silently as he talks over his radio. After a minute, the metal gateway slides up, and two more suited Outliers come out of it. They surround the skeletal rover with their bolt guns aimed and ready, the driver starts untying Clifford's wrists and ankles.

'Oh, for fuck's sakes, it isn't a trick,' Dylan mutters.

Clifford's body comes loose and falls from the side of the rover, landing on the uneven cavern floor. The driver jumps down, and lifts Clifford under the arms. One of the other Outliers picks up Clifford's legs, and the third keeps their bolt gun at the ready. They carry Clifford through the metal door, and it slides closed behind them.

The low oxygen warning blares in Dylan's ear. Her lungs are starting to burn, and she feels the rising panic of oxygen deprivation.

'Come on,' she gasps. 'Come on!'

The door slides open again, and the driver comes back out with another Outlier. He points a bolt gun at Dylan. The new Outlier, a young woman, climbs up onto the rover and unbinds her wrists. Dylan raises her hands in surrender, and drops down from the frame. As soon as she's on the ground the driver shoves her forward, and she stumbles towards the metal door.

On the other side of it is a metal chamber, five metres by five metres, lit with yellow light. When all three of them are inside, the outer door slides closed. Dylan feels air blowing against her suit, and noise from the outside world starts to return. The high frequencies come back first, making the world around her sound tinny. She hears the roar of incoming air, and the groan of the metal walls as they flex with the pressure.

Her skin is pricking and her vision is getting dark. As soon as she dares, she flicks the safety catches on the side of her helmet, and pops the seal. There's a stab in her ears as the pressure in her suit drops, but after a second the pain subsides, and Dylan breathes the air of the Outlier base. It's warm, even in the airlock, and smells faintly of burned plastic.

Dylan coughs, and gasps. She can feel her panic subsiding, and the dark spots in her vision start to clear.

She looks around at the Outliers. The driver reholsters his bolt gun, and takes off his helmet. His eyes are pale blue and he has a pronounced Adams apple. He looks at Dylan with a sneer.

'*Ty jen loco.*'

'Sorry, what?'

'He said you're crazy,' says the other Outlier, taking off her helmet. Her accent is unplaceable, somewhere between Russian and Chinese. She's as young as the driver, and her hair is cut in a tight black bob. A leaf-shaped burn mark runs from her cheek down the side of her neck.

The inner airlock door opens, and the two of them lead Dylan out onto a carbon-fibre platform at the edge of a huge, dark chamber. Dylan looks over the side and sees glints of light reflecting off a wet cavern floor, fifty metres below. She's never experienced vertigo like this before, even in the Grove in Hunter, and her body instinctively freezes. The woman grabs Dylan by her out-suit's collar, and pulls her away from the edge.

'*Mi anek mek wat?*' she says to the driver.

Dylan can't understand his reply, but she catches a few words that she knows from different languages: *guerre* from French, *plennic* from Russian, and what could be a few phrases of bastardised Mandarin. When the driver sees the way she's watching them, he glares at her.

'*Tos oi len ty,*' he says gruffly, and shoves her towards a thin bench at the back of the platform. The upper section of Clifford's suit is lying on a table next to it, along with the locket that had been hanging around his neck. The inner lining of his suit is crumpled on the floor in front of the bench.

The driver points his gun at Dylan while she takes off her suit. After she strips off her underlayer, the woman hands her light yellow trousers and a shirt from a bin of clothes next to the table. They're loose-fitting, but they give her a fraction of dignity.

The woman and the guard take off their own suits and put on the same loose clothes, taking turns to keep the gun aimed at Dylan. When they're done, the woman binds Dylan's hands again, and pushes her ahead of them down a steep ramp, to a wider platform below. A row of a dozen hammocks hangs down over it, held up by carbon-fibre rods that stick out from the rock wall of the chamber. Dylan sees the bulge of sleeping bodies inside them. At the centre of the platform, four Outliers are playing cards at long table with an open bottle between them. They watch Dylan silently as her captors lead her past, and down a second ramp.

As Dylan's eyes adjust to the dark, she gets a better sense of the scale of the cavern. It's more than a hundred metres wide, and its cross-section is roughly cylindrical. The walls curve in at the top and bottom to become the cave's ceiling and floor.

'Lava tube,' she murmurs.

'Quiet,' says the woman.

It's a vast, naturally occurring tunnel. Dylan has seen a few of them before, back in the south, but they were never more than a few metres across. The one the Outliers have found holds thousands, maybe millions of cubic metres of air. It's deep enough to protect the Outliers from radiation and micrometeorites. It's the closest thing to a natural paradise that a planet like Mars can provide.

The three of them reach the floor of the lava tube, and Dylan smells vegetation and rich soil. Fields of corn and wheat and paddies of rice are growing in long terraces, and water gurgles along a drainage channel next to the path. Dylan sees lights glinting ahead, above eye level, and hears distant music. Rhythms mix together over a thousand talking voices.

As they walk closer, she starts to understand what she's seeing. Ahead of them, the whole width of the cavern is filled with platforms, ramps and walkways. There are at least forty levels of them, held up on cables hanging down from the roof of the cavern, and from pylons jutting from the walls, and scaffolding rising up from the ground. As she gets closer, she can make out all the vital machinery of life poking out between the walkways: wide cylindrical vats for breeding bioplastics, rows of carbon scrubbers, vast water filtration stacks. The layers of platforms are unevenly spaced, and the connections are haphazard, like an organism that's mindlessly driven to fill every cubic metre of available space.

The smell of compost and vegetation mingles with the greasy scent of frying food. Dylan hears dozens of feet thumping on the platforms. She looks up through the scaffolding, and catches glimpses of people wearing the same kinds of loose clothes in muted shades of yellow, green and burgundy. There's a buzz of laughter, and the twang of a live band playing with unsettling joy.

Her captors lead her on, out of the fields and beneath the tangled mass of platforms. The underside of the town is dark, and water drips down from one of the levels above. In the patchwork of weak light shining down between the overhead platforms, Dylan can make out rounded shapes hanging down on either side of the path; more hammocks, filled with sleeping bodies.

Up ahead, the path passes a pool of light at the base of a pillar. Two figures are standing over an old man with a wild white beard, shining their flashlights down on him. He's sitting on the ground with his legs outstretched, holding a red ceramic container of drink that's spilling out onto the cavern floor.

Dylan recognises the situation instantly from all her months on the night shift. The older generation on Mars never really recovered from the Collapse, and are still trying to get off the planet any way they can.

'*Faka mama ty!*' the old man slurs, squinting up into the flash-lights.

Dylan expects the nightsticks to come down. Instead, the guards gently help the old man to his feet, and lead him over to the nearest empty hammock. They help him into it, and even take off his sandals for him. He mutters to himself the whole while, but his volume is greatly diminished. As Dylan and her captors pass the hammock, the guards give them a quiet greeting.

'*Ale.*'

Through the cables and scaffolding ahead, Dylan sees that they're approaching another wall of orange-brown ceramic. It rises from floor to ceiling, blocking off the whole height and width of the cavern. Light shines onto it in patches from floodlights on the platforms above her.

A second metal door is set at the base of the giant wall. Dylan's two captors lead her to it, and the driver taps a panel on the side. The door slides up, and the woman pushes her through a metal-walled antechamber: another airlock, but with both doors open.

When they step out the other side, the air is cold and smells of decay. Dylan's breath condenses into a cloud that glows in the light of a floodlight over the airlock door. They're still in the cavern, but there are no hanging platforms on this side of the barrier. The rock walls are far more uneven here, bulging inwards into the empty lava tube. Chunks of the cavern's roof have scattered across the floor as giant boulders. Two hundred metres ahead, the cavern constricts to a dead end.

Dylan looks around. To the left of the airlock entrance are stacks of crates, and piles of rock and scrap metal. On the right, twenty-five blue plastic sheets are lying in an orderly grid on the ground. Most sheets are coated in a thin layer of dust, but the closest one looks like it was recently disturbed. Each sheet has a long shape lying beneath it, and it doesn't take much imagination for Dylan to know what they are.

The woman with the scar points to the wall next to the airlock. There's a metal ring embedded in the ceramic, and a length of cable attached to it ending in two padlocked loops. 'Sit,' she says.

Dylan obeys. The Outliers pull the loops of cable tight around her ankles, and lock the padlocks closed. When Dylan's secure, they exchange a few quiet words in their hybrid language, and walk back out through the airlock. The metal door slides closed behind them.

In the silence, Dylan can hear the dull thud of her own blood pumping in her ears. For a moment she fears that the Outliers are going to vent the air out of this section of the cavern and suffocate her. But they've had every opportunity to kill her already, without wasting a million cubic metres of breathable air. She steadies her nerves, and the rhythm of her pulse slows. This isn't an execution chamber yet. It's just a prison.

The cold creeps in though her thin clothing, and the hairs stand up on her bare arms. She raises her knees and tucks her hands under her armpits to keep them warm, but she can't stop herself from shivering.

The closest blue plastic sheet is three metres away from her. When she can't hold out any longer, she lies down on her stomach and crawls towards it, as far as the cable will allow. It bites into her ankles, but her fingertips reach the edge of the plastic sheet. She hooks it with her fingernail and scratches at it, centimetre by centimetre, until she has enough of it in her hand to get a grip, and tug it away from the body.

It's Clifford. Of course it is. He's on his back, naked, with his arms at his sides and his legs together. His eyes are sunken and dry, and his mouth is open slightly.

Dylan crawls back to the metal ring in the wall and wraps the plastic shroud around herself, tucking the edges under her body until she's fully cocooned. The only gap is for her mouth, so she can keep breathing the cold air. After a few minutes she isn't shivering any more. A few minutes after that, with great relief, she feels the warm disorder of sleep creeping into her mind.

She wakes without any sense of how much time has passed. The floodlight over the door is still shining, and the cavern is still completely silent. Her body is stiff and cold, and her bladder is painfully full. She pulls the plastic tight around her as she sits upright.

'Hello? ...' she calls out. 'Anyone?'

Her voice resonates in the cavern, and dies away. There's no response, and no point in waiting. She unwraps herself from the plastic sheeting, and kicks it to the side. She squats down as far from the metal ring as she can get, and relieves herself. It's undignified, but given her situation, she feels no shame.

When she's finished, she grabs the plastic sheet again, wraps herself back into it.

And she waits.

She remembers being a child, six years old, joining her father in the bar in Solidaritas Base to meet up with one of his old friends. The man was a trader who had been imprisoned in the Orange Fortress for smuggling subversive literature, which was anything that hadn't been printed by the base authority. He told her father that he survived solitary confinement by going a little crazy, on his own terms. He would make up new imaginary people every day, and then pretend he was meeting them in the common room of his home base. He would have meandering conversations with them about music and politics and his favourite conspiracy theories.

Dylan isn't ready for that quite yet. But if the time comes, and she feels her mind fraying, she knows who she'll be talking to.

It's easy to imagine a chat with Frank. He'd be teasing her mercilessly, and looking for something to laugh about. He wouldn't stop until he'd found the darkest, sickest joke about their situation, and chuckle about it for hours. She used to roll her eyes at him for his inability to take the horrors of the world seriously, but she can see his point now. Sometimes, denial is the only way out.

The only other person she can imagine talking to right now is

James Clifford. He'd be laying the blame for all this onto her, and saying that if she hadn't tied him up, maybe they could have started running from the Outliers sooner. He'd be coming up with some kind of cynical survival strategy, some way for her to ingratiate herself to the Outliers before she stabs them in the back.

But Clifford isn't talking. He's right where she left him, staring up at the roof of the cavern through eyes as dry as marble.

# Chapter Ninety

Dylan hears a mechanical hiss, and lowers her hood of plastic sheeting to see the woman with the scar walk into the chamber with a bolt gun at her hip. She's wearing similar loose-fitting clothes to the last time that Dylan saw her, but these ones are pure white. She looks down at Dylan with a scowl.

'Legs,' she says.

Dylan takes a moment to understand. She straightens her legs out from under the plastic sheeting, and the woman leans down to unlocks the padlocks. Dylan considers kicking out, fighting back, grabbing the gun. But then she'd have to fight her way through a city of Outliers, and she isn't convinced that she would make it far.

'On your feet,' the woman says in her thick hybrid accent. Dylan stands, dropping the plastic shroud.

'I'm thirsty,' she says. 'I need water.'

'No. No time. *Dux tre* are waiting.'

The woman grabs Dylan by the wrists, and leads her through the airlock in the giant ceramic wall. On the other side, the cavern is in daylight. Geodesic spheres made from LED panels are hanging in the gap between the wall and the city, shining with bright, sun-coloured light.

The woman leads Dylan across the rocky cavern floor, and up a carbon-fibre ramp to the first layer of the city. It's made from platforms held up by pillars and pylons below, and cables that disappear into the gaps in the layers above.

On a nearby platform, some Outliers are cooking with metre-wide saucepans on a long line of stove-tops. Behind them, trays of tomatoes and strips of fruit are drying under heat lamps. Despite

Dylan's fear, her mouth waters at the smell of stew rich with peppers, cumin, onions, garlic, and soya.

The woman with the scar leads Dylan onto a second walkway. They pass over the top of a round vat of algae, where Outliers are using two-handed paddles to skim off the greenish scum rising to the surface, and feeding it into a chemical reactor to be refined into bioplastic.

There's an orange glow ahead, coming through the round portholes of a row of metal doors set into the rock face. As they get closer, an Outlier wearing a reflective heat-resistant suit opens one of the furnaces, and pulls out a ceramic crucible filled with molten metal.

Further on Outliers are tending to a milling machine that throws out showers of sparks as it carves a block of steel into the shape of a motor housing. Bins and crates are piled with ingots of steel, aluminium and titanium. On any other base they would have been under armed guard, but the Outliers here pass by without giving them a second glance.

They walk up another ramp, and Dylan catches more glimpses of life in the city: a team repairing a water pipe, Outliers sitting at consoles and standing around drafting tables, a group of elderly men and women, sitting in a half-circle, stitching sheets of mylar and electrostatic filament into the outer layer of an out-suit.

The city gets brighter as they ascend through the layers until the geodesic sun lamps are close enough to touch. The platforms of the upper level are more widely spaced to let the light shine down, but they're still filled with human activity: an Outlier is pulling fabric from a loom, a second is trimming another's hair with clippers, and some children are kneeling in a circle, playing a noisy game with steel bolts.

Dylan looks over the edge of their walkway. Through the gaps between the platforms she can see all the way down to the dark cavern floor, and once again, she feels her muscles freeze up from vertigo.

'*Gada*,' the woman with the scar says sharply, tugging on Dylan's wrists.

Dylan stumbles forward and catches the attention of one of the children. He points at her.

'*Kampani!*' he yells.

The children he's playing with look around and see Dylan. They start shouting, too, and their voices crack with rage.

'*Kampani, kila oi Kampani!*'

The shouting grabs the attention of the older Outliers, who turn and stare. Down below, more of them look up at the commotion. They kick off their sandals and begin climbing and swinging towards Dylan, leaping between the poles and cables and pylons. They fly up through the air with practised ease, arcing between handholds effortlessly and fluidly, and landing on the platforms around her to join the growing crowd.

'*Faka oi Kampani! Kila oi Kampani!*'

The woman with the scar turns and shouts at the crowd.

'*Tos ty!*'

But more Outliers keep swinging up from the lower levels. Adults and children, with red faces and bared teeth. They leap up onto the walkway, mobbing Dylan. She feels hands gripping her, and fingernails digging into her upper arm. A metal screw flies out of the crowd, aimed at Dylan's forehead, and she feels it tear her skin.

'*Hai!*' the woman with the scar shouts loudly. She pulls Dylan behind her, and faces the crowd.

'*Faka tos ty! Dux tre lei wit oi ta, yego lei gada oi dux tre!*'

It seems to work. The roar of the Outliers dies down to an angry murmur. A man at the front glares sullenly at Dylan and spits on the walkway by his feet. The woman pulls at Dylan's wrists, and marches her away from the crowd.

As they cross the top of the city, the platforms around and below them begin to thin out. After another thirty metres they disappear entirely. The city comes to an end, and the walkway stretches away from it, hanging alone from the cavern roof. A hundred metres below it are the fields of growing crops, a patchwork of green and yellow that rise up the curved sides of the cavern in long, thin terraces, glowing under the light of a thousand roof-mounted lamps. In the far distance, a scaffold crosses the width of the tube. Another giant ceramic wall is being constructed, and behind it, Dylan can see the haphazard layers of another hanging city.

The walkway sways gently under Dylan's feet. She keeps her eyes on the woman leading her, and tries to suppress the terror gnawing in her gut.

Hanging down between the grow lamps ahead of them is a circular platform, twenty metres wide. In its centre, three Outliers dressed in white are sitting at a table. The rover driver who brought Dylan in is standing at their side, glaring at her as she approaches. He is hugging his own arms, and his pale lips are pulled tight.

The table is raised. The three Outliers sitting at it glance up briefly as Dylan and the woman with the scar walk onto the platform, then go back to looking at some documents in front of them. It looks like some kind of courthouse, or maybe a throne room. She would have expected a council of elders, but none of the Outliers at the table are older than their mid-thirties. On the left is a woman with plucked eyebrows, and in the middle is a woman with piercing green eyes and hair tied back under a white cloth. The man on the right looks unremarkable, except for a neatly trimmed beard.

Dylan recognises them, or at least, their type. People like them flock to the Syria canteen at night, turning it into an informal bar: young, smart, and socially savvy, full of ideas of how to fix the base, always ready with an opinion, always butting heads. On Syria, they never get far. The old guard hold all the power, and have bureaucracy and inertia on their side. It seems like things work differently here.

'Do not speak to them unless they speak to you first,' the woman with the scar whispers. 'Do not lie to them. Speaking means death. Lies means death. Understood?'

Dylan nods.

The rover driver is still staring at her. When he sees Dylan looking at him, he bares his teeth with a snarl.

'He's on trial,' the woman behind Dylan murmurs.

'What for?'

'For not killing you.'

At the high table, the woman with the green eyes leans back in her chair. There's no discernible expression on her face as she looks Dylan up and down.

'*Ty kama.*'

The woman with the scar pushes Dylan forward to the centre of the platform, and the three seated Outliers look down on her.

'What is your name?' says the man with the beard, in heavily accented English.

'Dylan Ward.'

He runs his finger down a list in front of him, pauses on a line, and nods to himself.

The woman with the green eyes picks up the faded message that Dylan wrote, and holds it up with one hand.

'Did you write this?'

'Yes.'

The woman with no eyebrows leans forward and looks down at Dylan, tilting her head slightly.

'When we found you, what were you doing? Why were you on our border?'

There are many ways for Dylan to answer this. She settles for a self-servingly simple answer.

'We were stranded. Our rover was partially disabled after we attacked a Company train.'

'Why?'

'The man I was with had a vendetta against the Company.'

'What man?'

'James Clifford. Head of Internal Services.'

The woman with green eyes purses her lips. The man with the beard makes a note.

'Why would a Company head defect?' says the woman with no eyebrows.

'I don't know,' says Dylan. The woman with the scar gives her a nudge from behind. 'I do know that he was trying to reach your territory.'

'What for?'

'He was searching for a place called the Wintergarden.'

The bearded man looks impatient. '*Yego lei no oi ta, Rosa lei viv oi vil ta?*'

'Why did he want to go to the Wintergarden? What was he looking for?' says the green-eyed woman.

'Archie Fuller's out-suit. He believed it could damage the Company.'

Dylan doesn't know if it was the answer they were looking for, but all three Outliers relax noticeably. The man with the beard puts down his pen, and the woman with no eyebrows shifts back in her seat.

'*Yego lei no oi net,*' she says. '*Kila oi yego.*'

Dylan hears a click from behind her. The woman with the scar is unholstering her bolt gun. Her stance, with feet planted slightly apart, makes Dylan instantly alarmed.

'Would Rose want this?' she says desperately. It's a pathetic gamble, as futile as the Red Rose locket that Clifford kept around his neck, but the three Outliers at the table glance at each other.

The green-eyed woman speaks. '*Rosa lei dux oi ta, jen kampani lei kila or lei viv.*'

At the side of the table, the driver clasps his own hands, and his face sags with relief.

Slowly, the woman with the scar takes her hand off the gun, and steps away from Dylan.

# Chapter Ninety-One

Five domes, fifteen metres high and brown from dust, are clustered together in a bare stretch of the northern plains. They're the only visible landmark for kilometres around, other than the distant jagged hills of the Sulci.

The skeletal Outlier rover pulls to a stop twenty metres from the small base, and Dylan lets go of the side of it, and drops down to the ground. The Outliers back in the hanging city have given back her out-suit, and have even repaired the hole in her glove, but they bound her wrists again as soon as her suit was back on.

The woman with the scar drops the steering cables, and jumps down from the seat on the top of the skeletal rover.

'Come,' she says, striding towards the domes.

Dylan follows, watching her footing on the rocky ground. Her body aches from her night in the cold prison. She has been given water to drink, but no food, and the hunger gnaws at her. Stomach acid burns at her throat.

The woman leads Dylan around the side of the nearest dome. As they get close to its side, Dylan sees a spiderweb of ridges on its outer surface. It looks like it was glued together from curved sheets of hardened epoxy.

'Is this the Wintergarden?' Dylan asks.

The Outlier woman looks back at her, and nods in her helmet. '*Vintertuin*,' she says.

As they walk around the side of the dome, a round window the size of Dylan's helmet comes into view. The glass is dusty, but Dylan can make out some angular shapes inside.

'What's in there?'

'Look if you want,' says the Outlier. She's acting nonchalant, but Dylan catches the twitch of a smile at the side of her mouth.

Dylan wipes the window with her glove and presses her helmet against it. It's dark inside. The only light comes from another window opposite, which glows orange from a thick layer of dust.

Half of the inside of the dome is taken up by a two-metre diameter metal cylinder lying on its side. The hatch on the end of it marks it as an airlock. In front of the hatch is a guard rail, protecting a stairwell that disappears into the black depths below the base. As Dylan's eyes adapts to the darkness, she recognises another shape on the floor.

'There's a body in here,' she says. She make out a patch of pale skin under a mop of dark hair, but she doesn't see any blood or visible bone.

'I know,' the Outlier says. 'Come.'

'What happened here? Was there a blow-out?'

The Outlier doesn't answer, but walks away from her towards another dome. A glow is coming through its window, and for a moment Dylan thinks that there must be someone alive inside. But as they get closer, Dylan sees that a whole third of the dome is missing. The far side has burst completely, and hexagonal wall segments are scattered in every direction. The light in the window was sunlight, shining directly onto the glass through the open dome.

The Outlier woman walks to the broken wall, and beckons Dylan closer. The inside of the dome is empty except for the accumulated dust, and a hand-rail surrounding another stairwell. She climbs in through the hole.

'Come,' she says.

Dylan follows her into the dome. The dust inside it is fine and red, and about a metre deep. The Outlier goes to the central stairwell and starts climbing down. The dust has collected on the stairs, turning them into a smooth slope, and as Dylan follows the Outlier down, it comes loose under her boots. She grabs the handrail with both bound hands to stop herself falling.

'Careful,' says the Outlier.

She turns on her headlamp to show Dylan the way. Dylan holds the handrail and crab-walks down the steps until the dust is thin enough for her boots get a good grip. She relaxes, very slightly, and follows the Outlier down into the darkness.

The stairwell opens up onto the first subterranean level, and the Outlier shines her headlamp into an open pressure door.

'Almost there.'

She leads Dylan into a dining room. A single long table is scattered with used plates and coffee mugs. Dylan sees something large and orange on the floor. A second body in loose-fitting overalls is crumpled between the chairs on the far side of the table.

At the sight of the grey-eyed body, Dylan feels a leaden acceptance growing in her gut.

'This is what you wanted to show me, isn't it,' she says. 'Clifford was wasting his time. There's nothing down here.'

For the first time since Dylan met the Outlier, she hears her chuckle.

'No,' she says. 'Come.'

Dylan steps over the body, and follows the Outlier around the table to the back of the dining room. The Outlier points her headlamp at a small hatch on the far wall, next to the dining area's sink. It's marked with the universal symbol for environment control: a stick figure in a half-dome bubble. She pulls at the handle, and the hatch swings open. On the other side is a small cubbyhole, with a grid of circular indentations on the floor where the water and oxygen tanks should be.

'Picked clean,' says Dylan.

The Outlier ignores her. She tugs on a support frame at the back of the cubbyhole, and the rear wall swings aside. Behind it is a metal door. A green light above it marks it as an airlock.

'Everything out here is to throw off raiders,' the Outlier says. 'The real base is through there. Vintertuin. The Wintergarden.'

# Chapter Ninety-Two

On the other side of the airlock, Dylan and the scarred Outlier take off their out-suits in an antechamber and place them on a rack next to a dozen others. The Outlier unties Dylan's wrists, and binds them again after she's put on her light yellow shirt and trousers.

'This is a special place,' the Outlier says. 'Sacred. Holy. You must stay quiet. No loud noises. Understood?'

She leads Dylan out through a carved stone doorway, into a brightly lit cavern. The roof is only two metres above them, but the chamber itself stretches into the distance, so far ahead that Dylan can't see the end. Vegetation is growing everywhere, in an abundance and variety that Dylan has never seen before. Up ahead are wide beds of grasses and lilies, shimmering in a breeze blowing from angled vents in the cavern roof. To their left, cacti and succulents are growing in wide concentric circles around glowing orange heat lamps. The cavern roof is higher to the right, and a forest of trees rises up under the lamps; pines, maples, elms, and a dozen different species that Dylan has never seen before, even in pictures, with roots that hang down from their branches, and thin peeling bark that reveals the silvery skin of the tree beneath. Climbers and green vines twist their way up the trunks of the trees and hang between their branches. Mushrooms grow unchecked between their roots. The cavern is an explosion of organic shapes, colours, textures and scents, growing without limit, filling every available space.

All large bases grow their own plants, and they all treat the process differently. The greenhouse in Sinai is clinical, controlled and sterile. The Grove in Hunter was a diorama, for display purposes only. The Outliers' fields are expansive, but carefully cultivated. The Wintergarden is something else entirely.

The Outlier with the scar walks ahead of Dylan down a path of bare stone leading through the vegetation. In the flowerbeds, Dylan sees plants she never could have imagined. Flowers shaped like jugs and toothed mouths, green ferns with fractal leaves. Delicate flowers, smaller than her fingerprints, dotted with white and yellow. Small, bulbous succulents. Strong-scented clusters of purple flowers hanging from bushes of silver-green. Between them all, irregular rock columns rise up and spread out to support the roof, subtly carved to suggest the shapes of the plants and trees around them.

'Sacred,' she murmurs.

The Outlier walks slowly, and Dylan sees her twist her wrist, stroking the leaves on the bushes with her fingertips. They cross into a new habitat, with brighter light and pools of standing water. Other than these environmental zones, there seems to be no limitation to where the plants can grow. Everything is entwined with everything else. The thickets of bushes are dense and inaccessible. Why would anyone allow the plants to run rampant, when they could be so easily controlled?

Up ahead, she sees an old Outlier at the side of the path. His hair is grey and thinning, and he's kneeling on a woven mat with tasselled edges. He's holding a small brush with a handle made of wood, and his hand moves smoothly and steadily from flower to flower to flower, dabbing the bristles of the brush into the centre of each one. He doesn't look up at they approach.

'What's he doing?' Dylan whispers.

'Pollinating,' the scarred Outlier says quietly. 'Some plants need special attention.'

As they walk past, Dylan catches the expression on his face. He's completely relaxed. His breathing is slow, and his movements are precise. He's transfixed by his work.

They approach a grove of green bamboo, ten metres high. The roof of the cavern is carved out above it, giving it more room to grow. Walking through the grove is like walking through a tunnel.

Yellow leaves crunch beneath their feet, and high above, the poles creak as they sway gently in an artificial wind, bumping into each other with deep, hollow resonance.

'Why is there wind?'

'It's necessary,' the Outlier says quietly. 'The plants need to push against it, or they don't grow strong.'

They exit the grove onto a curving path. Ahead, Dylan can see another Outlier kneeling over the flowerbeds. It's a woman with grey hair, tied back in a bun. Just like the man she is wearing green, and is dipping the tip of a wooden brush into a row of purple flowers.

The scarred Outlier comes to a stop in the middle of the path, and clasps her hands in front of her. Dylan stops, too, looking around at the foliage. There are flowers on either side of them, and some vines hanging down from the cavern roof nearby, but she can't see any reason why they need to stop.

'She's here,' says the scarred Outlier.

The old woman puts down her brush at the side of the path, and straightens up slowly, wiping the dust from her knees. Her bare arms are covered with liver spots and dark freckles. The sun lamps overhead are hot, and sweat drips from her face. She wipes her brow on her sleeve, and turns to look at Dylan. Her cheeks are sunken, and there are fine wrinkles around her eyes and across her forehead, but she's still instantly recognisable. She leans in closer, and her eyes dart around Dylan's face. When she speaks, her voice creaks gently, like the bamboo.

'She wasn't lying. I can see it around her eyes. This is Netsai Chiwasa's granddaughter,' says Red Rose.

# Chapter Ninety-Three

Rosemary Fuller sits across the table from Dylan, with her head tilted curiously. She can't stop examining Dylan's face.

'I know you're not your grandmother,' she says. 'There are traces, though. I wonder how much of her there is in you.'

The table that the three of them are sitting at is wooden and unpolished. A fine moss is growing in the gaps between its warped planks. The ground below it is bare cavern floor swept clean of soil, but bushes and trees are squeezing in on them on every side.

'What happened to Netsai?' Rose asks. 'Is she still alive?'

'No,' says Dylan. 'She died seven years ago, according to the trader reports. I couldn't attend her funeral.'

'Oh,' Rose says. Her eyes go down to the table, and follow her fingertip as she runs it along the coarse grain. Dylan watches her closely. She's in her late sixties, as real and physical as Dylan is, but she's Red Rose. It feels like an optical illusion. Dylan can see the solid vessel, or the faces around it, but not both.

'And how did she end up with a family?'

'She met a French geologist named Mohamed.'

Rose breaks into a smile that leaves deep creases in her cheeks.

'She never struck me as a breeder,' she says. 'I guess the collapse of society did a number on all of us. What happened after that? I can't imagine her settling down.'

'She was the mayor of Rayleigh in the sixties and seventies. My dad told me that she was good at it. Rayleigh expanded massively while she was in charge.'

'Good,' says Rose, leaning an elbow on the table. 'It was a pokey little place when I left her there. Just three little domes and a handful of paranoid scientists. She was always a good leader. Did she talk about me at all?'

'No,' says Dylan. 'I'm sorry. Everyone else did, but not her.'

Dylan catches the pain on Rose's face. For a moment there's a slight extra wrinkling around the eyes.

'Ah, well,' she says. 'Are you hungry?'

'Starving.'

'Well then.'

Rose gets to her feet, and walks over to a tree at the edge of the clearing. Small green and orange fruit are hanging off its branches. She plucks an orange-coloured one, and peels off its skin.

'There's no way to tell if these are ready just by looking at them,' she says to Dylan over her shoulder. 'They can be green and be perfectly sweet and ready, and they can be orange, and still be bitter. The only way to tell is to taste them.'

She pulls out a wedge-shaped segment of fruit, and pops it into her mouth.

'How is it?' Dylan asks.

'As ready as it'll ever be.'

She reaches into the tree and starts plucking more. Dylan sees the way her eyes dart around, and her hand hovers as she selects the next fruit. For Dylan's whole life, she has imagined Rose Fuller as twenty-four years old. It's strange to realise that she must be close to seventy now, but all her movements are sharp and focussed.

'You're staring,' says Rose, not looking back at her. She reaches into the tree and pulls out another fruit.

'How are you still alive?' Dylan asks.

'Ah,' says Rose, turning away from the tree. 'That's the question, isn't it?'

She sits back down with a small smile, and puts six of the orange fruits on the table in front of her. She turns to the scarred Outlier, who has been quietly watching Dylan from the end of the table.

'Inessa, please. Untie her hands.'

'No,' says the Outlier. '*Dux tre* sent her to you to judge if she lives or dies. One way or the other, she is still our prisoner.'

'Inessa,' Rose says firmly.

The Outlier purses her lips, and stands. She takes a knife from her belt and slices through the cable binding Dylan's wrists. The blade reflects the yellow glow of the sun lamps above, and the curl of black cable falls to the ground. The Outlier stabs the knife into the table, point-first, and when she lets go of the handle, the knife stays upright. She sits back down and glares at Dylan.

'Thank you,' says Rose. 'Have a clementine.'

She rolls one across the table to Inessa, and one to Dylan. Dylan starts peeling hers eagerly, and the citrus scent rising up from it makes her mouth water.

'You probably heard that I was hit by a drone strike,' says Rose, peeling her own clementine. 'That's true. On the same night that I abandoned your grandmother, a drone hit my convoy. I was lucky, I was right at the back. I don't remember much of it, just a flash ahead of me, and then my whole rover was knocked backwards. I went outside to see if anyone had survived, but there was nothing left but twisted debris. After that, I kept running. I went as far north as I could. I ran out of food and water. Just as I was running out of air, I was found by a resource-scouting expedition from the Tycho Mining Base.'

Dylan bites into a wedge of the clementine. It's sweet, but tart enough to make her wince. She puts the rest of it into her mouth and lets its sour juices fill her mouth.

'But how could you join the Outliers? Have you seen what they do to innocent settlers?'

The scarred Outlier stands quickly, pushing her chair back, and snatches her knife from the table.

'Inessa, please. Sit,' Rose says calmly.

Inessa glares at Dylan, blade in hand. She spits on the ground, but pulls her chair in and sits down again. She puts the knife flat on the table in front of her and leans back, running her thumb across her scar.

'You're definitely Netsai's granddaughter,' Rose says to Dylan. 'You're not intimidated by me, are you? It's refreshing.'

'They kill families. Whole bases.'

'So does the Company,' said Rose. 'I don't like it, and I don't agree with it, but until you know what the Outliers have been through, you aren't qualified to point fingers. The Outliers saved my life. They wanted to use me as a pawn in their internal politics. When I refused, they cast me out. But they let me have this place, which isn't nothing. They still come here on a . . . I suppose you would call it a pilgrimage, to help me nurture the plants. But I'm not one of them.'

Dylan looks around at the jungle surrounding them.

'What is this place?' she says. 'There are species here that I've never seen before. Where did they all come from?'

Rose rolls a second clementine to her, and starts peeling another one of her own.

'This was my father's private seed bank,' she says. 'He was trying to preserve the genetic diversity of Earth. I couldn't let them stay dormant, so I'm giving them a chance to grow.'

'Why?' Dylan asks.

Rose looks up from her clementine, and gives Dylan a quizzical smile.

'What do you mean?'

'What's their purpose?' she said. 'Can you eat all of them? Make textiles? Medicine? What are they all for? Why are you doing all this?'

'Why nurture life for life's sake?' Rose asks. She tilts her head slightly and looks up at the vines growing on the roof of the cavern. 'Interesting question, I'll need to think about that one. But I'm meant to be interrogating you, aren't I? What brings you to the wild north?'

Dylan finishes her second clementine, and piles the peeled skin in front of her.

'I was brought up here by James Clifford.'

Rose looks off to the side, and shakes her head.

'Never heard of him.'

Inessa reaches into the pocket of her trousers and takes out a piece of paper. She unfolds it, and slides it across the table to Rose. Dylan cranes forward, and sees a black-and-white picture of

Clifford's body, taken on the floor of the cold prison. A flicker of a frown crosses Rose's face, followed by a look of terrible sadness.

'Oh,' she says.

'You knew him?' Inessa asks.

'Very well,' says Rose. 'He hurt me. He hurt my pride. I didn't think I had much of an ego, compared to the rest of my family. But he found it.'

She looks up at Dylan.

'What did he want up here?'

'He was trying to find the footage from your brother's out-suit.'

'Why?' says Rose. 'Trying to tie up all the Company's loose ends?'

'No. He was acting alone. He wanted to prove you didn't kill Archie Fuller.'

Rose studies the printout in front of her, and runs her fingertips down the image of Clifford's face.

'Bastard,' she murmurs. 'I hated him. I had every right. He's still pulling the same old shit, even after death.'

'Do you have your brother's suit?' Dylan asks.

Rose looks up from the page. It takes a moment for her eyes to focus on Dylan.

'No,' she says. 'I buried it with my brother near Pavonis Mons. I wasn't thinking straight, my brother was murdered in front of me and civilisation was collapsing. It didn't occur to me until I got to Tycho Mining Base that he could have been recording the whole thing. By then, it was far too late. I've been kicking myself. Every time the Company expanded north, every time they convinced the Settlements to let them build an outpost with promises of peace and order, I thought, if only I could show them that footage. If only I could show them what the Company truly is. I wanted to mount a mission to the south, to dig up Archie's suit from his grave, maybe even give him a proper burial. But it's pointless.'

'Why?' says Dylan.

'I don't have the code,' Rose says with a shrug. 'Archie encrypted all his footage at the source to keep it from the paparazzi. Without the code, there's no footage. So there's no point in going south to get the suit.'

Dylan stares right through Rose. She's dredging up her memory of Clifford's death. He was dangling from the side of the rover, hanging by his wrists, saying something that didn't make any sense, a word, written with numbers.

'Yes there is,' she says.

Rose frowns at Dylan.

'Why?'

'Clifford told me the code.'

# Chapter Ninety-Four

There are twelve other Outliers spread out through the Wintergarden. Dylan can see them in the distance, each one working alone, pollinating, planting, maintaining the air and water systems. Everything they do in the cavern is in accordance with the lives of the plants. Their toilets are set over a compost heap, behind some bushes at the edge of the cavern. Before Dylan uses it, Inessa tells her to scatter a thin layer of soil and wood chips over her excrement when she's done, in order to aid its conversion into fertile soil. After a lifetime of using sterile chemical toilets, Dylan finds the whole process upsettingly organic.

There are no showers, either. The sprinkler system is on a timer that waters different areas of the cavern in a predictable pattern. At the far end of the cavern, Dylan sees three of the Outliers stripping off their clothes without shame, and putting them aside in time to catch a five-minute shower of simulated rain.

In the evening, as the sun lamps dim over the cavern, section by section, they all gather together to dine at the wooden table. Rose introduces Dylan to the Outliers as her guest, and serves them all a range of fruits and vegetables that Dylan has never experienced before: avocados, mulberries, dragon fruit. Most of the flavours are delicious, or at least intriguing, but her sense of taste has been shaped by growing up on Mars, and some of the flavours are beyond the limits of her palette. She decides she never needs to try durian again.

Throughout the meal, the gathered Outliers stare at Dylan in stony silence. Occasionally, one will whisper to another. If Rose notices their hostility then she doesn't comment on it. Instead, she does all she can to keep the conversation flowing.

'My father was naive, when he started the seed bank,' she says, focusing her attention on Dylan. 'He thought that all you needed to grow plants was soil, water and light, but there's so much more to it. Many of these plants require very specific bacteria and fungi in the soil in order to connect them with all the other plants around, and no one thought to bring those specific species from Earth. It's taken us decades to successfully cultivate these plant networks. We've even had to engineer some of the missing bacteria and fungi from scratch. And there are other problems. Some species of plants are invasive, and poison the other plants' soil. As much as I want them all to live, I've had to choose sides. All these interventions have made me really question why I was doing this. If the plants can't truly live naturally, what's the point? But I can't pretend I don't exist, and that I'm not a vital part of this ecosystem, in my own way.'

After the meal, the grow lamps in the cavern continue to dim, some areas more slowly than others, to give extra light to the plants that need it. Soon, there's only a single strip of light coming from the far end of the cavern, shining between the tree trunks and the poles of the bamboo. Rose and the Outliers hook hammocks between the trees and stone columns, and settle in for the night.

Inessa gives Dylan her own hammock to set up where she likes. It's a sheet of orange-brown fabric woven from plant fibre, with loops of hemp rope at each corner. Dylan chooses a spot for it at the edge of the forest, not too close to the Outliers' hammocks, but not so far that she would feel vulnerable in the empty space. She ties it up between a stone column and the trunk of a sturdy pine tree, and climbs in. The sides of the hammock rise up, nestling her in a cocoon. The fabric is soft, and the air in the cavern is pleasantly cool. She closes her eyes, and hears a faint cough from one of the Outliers, and the hiss of the sprinklers in the distance.

Footsteps approach, crunching on fallen sticks and leaves. Dylan sits up. Over the edge of the hammock, she sees Rose coming closer, silhouetted against the last of the lamp light.

'Dylan?' Rose says. 'Can we talk?'

'Sure.'

Rose sits down near the head of Dylan's hammock, on the trunk of a fallen tree. Layers of mushrooms, moss and clover grow out of its sides, and over its exposed roots.

'I've been waiting here a long time, keeping myself busy, trying to forget the mess I left down in the south,' Rose says. Her head hangs down, and the faint light reflects off the side of her sombre face. 'I need to know something, and I don't think anyone else but you can tell me. If I go back down, if I get that footage, will it make a difference?'

'Clifford thought it would, I guess. Sealgair, too.'

'But will it, really? Will anything change?'

Dylan frowns, and runs her hand along the edge of her hammock.

'I guess so. The Company's myth is that it's the source of law and order on Mars, ever since you and the Free Settlements killed their hero Alex Fuller's only son. This demolishes that myth. Even if the Company doesn't believe the footage, the Free Settlements will. They won't be quite so willing to give up their independence to the Company.'

Rose looks out towards the distant light, through the silhouettes of the dense vegetation.

'I knew your great-grandmother, too. Her name was Grace. Did you know about her?'

'No.'

'She was amazing. She was the one who shaped me the most, besides my father. She taught me how to think clearly, so my emotions wouldn't always get the better of me. She said whenever I need to make a big decision, I shouldn't just ask what's going to happen if I do it. I need to ask the opposite question, too. So. What happens if I don't get the suit? Which way is Mars going, if I leave it be?'

Dylan shrugs. 'I'm just a Company guard.'

'But you've lived in Company Territory and the Free Settlements. You know them from the inside. What happens if I don't get the suit?'

'Honestly? The Company will win. Sealgair's making defence

treaties with new settlements every month. In five to ten years, there won't be such a thing as the Free Settlements. Not the way there is now.'

'And if the Free Settlements win? What will Mars be like?'

'Anarchy,' says Dylan. 'Anything could happen, good or bad.'

Rose raises her head, and Dylan sees the dim light reflected in her eyes.

'So what do you think I should do?'

'I can't tell you. I'm not my grandmother.'

'But you're part of it. You're as involved as anyone. You should have a say.'

Dylan stares into the darkness of the vegetation. 'Maybe what we do matters, maybe it doesn't. Maybe the Company's right, and nothing really matters except power and survival.'

Rose shakes her head, slowly and thoughtfully.

'I can't believe that,' she says. 'I have my own selfish reasons to get that suit, but I won't do it if it's only for my own ego. I need to know if there's a chance that it will set things right in some small way. That's why I'm asking you. What should I do?'

Dylan rests her arms on the side of the hammock and closes her eyes.

She thinks about the way that Raul and Chen robbed civilians, and the casual way Clifford had them killed. She thinks about the red list, and being condemned to death by association. The sound that's been playing on repeat in her head comes back to her; the noise of the guards beating her father in a crowded cafeteria.

Her eyes open, and find their focus.

'Find the grave,' she says.

# Chapter Ninety-Five

Rose leads Dylan out through a pressure door, and down a long tunnel that extends straight through the bedrock. The only light comes from a strip of LEDs along the upper right corner of the tunnel. It's the same width as a regular base corridor, about a metre wide, and every hundred metres, they pass a yellow pack the size of a cafeteria tray attached to the roof.

'Explosive charges,' says Rose, as they walk under one. 'So no one wanders in the back door.'

The tunnel goes on and on for more than a kilometre. Rose strides ahead of Dylan without any trouble, and takes her through a second pressure door, into a wide room, twenty metres across, with rock walls and a large airlock door opposite. The skeletons of two rovers stand in the middle of the room, and a third rover at the side is covered by a grey sheet.

'This was an abandoned mining base,' says Rose. 'We turned it into a rover workshop. It barely gets any use these days. Help me with this.'

She takes one side of the sheet, and Dylan takes the other. They pull it aside, revealing a boxy rover. It's only one deck high, with no airlock. One side of it is dented and scratched, and the other is covered with a blue logo. Most of it has been scraped off, but Dylan still recognises the diagonal launching rocket of Fuller Aerospace. The rover isn't much, but at least they won't have to travel south holding onto its sides.

'*Ty lei mek wat?*'

Dylan turns and sees Inessa standing at the pressure door, pointing a bolt gun at her.

'Oh, please, Inessa,' Rose says wearily. 'Put that down. Dylan's helping me.'

Inessa lowers the bolt gun, but keeps her eyes on Dylan.

'What are you doing?'

'I'm going south,' says Rose. 'To collect the suit.'

'No. You stay. It won't be safe. I will go with a team of soldiers.'

'This is something I have to do,' says Rose. 'It's my responsibility, and I'm the only one who knows where the body is buried. And I don't want you going on a murderous rampage in the south on my behalf.'

Inessa purses her lips, and points at Dylan.

'She can't go. She's my responsibility. She will escape to the Company.'

'Well, we can't have that happening, can we,' says Rose. 'So I guess you'll both be coming.'

The rest of the night is spent preparing. The rover has a single tiny sleeping cabin, so Rose brings two hammocks from the cavern. She fills a cold storage container with fruit and vegetables: pears, mangoes, apples, carrots, beans, grapes, jackfruit, and plantains. Dylan brings three out-suits, and Inessa carries a large metal locker into the rover under one arm. It has a security panel on the front.

'What's that?' Dylan asks.

'Bolt guns and knives,' says Inessa. 'Not for you.'

Once the rover is recharged and re-gassed, there isn't anything left to do except plan the route into the south. The three of them sit together at the front of the small rover, and Rose spreads a paper map out across the controls. It's a lot less detailed than Frank's map, and the whole area south of Outlier Territory is mostly empty space.

Rose traces a finger along the contour ridges, and taps on an empty spot.

'There's a plateau to the east of Pavonis Base and Hong Bao,' she says. 'It's on the lowest slopes of Pavonis Mons. At the end of it, there's a cluster of rock structures, worn down by the winds. Have you ever been there?'

Dylan bites the side of her lip.

'No, but I know how to get there. It's going to be tough to get that far south without being spotted.'

'We'll go slow,' says Rose. 'We're not looking for trouble. We'll take our time, get the suit, and be gone before the Company or the Settlements know that we're there. Are you both ready?'

# Chapter Ninety-Six

The rover's diagnostics terminate with a green light. From the driver's seat, Inessa glances over her shoulder at Rose, who nods. Inessa slides her finger forward on the control screen, and the rover rolls out of the bay and into the wide airlock. In the back of the rover, Dylan puts a hand on the wall to steady herself as they lurch to a stop. The doors to the bay close behind them, and after five minutes of depressurisation, the outer doors open ahead, and dusty morning light streams in.

Inessa rolls them out onto the rocky ground. Out of a small window set in the rear hatch, Dylan sees the airlock door closing. It's matt grey, and recessed into the side of a rock outcrop. Once the doors stop moving, it's practically invisible.

The rover turns right and heads southwards towards the distant hills of the Sulci. The northern plains are wide and empty, and there's no sign of any other vehicles on the horizon, or on the radio.

Rose comes to the back of the rover, half-crouched to avoid the low ceiling, and sits down next to Dylan. They don't talk, but rock back and forth together as the rover bumps its way across the uneven ground. Rose stares out of the rear window, watching the cloud of dust kicked up behind them. She fidgets with the fingers of her left hand, taking each one between her thumb and forefinger and twisting them back and forth, like she's trying to loosen a screw.

After an hour, they reach the northern foothills of the Cyani Sulci. Inessa drives them into a shallow valley and steers them through the boulder-strewn maze. Once again, Dylan is surprised how effortlessly the Outliers navigate the Sulci. She comes to the front of the rover and kneels down next to Inessa.

'How do you know the way?'

Inessa shrugs. 'I grew up here. All the True Martians can do it.'

'True Martians?'

Rose chuckles from the back.

'Outliers don't call themselves Outliers.'

For another two hours, Inessa weaves the rover through the Sulci. As they reach the southern slopes, Inessa abruptly powers down the rover.

'What is it?' says Dylan.

Inessa doesn't answer. She slowly reverses the rover until they're hidden in the shadow of a fallen boulder, and takes her hands off the controls. Dylan leans close to the front window, but she can't see anything ahead except scattered rocks between the southern foothills of the Sulci. After a minute, she catches the flash of sunlight on metal. A Fuller Aerospace patrol crosses the mouth of the valley in front of them, a kilometre ahead.

'*Faka oi Kampani*,' says Inessa, and spits on the floor next to the driver's seat. Rose shakes her head.

'You're cleaning that up.'

The Company rovers slowly crawl past the valley, and disappear out of sight behind the low hills. Inessa waits another fifteen minutes, then gets up and offers the driver's seat to Dylan.

'Your turn,' she says. 'This is your territory.'

Dylan sits and looks over the controls. Everything is run off a single touch-screen. The system is old, and looks like it hasn't been modified or updated in any way since the Collapse. But she finds the drive controls and eases the rover slowly forward, out of the valley and onto the barren plain that marks the start of the Free Settlements.

She keeps the rover aimed south. Even though she's driving slowly, she can't stop the rover from throwing up a cloud of dust behind them. All she can do is steer clear of the rippled ground where the dust is the deepest, and hope for the best. She keeps her eyes focused on the horizon, looking out for the tell-tale glint of sunlight on metal or glass, ready to steer clear if they get too close to a Free Settlement or a Company outpost.

Once in a while, she twists in her seat to check on her companions. Inessa is sitting on the weapons locker and watching her, with a bolt gun hanging off her hip. Rose is still staring silently out of the rear window with her chin resting on her hand.

After another forty minutes, Dylan comes to the light-coloured strip of recently turned dust that marks a regular track, and steers away from it. She doesn't want to meet any vehicles coming the other way. The regular tracks exist for a reason though, and past it, the landscape quickly turns treacherous. Rocks the size of out-suit helmets litter the plain, and Dylan has to keep jolting her finger left and right on the touch-screen to avoid them. When the sun finally dips below the southern slopes of Olympus Mons in the west, the extended concentration has left her exhausted.

'We should stop,' says Rose. 'If we drive at night they'll spot our lights.'

For supper, Dylan eats a pear. She's never tried one before. It's soft, ripe and juicy, with a faintly gritty texture. She has no plans to ever return to Outlier Territory, but she'll miss these new experiences.

After they all eat, they hang up the two hammocks from the Wintergarden forest. Rose takes the small sleeping cabin at the side of the rover, and Dylan and Inessa curl up in the hammocks.

After a few minutes, Dylan looks over the side. Inessa's hammock is still, but Rose's privacy screen is still open. The faint red of the rear hatch's emergency lights reflect in Rose's eyes.

'Can't sleep?' says Dylan.

Rose shakes her head.

'Too much to think about. Too many memories. Back when I was young, we thought we could cut ourselves off from the past. Earth's history is too painful. We tried to jettison it.'

Dylan lies back, and closes her eyes. She sees the landscape flowing past in her mind, and new boulders rising up in front of her.

'It didn't work,' comes Rose's quiet voice. 'But you can't cling to the past, either.'

'So, what can you do?'

'I don't know,' Rose mumbles. 'I'm as lost as anyone. Learn, I suppose.'

Dylan feels her thoughts melting, and drifts into a deep sleep.

When she wakes, her hammock is swinging. She looks over the side of it and sees Rose in the driver's seat. Through the front window, the horizon is glowing with the blue light of dawn. The cabin light is on, and Inessa is sitting on the weapons locker again, peeling mangoes with a steel knife.

After breakfast, Dylan sits at the back of the cabin. When the sun is high overhead, she spots a vertical column of dust on the horizon, on the far left side of the rear window. She keeps an eye on it, and it keeps growing. Soon, another dust cloud appears next to it.

'Shit.'

'What's that?' says Inessa, coming to the rear. She puts her head next to Dylan's and looks out of the window.

'Those dust clouds are following us.'

'Who is it?' Rose calls from the driver's seat. 'Free Settlements?'

Dylan lowers her head and clambers to the front of the rover, squeezing her body in next to Rose's seat. She leans against the front window, and looks as far as possible to the sides of the vehicle. A third column of dust is rising up in the west.

'Whoever it is, they're boxing us in.'

'Don't worry about the dust,' Inessa calls from the back. 'Just drive.'

Rose slides the accelerator forwards on the screen. The rover bucks on its suspension, and Dylan presses herself against the cabin wall to stay upright.

Rose points ahead. 'What's that?'

Dylan comes to the front again. Up ahead among the red-brown boulders of the Ulysses Fossae is a cleft in the ground. The mouth of it is wide and shallow, about five metres across, and it angles down into darkness.

'It's a death gully,' says Dylan. 'It's what the traders call them.

They're treacherous. Sometimes you get to the other side safely, sometimes you get wedged in place or fall into a pit. Death gully.'

Rose sucks air between her teeth. 'Well, we don't have a whole lot of choice.'

She steers into the open mouth of the gully, and the rocky walls rise up on either side of them as the rover drops below ground level. The sky becomes a strip of light overhead, and the world darkens.

Rose switches on the headlights. The gully curves to the left, and then sharply to the right. As Rose turns the second corner she locks the wheels, and the rover slides to a halt. Up ahead, one of the walls has partially collapsed. They're cut off by a rockslide.

'Fuck,' says Rose.

'We could wait here,' Dylan suggests. 'Turn off the lights and hope they don't figure out where we're hiding.'

'No,' says Inessa, squeezing past her to look out of the front window. 'Those rocks aren't big. The gully is clear on the other side. We move them.'

Dylan looks to Rose, who nods, and stands. Inessa pulls the suit rack open, and begins quickly and efficiently stripping out of her clothes and pulling on her out-suit's underlayer. Dylan follows her lead. When she has her upper segment in place she looks over to see if Rose needs any help, but she's hooking up all her own internal connection tubes without any trouble, and Inessa is already pulling on her gloves.

'Will we be able to communicate?' Dylan asks.

'No,' says Inessa. 'Your out-suit uses a different frequency from True Martians.'

When their helmets are in place and sealed, Rose vents the air from inside the rover, and opens the rear hatch. She steps out onto the rear ladder, but Inessa reaches out a hand to stop her. Dylan presses her helmet against Inessa's so she can hear what they're saying through the glass.

'You must stay,' Inessa says to Rose. 'Be ready to drive. We'll move the rocks. There aren't that many.'

Rose nods, and squeezes aside to let the other two out. Inessa drops down from the back of the rover first, and Dylan follows. The rock pile is ahead, lit up in the circle of the rover's headlights. It's about twice Dylan's height, and the largest rock Dylan can see is about as wide as her torso.

Inessa climbs to the top of the pile and starts throwing rocks down to the gully floor. Dylan scrambles up after her and joins her in tossing down the rocks and boulders, tugging at the larger ones until they come loose and slide down to the ground.

After ten minutes the pile of rocks is down to half its original size, but it's still too high for the rover's suspension. Dylan's arms and back are aching. She is preparing to tackle her next big boulder when she catches a glimpse of movement in the light above and freezes.

Silhouetted against the sky, an out-suit is looking down on her. It's black and white, the same as the guards in the train, and its gold visor is down. Behind it she sees the nose of a rover jutting out over the side of the gully, the blue Company logo on full display. The suit is unhooking a bolt gun from its belt.

Dylan throws herself against the wall of the gully, pressing her backpack against the rock. She looks around for Inessa, but the Outlier has disappeared.

Dylan looks towards Rose's rover, raising her glove to block the headlights. There's no sign of Inessa in the darkness around it, but through the window she sees Rose, lit up by the cabin lights, staring at something over Dylan's head.

Dylan looks up. Inessa is scaling the wall of the gully. Even in her full out-suit, she lunges from handhold to handhold with the same fluidity as the Outliers in the hanging city. She reaches the top of the rock wall and hauls herself up onto the surface, and out of Dylan's sight.

Dylan slides down the remains of the rock pile. When she looks up, she sees the black-and-white suit still at the edge of the gully, but its gun has swung around to a target out of sight. Dylan's motion must have caught its attention, because the suit's helmet turns towards her, just for a moment. That's all it takes. Inessa pounces into view, arcing through the thin air with her arms flung back, a knife the length of her forearm in each hand. The suit raises the gun to defend itself, but it's too late. The knife slashes through the layered fabric below its chest piece. The suit stumbles backwards, and loses its footing on the edge of the gully. It falls, flailing, scrabbling at the rock face as it tumbles down to the gully floor. The yellow bolt gun falls next to it, rebounding off the wall and landing amongst the scattered rocks.

Dylan approaches the body. Its leg is twisted back at an impossible angle, and blood is leaking from the fluttering tear on its abdomen. As she gets closer, it raises its visor and pushes itself up to a crawling position. She catches a glimpse of an orange beard through the helmet glass. The man scrabbles along the ground towards the yellow bolt gun, dragging a broken leg behind him. But Dylan is on foot, and she can run. She reaches the gun first, and snatches it from between the fallen rocks. Without thinking, she points it at the centre of the black-and-white helmet, and fires.

The suit drops back down to the ground. Dylan looks up to Inessa, who is watching from the edge of the gully. She nods at Dylan, then climbs back down, taking her time, choosing her handholds carefully. When she gets to the bottom she turns and holds out her open hand. Dylan hands her the bolt gun, and Inessa puts it into the pouch on the side of her leg. Dylan touches helmets with her.

'Are there more of them?' she asks.

'There was only one driver. But I saw the other rovers on the horizon. They're close.'

Inessa pulls away from Dylan, and turns the body over with her foot. She dips her fingers in the blood from its ripped abdomen, straightens up, and puts her bloody glove on the top of Dylan's helmet. She drags it forward, leaving four red streaks.

Before Dylan can process the baptism, Inessa pushes past her and scrambles back up the pile of rocks. Dylan follows her, and they return to demolishing the pile.

When the rockslide is down to the height of Dylan's waist,

Inessa taps her arm and points back. The headlights are moving as the rover crawls forward. Dylan stand back and presses herself against the gully wall. The rover drives past slowly, and its front-right wheel rides up the remains of the rockslide. The upper edge of the rover scrapes on the wall of the gully, but it gets over the hump and rolls to a stop on the other side.

In the privacy of her own helmet, Dylan whoops with relief. She runs to the rear hatch, and Inessa follows her in.

Rose crawls the rover forward slowly, deeper in the gully. As they drive, Dylan hears the hiss of the interior repressurising. After ten minutes, Rose taps the side of her helmet. She undoes the clasps around its neck, and lifts it off her head.

'We did it,' she says.

Dylan and Inessa remove their own helmets, and the three of them look out through the front window. Up ahead is yet another curve in the gully, but light is shining in from beyond it, reflecting off the jagged stone walls.

As they take the turn, the ground beneath them gives way to a scree-covered slope. The rover loses traction, and they slide forwards.

'Hold on!' Rose yells.

The ground crumbles, and the walls open up around them. The rover spins. Dylan sees a boulder approaching through the rear window, and before she can brace herself, the rover slams into it with a bone-crunching impact. She's thrown across the cabin, and the loose cold storage container lands on top of her. Rose and Inessa are on the floor of the rover next to her, and she can hear Rose screaming. And then there's sunlight, and the rover is sliding out of the gully onto the side of an open slope, carried in an avalanche of sliding rocks.

The rover spins to a stop, and the world is still. Dylan pulls herself upright. Her arm and jaw are bruised, but she's alive.

Rose sits up, nursing her leg. Inessa's lip is bleeding. She crawls to the window at the rear of the rover, and looks back into the mouth of the gully.

'They won't follow us through that,' she says. 'And we won't make it back that way, either.'

Rose strains, pulling herself back into the driver's seat. She sits there for a moment, catching her breath.

'Okay then,' she says. 'So we go onward.'

# Chapter Ninety-Seven

The extinct volcano of Pavonis Mons slowly rises up ahead of the rover. It's unimaginably vast, like its big brother Olympus Mons, three hundred kilometres wide and fourteen kilometres high, so big that most of it is hidden behind the horizon. The cliffs at the foot of it catch the afternoon sunlight, a wall of jagged brown interspersed with boulder-strewn slopes.

Dylan sits on the cold storage locker at the back of the rover with her helmet in her lap. Now that they're approaching Pavonis Mons, Inessa is taking driving duty, with Rose sitting at her side to guide her.

'Not far now,' Rose murmurs over the rattling of the rover. 'Drive close to the cliffs. It's somewhere down there, among the boulders.'

Dylan stares down at the top of her helmet. As they draw level with the plateau, Rose comes to the back of the vehicle and sits down next to her. She leans over, and sees the smear of blood that Inessa left on the helmet's crown.

'I should have let the guard live,' says Dylan.

Rose shakes her head. 'If you hadn't killed them, Inessa would. I'm complicit, too. That guard would still be alive if I hadn't chosen to come down to the south.'

'It isn't your responsibility. I killed him.'

'Because you were in a position where you had to. But I did this. All of it.'

Inessa glances over her shoulder at the two of them suspiciously. When she looks ahead again, Rose lowers her voice.

'I tried to deny my responsibility,' she says. 'I've tried to keep the Outliers at arm's length. But I can't pretend that I haven't benefitted from their protection and their secrecy. I'm complicit. And I benefitted from the Company, too. I grew up in luxury on the backs of people like your grandmother. I can't hide from the hurt I've caused. All I can do is decide what to do next.'

They drive parallel to the seemingly endless cliffs. In the late afternoon, as the sun hovers over the western horizon, Rose points ahead through the rover's front window.

'There,' she says. 'That boulder. The one shaped like a whale.'

Dylan comes to the front, and looks out between Rose and Inessa. She has never seen a whale before, but the boulder that Rose is pointing to is unmistakable. It's about thirty metres long, tapered at one end and rounded at the other, like a giant creature surfacing from the dust.

Inessa powers down the rover's wheels, and allows it to roll to a stop by the scattered boulders around the giant rock. Rose and Inessa put their helmets on, and Dylan follows their lead, locking it in place with a firm click. Rose says something muffled, and points at Dylan's neck seal. Dylan gives a thumbs up, and Inessa presses a red button on the control screen to vent the air out of the rover.

They open the rear hatch, and drop down onto the pebble-strewn ground. The traces of moisture in the jettisoned air leave a white cloud rising up from the vents at the top of the rover. Dylan looks up at it as it disperses in the light breeze.

'Let's hope that doesn't get us any attention.'

Neither Rose nor Inessa respond. Dylan glances back at them, and sees their mouths moving silently, talking to each other. The lack of a radio connection is getting frustrating.

Rose points southwards, to the scattered boulders at the foot of the volcano's plateau. She leads Dylan into the scree, and her helmet goes down as she searches the ground. There are thousands of rocks between them and the cliffs, ranged in size from pebbles to boulders twice Dylan's height. Inessa spreads out from Rose, searching further to the south. Dylan walks slowly between the two of them. She doesn't know exactly what Archie Fuller's grave looks like, but she assumes that she'll know it when she sees it.

There's a gentle tapping sound in Dylan's helmet. Dylan ignores it and keeps searching the ground, but after thirty seconds, it happens again.

She looks down at the communication panel on the forearm of her suit.

Incoming Connection Request
Accept Y / N

She looks up at Rose, but she's still searching the ground twenty metres away, at the side of the whale-shaped rock. Inessa is ahead, checking between the larger boulders at the base of the cliffs. Neither of them are paying her any attention.

Dylan presses the Y button on her arm, and the radio connects with a quiet chime.

'Dylan Ward?' comes a familiar voice. 'It's quite a surprise to see your name coming up on my communications screen.'

'Who is this?'

'This is Karl Sealgair, and you will address me as sir.'

Dylan straightens her back and looks around, scanning the horizon. Suits only have a limited communication range. He's close.

'I found the remains of Clifford's rover up in the north,' his voice says in her ears, clear and precise over the digital channel. 'I assumed you were dead. And then my people tracked this little rover coming out of Outlier Territory, with your radio signature on board. I had to come and look. Did Clifford survive?'

'No sir,' says Dylan. Her heart pounds as she searches the empty landscape. She can't see any trace of him.

'That's unfortunate. I'll have to get my answers from you instead.'

Dylan sees movement through the side of her helmet. Rose is standing straight, waving with both arms. Next to her is a boulder half her height, and the side of it is piled with helmet-sized rocks. Inessa bounds past Dylan towards Rose.

'Ward?' says Sealgair's voice. 'Are you still with me?'

'Sir,' she says, running towards Rose between the fallen boulders. 'I'm being watched. I can't talk freely.'

'Who's with you? Outliers?'

'Yes sir.'

Rose picks up one of the rocks from the top of the pile and tosses it aside. Inessa join her and lifts another, revealing jagged shards of broken glass that catch the light of the afternoon sun. Rose looks down into her brother's cracked helmet. His unblinking eyes stare back, red with dust.

'How many Outliers?' says Sealgair.

'One, sir. And one other.'

'Other? What do you mean?'

Dylan arrives at the graveside. Rose is frozen, staring down at her brother's unaged face, forever twenty-four years old. She closes her eyes for a moment, then looks away as Inessa throws aside more of the stones.

'You don't need to talk,' Sealgair says. 'I'm currently parked by your rover, on the north side of a very large boulder. I assume you're on the south side. My entourage hasn't arrived yet, but if there's only one Outlier then I'll be able to take them out easily. Just hold on.'

Dylan mutes her microphone and reaches across the grave, touching Rose's arm on the other side. Rose opens her eyes, and looks at her questioningly. She leans over the grave, until the glass of her helmet touches Dylan's.

'Sealgair's here,' Dylan says. She speaks loudly, so Rose can hear her through the glass.

'Where?' Rose says. Her voice is faint.

'He's on the other side of the whale rock. He's armed.'

Rose leans back, separating their helmets. She looks at Inessa, and her mouth moves silently. Inessa stops lifting the rocks, and her lips tighten. She unstraps a bolt gun from her belt and hands it to Rose, then takes a second one from her leg pouch.

Dylan reaches out a hand. Inessa meets Dylan's eyes, and shakes her head. She isn't arming Dylan.

Rose and Inessa run towards the whale-shaped rock. Inessa takes the lead, creeping around the tail of the whale, with the muzzle of her gun aimed at the ground in front of her. Rose is a few paces behind, and Dylan takes the back of the line.

Inessa freezes, and draws her helmet back. Dylan can't see what she's seen, but she waits as Inessa leans forward slowly, then beckons to Rose and Dylan.

As they round the whale rock, Dylan sees what made Inessa freeze. Thirty metres ahead, just to the right of Rose's rover, a small buggy is parked at the edge of the scattered boulders. It's dusty red, with four fat wheels and an enclosure that's only big enough for a single occupant. Its hood is open, and the seat inside it is empty.

Inessa runs towards the buggy with her weapon raised and ready, and takes cover behind a boulder twenty metres from it. There's no movement from the landscape, no hail of bolts fired at her.

Rose leans towards Dylan, and they press their helmets together.

'Where is he?'

'I don't know.'

Inessa beckons to the two of them. They run forward, and take cover on either side of her.

The radio chimes in Dylan's ear.

'I'm not surprised, Ward, but I am disappointed. I thought you might let me down.'

He sounds exhilarated, though, like it's a game. Dylan looks around, at the boulders, the buggy, and the whale-shaped rock. She still can't see him.

'What are you doing with these people?' he says in her ears. 'What are you trying to achieve? I assume it has something to do with Clifford's pet project?'

Inessa beckons to Rose. She points ahead, and quickly ducks for cover again behind her rock.

Dylan looks in the direction she was pointing, and suddenly sees it: a thin line of black against one of the red boulders. It takes a moment for her to comprehend it. Out-suits are traditionally bright, bold colours, like white, yellow and orange, to let them stand out from the landscape in case the wearer needs to be rescued. Sealgair's out-suit is dusty red, and other than the glass of his helmet, it lacks any reflective sheen. It's perfectly camouflaged in the rocky landscape. The black line is the barrel of a rifle that Sealgair is slowly levelling at Dylan.

Dylan ducks, and feels her boulder jolting. She looks around for her companions, and catches a glimpse of the top of Rose's helmet disappearing between the rocks on the right. When she looks to the left, Inessa has disappeared completely.

'I see your friends are trying to flank me,' says Sealgair. 'If you tell me where they are, I might forgive you. I might even take you off the red list.'

Dylan edges her helmet around the side of her rock. Sealgair is crouched down between the boulders, facing to the left. She catches a glimpse of Rose a few metres behind him, creeping closer.

Sealgair glances towards Dylan's helmet. It's only for a split-second, but it's enough. Inessa breaks cover in front of Sealgair, and opens fire. He fires back at Inessa with his rifle, but she ducks behind an upright boulder. Behind him, Rose runs forward with her bolt gun raised, and Dylan hears the distant pops as it fires three times. Sealgair hears them too, and spins around. His rifle twitches unnaturally in his hands like it has a life of its own, and its barrel swings to Rose's chest. The muzzle pops, and Rose jerks back, with a spray of puncture marks across her abdomen. She crumples to the ground.

'No!' Dylan shouts, her voice reverberating in her helmet.

Sealgair strides over to Rose, and looks down at her. Over the radio, Dylan hears his breath catch in his throat. He leans closer, and loses his grip on the rifle. It hangs loose on the strap around his shoulder.

'Is that...?' he says.

Inessa bursts out of hiding and charges at Sealgair, unleashing a flurry of bolts. Sealgair fumbles for his rifle, but can't raise it in time. He drops down between the rocks to avoid the onslaught. Inessa's mouth is open in an inaudible scream. She leans over Rose, shouting silently, then lifts her up under the arms and starts dragging her out towards the rover.

Dylan looks around for Sealgair, and catches a glimpse of his dirt-red helmet as he ducks away between the boulders in the direction of the cliffs. She runs to Inessa's side. Rose's eyes are closed, and her teeth are gritted. Her face is a mask of pain. Red blood seeps out from the holes in her suit. Dylan reaches for Rose's legs, to help Inessa carry her. Rose kicks as Dylan tries to lift them.

'Easy!' says Dylan, knowing that Rose can't hear. She catches Rose's legs, and holds them firmly under her arms. Together, they carry Rose towards the rover.

Dylan glances towards the boulders as they run. Once again, there's no sign of Sealgair. The rear hatch of Rose's rover is standing open. Inessa twists her body as she climbs up to it, holding Rose's torso. Dylan lets go of Rose's legs, and Inessa pulls her in through the hatch.

Dylan looks towards the boulders again. She catches a glimpse of movement in the distance, close to the cliff face, disappearing around the head of the whale rock. She starts to climb, but Inessa comes out and stands in the hatch, blocking Dylan's way. Her face is drained of colour. She takes the bolt gun from her hip, and tosses it down to Dylan. As she catches it, Inessa slams the hatch closed, locking her out.

'Hey!' Dylan shouts, pounding the hatch with her gloved fist. 'Wait!'

The wheels spin, kicking back stones, and the rover pulls away from Dylan. She chases it, slapping its side, but it accelerates and drives off along the edge of the vast plateau. She stops running, and watches it disappear around the curve of the cliffs.

She runs back to Sealgair's buggy and looks inside, at the controls. The cockpit screen is black. She reaches in and feels behind it for a hidden activation button, but there's nothing. Whatever method Sealgair uses to activate it, it's with him alone.

Dylan looks around at the whale rock, and then down at the bolt gun in her hand.

'Shit,' she murmurs.

She walks back to the whale's tail slowly, bolt gun raised, ready to fire at the first sight of motion. Her breath rasps in the helmet. She rounds the edge of the giant rock, and freezes when she sees

Sealgair. He's standing over Archie Fuller's grave, looking down into the open helmet. His rifle is slung over his shoulder.

He looks up at Dylan, and she ducks down behind the nearest boulder, holding her bolt gun tightly in front of her.

'Ward,' he says. 'I saw your rover leaving. Did your Outlier friend abandon you?'

Dylan keeps her head down, and dashes to a boulder ahead.

'Was that really Red Rose?' Sealgair asks. 'She was alive, and she led me right here to her brother's grave. Two chapters of history brought to an end, all at once. I don't think any of your generation can understand how important this moment is. The chaos is finally over.'

As she runs to the next boulder, a bolt strikes its top, throwing out splinters of stone.

'I should introduce my favourite toy,' Sealgair says in her helmet. 'This is an auto-tracking rifle. Custom made. Image-recognition-based target acquisition and gyroscopic self-aiming. Only the Company still has technology like this. Everywhere else is in decline, but the Company held on to the past. That's why we won.'

As Dylan runs to the next boulder, she catches another glimpse of Sealgair, with one hand holding the rifle, and the other reaching into a pouch at the side of his chest plate.

'I'd love to find out how you survived the Outliers,' he says, 'But I don't think I'm going to get the chance. Still, thank you for bringing me here. Whether you wanted to or not, you've done me a great service.'

She runs again. This time, as she dashes between boulders, she doesn't see Sealgair.

She gets to Archie's grave stone, and ducks behind it. Slowly, so slowly, she edges around its side, searching for movement among the scattered rocks. Archie Fuller's eyes stare up at her, and a faint green glow shines up from his helmet.

Dylan looks down. A white package is wedged into it, past the shards of cracked glass, squeezing against the side of Archie Fuller's face. It's soft and rectangular, about the size of a folded-up pad.

Two wires on it lead into a thumb-sized black radio receiver, with a single green LED.

Dylan looks out across the rocks. Sealgair is standing twenty metres away, with his rifle slung over his shoulder. In his glove he holds a white device, like a thick white pen, with a single button on the top. He lifts it into the air in front of him.

'Raise a fist,' he says quietly.

As Dylan turns to run, the thumb of his glove pushes down on the button. The explosive package in Archie Fuller's helmet detonates.

The world behind Dylan erupts into fire, dust and flying shards of rock. The ground is ahead of her, then the sky, and then she's on her back, looking up at rocks falling down at her through the thick cloud of dust. The ringing in her ears blends with the warning alarms from her out-suit.

She rolls onto her chest and looks around. At the side of the whale rock, there's a rough-edged crater where Archie's grave used to be.

She looks the other way, and sees Sealgair striding towards her through the dust cloud. He unslings his rifle strap from his shoulder, and she sees the barrel twitch, searching for motion. He pulls the trigger, and next to her, a falling rock shatters mid-air. The barrel swivels again automatically, following swirls in the dust and smoke. In the chaos of the explosion, the gun can't track Dylan.

Sealgair fires again. The bolt hits the ground in front of her, throwing up another puff of protective dust.

She puts a hand on top of the nearest boulder, and pulls herself upright. Her hearing is muffled, and everything around her feels dark and distant, except Sealgair.

Dylan raises her bolt gun and stumbles towards him. Sealgair fires a third time, but the rifle twitches, and the bolt goes wide. He glances down at the gun in his hands, and keeps firing. Bolts streak past her helmet, but she's far beyond caring. She steadies her gun. Sealgair ducks behind a cracked boulder, and her bolt glances off its side.

'Give it up, Ward,' Sealgair says.

Dylan catches a glimpse of movement through the crack. She fires, and the bolt rebounds off the right-hand side of the rock. A mechanical counter on the top of her bolt gun flips to the number two.

'You can't survive without me.'

She fires again, hitting the left side. The gun's counter flips down to one.

'Your father's still alive, for now,' he says.

Dylan fires her last bolt, and it ricochets through the crack. Sealgair stumbles backwards, with a white plume of gas erupting from the upper corner of his backpack. He drops his rifle and reaches both hands back over his shoulder, trying to stop the gas leak, but it's too late. His pack explodes, scattering fragments of metal canister and plastic casing. Gas fills the air, turning it white. As it clears, Dylan sees Sealgair stumble closer. His left arm is hanging down, held up only by a shred of torn fabric from his out-suit.

He puts his right hand out towards a boulder to steady himself. Then his arm goes limp, and he collapses against the rock. His body slides down it, and falls forward into the dust.

# Chapter Ninety-Eight

Dylan lets the empty bolt gun fall from her fingers, and limps forward. The warnings from her suit are buzzing in her ears, but they're distant and unimportant. She stops in front of Sealgair, and nudges his body with her foot. She rolls him over, and looks down into his helmet. His eyes and mouth are open, like he's gasping with surprise.

She stares down at him blankly for a few seconds, then turns around and limps back around the whale-shaped rock. A little past Sealgair's dusty buggy she spots the tracks of Rose's rover, driving parallel to the cliffs. She follows them, slowly, step after step, through the jagged landscape.

North of the whale, the boulders are bigger: great cracked lumps of rock, twenty metres high. The tracks weave between them, and disappear into a gulley in the side of the plateau.

Dylan leans against a boulder until her strength returns, then limps into the gulley. The golden evening light shines in behind her, casting her shadow onto the pebble-strewn ground.

Rose's rover is parked at the end of the gulley, past a gentle left-hand bend. Dylan squeezes her way past the side of the vehicle, and presses her helmet against the front window.

Inside, she sees Rose lying in one of the hammocks. Her out-suit is gone, and she has a grey strip of cloth wrapped around her waist, and another around her chest. Inessa is leaning over her, unrolling more bandages. There's an open orange med-kit on the floor next to her, and a pool of spilled blood under the hammock.

Dylan taps lightly on the dusty glass. Inessa looks at her and straightens up, wiping her brow with her forearm. She takes a pad of paper from a cubbyhole by the controls, and scrawls a quick message. She holds it to the window up for Dylan to see. Her handwriting is neat and jagged.

**SORRY**
**COULD NOT LEAVE ROSE**
**COULD NOT LET COMPANY MAN FOLLOW US**
**HAD TO LEAVE YOU**

Dylan nods numbly. Inessa lifts the pad back from the window. She folds over the top page, and writes another note.

**CAN'T LET YOU IN NOW**
**CAN'T PUT ROSE BACK IN A SUIT**

Inessa glances back over her shoulder, and Dylan sees Rose's lips moving. Her face is puffy, and her chest shakes as she breathes. Inessa's lips move as she replies. She flips the top page of the pad again, and writes a third message.

**DID YOU KILL HIM**
**IS THE SUIT SAFE**

Rose's whole body is shaking now. She pushes down the side of the hammock, and looks at Dylan pleadingly. Dylan raises the finger of her glove, and writes on the dust on the glass, in reverse.

**KILLED HIM**

Inessa's face crumples with relief. She writes again.

**AND THE SUIT?**

Dylan's finger hovers over the dusty glass. As much as she wants to, she can't lie.

## SUIT GONE

Dylan sees Inessa's mouth moving as she relays the message, and Rose grimaces in pain, arching her back. Inessa runs to her side. She takes a syringe from the medicine case, and stabs the needle into an ampule. But as she's drawing liquid into it, Rose starts convulsing. Inessa drops the syringe and leans over her, trying to hold her down. A minute later the convulsing ends, and Rose's body is still.

Inessa doesn't get up. She stays on the floor, on her knees, with arms across Rose's body, and her head hanging down between them.

A new alarm sounds in Dylan's helmet, high-pitched and wailing. She backs away from the window, and squeezes out between the side of the rover and the rock wall. As she limps around the bend in the gulley, light from the setting sun shines into her helmet, making the orange dust on her visor glow. She wipes it off with her glove, and sees large shapes driving towards her out of the sunset.

Three rovers converge on her, throwing back columns of dust. The largest one, in the middle, is two decks high and has six wheels. A cockpit extends out of the front of the upper deck.

'Rudolf,' she whispers.

But it isn't her rover. As it pulls to a stop at the mouth of the gulley, she sees the silhouette of a harpoon launcher mounted on the roof. The smaller rovers roll to a stop on either side of it, and four orange-suited figures drop down from the infantry platforms on their sides. Light streams in around them in rays of golden dust as they run towards Dylan with their bolt guns raised.

Dylan's radio chimes again. She looks down at the display on her forearm. A connection is coming in on an analogue channel. She presses a button, numbly accepting the call. The radio clicks in her ears.

'This is Sheriff Marchant of Pavonis Base,' says a familiar voice. 'You are currently trespassing in Pavonis territory. On orders of

Mayor Ravine, you're under arrest. Down on the ground, hands where we can see them.'

Dylan kneels, lowers her head, and puts her hands on the sides of her helmet. Two of the suits run to either side of her. They take her elbows and push her down, so the glass of her helmet presses into the pebble-strewn ground. As one of them binds her wrists with thick black cable ties, the other three run past her and deeper into the gulley, towards the rover holding Inessa and Rose.

# Part 8.5

---

# Seeds

# Chapter Ninety-Nine

Rose stood at her father's side, wiggling her fingers in her woollen mittens. The room they were in was freezing, and even though her hat and jacket were thick and fur-lined, the air was cold enough to make her body ache.

Her father didn't seem to notice the cold, or his thirteen-year-old daughter's discomfort. He wasn't even wearing a coat, or a cap to cover his ginger crew cut, just his normal long-sleeved dress shirt with thin blue stripes.

'We're magicians, Rose. I've been thinking about it, and it's the only good way to describe what we do. I say the right words and make the right gestures, and I change what people think. I'm casting spells.'

They walked through the freezing chamber, between endless metal shelves that went up to the rocky ceiling. The light was tinted blue, and it made her father's skin look old and wrinkled. Up ahead, three scientists in thick white snow gear, complete with hoods and goggles, were unloading transparent plastic cubes from a trolley and placing them carefully on one of the shelves. Rose hunched her shoulders and looked down at the floor as she walked past, so she wouldn't make eye contact.

'How's it going?' her father asked the scientists.

'Good, sir,' she heard one of them reply. 'They all survived the flight. Only twenty-seven more batches to go.'

'Great, great. You all are stars.'

She followed her father as he strode onward, deeper into the vast chamber. It was underground, in an abandoned mining base up in the far north. Rose hadn't wanted to come on her father's inspection mission. She had wanted to stay in her room in Aries

Base, playing anonymous online games, but he had insisted that getting outside would do her good.

He stopped at one of the shelves, and picked up one of the thousands of small transparent boxes that filled the chamber. Rose looked at some of the others, down at her level. Each one was labelled in Latin.

*Encephalartos sclavoi*

*Magnolia champaca*

*Sciadopitys verticillata*

'Did you know that I'm technically the poorest person on the planet?' her father said cheerfully, putting the transparent cube back on the shelf. 'The debt I'm in is astronomical. I owe the banks and investors billions. It doesn't matter, though. They're all happy. As long as everyone thinks we're rich, we're rich. If we want more money, they'll give it to us. It's magic.'

Rose's dad got this way sometimes, and it made her uncomfortable. Most days he would walk from place to place with his head down, barely noticing other people. But then, randomly, he'd have weeks where he'd be full of enthusiasm and excitement for every idea that came into his head, and the rest of the family would have to run to catch up with him.

'It works the other way, too,' he said, striding off down the line of shelves. 'If someone says I'm poor and other people believe it, it's like they're using magic against me. It's a curse, a hex, attacking my mystical form, and I have to fight back with lawyers and public relations. Magical warfare.'

'It all sounds like people telling lies,' Rose muttered, putting her mittens under her armpits and hugging herself. She had never been this cold in her life. She was going to die.

'No.' Her father stopped abruptly, and she almost walked into him. She thought she had annoyed him, and kinda hoped that she had, too. But he turned to her and bent down, putting his hands on his knees so their faces were level, and smiled. 'That's what I'm trying to explain to you. A lie is when you say something that isn't true. Magic is when you say something that isn't true, but it becomes true because you said it. I said we would get to Mars, and we're here. It wouldn't have happened if I hadn't said it.'

He put a hand on her shoulder, and pulled her in for a hug. His cheek was cold against hers.

'We're self-fulfilling prophecies, Rose. Anyone can be. People believe we're exceptional, so they put us in exceptional positions. We just have to work out who the world needs us to be.'

He leaned back from her, but kept his hands on her shoulders. When he saw her expression, he frowned, and his eyes darted around her face.

'What's wrong?' he said.

'I hate it when people look at me,' she said, hugging herself. 'I'm not special. I'm not magical.'

'Of course you are, and there's nothing wrong with that. People need you to make fantasies. Without fantasy, reality is as cold and dead as Mars was before we arrived. But you have to be making something real at the core of the fantasy, too. You have to be building something solid that will be revealed when the bubble bursts. That's why I brought you here.'

He straightened up and opened his arms, gesturing to the vast chamber around them.

'What are all these things?' said Rose. She walked to one of the shelves, and touched a transparent box with the finger of her mitten. There was something small suspended in the middle of it, like a smooth pebble about the size of the tip of her little finger.

'Seeds,' her father said. 'A million seeds, from a hundred thousand plant species from Earth. I'm hiding them here, far from the Earth, far from anywhere. I'm going to protect them, so that if something happens to Earth, in ten years, or a thousand, or a million, we'll be able to rebuild its ecosystems from scratch. I'm protecting the future. You love nature, don't you? I thought you'd appreciate this more than your brother.'

Rose felt a shiver run down her ribs.

'What's this got to do with magic?' she asked.

Her father looked down at her, suddenly serious.

'It's like I just told you. Under all the magic and the glamour there has to be some purpose, something real. You have to have a reason to do it that isn't all about you. Otherwise you get swept up in a hollow fantasy, and when the dream evaporates, you're lost. That's why I'm doing this. Make as many wild fantasies as you want, Rose, but always bring them back to reality. Always stick the landing.'

# Part 9.0

---

# The New World

# Chapter One Hundred

Once again, Dylan is held in the Pavonis bubbles. This time she gets a bubble all to herself, and a new, clean foam mattress. She pulls it under a vent that's blowing warm air in from the base, curls up, and sleeps.

She needs to recover, and the bubble gives her plenty of time to do it. She spends whole days sitting on the mattress, looking out of the transparent plastic at the barren landscape, watching the rovers coming and going from the docking bay. Occasionally, a deputy comes along the connection tube to bring her a meal and replace her waste bucket. He's a fidgety young man, and the orders he gives her are polite, as if he can't work out if she's a prisoner or a guest. He brings her a selection of simple flatbreads and roasted vegetables from the stalls on the Pavonis concourse, neither impressive nor offensive. It's limbo.

The only person Dylan talks to regularly is Mayor Ravine. The former sheriff comes out to Dylan's bubble every morning with an armed guard, and politely questions her on her last visit to Pavonis, her time with Red Rose, and her part in the incident at Whale Rock. Dylan answers her honestly, and after each session the mayor nods and goes away, returning the next morning with more questions.

During their little talks, the mayor reveals something that Dylan finds interesting.

'The Settlements have caught word of Whale Rock. The Company's trying to say that Sealgair was assassinated by the Outliers, and the woman he killed weren't Red Rose, but their rumours don't fly no more. They got no traction. The truth's more interesting. It's got betrayal and broken hearts and secret histories. They can't beat that.'

When Dylan asks about Inessa, Ravine is cagey.

'She's safe,' she says.

But Dylan keeps asking, and over the days Ravine gives in.

'It's rare that we catch an Outlier alive,' she says. 'And even rarer that they don't kill themselves when we do. We're looking after her. We know so little about them. Anything we can find out from her will be valuable.'

'She isn't an animal. You can't dissect her.'

'We ain't going to torture information out of her, if that's what you're thinking. Red Rose trusted her, and that counts for something. We're taking her to a small base in the south-west, where we can let her roam free without any danger. Don't worry. We'll treat her with respect. Think of her like the first Outlier ambassador.'

On day twenty-one, Dylan is released from custody with an official pardon from Pavonis Base. Mayor Ravine gives her special dispensation, under observation, to contact Company Territory. She sits in the mayor's office, and talks to her father on a static-fuzzed screen.

'Well,' he says. 'That sounds like a total fuck-up.'

He's sitting up in bed in a medical bay, stroking Burma, who is curled up patiently on his lap.

'I guess so,' she says. 'But we're both still alive. How are you recovering?'

'Fine enough. I mean, if you want to hear my long list of complaints I'll be happy to oblige. But I'm lucky that the Company beat the shit out of me so publicly. After that video everyone got all riled up, so they shipped me off to the medical facilities in Sinai Base and Vinnie got two week's paid leave. I'm getting my physio and meds, and that's all I can ask for, I guess.'

'And what's happening in the Company?'

'Oh, it's total chaos without Sealgair. The board are stabbing each other in the back for the top job. I don't think the Free Settlements have to worry about them. They're going to be squabbling for a while. And you? Are you coming back?'

'I can't,' Dylan says quietly.

Frank tousles the tuft of hair on Burma's chin, and stares past the camera vacantly.

'Good,' he says, eventually. His voice cracks. 'I should never have brought you to the Company, Dylan. You weren't meant for this life.'

An alert beeps from the screen, telling them their time is up. Dylan wipes her eyes on her sleeve.

'Bye, Dad. Look after yourself.'

'I always do.'

'Properly. No more of Guthrie's rot-gut.'

'Okay, okay. Sheesh. Bye, kid. Have fun out there. Do what you want. I'll love you forever.'

The video cuts out.

Over the next few days, black-and-red posters of the young Red Rose go up all around the base. They're everywhere: on the walls of the concourse, on the sides of the vending stalls, inside the bars, and on placards over the main stairwell. Delegates arrive, representing every faction in the Free Settlements, from the largest hegemonies all the way down to the smallest independent outposts. The population of Pavonis doubles, and more bubbles are inflated outside its walls to cater for the overspill. It's an unofficial congress for the Free Settlements. They're meeting on neutral terms, with nothing to prove except their respect for Red Rose.

On the twenty-fifth day after Dylan arrived, Red Rose's funeral is held in the central hub of Pavonis Base. The food stalls are cleared for the event, and the delegates and base inhabitants all gather before the coffin, which is laid at the foot of the glass mural of the young Rose, surrounded by red handprints. The service itself is nondenominational and, frankly, unmemorable. The leaders of the five largest alliances in the Settlements are all allowed to speak. When they're done, they press their hands onto a tray of red paint, and add their palm prints to the fiery halo surrounding the mural. The coffin is lifted by four out-suited Pavonis guards, and carried at the front of a procession through the concourse, all the way to the airlocks. The guards take it outside, to be buried on a low hill just past the boulder fence. At Ravine's suggestion the delegates have brought stones from their own territories. After the funeral, they take turns to don their own out-suits and make the pilgrimage out to the grave on foot, to place their stones on it.

Even after the delegates leave, the ritual continues. Traders and travellers who didn't attend the funeral are encouraged to make their own pilgrimage to pay their respects to Red Rose.

Dylan waits two more weeks before she takes the walk. She tells herself repeatedly that it's meaningless, and a waste of valuable time and oxygen. Eventually, though, almost against her own will, she finds herself in her suit, standing in the Pavonis airlock.

The outer door slides up, and the daylight shines in. After weeks inside she had forgotten how bright it was. She lowers her visor, and steps down onto the rocky ground.

The hill is a kilometre away, past the line of boulders. Even from this distance she can see the cairn of stones on the grave, a triangle pointing at the sky.

It's only a meaningless ritual if she lets it be. As she walks she looks down, searching for a suitable stone. She finds what she's looking for just before the border fence. It's a medium-sized rock, rounded on one side, and so perfectly fist-sized that Dylan wonders if one of the travellers brought it with them from a far-flung base and dropped it on the way. But, no, it's the same colour and texture as all the other rocks around Pavonis.

As she carries it up the hill, she thinks about Red Rose as a symbol, and her grandmother as a real person, and herself, and what she could be. She reaches the top, and looks out at the landscape. The dust in the air bathes the world in an orange light. Mars may be cold and dead, but the dead can be beautiful, sometimes.

She looks at the cairn on Rose's grave, hundreds of stones high. She passes her own rock from one hand to the other, feeling its heaviness through her gloves.

'You don't need any more weight on you,' she says.

She throws the rock out across the landscape. It falls slowly, and bounces off the hillside below.

She sits down by the cairn, enjoying the silence. More pilgrims are walking towards her in a thin line from the base. They're just white specks, but soon enough they will arrive, and pay their respects, and Dylan will be expected to talk about unimportant things. And after that, she'll return to the base before the sun sets, and she'll start her search for work. She'll look for a group of traders that's willing to take her on board, and she will learn how to fit in with them, and work around them, and become one of them. If she lets them mean something to her, they'll feel like family.

For now, though, she sits, and stares out into a great wide openness.

END

# Acknowledgements

Back in 2015, along with some of her friends, my wife Kerry ran a monthly event called Science Cafe, where they would book out a coffee shop in Cape Town and have scientists give open lectures to a general audience. The venue was always packed, and there were some excellent talks about subjects like gravitational waves, string theory and personalised medicine, but one of my favourites was a lecture given by Kai Staats.

Among other things, Kai is an expert on the ways that humans might live on other planets. He is one of the project co-leads on SAM, the world's highest fidelity simulated Mars habitat, and his talk was about Mars colonisation. He ended it by saying the following (and, because it was seven years ago, I'm going to have to paraphrase):

'When people first arrive on Mars, things will be simple. There will be a small group of scientists, all working towards the same goals. Everyone will know each other, and everyone will trust each other. But slowly, the population will grow. People will be born, and people will arrive from Earth, and eventually things will stop being simple. There will be growing inequality and distrust, there will be politics, there will be crime, and eventually, there will be murder.'

And, sitting in the audience, I thought, 'ha!' So thank you, Kai, for getting this whole ball rolling.

Thank you to my family, Tony, Diana, and especially Kerry, for being my beta readers, and more importantly for allowing me to disappear so I could write. I know it wasn't easy, and I'll never be able to pay back the time you gave me.

Thank you to Jacqui and Phil Cunningham for letting me use

the studio on weekends. Thank you to Lauren Beukes and Sam Beckbessinger for the long silent Zoom calls during lockdown, when we would watch each other write and make sure that no one wandered away to eat everything in the fridge. Thank you to my tireless agent, Oli Munson, and my editor Emad Akhtar, whose advice and guidance were, once again, incredible.

The grammar of the Outlier language is loosely based on Toki Pona, created by Sonja Lang. Many thanks for inventing such a wonderful language.

I'd also like to acknowledge Floss Mitchell, who allowed me to interview her as a consulting child psychologist. Even though she knew very well that the young Rose Fuller was fictional, she was still concerned she would grow up to be okay. Sadly, Floss passed away before she could read the final manuscript, but I hope she would have been content knowing that she helped set Rose on an interesting life path.

Sam Wilson, Cape Town, 2022

# Credits

Sam Wilson and Orion Fiction would like to thank everyone at Orion and our other teams who worked on the publication of *The First Murder on Mars*

**Agent**
Oliver Munson

**Editorial**
Emad Akhtar
Celia Killen
Sarah O'Hara
Millie Prestidge

**Copy-editor**
Jamie Groves

**Proofreader**
John Garth

**Editorial Management**
Jane Hughes
Charlie Panayiotou
Tamara Morriss
Claire Boyle

**Contracts**
Anne Goddard
Ellie Bowker

**Audio**
Paul Stark
Jake Alderson
Georgina Cutler

**Design**
Nick Shah
Tomas Almeida
Joanna Ridley
Helen Ewing

**Rights**
Rebecca Folland
Ben Fowler
Alice Cottrell
Tara Hiatt
Marie Henckel

**Inventory**
Jo Jacobs
Dan Stevens

**Communications**
Katie Moss

**Operations**
Group Sales Operations team

**Finance**
Nick Gibson
Jasdip Nandra
Sue Baker
Tom Costello

**Picture Research**
Natalie Dawkins

**Production**
Ruth Sharvell
Katie Horrocks

**Sales**
Jen Wilson
Victoria Laws
Esther Waters
Group Sales teams across
    Digital, Field Sales,
    International and Non-Trade